THE GHOSTS IN MAPLE LEAF GARDENS

∽RICK FERGUSON∽

iUniverse LLC
Bloomington

The Ghosts in Maple Leaf Gardens

This is a work of fiction. All of the characters, names, incidents, organizations, and dialogue in this novel are either the products of the author's imagination or are used fictitiously.

iUniverse books may be ordered through booksellers or by contacting:

iUniverse
1663 Liberty Drive
Bloomington, IN 47403
www.iuniverse.com
1-800-Authors (1-800-288-4677)

ISBN: 978-1-4917-0710-4 (sc)
ISBN: 978-1-4917-0712-8 (hc)
ISBN: 978-1-4917-0711-1 (e)

Printed in the United States of America.

iUniverse rev. date: 10/23/2013

Table of Contents

He Shoots...He Scores

"**T**here are less than three minutes remaining in this one Robert and it looks as if the Leafs are finally going to break out of their five-game losing streak!"

"Well that's right Jim, and it couldn't have come at a better time, what with the Leafs having *lost* their last five."

Leaf fans that followed their team on the radio felt sorry for play-by-play man Jim Gerber. They felt sorry for him because Gerber had to work alongside and carry a clown like Bob Swanson. They knew that the only reason why 'Big Bad' Bob Swanson was able to keep his job as radio colour man was that he was willing to work for almost nothing. Bob Swanson worked in the largest media market in the country and held the second most prestigious job in sports radio, second only to Jim Gerber's job as play-by-play man. Even though he was driving, Ron Bailey closed his eyes for a second while shaking his head. Ron listened as the diatribe continued. He was as interested in anticipating 'Big Bad Bobby's next screw-up as he was in the score and the time remaining in the game.

"Here's Sullivan stealing the puck at the blue line, a shot right on, the rebound,

THEY SCOOOORE! Stevie Sullivan brings the Chicago Black Hawks within one as he picks the pocket—"

Ron Bailey pushed in the power button on his car radio so hard it might never come out. He did not want to hear which one of the Leafs defensemen were responsible for the giveaway that led to the goal. He would hear about it over and over again, on the half hourly sports updates, he would read it in the paper the next morning, and he would see it on *Sports desk*, probably twice. He turned the radio back on. He had to know what was going on.

"Awwww, you know Jim this is starting to look a lot like last week in Pittsburgh when the Leafs were up 4-1 with about half a period to play—I just don't understand!"

That part Ron believed, that "Boob" Swanson just didn't understand anything. He once asked his boss why a moron such as Bob Swanson was allowed to pollute the airwaves, but the Leaf General Manager justified it this way: "I think that Bob Swanson makes everything Jim Gerber says sound that much more intelligent." Ron had to agree. It was part of Ken Butler's job as General Manager of the Toronto Maple Leafs to decide who was awarded the rights to the Leaf radio broadcasts, but it *wasn't* up to the general manager to choose who the on air personalities were. He could influence the broadcasters' decisions if he chose to do so. It *mattered* to the hockey junkies in Toronto that the colour man on the team's radio broadcasts knew what he was talking about. The fact was that Bob Swanson was nothing but a schmoozing, blithering, homer, afflicted with verbal diarrhea that made the listeners ill.

"If the radio ratings are suffering because of who we have as colour man then I have a small problem," Ken Butler said, "if however the ratings are suffering because of how *our team is playing*," he told Ron, "Then we *all* have a *big* problem."

Ken Butler's position was not an easy one, Ron concluded. The General Manager of *any* business had to be right about all of the decisions he made, but with a hockey team, the 'customers' are the fans, and are so much more passionate about the decisions, as if each one affected them personally. The Leafs' GM had to be right about whom the team selected in the entry draft, right about the trades he made, and right about whom he chose to coach the team. He had to answer not only the team's ownership but also to the fans for these decisions. He would also have to answer for who was chosen as the on-air announcers.

"Two Fifteen left to go in this one as they drop the puck at centre ice, from the face-off

And OH MY! Dave Moore is NAILED by Ryan Vanden Bussche of the Hawks!"

"Awwww Jim, Moore was just nailed by Vanden Bussche and there's no penalty! I can't believe it!"

"Well there *is* going to be a penalty as the referee raises his arm. The play is called and Dan Marouelli signals an interference call. So at least the Leafs will be on the power play as this one draws to a close."

Ron was happy about that. If the Leafs had the man advantage there was less chance of them blowing a one-goal lead.

"The Maple Leafs with the extra man, are 0 for 6 tonight, Robert."

"That's right Jim—they have yet to score a power play goal in this game."

Ron wondered if every Leaf fan thought Bob Swanson was the worst case of halitosis that had ever fouled a microphone.

"The Leafs win the draw, the puck goes back to the point, and Korolev picks up the loose puck. It's going to be a race to the net, he's in on goal—he shoots he scores! Igor Korolev! Korolev ties the game on a breakaway as Terry Oddy couldn't handle the pass at the point and was left in the dust. Mother of pearl they have found a way!" the play-by-play man described.

Bob Swanson couldn't help himself. He added, "They've found a way to snatch victory from the jaws of defeat, Jim."

"I think you mean that the other way around, but in any event the Toronto Maple Leafs have seen a two goal lead evaporate here in the dying minutes and the only question that remains is can they hold on for the overtime that looms and salvage at least a point out of this one."

Ron had listened to this type of ending too many times this season. Like every other Leaf fan, he knew that ex-Leafs have a way of coming back and killing their former team. It's true that when *any* player gets traded he wants to show his former bosses that they were wrong—that they still have something left. But with ex-Leafs it was even worse. It wasn't just a coincidence—it seemed that the minute a player got out of Toronto that their play picked up, and the guy looked and felt like he was ten years younger.

"We'll use it to our advantage," the General Manager would tell Ron. "We'll remind the clubs we're trading with that the guy we're dealing will be *reborn* once he gets out of town."

Ron wondered which one of the Black Hawks was likely to score in overtime, and then it occurred to him. Yes, there were six ex-Leafs on the Chicago roster and two of them, Steve Sullivan and Igor Korolev had already scored in this game. So it stood to reason that one of the others would get the winner in overtime.

"The buzzer goes to end this one. Wait a minute, to end the third period!"

There, it had finally happened. After two seasons of working with *Boob Swanson*, Jim Gerber was finally being affected. The incompetence was contagious.

"And we'll be back with the overtime in just a moment. You're listening to Toronto Maple Leafs Hockey on the voice of the Leafs, 1430 CKFH."

Ron turned off the radio again as he reached the stop light at Bloor Street. The traffic on his route home from Maple Leaf Gardens did not usually move this fast. But then Ron wouldn't normally be leaving a game before it was over. He had been the Leafs director of player personnel only since the start of the season. The position involved many duties related to the team's roster of players, including the evaluation of prospects, both present and future. It was this duty that was taking him away from tonight's action on the ice. And from the sound of things he would have found it hard to sit through. In fact many of the Leafs games so far this year had been hard to sit through. He felt almost relieved that he had to leave the Gardens early in order to prepare a report for the next morning's organizational meeting. The meeting was to focus on the next step in the 'new direction' the hockey club would be taking. This so-called 'new direction' wasn't really all that new, and it wasn't so much a direction as an admission that they had made a mistake and overestimated the talent at hand.

Ron could not stand the suspense. The overtime would just be starting. If the team could hold on for just five more minutes, and at least come away with a tie, they would end the losing streak.

"We're in overtime," he heard Jim Gerber say, his voice always sounding raspier the longer a broadcast lasted, "and so far this year the Leafs record in the extra frame is 0-7 and 0."

Bob Swanson needed to fill the listeners in on this one. "Jim, the Leafs haven't earned as much as a single point in overtime games yet this year, which is a strong contrast to last season when they were 0-0 and 8. No, wait a minute; that was *two* years ago. Last season they were 4-2-and 12. Hey, that's not bad!" he commented.

Ron headed up Mount Pleasant Road, and as the play resumed it became painfully obvious that the Leafs were not going to recover from blowing a lead. As Jim Gerber was fond of saying (when referring to the opposition) 'Their collars are becoming just a tad too tight at this juncture.' They were choking, indeed.

"Bryan Berard has just scored from the face-off, and he's being mobbed by his teammates. While we were away, Steve Sullivan won the face-off after Igor Korolev was thrown out of the face-off circle and he drew the puck back to Berard at the point who blasted a shot at the 1:21 mark of overtime! Can you believe it?"

Sadly, Ron Bailey *could* believe it. He had predicted that an ex-Leaf would score. He had just predicted the wrong one. He forgot about Berard, who left the Leafs after his tragic injury in '99-00. Ron's thoughts turned from the game (a loss which kept the team at winless in January) to the topic of tomorrow's meeting. He could almost hear the General Manager's low steady voice telling his brain trust of his latest decision; the much speculated rebuilding of the team.

"Much was expected of our players as we headed into training camp," the GM would begin, and then would stop to drink from a glass of water he always kept close by. He thought it comical for the GM to begin this way, as it almost looked like a ventriloquist performing the drinking-from-the-glass-while-the-dummy-sings routine. "It looks," the GM would continue, "like the talent on the present roster is not going to be good enough to get us in to the playoffs."

'Yes, it does look that way, even to a blind man,' Ron thought. This decision had been reached about two months earlier, by most fans, and even as far back as last summer for many, when the Leafs failed to sign any free agents or make any major deals to improve the team. In fact it seemed as if they were going in the opposite direction, trading away a couple of the team's leading scorers while getting little in return. The media had portrayed it that way—that the team had been dumping big contracts in order to improve the bottom line. It was no secret that the team was for sale. Owning the Toronto Maple Leafs would be the ultimate sports high for any deep-pocketed suit in Toronto. The club had been for sale since its former owner had died from cancer, and left the team to the Salvation Army in his will. The charity was eager to complete the sale and use the funds to construct a new hospice for the homeless. The conditions of the will were bizarre, however, and called for many convoluted conditions to be met before the charity could sell the team. The will was being contested in court indefinitely.

"If a deal goes through, a new ownership group will want their own people in place, and we may *all* be looking for work," the GM had once said. "It may not matter—we may all be dead and buried before ownership changes."

Ron wasn't afraid of being out of work—it's just that it was a treat to finally be able to work in his home town.

As he neared his Avoca Avenue apartment, Ron began to mentally organize the project that had him leave the Gardens early that night. The club was preparing to make a big trade, and while the trade deadline was more than two months away, the offers had already started to become interesting. Part of Ron's job was to organize and collect all data relating to the evaluation of the players involved in prospective trades. His report would help to assess offers the club had received; the first one, from the Pittsburgh Penguins involved Vaclaz Artis, the Leafs leading scorer. Artis was a young Czechoslovakian who was having his best season since his rookie season four years ago, but who was unhappy with his contract, and had demanded a trade (although the media were not yet aware of this.)

Artis was a skilled play maker, but he wasn't a hard worker and this was a team desperately in need of leadership. Ron had to update the file on the three young prospects being baited.

The second trade offer came from Dallas, and the Stars wanted the Leafs goalie, John Dennis, who was a spectacular playoff performer but who had struggled recently, and who was now considered expendable. Another big contract was the obstacle here. Dallas was offering a decent defenseman, but there was some concern about the player's health.

The third offer was from Carolina, and was perhaps more to the Leafs liking. The Hurricanes wanted Artis and David Burks, the one-time point man on the power play who now was getting a bit grey in the whiskers, and who also was making big bucks. The Hurricanes offered two former first-round picks *and* a second-round draft choice. The General Manager wasn't too interested in draft choices, which he called, 'Like stock in a company that no one has ever heard of.' The two prospects involved hadn't panned out in the NHL, and Ron had to dig up every shred of dirt that there was on these two. He also had to research all of the draft information available from three years ago, and try to find out if there was any reason to think that they might still be worth their draft selection.

As Ron entered his apartment he noticed that the red light on his answering machine was flashing. He hit the replay button while he thumbed through his mail. Only the new copy of *Canadian Sports card Collector* caught his attention as he heard the first message.

"Ron, its Ken Butler. I just wanted to remind you of our 9:00 tomorrow. I'll need that report on the analysis of the three offers. See you!" That was it, short and to the point as most of the General Manager's messages were. Ron could never understand why the General Manager found it necessary to call and remind everyone of the meetings he scheduled. The last thing that was said to him as he left the building was, "See you at the meeting tomorrow, 9:00 sharp!"

It was almost as if the General Manager thought he wasn't *important* enough for people to remember to attend his meetings—he was constantly sending reminders as if his worst fear was to walk into a meeting room and find no one there.

Ron listened to the next message: "Hey Bailey, its Moore. I wanted to thank you for those shitty seats you got for my in-laws. Thanks a lot—awful nice of you, *asshole!*" CLICK.

That was expected of David Moore, Leafs defenseman (who was known as *Shithead* Moore in the dressing room.) He was the one who bitched about everything, from the kind of drinks in the trainer's room to the length of the bus ride from the hotel to the practice rink. Now he was complaining about the complimentary pair of gold seats he had been given for his in-laws. They were Ron's *personal* season's tickets, which although in the corner, were still close to the ice.

"How did they like the price, Shithead?" Ron wondered, as he fired up his lap top and began to prepare his report for the morning.

"Maple Leaf Gardens, this stop"

Ron took the TTC to the Gardens the next morning. Riding on the subway was a welcomed change from driving. He appreciated the opportunity to read the morning sports rather than trying to listen to it on the radio. As he turned the pages of *The Globe* he noticed the headline around Neil Power's column LEAFS TO DEAL ARTIS FOR FUTURE? The article went on to state

"The future is not now for the Toronto Maple Leafs but rather tomorrow, or the next day. This is a franchise that has many tomorrows but not very many todays. Since Ken Butler took over this club he has made many shrewd moves, including stealing Vaclav Artis from the New York Rangers for some yesterdays. But now he must admit that while this team was built for today (meaning the present) the Leafs present is not very pretty. They sit three points out of 30th place in a 30-team league. This team was designed around playoff-savvy veterans for today, and the hell with tomorrow. But tomorrow is finally here, and the Leafs are not. Ken Butler has realized that this team is not even good enough to make the playoffs and so the direction has changed again; they will trade today for tomorrow. Artis will be dealt, likely to the Carolina Hurricanes for Radim Vrbata, Mike Zigomanis and a draft choice. These players are not household names now, but perhaps they will be. After all, as Scarlet O'Hara said, 'Tomorrow is another day'"

Ron sighed and closed the paper. He would never stop being amazed by the ability of the media to uncover facts like the details of a trade that was supposedly confidential. Every team had what the media referred to as a 'mole', and the Leafs were no different.

No one knew for sure, but the suspected mole on the Toronto club was the media relation's director Tommy Stukko.

If he *was* the mole then at least it was fitting that Tommy Stukko also looked the part. He had small, dark eyes highlighted by small granny-glasses, and a thin pointy nose. His hair was black and always slicked down. He gave the appearance more of a seedy pool hall hustler than anyone connected with an institution like the Toronto Maple Leafs. It was no coincidence that he held this position because he was the nephew of club's director of finance. Ron had to deal with Tommy Stukko every time a player move was announced, for every signing, for every transaction, for every call-up from the minors and for every contract extension. Tommy Stukko was the kind of person who was personally offended if he was not the first to know of any move. Tommy Stukko would whine, "You have to give me time to get this out" every time some late night personnel decision was reached. These decisions were mostly made after Tommy's 'banker hours', by the 'gang of four' committee, which consisted of the Coach, the General Manager, the Assistant General Manager, and the Director of Player Personnel.

It was often an hour or so after game time that Ron would *have* to come to Tommy and announce the move. Of all of his duties it was this one that he disliked the most. The General Manager would always handle the awkward call to a player to tell him he'd been traded. That was a duty that *no one* wanted to do.

The Coach would always handle the equally difficult, 'We're sending you down to St. Johns' but if you work on blah blah you'll be back up here in no time' speech. The Assistant General Manager had the easy task of calling players up from the "rock" and telling them what plane to catch to make it to wherever the Leafs happened to be playing. And Ron got the only other duty: letting Tommy Stukko in on whatever the media had to be advised of. Tommy could gripe in any way he wanted, because he didn't have the balls to complain to the higher-ups; so he ranted on Ron Bailey.

"You never give me time to prepare a proper press release," he would say, to which Ron would reply, "Just make sure that you give them *all* the details—the ones that matter to the fans, like whom we got in return, where they played their junior hockey, what their stats were, which way they shoot, and what they bring to the team. Never mind speculating which line they'll play on. The fans like to figure that one out on their own."

Tommy Stukko resented being told what the fans wanted to hear. *He* would decide what information was necessary, *not* the director of player personnel, who was a scout with a title as far as Tommy Stukko was concerned. As far as Tommy Stukko was concerned, the media could look up all that information stuff for themselves. That's what media guides were for. But the thing that Tommy Stukko lived for was being the one to put the bug in the ear of whatever 'TV head' or Leaf beat reporter covering the Leafs who was most likely to kiss his ass.

By being a fly on the wall at all personnel meetings he had the pipeline developed to whatever moves were in the works, and would let these juicy tidbits of information out from time to time. The media gurus would hang around Tommy, either at *Tim Riley's Bar*, the watering hole frequented by players and fans alike or in hallways or dark recesses, the kind of places all moles resided when they weren't in their holes. Tommy Stukko was a cheap drunk. Buy him a glass of his favourite white wine and he'd spill almost any piece of information (and the occasional glass of wine) to any available reporter. He would stop just before naming the name that would make the piece complete for the writer. He would almost always keep that last bit for another time, another drink, and another reporter. Ron knew that this was going on but he wasn't going to be the one to out Tommy Stukko; he would leave that for someone who had a real grudge against Tommy Stukko. And there were many of those.

Ron also knew that other people in the organization, specifically the General Manager, suspected that Tommy Stukko was the mole. But until it caused the organization some real embarrassment, or until it could be proven without question, Ken Butler was content to let things remain as they were.

Ron stood up as the train pulled into the College Street station. As he got off the train he noticed that the décor suggested this was the stop for the Gardens. He wished that the name of the station would be officially changed *to Maple Leaf Gardens* the way the University and Bloor Street stop was called 'Museum' because of its proximity to the Royal Ontario Museum. The College Street station's walls were painted with huge, larger than life murals of Leafs players from the past and present. The vivid blue and white colours were a sharp contrast to the rest of the station that also featured framed photographs of great moments in Leaf history. There was a picture of Darryl Sittler, from the February night in 1976 when he scored six goals and added four assists, which still stood as a NHL single-game record. There was also a picture of Leaf captain George Armstrong being awarded the Stanley Cup in April of 1967, the last championship that the team had recorded to date.

Thirty-plus years ago, Ron was only three years old when the Leafs won that cup. He could still remember his brother waking him up the next morning to tell him that Toronto had beaten Montreal 3-1. He remembered sitting at the kitchen table in his parent's home, eating his Muffets with brown sugar, while the radio played the musical introduction to 'CFRB Sports' with Bill Stephenson at the Canadian Tire sports desk, who came on to tell us that the Leafs were champions again, and that did we know that this week at Canadian Tire spring tune-ups were being featured for only $9.95?'

Ron could picture the kitchen, decorated in the familiar turquoise and pink colours that were so popular when he was a kid. It was the very kitchen that he came running to for dinner after endless hours of road hockey. Ron and his brother would play in their driveway, until it got too dark or until they were called in for dinner.

They would take shots on each other, though Ron was almost always the goalie, pretending to be Johnny Bower. His brother would be any of the hated opposition, from 'Boom Boom' Geoffrion, to Stan Mikita to Alex Delvecchio. His brother could rarely score on Ron when he was Bower. But when his brother became Frank Mahovlich, and Ron was Gump Worsley or Gerry Cheevers, he found it impossible to make a save on the 'Big M'.

It was thirty-plus years ago but it was still fresh in his mind since the media continually reminded the public that the last cup victory was thirty-plus years ago. And the laughing speculation of the typically cynical Canadian fans and media was that it might be thirty-plus years before the Leafs would win another one.

As Ron walked along Carlton Street to the Gardens he saw Walt Fisher approaching him.

"Good morning Ronnie," he smiled.

Walt Fisher was the team's Assistant General Manager, but he could easily be mistaken for a corporate lawyer. His grey at the temple look was enhanced by his haircut, which always looked as if it had been done earlier that day. His choice in suits was impeccable, always the right cut and style. While he could be fitted right off the rack, his suits were always custom tailored. Walt was a former defenseman in junior hockey and even had a brief stint as a fullback with the Argonauts. He tried to make everyone forget that he had also spent three years on the professional wrestling circuit in Ontario. His physique however did suggest that of an athlete. He was still in good enough shape to be wrestling at the Gardens.

"All ready for the big meeting?" he asked though Ron knew that the sarcasm in Walt's voice was genuine. Walt Fishers title was 'Assistant' and although he had no designs on his boss's position he did take great pride in filling in for Ken Butler whenever he could. An his sarcasm today was due to his favourite pastime of scrutinizing the Leafs trade offers and suggesting his own deals which would be 'in the better interest of the hockey club'.

Walt led the way through the front door before Ron could answer, as if he was barging through the Ottawa Rough Riders defensive line for a first down.

As they walked along the corridor they both said their 'good mornings' to the various workers they saw on a daily basis. It pleased Ron that so many of the Garden's employees were long time employees. Almost everyone took great pride in being associated with the hockey team. There was a time when those were the *only* benefits to working there, because the teams previous owner, while known as a benevolent soul for any charity or cause, treated his people with little regard or financial reward. That began to change after his death, when the foundation that now controlled the team began to make amends for those past oversights. All employee contracts were reviewed even the Garden's agreements with the unionized employees. This was the foundations way of bringing the Gardens' into the twenty-first century.

Ron and Walt Fisher entered the director's room together and noticed that the coach, Spencer Smith, was already seated.

"I told you that we should have kept Sullivan" Walt Fisher began. He caught the coach's attention immediately.

"Good morning to you too, Walt," he grimaced. Spencer Smith put his glasses down on the table.

"He's a damn hard worker that Sullivan. I would've loved to have found a spot for him, but you guys wanted a tough guy." Spencer Smith leaned comfortably back in his chair. He was leaning a bit too comfortably for a coach of a team only three points out of 30th place, Walt Fisher thought. If this was his team, there was no way someone like Spencer Smith would still be the coach. Walt Fisher held no personal grudge against Smith, and even thought that he was doing a reasonable job under the circumstances. But Walt Fisher wanted to see someone behind the bench who would make this bunch of overpaid underachiever's earn their seven-figure income. At every opportunity he told the General Manager that once Smith's contract as coach had expired that they should re-evaluate the position.

Ken Butler had hired Smith, and wasn't about to admit that he *wasn't* the right man for the job. Walt Fisher was about to pursue the Sullivan thing, but dropped it when the General Manager entered the room. Ken Butler was dressed in a suit that looked as if it came of a mannequin in a discount store. The shirt barely matched, and the only thing that appeared as if it was new was the tie with the Maple Leaf logo all over it, which looked like one of those items in the souvenir stand that the public rarely bought.

"Good Morning, Good Morning," Ken Butler said to no one in particular. "We have a great deal to cover in very little time so let's get right to it. Spencer has a practice to get to and I have a plane to catch to Chicago," he said as he began to search for his glass of water. The news about the plane to Chicago caught everyone by surprise, as they had heard nothing about it up until now.

Walt Fisher *had* to know, so he was the one who asked. "Getting in a little ice fishing in the windy city, Ken?" Ken Butler was still searching for the water pitcher, which he found to be empty. He was about to ask someone to go and fill it when he realized that he had been spoken to.

"What? No! I have to meet with the league committee on... where's Crowe?" he asked, instead of answering Walt Fisher's question. Indeed the meeting wasn't ready to start because the Chief Scout was absent.

Fred Crowe wasn't an integral part of the organizational meetings when it came to evaluating trades. His title was 'Chief Scout', although he didn't report directly to the director of player personnel, as was common in most organizations. Instead, he reported to the General Manager, but was listed below Ron Bailey on the organizational chart. This was because of a long-standing relationship that existed; Fred Crowe had actually hired Ken Butler for *his* first job in pro hockey, as a scout for the Detroit Red Wings. And years later when Fred Crowe found himself looking for work, Ken Butler wasted no time in hiring him. Chief Scout was the only position with enough of a title to still let Fred Crowe keep some dignity. In reality Crowe was something of a joke in the organization. Most of the clubs' scouting was handled by NHL central scouting, except for Europe, which was looked after by a group put together by a former Leaf player from Finland. All of the clubs professional scouts reported to Ron Bailey, as did the scouts in eastern and western Canada, and those covering the US colleges. Fred Crowe attended junior hockey games in the Toronto area only, covering Brampton, Mississauga, Oshawa and Barrie.

Walt Fisher was getting impatient. "Can we begin, Ken?" he asked, knowing that Crowe was only there to add a yes vote to anything that the General Manager proposed.

"I think we can, and we'll bring Fred up to speed when he gets here," Ken Butler drawled. He was ready now that he had water in the pitcher. And Walt knew that it was impossible to *ever* bring Fred Crowe up to speed without rewinding his armature and overhauling his motor completely.

The General Manager cleared his throat. "I think it's time to re-examine our mission statement as it was outlined when we began our plan three years ago. We set a timetable of five years to make this team competitive," he said, focusing on the coach for no apparent reason. "After reaching the conference finals two years running, a couple of years earlier than we all expected I might add, we decided to retool parts of this team to be able to win *immediately*. If that meant sacrificing a little bit of the future for the present, then so be it. When you get as close as we were to winning the Stanley Cup, the next hurdle should be the easiest."

Ken Butler took his first glass of water. "We know this is not always the case, however. The moves we made to push us over the top have not worked to our liking; it's safe to say. Perhaps the talent on this team may have been overestimated by all of us? I feel that while we still have a good chance at making the playoffs, the purpose for which this team was constructed—that goal for this season, is no longer within our reach."

Everyone in the room had to agree. None of them would say so, however. He continued

"We have a unique opportunity now *because* of the situation we find ourselves in, to redefine the mission statement and to re-evaluate the personnel we have. It's no secret that every club in this league knows exactly the predicament we are in, and they will try to exploit it if we choose to panic. I am suggesting the opposite." Ken Butler paused here to see if those around him were in agreement so far.

He looked at Spencer Smith, who absolutely *disagreed* that the talent had been overestimated. He looked at Walt Fisher, who considered the word panic to mean something that others would resort to in a crisis. And he looked at Ron Bailey, who thought that the retooling resulted in all of the *wrong* moves being made. It was not Ron's position to second-guess his boss, however. He left that to Walt Fisher, and the club's owners.

It was time for the second drink from the glass. Ken Butler continued. "We have several trade offers to consider, and we'll go over them. But I'm throwing this idea out for all of you to consider, the idea that we hold off until we *know* that the playoffs are out of reach and that we use our trump cards, the veterans of trade able quality, to secure ourselves some younger players with which to build a foundation of contention for three to five years down the road."

Most of the others were shocked by the General Manager's candour. It was rare for him to speak about the organization without putting a more positive spin on it.

"Now I'm just throwing this out for discussion," he continued. "We have to consider that the closer we get to the trade deadline, the more desperate clubs with a chance to improve themselves will be. It stands to reason that we can make the best deal for ourselves by playing one contender against the other and in doing so wind up with something to build on for the future. What do you think?"

Walt Fisher rushed into the opening in the line as if a Winnipeg linebacker was in pursuit.

"I don't think that anyone in this room will disagree that the performance of this team on the ice has been a disgrace. And that's no disrespect to the coaching staff," he added. Of *course*, it *was* a disrespectful thing to say about the coaching staff. But Walt Fisher was at least being honest.

"I say we weigh each against each other. And like Ken says, wait until the appropriate time as the deadline approaches and close the deal that makes the best sense for the future." Walt already sounded like this was *his* decision, and therefore that was the way it was going to be. Ken Butler continued, after sipping some more water.

"The redefined mission statement is this; our goal now is to make this team younger, faster, tougher and guided along a learning curve to make it competitive in five years' time."

The silence that followed was like that of a DVD being paused; no one even breathed. Spencer Smith had to say something now. "Let me understand this," he began as if he was paying attention for the first time, "we were heading on a five year plan that *was working* after only three years and now we're going to abandon it to start on *another* five year plan, that's it?"

Walt Fisher felt he had to defend the General Manager. "Not exactly Spence. You're taking it a bit out of context. I think we all agree that the original plan was *not* working; if it were we wouldn't be chasing a playoff spot—we'd be secure, and strengthening ourselves as the regular season winds down. But here we are in January and already so far out of a playoff spot that only some kind of miracle could get us there."

Spencer Smith didn't like the condescending tone that was always present when Walt Fisher spoke. "Walt, I was behind the bench when this team made it to the final four those two years, and I'm willing to go with them again; all we need is a few band aids, not major surgery. I don't think we have to throw the baby out with the bath water."

Walt Fisher screwed up his face as if he had no idea what the coach meant.

"Are you trying to say that you think this team has the talent to make the playoffs?"

Spencer Smith glanced around the room for some backup on this, but the faces of Ron Bailey, Ken Butler, and Fred Crowe (who had now joined them) showed no such agreement.

"Yes, with a little help, I think it does," he answered. "All we need is a chance to get some guys healthy, maybe add a third line centre and another defenseman, and just *make* the playoffs. Once we're in, anything can happen. A veteran club like ours can do a lot of damage in the playoffs."

To our reputation, Walt Fisher thought. "Are you willing to stake *your* job on that, Spence?" he asked.

"Damn right I am!" he fumed, while pounding the table with his huge fist.

Ken Butler stepped in. After all, it was his meeting. "Just a minute fellas—let's not let this get out of hand! As I said earlier, making the playoffs with this club is not likely. We all know where we need help. The trade offers that Ron will present show that we can improve ourselves where we need to. All I'm saying is that we should consider them, but with the idea that we'll make our moves closer to the trade deadline to maximize what we get in return. Seeing what's on the table now will give us some idea of what we can get at the deadline."

The meeting continued with a discussion and evaluation of the trade offers. The group agreed that talks would continue with Pittsburgh, Dallas and Carolina, with the Carolina deal considered the most attractive. Nothing however was likely to happen until the trade deadline.

The Centre of the Universe

As the trade deadline approached (and the club found itself all alone in last place) it became obvious even to the most 'blue and white bleeding' Toronto Maple Leaf fan that the club was *not* going to make the playoffs.

Ron Bailey sat in his office one morning reading *The Hockey News*. This particular issue was most intriguing to him because it included a league wide assessment of each club's prospects, both the players who were still playing junior hockey and those at the minor pro level. Out of thirty clubs the Toronto MapleLeafs were rated 23rd, and Ron took considerable objection to both how the article was written and the method at which the so-called 'ranking' was determined. The survey was conducted among a panel of 'experts' from around the league, consisting of a current General Manager, a current assistant coach, a broadcaster from Fox TV and several current and former scouts and player agents—also included were the paper's group of experts. Ron was sure to be asked to comment on the article and while he sat playing with his computer screen saver, he tried to think of one.

Ken Butler passed by his open doorway, and when he realized that Ron was at his desk, he stopped and lowered the glasses on his nose and said, "How'd you like to leave early today?"

That question was typically followed by a request to travel— either to pick up some newly acquired player at the airport or to go and catch a game somewhere. Ron liked the travelling part of his job, especially when it meant an assignment to a big-league city.

"What's up?" Ron asked as he clicked the mouse to leave the desktop. He hoped it would be Miami. That was one of the few NHL cities he had yet to visit.

"I'd like you to go down to Kingston and have a look at an over-age player we've heard some good things about. It doesn't look like the Kingston club will make the playoffs, so we should be able to sign the kid soon if he pans out. It'll also give you a chance to have another look at Dylan Prevost."

Ron remembered the name; this was a kid who could go in the middle of the first round of the entry draft, which is where the Leafs would be selecting even if they maintained their last-place finish. During the previous off-season (when they expected to be a potential cup finalist) they traded their first round pick and a player to Calgary for Tommy Rettig and the Flames' first round pick. The move now was an extreme embarrassment to the club. Rettig turned out to be little more than a 'baggage smasher', who collected more fighting majors than points, and the Flames first round pick would be no better than about 15th overall. If the Leafs finished last Calgary would be blessed with the best player available in the draft. Ron could just see the headline in the *Toronto Sun's* sports section: LEAFS LOSE OUT ON #1 FOR RETTIG!

"Better get going, Ronnie. You'll have the traffic beaten out of the city if you hurry," Ken Butler said.

Ron agreed. As he backed up his car, his eyes fixed on the blue and white sign above his personalized parking spot that read 'R.BAILEY'. He never stopped admiring that sign on the days that he drove to work. It made him feel like an important part of the organization. As he drove up the Don Valley Parkway to highway 401 he tuned in to the banter on the all sports station.

The afternoon host, Eddie LeBec was discussing the *Hockey News* article that Ron had been reading earlier. "We're in studio with Bob McWilliams of the Hockey News, talking about his article '*Rating the NHL Prospects*', which is really a report card if you will, of the scouting and player development staffs around the National Hockey League. My guest is the man who wrote the article, and if you're a Leaf fan you may want to find a bullet to bite on!"

Ron turned off the radio. He didn't mind Eddie LeBec, as a rule. He was one of the *less* irritating 'radio heads' as they were called. He was still upset by the criticism in the article he had read earlier.

Ron Bailey's career had not exactly followed the course he had set out on. He was a pretty decent high school hockey player with Winston Churchill Collegiate. He dreamed of playing for his hometown Toronto Marlboros, which were the stepping-stone to the Maple Leafs, but he was a little lacking in size and was never even given a tryout as a junior. His academics were good, however, and the athletic director at Massena College in upstate New York noticed him. He was offered a scholarship there and loved the idea of playing hockey to earn an education.

The setting was ideal for him. Massena was a sleepy college town dotted with old brown brick buildings covered with ivy, tall steepled churches and white clapboard homes like those on Christmas cards. There were no distractions like there were in Toronto—nothing to do but study and play hockey. Ron became a good student. And he was learning on the ice as well. He was fortunate enough to be tutored by one of the most innovative coaches around at the time, though Red Garrett's methods were considered somewhat preternatural.

Red Garrett would listen attentively to the complaints of his players. And just when they thought they had his sympathy he would ask a question like, "How'd ya like to have a child by me?" The bewildered player would instantly forget whatever objection they had. He would also not permit his players to use curved sticks in practice. When they would whine that they couldn't raise the puck enough with a straight blade he would lament, "It's a poor workman who blames his tools."

Red Garrett's obstinacy paid off. His players were the only ones in the league who were able to take a decent backhand shot as a result his staunchness. Ron was progressing nicely towards a minor-league career until the evening of January 20th, 1983. The Massena Mohawks were playing at home against the Overland College Blue Blazers when Ron was blind-sided while trying to ice the puck. He fell over backwards and would probably only have sustained a bruised tailbone had his left skate not caught a rut in the ice. Instead he tore both the medial collateral and anterior cruciate ligaments in his knee. His playing career was over.

Ron spent the rest of the college year helping out behind the bench, and became useful as an assistant coach. Red Garrett offered him the position on a permanent basis and they were a tandem for four years at Massena. When Garrett moved on to the Windsor Spitfires in the OHL as coach and General Manager he took Ron with him as his assistant. And after another four years they moved on together to Rochester of the American League. It appeared to those on the outside that Red Garrett and Ron Bailey was an inseparable pair, and it was common knowledge that Ron was dating Red's oldest daughter Kelly.

The fact was, though, that Red was not an easy person to get close to. He shied away from the spotlight as much as was possible for a head coach, instead directing it on his players, his assistant coach and the team owner. To him his life away from his job was nobody's business. Whether that was the reason why he seemed to move regularly from position to position was anybody's guess. Still Ron was not surprised when Red Garrett accepted the position that would eventually separate them. When he became the assistant General Manager of the Calgary Flames he knew there was no spot for Ron. And Ron knew that as much as he had relied on Red Garrett's advice over the years, maybe there was something to be gained by studying with someone else. Red Garrett was not finished advising his *unofficial protégé* when he suggested Ron apply for the position of Director of Player Personnel with Toronto.

"You have all of the qualifications, experience in US College, junior and minor leagues. Not many guys your age have had a taste of all of that—coaching, managing and some scouting to boot!" Red reminded him. Ron knew that he had Red Garrett to thank for his diverse background. And it was Red Garrett that probably sealed the interview by providing such a glowing recommendation on his resume. Ken Butler respected the opinion of Red Garrett, as they had briefly played together in the WHA.

Ron turned the radio on once again to keep from being hypnotized by the road.

"We're back with Bob McWilliams of the *Hockey New,* talking about the article '*Rating the NHL Prospects*' and Bob you have something special to say about the local team, the Toronto Maple Leafs." McWilliams took over the microphone.

"Well it's no secret Eddie that this team ranks near the bottom of the NHL standings, but if you look at how they have drafted and developed players over the last few years you begin to get an explanation."

Ron was frozen by these words. "The current NHL roster only includes six home-grown players, while there are twelve players currently playing elsewhere in the NHL who were drafted by this regime." Ron was bristling to get a word in, but the call-in portion of the show hadn't begun yet.

McWilliams continued. "So you have a dozen players who aren't good enough to play in Toronto but *are* good enough to play for other clubs which are *ahead* of the Leafs in the standings—very strange." McWilliams was doing a good job of skewering the club's management. And he wasn't finished.

Eddie LeBec tried to interject some impartiality. "I think you'll agree Bob that these twelve players you speak of weren't just *given* away by Toronto. They did get something in return."

"Of course," McWilliams conceded. "But the players they got in return are the ones who have them in 27th place! I think you have to go beyond *that* and look at why this clubs' draft picks haven't panned out and *furthermore* why the players they currently have in the minors and the ones they have drafted but are still playing in junior are rated so lowly. As an organization this study rates them only 23rd in the league."

Ron was fuming. He managed to keep his anger revved up until the call in portion of the show began. He kept pressing his re-dial button with frenzy, until he got through.

"We'll take another call now. Ron is on the car phone in Toronto. Ron you have a question for Bob McWilliams of *the Hockey News?*" Eddie LeBec boomed.

Ron started slowly; he didn't want emotion to ruin the credibility of his argument.

"Yes. I'm very interested in *how* you arrived at the rankings in your article, which I've read. I seem to remember something about a *survey?*"

"Not a survey per Se," McWilliams corrected, "but a consensus of hockey people in the know."

"That's very interesting," Ron continued, "but I suspect that not *all* of these 'people in the know' have seen *every* player in every club's development chain *play*. I mean even *scouts* only get to see these guys maybe three times a year, and if that's the case, how can you—"

"We're running a little short of time, Ron. Thanks for the—"

Eddie LeBec wanted to cut Ron off but he pleaded, "Can I just say one more thing? If these self-proclaimed experts haven't seen *all* of the players they are including in their assessment, how can they to pass off their opinions as if it's some kind of scientific study or analytical survey? Don't these idiots realize the influence they have over the public? People that read the article will assume that some organizations are incompetent because of this article—to condemn a whole organization of people because of someone's opinion?"

Eddie LeBec hit the kill button and Ron was cut off. "We really touched a nerve with that guy!" McWilliams chuckled, "he must be a Leaf fan."

Ron didn't hear the last comment because he hadn't turned the radio back on. But *he* felt that he had made his point, even though the two "talking heads" had not. Ron was continually surprised by the public's perception that, 'if it's in the paper then it must be true.'

He frequently would be approached in some small town arena, and hear such gems as

'So I hear where you're going to draft, '*insert name here*' with your first pick, all because it was in the paper.

'Oh of course' he wanted to answer, 'we always tip off the papers in advance. That way the other teams will know who we're taking too, so they can concentrate on someone else.'

The love / hate relationship he'd had with the media over the years was a lot more of the latter. "Just once I'd like the media play up the stories that really *deserve* it instead of digging up dirt or stirring up controversy. But I guess you can't sell too many newspapers with good news," he lamented.

Ron was glad to be going to a junior game for a change. Sometimes the hype that surrounded an NHL game overshadowed what took place on the ice. After all, hockey is a *simple* game; his old coach Red Garrett used to remind him. "It's not complicated" He used to tell his players when they would look confused about one of his directions. "Hockey is the simplest game on the face of the earth. You put this old rubber cookie past the goalie at the other end of the rink more times than they do it to us, and we win!"

Red Garrett was a master of the understatement. When an official would miss a call, he wouldn't get upset. He would stand calmly, almost disinterested behind the bench while stroking his red beard as if a solution was hidden in the sprinkling of grey whiskers. And then when there was a break in play he would slowly lean over the boards and ask the official that blew the call: "Steve, would you rather do what you do, or work for a living?"

Even at the junior level the game of hockey was still a business. But in rinks like the Kingston Memorial Arena where he was headed, the business side was easily forgotten once you were in the building. The portrait of the queen at the end of the rink, the vendor hawking tickets for the 'fifty-fifty draw' that would fund the midget team's trip to the Air Canada Cup, and things like 'sweater bingo', where you could win a prize by filling out a bingo card in the program by checking off the sweater numbers of players who scored. Ron enjoyed the closeness to the game that these small town arenas offered.

The overage player that Ron was there to see didn't disappoint him. His name was Rylan Thomas, and he did everything he could to make the scouts notice him. He delivered a big body check to the other team's top scorer, he played some decent defensive hockey by intercepting a pass on a power play, he scored a goal by using some good puck sense in stealing the puck on a line change and he even got into a fight with the other team's enforcer. And he won the fight. Ron was looking for a warm body that could do just *one* of these things.

And here was an overage junior that went un-drafted who was ripe for the picking. If Rylan Thomas signed with Toronto he would be dispatched to the St. Johns' Maple Leafs at the conclusion of the junior schedule in mid-March (since it didn't appear that the Kingston Frontenac's would make the playoffs.) The kid could probably be had for a signing bonus of fifty thousand dollars, and offered a minor league contract. He would be easy to sign because he probably didn't have an agent or was likely represented by his father.

Ron was making some notes in his program about the need for the kid to go deeper into the offensive zone when he *didn't* have the puck. His attention was re-directed to the public address announcer, who said, "Ladies and gentlemen, if you'll turn to page 23 in your program we'll give you the first of tonight's lucky program numbers."

Ron was trying to focus on the *other* player he was there to see Kingston's leading scorer Dylan Prevost, when he noticed that his program was turned to page 23.

"Tonight's first lucky number is 1927. If you have that number you can claim your prize at the Frontenac's souvenir booth."

Ron laughed as he stared at his number: 1927.

"The first prize is dinner for two at Red's Hotel in Cobourg."

Ron scowled as he tried to figure this one out. He wondered why they would give away a dinner in Cobourg; it must be sixty miles from Kingston. He dismissed the idea, but he remembered to cash in his prize as he left the arena. He stopped by the Frontenac's dressing room after the game to talk to the coach about Rylan Thomas. The coach remembered Ron from his days with Windsor.

"You better move quickly on this one Ron! Thomas's had some interest from Boston. Cap Raeder was here on Friday night."

Ron thanked the coach. If the Bruins had sent their assistant coach to check the kid out then they must be *very* interested. As he drove back to Toronto he tried to call Ken Butler on his cell phone. When he pressed the power button, nothing happened; it didn't even light up. He couldn't remember the last time he had charged the battery. It was now 11:15 PM by the clock in his car. He started to think about where he could pull off the highway to find a pay phone to call his boss. Then he remembered the 'lucky program' prize. He doubted if 'Red's Hotel' would have a kitchen open this late; he really wasn't that hungry anyway, what with having devoured an arena hot dog, popcorn and ginger ale.

But Cobourg was only 15 kilometres away according to the sign on the 401, so it was there that he planned to get off the highway. He stopped to use the phone and to ask directions at the Petro Canada station, and then drove into the 'downtown' section. It consisted largely of a few store fronts on the main drag 'King Street' that was common to almost any small town in southern Ontario. The street was deserted, but well lit. He found Red's Hotel without any trouble. It was distinctly red on the outside. But it was anything but a hotel on the inside. It was nestled between the Cobourg jail and a chiropractor's office, in what was formerly a residential part of the old downtown.

Ron was able to park on the street right outside the front door. The place still had the antiquated signs for 'MEN'S ENTRANCE' and 'LADIES ENTRANCE' from a time when they were necessary. He stepped inside and was overcome by aromas of stale cigarette smoke and beer. If he had been a connoisseur of these smells he would have recognized them as Export 'A' cigarettes and Export Ale draft. The walls were littered with beer signs—both neon and electric, of brands that had either lost their appeal or were no longer brewed at all. And there were also pennants and posters of teams that were past their glories, a Detroit Tigers pennant depicting them as '*1984 World Champions*' and also a poster of the '*Super Bowl Champion*' Washington Redskins. Ron felt like something was missing. In every watering hole from Sudbury to Brockville and from London to Gravenhurst you could find something with the Toronto Maple Leafs logo on it. Whether it was a Molson Canadian WATCH THE GAME HERE sign, or a picture of goalie John Dennis or winger Joel Kent, there was always *something* to say that this was Ontario, and the hockey team almost everyone followed was THE LEAFS! The walls held only team pictures of the Stanley Cup champion Edmonton Oilers (all five of them) and a pennant of the New York Islanders. Ron stepped up to the bar and tried to get the attention of the bartender, who was filling a pitcher with draft while carrying on a conversation with a man at the other end of the bar.

"Excuse me," Ron interrupted, "But can you tell me—?"

The bartender didn't even look at him as he replied, "Be right with you," as he took the full pitcher to the end of the bar. As he gazed around the area behind the bar he was taken aback by the presence of a couple of hockey sweaters that he recognized; side by side were a Rochester American's white sweater and a maroon Peterborough Pete's sweater, both with the number 16 on them. Both sweaters appeared to have writing on them as if they were autographed and personalized.

The bartender appeared and asked Ron, "What can I get you?" Ron wanted to ask about the sweaters but he suddenly remembered *why* he came in. "I don't suppose that the kitchen is still open?" he asked.

The bartender shook his head. "Kitchen closes at ten. But if you want something to *eat*," he answered as he waved his hand over a jar of pickled eggs. They reminded Ron of the jars of formaldehyde-preserved specimens from high school biology class.

"No thanks. I'll just have a Canadian," he said as he took out some cash. The bartender returned with a bottle and proceeded to remove the cap by holding it against his forearm while giving it a twist. He placed the bottle in front of Ron and asked, "Need a glass?"

Ron said no, and asked the bartender "What's the significance of the Peterborough and Rochester sweaters?"

The bartender half smiled, the way someone does when they know something that you don't but should know (unless you're a tourist.)

"They were Dale McCaine's," he replied, as if *that* answer was enough. A cynical person would have asked who the hell Dale McCaine was, but Ron wasn't a cynic. He looked closer at the sweaters and realized they were old, as in maybe *forty years* old. The style of the Peterborough sweater (which had changed from the old 'TPT' front, which stood for Toronto-Peterborough Trucking to the current 'Petes' logo about thirty-five years ago) *looked* old—how old was difficult to say. The Rochester sweater (with the stylized Stars and Stripes shield but *without* the scripted 'Americans' on it) hadn't been used since before he was a coach with the Americans. Below the sweaters was a small black and white photograph showing a profile of a player skating in alone on a goalie. Ron squinted to recognize the teams involved; the goalie was wearing a Leaf's dark uniform, while the forward was wearing what looked like a white Rochester sweater. Ron was amazed—why would the Leafs be playing the Rochester Americans? Below the picture was a small plaque, but Ron could barely make it out. He had to know, so he leaned across the bar and read, '*Dale McCaine scores for Rochester as they beat the Stanley Cup Champions 9-1*'

"Everything okay?" the bartender asked, as Ron realized he *shouldn't* be leaning *that far* over the bar. "I was just noticing the picture. I didn't know that Rochester ever played the Leafs, let alone beat them. And I don't remember a Dale McCaine. Is he from around here?" Ron asked.

The bartender gave him the same knowing smile. Before Ron could answer a voice boomed from the end of the bar, "DAMN RIGHT HE'S FROM AROUND HERE!"

The voice belonged to the man the bartender had been conversing with. Ron was embarrassed that his words had been overheard, but even *more* embarrassed that he didn't know who the local yokel hockey player was. He thought about introducing himself as a member of the Leafs organization, but something told him not to. He took his beer and walked over to the man.

"I'm sorry, but I used to be with Rochester, and I didn't recall the name. He was with them long before my time," Ron offered more as an explanation than as an apology. He didn't think he should apologize for being ignorant of the history of a local hero who had his uniform in a bar for scoring a goal in an exhibition game, even if it *was* against the Stanley Cup Champions. The grey-haired man looked at Ron in disbelief. "If you played in Rochester you would have heard of Dale McCaine!" the man insisted.

At this point the bartender intervened, as if to keep the peace.

"He said he wasn't with the Americans when Dale was there. That was a long time ago, Thorny."

The man they called Thorny took a long gulp from his glass of draft and didn't even wait for the foam to leave his lips before he started to speak. "Dale McCaine was the best hockey player who ever played in Cobourg!" he paused, looking as if it was painful to remember what he was about to say. "He was the best hockey who ever played in *Peterborough!*" he paused again as if the words were on a distant blackboard that he was having trouble reading. "He was the best hockey player who ever played in Rochester!" he stammered, "and, he would have been the best hockey player who ever played for those god damned Maple Leafs!" he concluded.

Ron was glad that he *hadn't* introduced himself as a member of the Leaf's organization. He was unsure about pursuing this conversation with the slightly drunken man. But he suspected that Thorny wouldn't let him leave until he had convinced Ron that Dale McCaine was everything he said he was. Ron looked around for a way to escape but there was none. Thorny waved for him to sit at the empty barstool to his left and Ron obliged.

"You asked about Dale McCaine so I'm gonna tell you about Dale McCaine, so sit down! What're ye drinkin there?" Thorny asked.

Ron said, "Its okay—I'm fine, really. Why don't you let me buy *you* a beer if you like?"

Thorny liked that just fine, and the bartender delivered him another large Export draft. Thorny adjusted his threadbare green John Deere baseball cap so that it rode further back on his head and he continued.

"Whenid you play in Rochester?" he asked.

Ron admitted, "I didn't play—I was an assistant coach for eight years—from '92 until '02"

Thorny sneered at Ron. "You were never there when they was any *good!*" he slurred.

Ron didn't want to argue, but they *had* won a Calder Cup in that span. Thorny put his thumbs behind his suspenders as if to find his balance and offered, "I mean when they was the number one farm team of Tronta. When they won three cups in four years... when they beat the Leafs right in the Maple Leaf Gardens!" he said as he gulped the last of his draft and proceeded to sip the one that Ron had bought him.

"Dale was there then," he continued, "he started right when he finished in Peterborough. He went right from the Petes to the Americans and shoulda gone on to Tronta," he concluded.

Ron's curiosity was piqued. He thought that he could interrupt now. "So what became of Dale McCaine?" he asked.

Thorny got quiet for a change and stared into his beer for the answer. "That is a sad story, is what it is. Dale never did like being too far from home, 'cause his dad, Dougie, was kinda sick. He was a tin knocker and he had asbestosis. When Dale was playin in Peterborough, and even when he was in Rochester, he wasn't too far away and Dale could be home from time to time. And if he made it to Tronta, well that would only be an hour and a half's drive."

Thorny seemed like he was going to be a while getting to the point so Ron took a long sip of beer.

"Dale had a good year in Rochester, He led all the rookies in scoring, but he was homesick. He always played better when he knew he was gonna be home for a few days. Well after his first year in Rochester, the Leafs decided to sell the team, from asshole to breakfast, and they moved all of their players, the ones they didn't sell, to Tulsa. Well that meant no more drives home for Dale. He was ascared that his dad was gonna take real sick when he was way off in Oklahoma City or Houston or someplace and wouldn't be able to get home in time. He was always worried about his dad, and his play started to go for a shit. He only lasted one year in Tulsa before the Leafs let him go."

Ron seemed to remember something about the Leafs having more than one farm team when he was a kid, but he didn't know how or when their farm team changed from Rochester to Tulsa. "So he never made it to the NHL?" Ron asked.

Thorny looked as if his eyes were about to water, but instead he took another swig of his Export. "He never even made it home from Tulsa!" Thorny cried.

Ron was shocked. For a moment a horrible thought came to him that maybe Dale McCaine committed suicide, but he decided to ask what really happened.

"I remember that night like it was yesterday. He phoned Dougie from training camp. He was too ashamed to tell him that he'd been cut. He told Dougie he was comin home for a visit," he stammered.

"He was cut from the team and he couldn't tell his dad over the phone. So he decided to tell him face to face. But on the way home he got into a wreck and he's killed just outside of Tulsa."

Ron stared down at the bar and then glanced up at the picture of Dale McCaine scoring against the Stanley Cup champions.

"At the time I couldn't help but think how he'd still be playin if it weren't for them no longer being in Rochester," Thorny continued, "but no matter—when you're times up. And Dale, it was just his time I guess."

The old grey haired man rubbed the silver stubble on his chin. "It's an awful thing for that family to have gone through. Everybody *knew* Dale was good enough to play in Tronta; he just never got his chance," he sighed.

Ron had to agree that it was one of those 'if only' tales like the story of Norman Levielle or George Pellawa. Thorny pounded his chubby fist on the bar so hard that it made Ron's half-empty bottle spin.

"To this *day* old Dougie is bitter—do you know that he was so torn up inside by losing his only son that he vowed that team would

34

never win another Stanley Cup because of what they had done to Dale?"

Ron was speechless and shook his head in disbelief. "He vowed they would never, the Leafs would never win, because of *what*?" he shrieked.

Thorny shifted his bulk on the bar stool as he confronted Ron. "Dougie McCaine was the biggest Leaf fan there ever was. He had the Maple Leaf tattooed on his arse. More than anything he wanted Dale to play for Tronta. And that's why Dougie cursed them. He blames the Leafs for his son's death, you know, because" he trailed off.

"You mean because they moved their team from Rochester to Tulsa!" Ron exclaimed.

The old man grabbed his glass and gestured to Ron with it. "Dale McCaine'd been called up to Tronta after one more year in Rochester and he'dve stuck with the Leafs; he was that good! He'd never have been cut and he'd never've had to drive home with all of that shame," Thorny wailed.

Ron was amazed by this tale. Of *course* it was sad how this kid's career and life had ended. But how on earth could his father blame it all on the organization, just because they moved the farm team from Rochester to Tulsa? And to vow that they would never win another Stanley Cup!

"This is incredible!" Ron ranted, "I mean it's a shame what happened to Dale McCaine but to blame it on the Leaf organization—don't you think that's a bit *severe*?"

Ron was asking the wrong person. Thorny was all wired up now. He didn't even need a gulp of draft to respond to this one.

"Son, you don't know how things was back then, do you? That team was making money hand over fist but the owners of the Leafs would do anything for a buck. They didn't care that their future was the farm teams. They sold Rochester and Victoria just to raise

35

the profits. They didn't care that it left the team short o' players, especially with the expansion coming up. A team like Montreal, now they knew they had to keep their farm clubs so they dealt their extra bodies for draft picks. That's what kept them going long after their Montreal Juniors was gone. It was the worst deal the Leafs ever made."

The scary part of it to Ron *now* was that Thorny was making sense. Ron knew that the end of the sponsored junior clubs era was harder on Toronto than it had been on Montreal but he had never really known why.

"You said that Doug McCaine is bitter to this day. So I take it he's still around?" Ron questioned.

"Damn right!" Thorny affirmed, "He's the toughest little sonofabitch I ever knew. I've been a pipe fitter for forty years and I've seen a lot of big men, strong men. But I've never known any as fiery, and tough up here," he said while tapping his temple, "and Dale McCaine was like his old man. He wasn't the biggest or strongest kid on the ice. Hell, he wasn't even the fastest. But he was tough, not dirty mind you, but he'd always take a hit and give one back, but clean, you know?"

Ron didn't exactly know. The kind of player that Thorny was describing was not exactly suited to the NHL today. If you weren't big or fast, you didn't have much chance of sticking unless you were exceptionally skilled. "Who would you liken him to that is playing today?" Ron asked.

Thorny scoffed, "Aw there's nobody, not now. Hey Vern," he called to the bartender, "who'd Dale remind you of that's playin today?"

The bartender came over and joined the conversation. "The only guy that *plays* sort of like Dale is Gilmour. I mean Dale was small and slight like that, not fast but a *good* skater, a guy who was hard to hit, and a good play maker. Dale was maybe a better goal scorer—he would get you a big goal when you needed it most."

Just the kind of player the Leafs could use *now*, Ron thought.

Vern recalled, "And he had it here," he said touching where his heart was. "And he was smart; just like his Dad," he laughed.

Thorny laughed too. Ron wanted to laugh as well, but he didn't know what the joke was about.

"His dad, his name is Doug?" Ron asked. "You said he was still around. I'd like to meet him," he continued. "Where would I find him?"

Thorny was a little surprised. "What for?" he asked

Ron wanted to be honest, but he was afraid Thorny would take it the wrong way.

"I'd just like to know more about Dale." What Ron *really* wanted to know was why anyone that had once such a Leaf fan would vow that they would never again win the Stanley Cup. How could anyone be that bitter?

Thorny didn't answer, and got up to go to the men's room, so Ron decided to ask the bartender where he could find Doug McCaine.

"He's right here in town. He lives at the Golden Plough. It's a retirement home," Vern offered, "But if you're gonna go visit Dougie, I wouldn't mention anything about being with the Leafs," he advised.

Ron was shocked. He hadn't said a word about being a member of the Leafs organization.

"How on earth did you know that?" he demanded.

Vern smiled that smile again. "I don't remember names all the time, but in my business you remember faces. And I remember yours," he grinned, "You were at the Memorial Cup. My brother and you were talking when I came up. My brother is the GM in Hershey."

Ron wasn't good at remembering *faces*, but he could remember names. And he knew that Dave Redden was the GM of the Hershey

Bears. So he must be talking to Vern Redden. And he must be the 'Red' in *Red's Hotel*.

"That's right. I was there, and I am, with the Leafs. And I know your brother. I just can't believe you remembered *my* face!"

Vern smiled again, as he began to dry some glasses with a cotton rag. "I didn't place you until you started talking about the Leafs. You see the Leafs are not popular around here. There aren't many Leaf fans here now. But when Dale was playing, well that was a different story. On a Saturday night this place would be packed. Dougie McCaine would be at that end of the bar, right beside where Thorny was sitting, and let me tell you he'd be leading the cheers, and telling everyone who'd listen that someday Dale would be out there. And nobody would doubt him. Dougie was a respected man around here. He was a smart man who gave Dale all the best advice. He loved that boy more than life itself, and when he lost Dale he lost interest in life. I don't really know why he's hung on all these years. He's been sick for almost forty years, but he kept working for most of it. Like Thorny says, he's tough."

Ron began to reconsider visiting with Doug McCaine. But the curiosity was getting the better of him. "Where's a good place to stay around here?" he asked.

Vern wasn't going to convince Ron not to go. "There's a Best Western across the street from the Golden Plough Lodge. Just go up here to William Street and it's just past the second light. Turn right on to Burnham and its right there at the corner of Elgin and you're there."

Ron thanked Vern, and he waited for Thorny to come back from the men's room so that he could thank him too. He pulled the collar up on his overcoat as he left the bar. The frigid night air was a reminder that winter couldn't be escaped for very long by taking refuge in a warm bar. But winter always made Ron think of hockey, and hockey was the biggest thing in his life.

The Way It Was

Ron checked in to the Best Western and the next morning he had a quick breakfast of scrambled eggs and sausages at the hotel. He paused to call the Garden's office for his messages before proceeding across the road to the Golden Plough Lodge. Just exactly what he was going to *do* when he got there he wasn't sure. But he was intrigued by the fact that anyone who had been such a die-hard Leaf fan could wish that they would never again win the Stanley Cup, no matter *what* the circumstances of their son's death. After all, Ron reasoned, it wasn't like the Leaf organization of *today* was responsible. He didn't truly believe that the reason the Leafs hadn't won a Stanley Cup since Dale McCaine had died was because Doug McCaine had *vowed* that they would never win another one. The Leafs had been a poorly run organization for much of the past forty years—that was an opinion widely held by most fans and hockey people. But the idea that this man had somehow jinxed them, well, that was too fascinating for Ron to let pass.

The game of hockey was full of superstitions, maybe more than most sports. Players, coaches and fans alike all believed in good luck and bad luck. How many times had Ron Hextall and Patrick Roy performed the same on-ice ritual before games? And how true were some of the legendary tales Ron had heard, like the 'Curse of Muldoon', about the Chicago coach who was fired after one season and who vowed that the Blackhawks would never win another cup? The superstitious aspect of the idea was intriguing, that someone could alter the future of the game by their ill will, or by their belief in good luck or bad. Ron couldn't comprehend the notion that someone who once 'bled blue and white' could want them to fail for eternity. He wanted to know more about what was behind Doug McCaine's vow.

Ron ventured up to the front information desk. "I'd like to see a patient," he stated.

The middle-aged woman at the desk smiled at him and lowered her glasses, which were fastened around her neck by a chain.

"We don't refer to our residents as *patients*, dear," she corrected. "Tell me who you would like to see and why you are here."

Ron wasn't good at lying, at least not convincingly. He wasn't prepared to come up with a plausible excuse. "I'd like to see Mr. Doug McCaine," he said.

The lady was waiting for him to state his business when the front desk phone rang and she motioned for him to wait. While the woman talked on the phone he got the crazy notion to pass himself off as an investment counsellor. He even had a business card of his *own* investment counsellor to offer as evidence, but he came to his senses at the last second. When she hung up, she asked, "Is Mr. McCaine expecting you?"

"No," Ron answered truthfully, "but I've come all the way from Toronto to see him," he lied. "It is very important that I speak to him."

The lady didn't comment, but instead punched a few numbers on the telephone.

"Can you ask Mr. McCaine if he wants to see a gentleman, a Mr. Ron Bailey?"

There was a long pause as whoever answered the phone must have been searching out Mr. McCaine to ask him if he wanted to see someone he'd never even heard of. Ron began to sweat. He was waiting for the axe to fall on this one. Finally the woman said, "thank you" to whoever was on the phone and looked Ron squarely in the eyes and said, "Mr. McCaine says that he doesn't know a Mr. Ron Bailey."

Ron was embarrassed. It was a stupid idea to come here. "But he *does* want to see you," the lady added.

Ron raised his head, thanked the lady and asked for directions. He waited for what seemed like an eternity for the elevator. As he rode to the third floor he was overcome by fear—

not the fear of meeting Doug McCaine, but of the fear of getting old. He passed by old people in walkers, wheelchairs or those shuffling along, doing their best to cope with the ravages of old age. And there was a smell of old age in the stale air, whether it was Geritol or Dentu-Crème, Ron didn't know. But it reminded him of the dreaded visits to his Grandfather's old age home.

He approached the room he was directed to and saw the name on the door 'McCAINE'. He stopped and knocked at the open door, but heard no response. He entered the small single room slowly and approached the bed where a man appeared to be sleeping. He wasn't snoring but instead lay with his mouth wide open and was making a noise like the whistling of wind through a partially open window. Ron gazed at the peculiar looking body that lay there before him. The head was small and round, sort of like a chimpanzee's, and had stringy hair like that on a coconut. The brown skin was drawn tightly across it like parchment and it had an oily transparency about it. The body appeared like that of an Egyptian mummy. Suddenly the man stirred and reached quickly for the glasses that lay on the bedside table.

"Who the devil are you?" the man asked crossly. Ron froze in his tracks. The small old man in the bed had eyes that pierced through to your very soul. He stared at Ron and waited impatiently for an answer.

"Well come on!" he urged, "What do you want?"

"Mr. McCaine, my name is Ron Bailey."

"Well that doesn't tell me anything! Why are you here?" he snarled. Ron paused to get the courage to mention who he was when the small man said, "Well, you must be that guy with the Leafs!" He gasped.

Ron raised his eyebrows in such a way that he was unsure if he'd be able to lower them again. "Red told me you were in there last night asking about Dale. Well sit down!" he snapped.

Doug McCaine began to cough so hard that he trembled. He rolled half out of bed and reached for a glass on the bedside table. His medic alert bracelet clinked against the glass as he reached for it. Ron couldn't help but notice how the small old man's hands shook as he drank from the glass slowly, as if to keep its contents from spilling. He said, "You want to know about Dale—what for?"

"Mr. McCaine, I was interested in the story about what happened to your son. I mean when I heard about how he died, it made me—"

"It made you sick, didn't it? Look son, it happened a long time ago. No one cares about how he died now. So why is someone from the Leafs coming around here and asking questions forty years later? It's too late to do anything about it now."

The bitterness was coming out like a festering wound. Ron felt he could never get past it.

"The way the organization handled things back then was wrong, I mean if it happened today—If your son played for our farm club today and needed to be closer to home, I'm sure we'd do something to accommodate him."

"So what's your point, son? You can't make amends for it now! Dale's gone and the Leafs made their bed and now they have to sleep in it," he snarled. Ron looked across the room. Doug McCaine began to direct his attack personally.

"Did they send you here to try and patch things up after all this time? That's pathetic."

Ron tried to deflect the criticism.

"No one from the organization sent me, Mr. McCaine. I heard about the, about your son for the first time last night. I was amazed.

But if he was such a great prospect, how is it that he never got a chance to play in Toronto?"

The small old man parked himself in a chair beside the bed, and pulled tight the drawstring on his bathrobe. He began to cough more violently than before. Ron wondered if he should call someone but the small old man waived him off.

"You really have no idea how things were back then do you son?" he asked.

"No, I guess I don't," Ron replied.

"Well let me tell you, hockey was a business then, and it's a business now." He talked fast, as if he had to get the words out in a hurry, or he would *never* be able to get them out.

"The difference is that back then the *players* weren't in it only for the money, but the *owners* were. Kids grew up playing hockey for the fun of it and wanted to be just like their heroes on the Leafs or the Canadiens."

"It's pretty much the same now," Ron interrupted, "except now their heroes probably play for Philadelphia or Detroit."

Doug McCaine ignored the interruption. "There were no player agents hanging around, no endorsements to speak of, and no strong-armed players association to get them whatever they wanted. If you wanted a job in hockey, well there were only 120 of them. So if you wanted one you had to take it away from somebody else. If you were sent down, you stayed down maybe for your whole career, and waited until someone else got hurt of lost their edge."

The picture Doug McCaine painted of an original six NHL was nothing like the league that Ron knew today. The small old man pointed a finger at Ron.

"It was all about dedication. You played because you loved to play. No one was going to hand you anything. There were no guarantees, no long-term contracts. You made good money by the standards of the day. You were getting paid to play a kid's game. What more could a kid ask for? But there were no good pensions, and if you got hurt they'd pay your doctor bills and that was the end of it. If you were lucky they'd pay for a train ride home, and once you recovered, if you could never play the game again, well you better find a day job."

Ron wanted to know what happened to Dale McCaine. He hadn't suffered a career ending injury, or had he? "Is that what happened to Dale?" Ron asked.

The small old man's face turned sour. "Dale was treated like chattel. He worked hard to make the team and got sent down. That was fine. He'd just have to work harder and maybe get called up. He led all rookie scorers in the league that year in Rochester. He was ready to be called up but on a Stanley Cup champion, well you just don't walk in and get handed a job. You had to beat out a veteran. His time would have come. But the bastards that owned the team thought they were smarter than everybody else. Why have two farm teams full of prospects when one would do? Why not sell both of them and half your players and put them on a team that somebody else owned. Let them take the risks running a minor league operation that didn't make much money. They sold out, do you understand? They sold the future of the Toronto Maple Leafs for $900,000!"

"And because of that, Dale had to go to Tulsa to play?" Ron asked.

"The new owners in Rochester bought some of the old contracts, of veterans mostly. The Leafs kept Dale and sent him and the other kids to Tulsa. They didn't own the team, only the player contracts. Dale was too far from home. He wasn't happy there. He didn't play like he could, and he got distracted."

Ron sat down on the bed and had to ask the question that intrigued him. "But Dale's death, it was the result of an accident. It could have happened anywhere. Do you really blame the team for his death?"

Doug McCaine eyes burned through his glasses at Ron. "It wouldn't have happened had he not been sent there. Their greed was what took Dale and they will never win another Stanley Cup because of it!" he screamed.

Ron tried to be the voice of reason. "Mr. McCaine, the Leafs made a terrible mistake. If your son was in the system now and needed to be playing closer to home for a reason such as your situation, well we'd do everything we could to accommodate him. We would make a deal to place him on another team, closer to home. I think that your feelings for the management at the time are genuine. But I think you are doing all of us now, including yourself a disservice by condemning the whole Leaf organization."

Doug McCaine wasn't about to change his opinion. "It's too late for that. If you could do it *now*, if you could give him a chance *now*, that would be different."

For the first time Ron considered that perhaps Mr. McCaine was in the *wrong* kind of home. What on earth was he talking about? "I'm not sure what you mean!" Ron exclaimed.

The small old man looked at Ron suspiciously. "You say you're with the Leafs. Well what the hell do you *do* there?" he asked.

Ron handed Doug McCaine his card. "I'm the Director of Player Personnel," He answered proudly. Doug McCaine took the card but regarded it as if it was Monopoly Money.

"What do you *do* there?" he repeated.

"I'm responsible for coordinating the amateur and pro scouting with the general manager, and for all player movements. I look after registering all of the contracts. I'm in charge of compiling all statistical data and files on all of our players, both at the NHL and minor-league level. I help the GM and coaches to evaluate talent," he concluded.

"You sound like a clerk to me. Did you ever play the game?" Doug McCaine questioned.

Ron told him about his brief college career, and his coaching background. "Well, if you are responsible for evaluating talent, you'd be a fool not to recognize a talent like Dale's. He's just the kind of player your team needs right now!"

Ron had to agree, if Dale McCaine was *half* the hockey player that these local people claimed he was. "You're right, Mr. McCaine. If Dale was here we *would* be foolish not to recognize talent like that. But he's not, and I hope that you'll forgive the present Leaf organization for the mistakes made in the past. I hope you'll not wish us any bad luck."

The small old man was unconvinced. "The only way the Toronto Maple Leafs will *ever* win another Stanley Cup is if they get my son to play for them!" he snapped.

Ron knew he wasn't going to get anywhere. The past gripped Doug McCaine too tightly.

"I really, *really* wish that could happen, Mr. McCaine. I wish we could change the past. But we can't. I'm very sorry that you feel so strongly about this."

Doug McCaine offered no apology for his feelings. "You married? Have any kids?" he asked Ron.

"No, not married, no kids," he answered.

"You shacked up with some broad?" the small old man asked.

"No," Ron laughed. "My fiancée goes to school in B.C."

"B.C.!" Doug McCaine shrieked, "How the hell can you carry on a relationship when she's in B.C.?"

Ron wondered why it mattered to the small old man. "Long distance love, I guess. I see her whenever we have a west coast trip, and on holidays and vacations. We're going to be married as soon as her term is up, and then she's moving back home to Toronto."

Doug McCaine continued his thought. "Well, if you're not married and have no kids, you can't appreciate what it's like to lose one. He was a great kid, Dale was. And his dream was to play for the Leafs—to win a Stanley Cup in Maple Leaf Gardens. Unless you can make *that* happen, that team is *never* going to win another Stanley Cup!" He swore.

Okay, Ron thought, I tried to be nice to him. "Thorny said you were a tough old son of a bitch. He was right."

Doug McCaine scoffed, "Thorny! He's so full of shit his eyes are brown!"

He began to cough again, and this time Ron was alarmed. It lasted much longer than before, and he didn't answer when Ron asked him if he was okay.

"Sure, I'm just dying, that's all. My lungs are full of asbestos. I was a tin-knocker, years ago. I used to work in Toronto in those god damned office towers, where the ceilings were full of asbestos insulation. We didn't know any better at the time. The money was good, lots of double time for everybody. But look at me now!" He said while wiping the spittle from his chin. "I had to retire when Dale started playing in Rochester. He was afraid I was going to die! I kept telling him not to worry, that I was going to hang on until he got to skate around in Maple Leaf Gardens with the Stanley Cup!" He stopped coughing, but began to drool. He wiped the spittle from his mouth, but kept on talking as he did so. "And I'm still hanging on."

"I should get going. It was nice meeting you," he said while offering his hand for the small old man to shake.

The handshake he was offered was not that of a man who was either tough or fiery, as Thorny had described him. It *was* the handshake of a man who was dying, Ron thought.

"Heaven knows I'm not an angel, Mr. McCaine. But if it were possible we'd have your son in training camp in a second. And I'm sure he'd help us win a Stanley Cup."

"You'll need a lot more than that, son. You better get rid of some of the dead wood. Randy Rettig, Lorne Graham, they're just baggage-smashers; people who smash other people's baggage. And that Shithead Moore, doesn't he lead the league in stupid penalties? And while we're at it, that Terry Oddy! Is he a pylon out there to skate around? The team needs to get tougher on defense. You need some more skilled forwards, and while you're at it get a backup goalie to challenge John Dennis. Maybe a little competition will make him play like he used to."

Ron thanked him for the advice. He turned to leave, but the small old man wasn't finished.

"And you need to do something about your scouting too. You know you only ranked twenty-third in the *Hockey News* poll of prospects."

Ron was still trying to head through the door, but Doug McCaine wasn't finished.

"And Ken Butler's a *fool* if he can't do any better than Vrbata and Zigomanis and a draft choice for Artis! You guys would screw up the draft choice anyway!"

He thanked Doug McCaine for the advice, and left the building. Ron pressed the speed dial button to reach the Gardens' office. He had to report to Ken Butler about his favourable review of Rylan Thomas.

"So what'd you think of the kid?" the General Manager asked.

"He showed a lot," Ron answered, "But we better move fast. I understand that Boston has been sniffing around him."

"Leave it to me," Ken suggested, "I'll call the GM in Kingston. Anybody else down there you like?"

Ron wanted to mention Dale McCaine. *He* was a player that could help them all right, if he was still alive. "No," Ron replied, "I'll be back in the office around lunch time," he said and he pressed the end button on the cell phone.

As he headed along the 401 to Toronto he thought about the 'curse' as Thorny put it, that Doug McCaine had placed on the Toronto Maple Leafs. He also though about how superstition has played such a big role in hockey players minds, even today. He thought about all of the players he had known through the years who would go through periods where they didn't want to change anything if they were on a hot streak. Guys who would wear the same shirt (regardless of the smell) or always put their right skate on first. Even great players, like Wayne Gretzky with the 'sweater out of the pants thing on one side' were superstitious. He knew that superstition could extend beyond the individual player to team play as well. When he was with Rochester the team hadn't lost a game in Hershey in over nine years. Even though players had come and gone (there actually wasn't a single player left on the Rochester team who had played in the first win at Hershey) the players believed that they would win every game there. When the streak came to an end, many of the players honestly believed it was because they had failed to continue some pre-game ritual that was responsible for their success.

By the same logic, it would be easy to explain the Leafs thirty-plus year Stanley Cup drought. It wasn't because the team had lacked good management for years or because they practised penny-pinching financial practices and wouldn't spend money on players. No, *those* were not the reasons that they had gone so long without a cup. It was all because of Doug McCaine and his 'curse.' Ron laughed out loud at the thought. Maybe the media would like to get hold of this story. Ron thought that the whole scenario of Doug McCaine and his curse would make great sense to long suffering Leaf fans. If they knew that their team was cursed, well then maybe they would find losing easier to accept. And if the curse was real, then no matter *what* player moves the club made they were still never going to win another Stanley Cup until they brought Dale McCaine back to Maple Leaf Gardens. The more he thought about it, the more he wondered if it would be easier to bring a player back from the dead than it would be for them to win another Stanley Cup, considering the present talent pool. Surely that would be the headline of a newspaper column if this story ever got out; '*Leafs curse means no more Stanley Cups*'. Ron even wondered why it hadn't made it to the papers already, considering they everyone in Cobourg seemed to know about it.

As he drove past the suburbs of Whitby, Ajax, and Pickering, Ron thought about Dale McCaine. The description of the way the kid played made him think of the Kingston junior he has seen last night, Rylan Thomas. If Doug McCaine only wanted his son to play for the Leafs again at Maple Leaf Gardens then maybe Ron could oblige.

Maybe all I have to do is ask him, he thought, "Dale McCaine, if you can hear me, the offer is open. Just show up at the Gardens for tomorrow's practice and we'll see what we can do about you making this team," he said to no one present. There—he had made the offer. Now it was up to Dale McCaine to contact *him* if he wanted a tryout with the Leafs.

Ron speculated that if they did sign a player who was already dead they wouldn't have to break the bank in offering the guy a contract. Maybe a ghost would play for nothing, he guessed.

Wake Up and Smell the Coffee

Ron awoke the next morning and bolted upright in bed. He panicked as he wiped cold sweat from his brow. The things he had just seen were a dream, he told himself, though it was as real as if he had been watching a movie. He struggled to remember everything that had just happened, or rather that he had just dreamt.

He was at Maple Leaf Gardens. He was in his office and he wanted coffee. The place was deserted, and he walked by the corridor the led to the ice. He was surprised to find that the lights were on, including the television lights. On the ice was a junior-age player taking shots at the empty net. He wore what looked like a Tulsa Oilers jersey. As Ron approached the kid stopped and Ron asked him what he was doing there.

"It's okay. I have permission from the team," the kid answered. Ron was suspicious.

"How long have you been coming here and practising at night?" he wanted to know.

The kid looked at Ron as if Ron should know, but replied, "I come here all the time."

Ron didn't believe the kid, so he went to find security to check the story out. He found a security guard having a coffee and a donut at a Tim Horton's concession, which to his surprise, was open, although everything else in the Gardens was closed. Ron didn't recognize the guard but asked him about the kid.

"That's impossible!" the guard bellowed, his mouth full of a Boston Crème donut.

Ron wished that he had stopped to get a coffee, but he accompanied the guard who was racing down the corridor towards the rink. Ron caught up with him as they reached the ice surface. Everything was dark. No one was around.

"What are you talking about?" the guard shrieked. "You know you almost made me choke?"

Ron knew he had talked to the kid. He knew he hadn't dreamt it, he told himself. He wondered how the kid had gotten out of there so fast. Then he remembered that the Tim Horton's was still open. He hurried back to where it was, and *it* was gone. Ron could still smell the coffee.

That was when he woke up. He didn't want to look at the clock radio because he was still tired and he hoped that it wasn't almost time to get up. But he *could* smell coffee. It meant that the automatic coffee maker in the kitchen had started to brew, which also meant that the alarm was about to go off. The dream had seemed so real, he thought.

"Time to wake up and smell the coffee," he laughed. He reluctantly looked at the clock that read 6:15. He strolled down the hall to the bathroom, and thought about coffee. It's too bad that there *isn't* a Tim Horton's in the Gardens, he thought. That would be a great idea!

As he showered, he thought about asking the GM if it was feasible. Why not? After all, Tim Horton *was* one of the greatest players in Leaf history. It just seemed right. He reminded himself that he did some of his best thinking while in the shower.

When he got to the Gardens that morning he was met by Ken Butler before he could even unlock the door to his office. That told Ron of a looming sense of urgency.

"We have a decision to make," the GM said instead of a good morning.

Ron Bailey stood with his mouth wide open, as if closing it would prevent Ken Butler from continuing.

"Come on in my office," he ordered, while leading the way to the row of executive offices, located beside the director's room. Ron loved spending time in Ken Butler's office because it *looked* exactly like a General Manager's office should look. The walls were arranged with tastefully framed photographs of the many teams that Ken Butler had been involved with, as a player, coach and GM.

The selection of pictures was significant too—they were hung in chronological order of Ken Butler's career. One wall began with a team picture of the Memorial Cup champion Guelph Biltmores, and continued with a shot from his brief stint in the NHL with the Oakland Seals, scoring a playoff game-winning goal. There was a photo of him assisting on a goal by Bobby Hull when the WHA version of Team Canada played the Russians in the fall of '74. And there was a shot of him congratulating Roger Neilson when the Vancouver Canucks made it to the Stanley Cup final in '82.

The opposite wall displayed his accomplishments with the Toronto Maple Leafs (granted there weren't as many as with other organizations.) There were pictures of the Leafs overtime victories over Detroit and St. Louis in '93 and San Jose in '94. And there was a photograph of the GM receiving the *Hockey News* 'Executive-of-the-year' award in '92.

The GM got down to business. "We've had interest heating up in Artis," he said, referring to the Leafs leading scorer.

"Carolina?" Ron asked, referring to their earlier trade offer from the Hurricanes.

"No," the GM responded, "they've decided to go another route, it appears. The Penguins have upped the ante now that Recchi has gone down with a knee injury. He might be out until the second round of the playoffs. Their thinking is that Artis would be a nice fit with Lemieux until Recchi returns. In any event," he said, while sliding his glasses down on his nose to see Ron "They have offered an interesting package. I want you to take a look at it and get some updated scouting reports on these guys." He handed Ron a hand written list of player's names.

Ron recognized the first two; they were on the Penguins' roster and could help the Leafs he thought. The third name was of a player who was either still in junior or in the minors, but not a name Ron recognized. He would have to prepare a trade report, but more often than not these potential trades never materialized. The research had to be done anyway.

Ron retired to his office and began working on updating the files of the players involved in the trade. One of his personal pet peeves was that the team was barely in up to speed in computer technology. Before Ron had accepted the position of director of player personnel, the team had none of its personnel files on computer. And the fact that all of the Leafs pro and amateur scouts were age fifty and over and not computer-literate meant that all data he was currently receiving had to be transferred electronically in order for Ron to access it from his data base.

He had been working for over an hour when he recalled what the people he had met in Cobourg said about Dale McCaine. He wondered if there was a scouting report in existence that would shed some light on how good this player *really* was. He knew that the player personnel files in the office went back many years, but how far, he didn't know. Ron needed a break and went down the hall to the GMs' office, where he knew he would be able to get some coffee at the GM's secretary's office. He found Ken Butler at the coffee maker, apparently doing the same.

"You winning?" the GM asked. Ron disliked this expression intensely, but never let the GM know it.

"Yeah," he replied, "I should be done in an hour or so. I have a question for you, though," Ken Butler ran his hand through his silver hair, as if to make sure it still was all there. "Do player files, scouting reports and the like exist from, say, forty years ago?"

Ken Butler stared up at the ceiling as if the answer was written there. "I don't think that *any* files of *any* kind have ever been thrown out, to my knowledge," he answered. Ron shook his head. "When I started this job the office was jammed full of filing cabinets that dated back, I think, to the time the building opened," the GM continued, while stirring his coffee slowly. "All of the stuff got moved to the storage room on the third floor, where all of the accounting records are kept. As far as I know they're still there. Why are you asking?"

Ron thought it best to answer honestly. "I ran into the father of a player who was in the Leaf system, about forty years ago. I just wanted to find out if the kid was as good as his old man said he was." Ron laughed.

Ken Butler began stirring his coffee clockwise.

"What was the kid's name?" The GM asked.

"Dale McCaine," Ron replied.

Ken Butler stopped stirring his coffee. He looked at Ron as if Ron had fused the connection of a long dead synapse. "I played against a Dale McCaine. He was in the Leaf system when I was with the Montreal Voyageurs."

Ron looked puzzled. The GM noticed his confusion, so he attempted to explain.

"The Voyageurs were the Canadiens farm club in the American league at the time."

The GM thought that the name Montreal Voyageurs had confused Ron. In reality Ron was surprised that the GM had remembered Dale McCaine.

"What do you remember about him?" he asked.

Ken Butler took a sip of his coffee without looking at it, before realizing that it was still too hot to drink. He barely reacted to it, however. "You play against so many guys in your career, and

55

usually only remember the ones you had success against, or whom you battled with. And you remember the ones who went on to really make it. I remember him because I thought he was too good to be playing down there. It was just a matter of time before he got called up. I remember that he had pretty good success against us. But that was it. I made it to the Canadiens, for a time, and I expected to see him up with the Leafs, but we never heard from him again."

Could there not have been a spot on the Toronto Maple Leafs roster for a player who had left an impression in the mind of such an acute judge of talent as Ken Butler, especially after forty years?

"Do you *know* what happened to him—why he didn't make it to the NHL?" Ron asked.

The GM shook his head. He began to head off in the direction of his office. "Just one of thousands who never get to realize the dream, I guess," Ken Butler said.

Ron agreed with the notion that Dale McCaine never got to realize the dream. He was still consumed by the need to read a scouting report on Dale McCaine. He got the key to the third floor storage room and unlocked the door and flicked on the light. He was almost overcome by the pungent mustiness of the room as if he had cracked open an ancient tomb. The scratched and rusted filing cabinets had labels on them that were faded and barely legible. Ron noticed that the cabinets were organized by year. He wasn't sure which year he should be looking for, so he searched for a media guide. He began with 1965-66 season, but there was no mention of Dale McCaine. He checked the 1966-67 media guide—the season the Leafs last won the Stanley Cup. Listed on the training camp roster was Dale McCaine; Height 5 feet 11 inches, weight 180 pounds, shoots left: Place of birth, Cobourg, Ontario, date of birth: November 21st, 1946. 1965-66 Club: Peterborough Petes (OHA), 35 goals, 46 assists, 81 points, 21 penalty minutes. That was all there was in the media guide, not even a picture.

At least now Ron knew where to look. He found a filing cabinet with its bottom drawer labelled '1966–67'. Ron began looking for the personnel files. He opened the drawer to find folders labelled 'REGULAR SEASON GAME STATS', 'PLAYER TRANSACTIONS', 'MEDICAL REPORTS', 'TRAVEL ITNERARY', and finally 'PLAYER PERSONNEL'. He opened the file, and found sheets inside for each player. But Dale McCaine wasn't among them. All of the names in the file were recognizable. They were all-star players, like Armstrong, Baun, Ellis, Mahovlich, Pulford, and Sawchuck—there were no names of minor leaguers.

He continued searching, and then found another file folder titled MINOR LEAGUE PROSPECTS. Inside he found a sheet with Dale McCaine's name on it.

As he read the glowing report 'Smooth, effortless skater, good play maker, excellent puck sense, hardworking, willing to get tough when he has to', he realized that, except for the last two parts, it sounded amazingly like the scouting report he had just finished reading on Vaclav Artis, the young player they were about to trade away. Ron also found some background information. 'Drafted in the fourth round, number 22 overall' it read. Ron was amazed. He had just assumed that Dale McCaine had been the Leafs first choice. In fact they had selected three other players ahead of him. It didn't make sense; if he was such a great player, and had such great statistics in his last year with Peterborough, why were three other players taken ahead of him?

Ron read on and got some answers. The scouts were afraid that the kid would not be able to adapt to the NHL because of Dale's concern over his father's poor health. It was stated in the report that Dale was considering *not* turning professional if it meant he had to leave Cobourg. While playing in Peterborough he continued to live at home. If he played in Toronto, this would not be a problem, as he would be close enough to Cobourg to visit regularly. If Dale was drafted by another organization where he would be farther from home he was seriously considering turning down a chance to play in the N.H.L.

"I just can't see this happening today." Ron thought.

He envisioned a situation where a deal would be worked out to allow him to play closer to home—perhaps leaving the kid in junior for another year. But from what Ron could remember hearing about the league at the time, consideration for a player was not at the top of the list of team's priorities. He closed the file folder, but removed the sheet on Dale McCaine. He wasn't sure why but he decided to hang onto it for a while.

"I don't know what happened to you back in '68, kid but it would be different in now," Ron promised. "We'd give you every opportunity to play closer to home; we'd even move your sick father to Toronto if that would make things easier," he vowed.

Got 'em...got 'em...need 'em

The day the trade was made 'would mark a new beginning for the Toronto Maple Leafs' Ken Butler had said. What was wrong with the old beginning was the question most Leaf fans wanted to know. The story broke quickly. It was first aired on radio station CKFH in a noontime bulletin.

"The long awaited deal has finally happened!" was how play-by-play man Jim Gerber called it. "Vaclav Artis is off to the Pittsburgh Penguins. In return the Leafs acquire center Tobin West, defenseman Ian Moriarty and left-winger Greg Sawchuck. Only West and Moriarty are currently on the Pittsburgh roster and of the three only Sawchuck, who has just turned 21, can be considered youthful."

Officially the Leafs had addressed some big needs, getting another centre man (although West was on his third NHL team now in five seasons) a defenseman (Moriarty was just 5'11) and adding a prospect (even if no one outside Sawchuck's immediate family had ever heard of him.) *Unofficially,* the Leafs had dealt away a player who had demanded a trade, who wasn't producing like in the past and was becoming a huge pain in the ass with his dressing room tantrums; and the combined salaries of the three newcomers were *less* than Vaclav Artis would earn in bonuses.

The reaction to the trade was startling; it was a deal that fans either loved, or they hated. There was no middle ground. The consensus (if you believed the poll conducted in the pages of the *Toronto Sun*) was that the Leafs could have received more for Artis. Some looked at it this way; the Leafs practically *stole* Artis from the

59

Rangers, and now they were perhaps not taking advantage of their good fortune. Ron Bailey was sitting on the fence on this one. Of the list of players the Penguins were offering there was one player that Ken Butler insisted on; defenseman Moriarty. For the other two players in the deal, he relied on Ron's intuition. The director of player personnel was familiar with Tobin West, who had played for Ron in Rochester when the kid was in the Sabres system. Ron always felt that West had never really been given a chance to prove himself at the NHL level. Greg Sawchuck, the third player included, was a good scorer in the Western league as a junior. His former coach once confided to Ron that the Penguins had been expecting the kid to score goals at the same clip. In reality, the kid had been placed on a line with some good play makers; his real talent was as a two-way player, but had never been utilized as such.

The interesting thing about the trade was that initially, Ken Butler was going to accept two other players. At the last second he chose to consult Ron, and instead, on Ron's advice, decided to go with the deal that was eventually made. Ron thought that he'd file that one away for himself; one day he would look back on the deal and see if *his* version of the trade was better than the General Managers. That kind of second-guessing wasn't really fair, but he could have some fun with it someday just the same.

With the deal now consummated, the Leafs still had fourteen games left in the season, and trailed a couple of teams for the last playoff spot, albeit by 12 points. Mathematically they could still do it. Mathematically also the players could all have the winning numbers in the 649 lottery. The likelihood of either occurring was about the same. As far as the organization's brain trust was concerned things were proceeding as planned. Improvements had been made 'to make it a better hockey club' and the long-term goal was the future. As far as the fans are concerned, this wasn't good enough; a popular player had been dealt for an unknown quantity. The media were going to grab this one and impale it on a pike for all to see. The newspapers were kind in comparison to the all-sports radio station. After each Leaf game aired, there was a call in show call, predictably, 'Leaf Talk', hosted by a self-described, dyed-in-the-wool Leaf fan and commentator, Gilbert Baines, or 'Gil the thrill', as he called himself.

Ron Bailey avoided listening to the show as a rule, but on the nights when the team was on the road, especially when the game wasn't televised locally, he would often leave the radio on after the broadcast had ended. He felt that listening to what the fans had to say would give him some insight into how they perceived the hockey club. Ken Butler's spin on this was decidedly different. "While it's enlightening to hear what they (the fans) think," he'd say, "Remember that they are not responsible for their decisions." He added, "*We* are the ones who have to account for the moves we make, and we accept the criticism and the plaudits equally. Running an institution like the Toronto Maple Leafs is a huge responsibility. We have to be responsible to the 16,500 voices that call out to us at each game, and consider all their opinions; but also with the best interests of the club in mind. We can't simply react to fan pressure to move someone who isn't performing up to expectation by trading or demoting him without considering the overall picture. All of our moves are made to improve the situation incrementally. We have to consider that above the fan knee jerk reaction. We listen, but we have to listen with open ears and a closed mouth."

As far as the voice of the Leafs was concerned, they listened with an *open* mouth. And 'Gil the Thrill' had the *biggest* mouth.

On the night when the Leafs dropped a close 5-4 decision to the Red Wings in Detroit, and were mercifully eliminated from the playoffs the switchboard at CHIL lit up like the night sky over the Toronto waterfront on Canada day. Ron listened as he sat at his computer, working on entry draft player updates.

"This is '*Gil the Thrill*' Baines, and for the next forty minutes were going to take your calls and we want *you* to tell *us* just exactly what you think about how the Leaf season is ending. Are you happy with how the team is playing, the moves that have been made? Do you think Spencer Smith is the right man to coach this team? Should Ken Butler be back as General Manager? Do you think the club is going in the right direction? We'll let *you* answer these questions—right after we take this break."

Ron shook his head, "Yes, we'll let you answer these question just as long as they fall in line with the theme of this show which is to stir up a little controversy and get some more listeners involved, he thought.

The first few calls were non-specific, and each caller tended to agree with the tone set by the previous one, as if their opinions were scripted. The general consensus was that the team was underachieving, some of the moves that had been made were good, but that they should have received more in the Vaclav Artis trade than they did, that Spencer Smith was the wrong man for the job, and that Ken Butler should not be back as GM. Ron listened to the calls, and tried not to laugh. Most of the callers had difficulty completing sentences and had trouble comprehending why other teams such as New Jersey and Colorado could win the Stanley Cup after having only been around for a few years, and not Toronto who had been around since the league began.

That's it, Ron thought. All we have to do is to move the team. It worked for the Devils and the Flames. Why surely Carolina should be the next favourite now that they are out of Hartford.

It amazed him that some fans believed that winning the cup was so easy. The fact was that the Kings, Blues, Canucks, Sabres, and Capitals had all been around for more than thirty years and had *never* won a Stanley Cup, and that other original six teams like Chicago, Detroit, Boston and New York had gone through droughts of between twenty-five and forty years before winning.

To the fans the formula for success was not rocket science; simply hire a good hockey man who will in turn hire the right man to coach and select the right mix of players to mould a team with the right ingredients to win. While this was certainly true, there is so much more to assembling a championship team. On top of everything else, a great deal of luck was also needed, such as the ability to remain injury free and the patience of ownership and fans to put up with the development (*read losing*) years necessary for a team to mature. An article had appeared earlier that day in the *Globe and Mail* which suggested that once the team was sold (which could be as early as the new year) the current management group would be gone, and that the new owner was ready to spare no expense to hire 'the best hockey people that exist' away from other organizations.

The next caller shed some light on the subject.

"This is Gil the Thrill back with you, and we go to Jerry in North York—Jerry what's on your mind?"

"Gil! I hear that it won't matter anymore, what this team is doing now. The new owners' going to—"

"Wait a minute, Jerry—new owner?"

"Well, I hear that the team is being sold in April and that all these guys are gone. Butler and Smith, and that they're gonna get Glen Sather as manager and Mike Keenan as coach, and—"

"Whoa, wait a minute Jerry. Where on *earth* did you hear that? Do you have a crystal ball?"

"No, no, it was in the *Globe and Mail!* They are gonna spend the money to get—"

Gil the Thrill interrupted. "Jerry, please! For one minute do you think that this ownership schmazzle is going to be solved by Valentines' Day and that Glen Sather and Mike Keenan are going to be snapped up by then? Jerry really—what are you smoking? We go to Oakville..."

Ron had to agree with the Thrill. And everyone was missing the *real* reason why Toronto hadn't won the Stanley Cup since 1967. "It's because Doug McCaine placed a curse on them!" he shouted at the radio.

Even though the season was ending on the ice, it was just beginning to heat up for the scouting staff. The playoffs were a busy time for the pro scouts as they had a unique opportunity to watch players under the kind of pressure that only the playoffs delivered. For players that would become free agents on the first of July, it was a kind of window-shopping for the scouts. The amateur scouts had been watching playoffs for a few weeks as the junior leagues, colleges and European leagues were already well into their 'second seasons.' And the world championships were starting in Helsinki. Hockey Canada had approached Ken Butler late in January to be part of the Canadian World Championship team's management group, but he turned them down.

"I expect to be very busy with our run for the playoffs," he replied, in declining.

In retrospect, he needn't have worried. As it turned out, the General Manager *would* be going to Finland; to view some of the teams unsigned draft choices. The Leafs were exceptionally well represented, by prospects that were not eligible or ready for the NHL. They had players on each of the Finland, Sweden, Slovakia, and Russia rosters, even though no current Leafs were selected to play in the championships. This was an obvious reflection on the current rosters' talent level.

While Ken Butler was away in Europe, Walt Fisher remained busy in St. Johns' overseeing the farm club's Leafs run for the playoffs. While the parent club was heading for cottage country, the farm team was still challenging for first place. Ron planned to take in games from the Calder Cup, NCAA championships, Memorial Cup and even the Centennial Cup playoffs. He estimated that from April 14th to May 30th he could potentially see 30 to 35 games and travel 4000 miles. He would use the air miles he earned to visit his fiancée, though with so much travelling in such a short period of time he would be longing to spend some time at home at the end of May. That would have to wait however, as he would then begin to assemble the scouting reports for the June entry draft.

The prospect from Tulsa

The draft was not as exciting an event for the Leafs as it was for most of the other 29 teams in the league. Toronto had unwisely dealt their first pick in the draft previously to Calgary, for tough guy Randy Rettig, who turned out to be not-so-tough.

Ron couldn't really look forward to any time off until the middle of July. By then the week long prospects camp would be over. This was a relatively new idea; the club had never done this sort of thing before. And Ron took great pride in it, because it was *his* idea, although he had borrowed it from baseball's formula for the fall Florida instructional league. By having the camp in July it gave the club an opportunity to invite the players selected in the entry draft who had been signed as well as the youngsters acquired late in the year in the Artis trade as well as the players drafted in previous years who had never played professionally, or had only made brief appearances with the St. Johns' Maple Leafs. The coaching staff didn't appreciate having to interrupt their summer vacation for a week, but Spencer Smith at least was anxious to see what fresh meat was going to be fed to him at training camp in September.

Ron was having coffee one morning in the Garden's coffee shop when a familiar face appeared at his table.

"Good morning Ron," he was greeted. Ron recognized Mike Lengell, who was the club's director of marketing.

"Hi," Ron answered; somewhat surprised that one of the 'suits' recognized him.

65

Mike Lengell got right down to business. "I guess that with Ken and Walt away, that pretty much leaves you in charge of hockey operations." He smiled.

Ron's eyes went wide for a moment. Ken Butler was on a two-week vacation in Europe, and Walt Fisher was at the American Hockey League meetings in Charleston, South Carolina. From an organizational chart standpoint, Ron *was* the next in command. "I guess I am!" he said, returning the smile with unmistakable authority.

"I wanted to run something by Ken, but I'll try it on you. We have the best future prospects here for a few days, correct?"

Ron nodded in agreement.

"We'd like to feature something on them for this years' media guide; maybe some shots of them going through their first pro camp, so to speak. Or maybe a team picture, sort of what the Leafs might look like in the future!"

Ron *loved* the idea. After all, the prospect camp was his baby. "I'm sure we could suggest it to Spence. It has to be OK'd by the coach. He only has these guys for a little less than a week—but how much time can a team picture take?"

"Exactly," Mike Lengell agreed, "and it will give us a chance to have the guys photographed it the new version of the sweater."

Mike Lengell was referring to the NHL's newest cash grab; changing the team uniforms every few years in order to capitalize on the public's "gotta-have-one-like-the-pros-wear" mentality. The new Leaf style changed the number and name font to match the one on the crest. Ron didn't like the latest Leaf sweater, and wasn't even especially fond of the one that preceded it, which he thought was a half-assed attempt to blend the old design (the one he remembered growing up) with the modern one that was created for 1970.

"Tell me again why the Leafs *can't use* the old original-six sweater anymore?" he asked Mike Lengell.

He sighed. "The old 35-point maple leaf you are referring to was replaced with an 11-point maple leaf in 1967, sort of a salute to the new Canadian flag that was introduced before the Centennial. Neither one of those leaf designs can be copyrighted, any more than say a circle shape or a square" he explained.

"You remember that movie *Ghostbusters* a few years ago?" Ron nodded affirmatively.

"Well they were taken to court by the creators of, I think, *Casper the Friendly Ghost* over copyright to the ghost design. The court ruled against them, because there are only so many ways you can draw a ghost. You can't copyright shapes, colours, designs that are non-specific. That's why we came up with the style of maple leaf we have had since 1970; it's distinct and can be copyrighted. And to pay homage to the past we put the old leaf on the shoulders of the sweater—to keep the traditionalists like you happy!"

Ron felt as if he was being compared to a stodgy old Leaf fan, like Doug McCaine.

"So you want to have the kids photographed in the new uniform. Sounds okay to me," Ron agreed.

"Good," Mike continued, "I'll talk to Spence about it if you want."

"Oh I can talk to him about it. I have to get down to practice this morning anyway. I want to have a look at these kids."

Ron thought this was a great opportunity to run another idea of his through the marketing department.

"Mike, a couple of years back we brought back the original—six uniform, the one with the *old* maple leaf we can't copyright on it."

"It was for the league's 75th anniversary," Mike Lengell interrupted.

"Right," Ron agreed, "and recently we brought back the 1932 version of the sweater-"

"For the Gardens' 65th birthday, Mike Lengell noted.

Rick Ferguson

"Yeah, now I was at a game a couple of years ago. It was an afternoon game. It was St. Patrick's Day, March 17th"

"Irish Spring towel give-away day," Mike Lengell corrected.

"That's right. But I was thinking, the Leafs *used* to be called the St. Patrick's, and I thought what a wonderful idea it would have been for them to come out with Toronto St. Patrick's uniforms for that game only. I was down at the hockey hall of fame a few weeks ago. The have the old sweaters in the gift shop, all green and white with a shamrock on the front. It could have been a great promotion."

Ron wondered if he had offended Mike Lengell, until he could see the dollar signs reflecting in his eyes.

"What a great idea—damn it! We' have a home game scheduled for March 17th with Minnesota. We still have time! I'll have to get a hold of Walt, no, better yet Ken! I can reach him in Europe!"

He left his unfinished coffee on the table and hurried off down the corridor to his office.

At practice the next day, Ron ventured down to the coach's office to chat with Spencer Smith about the practice. The subject of the team picture came up and Ron noticed that the players were not wearing the new style jersey as Mike Lengell had suggested.

"The new ones are in the dressing room," Spencer Smith informed Ron. "I didn't think Lengell'd want us to mess them up before the picture. I'll get them to change after practice. Go have a look at them—they're hanging up in the room."

Ron was curious to see the new uniforms up close. He walked into the dressing room slowly; as if he was entering a church and the service had begun. He cast his eyes around the room, appreciating the history that the room held. Stanley Cup victories had been plotted here, and celebrated here as well. It was a room that thousands of kids across Canada had dreamed of sitting in to lace up their skates, and to pull on one of those magnificent in their simplicity blue and white uniforms. The words 'DEFEAT DOES NOT REST

68

LIGHTLY ON THEIR SHOULDERS' were still emblazoned on the wall, although there had been talk of replacing this motto with something the current generation could better relate to. Ron moved into the centre of the room, reading the honour roll of Maple Leaf captains on the wall.

The names Conacher, Apps, Kennedy, Armstrong, Keon, and Sittler, created visions of men proud to lead others while wearing the distinctive 'C' on their sweater. He reached for one of the new sweaters and stood near the doorway. A full-length mirror met the doorway on two sides there (although it should only have been on one side—workers had mistakenly installed two mirrors instead of one.)

Ron held the sweater over his chest and admired it. It was the jersey that he had dreamt of wearing one day, but had never come true. He stood transfixed by the sweater in the mirror when he suddenly felt that he was no longer alone in the room. He lifted his eyes to see that a player was behind him, watching him admire the sweater. Ron was more embarrassed than startled and he looked over his shoulder to offer an explanation, but no one was there. He glanced around the room, but it was empty, except for the roll of discarded hockey tape, folding chairs and clothing hung at each cubicle. Ron gasped for air and quickly looked back in the mirror. The player was still there, and was now closer to him, as if Ron could turn around and touch him. Ron spun around quickly but there was no one behind him. He turned his back on the mirror for a second, and then turned back towards it as if he was being followed. The player stood right in front of him, like a reflection, and then moved directly toward him. Ron shivered as he felt cold envelope and penetrate his body at the same time as if he were in a pool of water. He could barely stay on his feet, but he was unable to move. He heard someone speak, softly like a whisper, and then the voice became more gravely. He could not make out the words, until the voice became clearer.

He heard the voice calling "Mr. Bailey," and he tried to answer but his throat could only tremble and his lips could only quiver. He did feel now that he could move and he was able to turn around. Before him stood a player, about Ron's height but appearing much younger. He wore a uniform in blue and white, and while it was styled like a Leaf uniform, it was not. Instead of a Leaf crest on the front it had a large oil derrick. Ron looked deeply into the player's eyes, which were bright but were an eerie bluish grey colour. The player's face was young, perhaps only twenty or so, but it had a worried expression. Again Ron tried to speak, but no words came. The player began to speak.

"Mr. Bailey, I'm here to try out for the team, like you offered," he said.

Ron was still speechless. Then he remembered the drive back from Kingston, and all he could think about was the offer he had made to Dale McCaine. 'Just show up at the Gardens for practice and we'll see what we can do about you making this team.' he had said. Ron took his eyes off of the player, and expected him to be gone, but he was still there.

"Who *are* you?" he was finally able to say.

The kid smiled. "I know I can help this team win the Stanley Cup if you give me the chance," he answered.

Ron leaned against the dressing room wall and helplessly his body lowered to the ground as he felt his legs wobble and weaken, until the carpeted floor caught him. If he hadn't seen the kid move from the mirror he would not have believed it. Ron was no longer afraid, but he could not believe what was happening.

"I see you here in front of me! Can other people see you, or is it just me?"

The kid did not appear to know *how* to answer the question. Before the player could respond their solitude was broken, as Ron realized that the two of them were no longer alone. Spencer Smith stepped gingerly into the room still wearing his skates.

"Here you are Ronnie! I thought you were coming to practice," he said, while looking around the room as if he had lost something. Ron was unsure of what to do or say next. Spencer Smith broke the silence.

"You going to introduce me to your friend?" he asked, looking at the player.

Ron jumped immediately to his feet. The question of whether he was imagining all of this had been answered.

"You *see* this kid?" he asked Spencer Smith. He realized that Spencer Smith *could* see the player, and attempted to make an introduction. "I offered this kid a chance to try out with the team, Spence, and he took me up on it. That's why he's here!"

Spencer Smith was perplexed. "Ron, we have a procedure that we're supposed to follow. All the other kids here have gone through their medicals, fitness tests; they have had their evaluations. I've had a chance to meet with them; aren't you jumping the gun a bit? You haven't even introduced me. By the way son, I'm Spencer Smith," he said, extending his hand.

The player offered his. "I'm Dale McCaine," he responded.

Ron felt it necessary to stretch the truth in order to make the situation easier. "He's been checked out. I'm sorry you haven't had a chance to meet him before this. Dale's just arrived," he said.

"Well practice is starting, so we better get you out there—nice uniform!" he commented on the kid's Tulsa Oilers outfit.

"Say Ronnie-get a hold of Carpenter," he said, referring to the trainer and equipment manager, "and get this kid a practice jersey."

Spencer Smith turned and left, forgetting whatever it had been that had brought him into the dressing room in the first place. Ron turned his attention again to the player.

"You are *not* Dale McCaine. You are not Dale McCaine because Dale McCaine is, is not alive today," Ron told himself. He was only telling himself, though because he still didn't believe that he had seen this kid pass through the mirror. It appeared to happen, right in front of his face, but he still had not accepted it.

"You can't be Dale McCaine. I met your dad in Cobourg. He told me that you were killed in a car accident outside of Tulsa, in 1968."

The player looked worried again. "You said that things would be different this time," he replied. Ron felt that the kid was not getting it.

"You say you are Dale McCaine—how is it *possible?*" he asked.

The kid moved closer to Ron and looked him right in the eyes, the way a child does.

"You asked me to come here and I'm here," he replied. "I want a chance to make this team, just like you promised," he pleaded.

Ron realized that he was not going to get his answer, at least not now. For the moment the curiosity he held about how the kid happened to be here was being replaced by his curiosity about how good a hockey player Dale McCaine really was. More than anything he wanted to see what this kid could do on the ice.

"Okay, I made you a promise. And I try to keep my promises. The coach wants me to get you a practice jersey—I'll get you a practice jersey. Let me go find Carpenter. Just don't go disappearing through that mirror while I'm gone," Ron ordered.

Ron grabbed the first jersey he saw, not even bothering to see what size it was. He was gone for less than a minute, and when Ron returned to the dressing room the kid was not there.

Ron stood hanging his head for a moment, as he felt the blood rush to his head, and his mouth began to go dry. He cautiously moved in front of the mirror again and began to rub his hand carefully on its surface. He was distracted by the sound of the whirlpool running in the trainers' room, so he went to investigate.

The kid stood beside the tub, watching the water froth and bubble.

"This is great!" the kid exclaimed, "We never had anything like this in Tulsa!"

Ron smiled. "There are a lot of things around here that I bet you never had in Tulsa."

He handed the jersey to the kid and watched as he carefully placed the Tulsa Oilers jersey on a bench. Ron noticed for the first time that the kid's equipment was old looking. The shoulder pads, elbow pads and pants looked like they belonged in the sixties. And he noticed the skates the kid wore. They were the old tube type of blade support, like the ones Ron had learned to skate in when he was a kid. He notices the words 'Tackaberry by CCM', emblazoned on them. He remembered that when he was a kid these skates were to die for. Everyone wanted CCM Tacks, as they were known, but few kid's parents would spring for them; 'Made of real kangaroo hide' he remembered the advertisements reading.

As the kid pulled on the purple mesh practice jersey it occurred to Ron that the kid didn't have a helmet.

"I don't suppose you brought a helmet with you?" he asked.

The kid looked at Ron with that worried expression again. "It's a rule now kid. Everybody has to wear one. Let me go back and check with Carpenter," he said before he exited again. "Don't wander off anywhere."

Before Ron could leave, the kid made a request. "Mr. Bailey, if it's possible, could you get me a new stick too?" he asked.

Ron noticed the kid's stick. It was a wooden Sherbrooke model, which hadn't been made in probably thirty years. It had a straight blade.

"Let me remember, don't tell me; you shoot left?" he asked.

The kid nodded, and Ron went back to the equipment room. Nevell Carpenter was surprised to see Ron again. "Bring the kid in here!" he ordered. "We'll have to fit him *properly* for a helmet, Ron."

73

Ron rolled his eyes. He was so anxious to see this kid on the ice that he was forgetting everything else. He returned to the trainer's room, and this time the kid was just where he had left him.

"Come on with me," he directed. He introduced the kid to the equipment manager.

Nevell Carpenter, whose hair practically stood on end when he saw the kid, greeted them in horror.

"Where on earth have you been playing with this stuff?" he demanded to know. Neither Ron nor the kid was ready with an answer.

"Australia!" was the first thing that came out of Ron's mouth.

Nevell Carpenter looked up at Ron, who stuck by his story. "You don't say?" the equipment manager asked.

Ron was still thinking about the kangaroo hide Tackaberrys when he cooked up this lie. It would explain the skates, he thought.

"Yeah, we found him down there," Ron lied.

Dale McCaine didn't react to this latest bulletin. He gazed around the room like a kid unleashed in Toys R' Us on the day before Christmas.

"This stuff must be forty years old," Carpenter muttered, as he began outfitting the kid from head to toe.

Not far off, Ron thought. Ron stood by and watched the kid try on new shoulder pads, elbow pants, socks, and skates. For the first time he realized that *he* must explain the existence of Dale McCaine. The truth, if it was the truth, was too bizarre he reasoned. Better to make it look like this kid was from somewhere unusual, where nobody could check up on him.

"There any more like you where you come from kid?" the equipment manager asked.

Ron answered for him. "No," he replied. "We sort of found him by accident," he said truthfully for the first time.

The answer seemed to make sense, so Ron added to it. "Australia's not exactly a hockey hotbed, as you can imagine", he continued.

The kid didn't refute what Ron had said. He was more interested in flexing his arms, and getting used to the feel of this new stuff.

"I feel like a football player," the kid said.

"You're not *from* Australia, are you kid?" Carpenter asked.

Ron wondered if the story did sound phony. If the kid was from Australia, why didn't he have an accent? Ron was ready to reply on the kid's behalf but he was too late.

"No," the kid responded, "I'm from Cobourg."

A Canadian playing in Australia—now *that* sounded reasonable, Ron thought.

Nevell Carpenter continued to fit the kid. "I didn't think you were an Aussie. You don't sound like that Crocodile Bundy," the equipment manager remarked.

"I think that's *Dundee*" Ron corrected, now that he was suddenly an expert on all things Australian.

"Whatever made you go way the hell down there to play hockey?" Carpenter asked.

Ron wasn't going to miss the next opportunity.

"School," Ron replied. He looked at the kid, who was getting the feel of the new skates he was trying on.

"Don't they feel great kid—not like the piece of crap ones you had. These used to belong to Artis. He was in such a hurry to be out of here he left them behind. How do they feel?" the equipment manager asked.

The kid walked around on them, and said they felt just fine. "Who is the *artist*?" the kid asked.

Nevell Carpenter laughed so hard he almost fell off his stool. "Hey Ronnie, that's great," he chuckled. "Maybe this kid will make everybody forget Artis!"

Ron chuckled too. They were certainly going to need someone to make the fans forget the loss of Vaclav Artis.

"If this kid is half the hockey player that little selfish snot was, we'll all be laughing," the equipment manager continued.

Ron had to agree. If this kid was half the hockey player that he had heard that Dale McCaine was in his prime then no one was going to laugh. If he was as good as everyone said he was then this kid was going to make an impact on this team, and maybe even the league. He was going to be noticed. And as Ron recalled what he had told Nevell Carpenter he realized that he would have to keep his story straight.

"There you go Australia!" the equipment manager said, as he was finished with the kid. "Go out there and show Spence how they score down under."

Ron led the puzzled kid out of the equipment room and down the corridor to the rink.

"I didn't know how else to explain who you were or what else to say," Ron apologized.

"We'll just have to stick with this. For the record, I guess we scouted you in Australia. I don't really think anybody will challenge us on this," he added.

They had established that the kid's name was Dale McCaine, that he was from Cobourg and that he was discovered playing school hockey in Australia. Ron would have to do a much better job in creating the rest of the kid's background.

For now though who he was and where he came from wouldn't matter if he couldn't show anything on the ice. As they approached the rink, Ron grabbed the kid by the arm and told him

"I believe some things happen because they're supposed to. Maybe you weren't supposed to make this team forty years ago? Anyway you have a chance to impress the coach now. This isn't training camp but it is a chance to show them what you can do. Good luck."

Dale McCaine said, "Thanks," and skated out to join the others.

Spencer Smith and his assistants Ralph Newton and Brian Ridley were conducting stretching exercises before the skating drills would begin. Ron took a seat in the middle row of red seats.

He liked sitting up high enough to see the play develop as it moved from end to end. With the building empty of spectators he would be able to hear every order barked out by the coaches, even at this distance.

As the skating session ended, the coaches organized the players into groups to begin some passing drills. He kept his eyes on the kid from Cobourg, forgetting that his job at this practice was to watch, evaluate and report on all of the prospects. He sat riveted as he watched Dale McCaine give a pass for the first time. It was fast, and smacked the blade of the player's stick right on the middle of the blade, perfectly. He watched in awe, as every pass was exactly the same, like choreography. The passes he took were just as graceful, even when they were too far ahead of or behind him. He would reach back and draw the puck ahead without breaking stride.

At one point Ron noticed the two assistant coaches carefully watching Dale McCaine. The groups then moved on to some two-on-ones, and when it was Dale McCaine's turn he got Spencer Smith's attention for the first time. Most of the kids would either shoot when they should have been passing or vice versa, but not Dale. He would carefully draw the defenseman just a little too far out of position, and then rush back quickly towards the net. His passes were so quick that several times his partner could not react in time to get a good shot away. When it was Dale's turn to receive a pass he wasted no time in getting the shot away, snapping his stick towards the net in one flexing motion as he anticipated the puck before it was there. That kind of puck sense couldn't be taught, Ron thought. The kid had a deceivingly quick release. His shot did not seem to move all that fast because he took such a small windup, but the release was like a whip cracking. He put the puck past the startled goalie several times this way. The poor goalkeeper misjudged each of these shots as the speed changed in a seemingly impossible way.

As the session drew to a close, Ron noticed Spencer Smith conferring with his assistants. Ron had seen everything he had hoped to see. He was anxious to know if coach's impressions were as favourable.

When the coach ordered the players off of the ice, he skated over to the boards and called up to Ron. "Get down here, Ronnie!" he screamed.

When a coach bellowed like that, the order was followed without question. Ron hurried down to the player's bench, as Spencer Smith leaned on the boards.

"Tell me the truth; where did you dig up this kid?"

Ron shivered a bit. "Dig up? That's such as strange choice of words, Spence!"

Spencer Smith seemed almost angry. "I mean we don't draft this kid, I don't see a scouting report, I don't get to have an interview with him, and he shows up at the practice with no notice. So who is he, the nephew of one of the suits?"

Ron laughed. He knew that when it came to the bodies on the ice there was no bullshitting Spencer Smith. He may no longer be coach of the year, Ron thought, but he still is an amazing judge of talent on the ice.

"You're too suspicious," Ron suggested. He tried to get the coach's opinion, rather than explain the presence of Dale McCaine. "So what did you think of him?"

Spencer Smith almost lost his Leaf baseball cap as he scratched his head. "I've rarely seen anything quite like him. He's such a great skater, moves the puck so well. Good shot. I can't wait to get this kid in camp. If only he had some size."

Those words caught Ron like a butt end in the gut that knocked the wind out of him. Ron had not given any regard to the fact that Dale McCaine was slight. He was maybe 5 feet 10, 170 pounds, though the media guide had listed him larger. If that was going to be the only knock against the kid, Ron could overlook it; he only hoped the coach would.

"You're not going to hold *that* against him, are you?" Ron asked.

Spencer scratched his scalp with the bill of the baseball cap again. "I just want to see him in a camp with contact. I want to see how he carries himself in front of the net, with traffic. I need to see if he can take a hit, or give one. Can he play without the puck? More questions than answers, Ronnie."

Spencer Smith did a little pirouette in front of the boards, and then came back to where Ron was standing. "You found this kid yourself, Ronnie. I can tell by that poker face of yours!" The coach smiled.

Ron probably blushed, but he couldn't tell.

"You're a modest son of a gun," the coach needled. "I'll make sure that Ken gets lots of praise about the kid from me. Kenny will give you a good pat on the back for sure. Don't worry Ron. You've always stuck up for me."

Ron thanked the coach for his vote of confidence. He decided to hang around the dressing room after practice and wait for Dale McCaine to come out. He finally got tired of waiting and entered the room, and found the kid still wearing his practice jersey, sitting on a folding chair in front of a cubicle.

"Are you okay?" Ron asked. The kid didn't even look up.

"I have to go," he answered solemnly.

Ron became a little distraught. "Exactly where are you going, or do I want to know? Are you coming back?" he shrieked.

The kid smiled. "I want to come to training camp—if I'm invited," he said.

Ron sighed. "Yes. We always mail out the instructions a few weeks before camp." He had no sooner finished hearing himself say these words than he realized how ridiculous they sounded.

"I don't suppose you can tell me where to mail it?" Ron shook his head.

"How will you know when to come back? I don't even know how you got here!"

"I'll be back. I'll be back when you want me. But I do have to go now. I have to see my dad first," the kid answered.

Ron remembered how close they were. "You're going to Cobourg?" he asked.

Dale McCaine didn't lift his head, but answered softly, "Yes. He's not doing very well now."

Ron was shocked. "Are you sure? How do you know?" he asked.

The kid wouldn't say, "I have to go see him now, but I'll be back for camp in September, you can count on that."

Ron had to believe him; he had no choice in the matter. He left him in the dressing room, where he had first laid eyes on him.

A week later Ron received a message at the Gardens—it had been left by Vern Redden of Red's Hotel in Cobourg. The message was that Doug McCaine had passed away, from emphysema. Doug had not lived to see his son get a chance with the Maple Leafs after all.

Where everybody knows your name

Ron needed to get away and collect his thoughts, so he headed for the place where all of the people in 'the business' went to relieve the pressure and drown their sorrows: *Tim Riley's Bar.* He was too late for lunch and too early for dinner, but he did not like to drink on an empty stomach.

When Ron walked into the bar the familiar mahogany and green marble decor made him feel as at home as if he were in the basement rec room of a friend's house. Even though Ron was not as regular a patron as were many associated with the Leafs, he was still recognized by most of the waitresses and bartenders, especially those who worked the late night shifts.

Ron went to sit at the bar, which he felt was a more private place to eat when he was alone.

He had no sooner seated himself than a reporter (or "scribe" as they were called by some of the Leaf management) recognized him.

The elderly man that sauntered over to him didn't look like a reporter. Most people who saw Billy Sinfield for the first time were struck by uneasiness. It was a kind of *deja vu*, not only that you had seen him before, but that you knew this person well. He reminded most people of Alistair Sim as *Ebenezeer Scrooge.* It wasn't that the reporter was mean or miserly; it was just his physical appearance, although he was becoming more cantankerous with his advancing years. And while he wasn't a miser he was the subject of much speculation as to why he was still drawing a pay cheque when most men of his age had long since retired.

When it came to his relationship with the media Ron Bailey was circumspect. He was not in the spotlight as much as the General Manager, or even the Assistant General Manager. Ron would only be interviewed when no one else was available, or when a rookie reporter, who was unable to get anyone of importance to return his calls, needed a quote. He was also the most likely suspect to be interviewed between periods of the TV broadcasts on the road games from the coast, when comparatively few fans would be watching.

Ron's relationship with Billy Sinfield was decidedly different. When Ron first arrived on the scene in Toronto, Sinfield was one of the first media types to greet him. They met at a 'Meet the Leafs' luncheon, an early season charity function where the fans are introduced to the newest Leaf players, and get an opportunity for autographs and photos. Ron was wandering aimlessly around the huge ballroom at the Harbour Castle Westin, not being recognized by either fans or media. Billy Sinfield was helping himself to the complimentary refreshments afforded the media when Ron was directed to the bar by one of the scouts, a former Leaf player who had been one of Sinfield's favourites when the player skated for the 'Blue and White'.

"This is the Old Goat," the scout said, introducing Ron to Billy Sinfield.

The nickname was a reference to the name 'Billy Goat' and the fact that everyone believed that Sinfield was an old as the earth's cooling period. It was widely believed that Billy Sinfield's first reporting job was covering the selection of animals chosen by Noah as he filled the Ark. Ron had come to respect Billy Sinfield's experience. And he remembered him fondly from childhood, as a newspaper beat writer for the Leafs and as a ghostwriter for several Leaf player biographies in the sixties. Nowadays he was semi-retired. His column, *The Sin Bin* appeared occasionally in the *Toronto Star*. Ron disliked the papers' trenchant slant on the Toronto Maple Leafs although he was fond of Sinfield's style, which was from the old school of reporting—the only thing missing was the fedora.

"I haven't worn one of those damn things in years," Sinfield told Ron, "and even when I did I hated them. I was always leaving them on the seat on the train where some fat guy would sit on it. Or it would get flattened when I would put it in the overhead storage compartment on a plane."

Billy Sinfield lumbered along the bar, and Ron couldn't help but notice how stooped his posture was—this was exaggerated because he was a man who stood about six foot five, *if* he was standing straight.

"Good afternoon, Ron," Billy Sinfield greeted him, "is it official business that brings you here today?" he asked.

Ron realized that the reporter was wasting no time in getting to the point. Reporters, he guessed could not help being reporters even when they were socializing.

"Just stopping by for a late lunch," Ron replied.

Billy Sinfield seated himself on the stool beside Ron, but not without some difficulty. Ron wondered how a man of the reporter's advancing years and apparently declining physical condition could continue working. Billy Sinfield was an enigma in more ways than one. "Well let me buy you a drink to go with it, my friend," he offered.

Ron knew that meant that Billy Sinfield was not socializing but rather was on the trail of a story.

"It must be a slow news day when you have to bother a director of player personnel of a hockey team in the *off season* for a column." Ron needled.

Billy Sinfield ignored the barb. Instead he ordered a gin and tonic for himself and a Creemore Springs draft beer for Ron.

"That's what I like about you, Billy. You often forget my name but you *never* forget what I like to drink."

"You're right about it being a slow news day. All is right with the Toronto Raptors, the Blue Jays still haven't made a trade or fired the manager, the Argonauts are still in first place and no one seems to give a damn, and there's still no one owning the Maple Leafs."

Ron could see where the conversation was headed, so he wanted to put a stop to the fishing expedition. He ordered some halibut and chips, a side salad without dressing, and proceeded to give his friend some useless information.

"You know as well as I that the ownership situation isn't going to be settled until after the hearing begins on October 31st. The contracts of all management personnel were renewed July 1st, for one year."

The drinks came, and although Ron offered to pay Billy Sinfield wasn't finished fishing. When he was, Ron could buy the next round.

"So, do you have any comment on the rumour that AGM Communications is going to buy the team and put the majority of the games on pay-per-view television?" Sinfield asked.

Ron almost choked on his beer. "Where do you guys *get* this stuff?" he asked. The reporter didn't consider that a fitting response to his question.

"Billy, *if* I had any inside knowledge, and I don't, I would not be able to divulge it; not that *I* would have any knowledge. I'm involved in the hockey side, not the business side."

The reporter still hadn't gotten anything he could use. "Let's face it, everyone knows the team is going to be sold, and that the new owners are going to need big bucks to compete for players with the other owners that have deep pockets. And to get that kind of coin they'll have to find new ways of squeezing the public. And what better way to do it than pay-per-view television?"

Ron laughed, "What about a new arena that seats 20,000 fans with 150 private boxes and 3000 club seats with personal seat licenses?"

Billy Sinfield put down his drink for the first time. "Now you're talking. So where is this new arena going to be built, and who's going to build it?"

Ron wasn't finished having fun. "I didn't say there *was* going to be a new arena. I read that in your paper, so it must be true."

The reporter wasn't discouraged by the sarcasm. "If your people would only let the public in on what's *really* going on then we wouldn't print speculation!" he countered.

"Then you *admit* that what you're printing is speculation!" Ron challenged.

Billy Sinfield shook his head, "Not at all. We print what we hear, sometimes we can't quote our sources because they don't want to be quoted," he defended.

Ron didn't appreciate the workings of the media, so he offered to let it go. "When I have something to let you in on Billy, I will," he promised.

The reporter wasn't finished either. There was one more subject on which he could definitely get a comment on the record from Ron. "July the first has come and gone and I can't help but notice that your team is one of the few that haven't made offers to any free agents. You mean to tell me that a team that finished 23rd overall in the standings can't possibly improve themselves by adding a player or two?" He demanded.

Ron wasn't expecting a verbal assault like this from Billy Sinfield, at least not while he was eating his lunch.

"Give me a break, Billy," he implored, "we haven't even had a week to tender any offers. We have our eyes on a few players, but we don't want to tip our hand right now. No need to let the competition in on what we're doing."

Billy Sinfield laughed. "Oh, come now! Your boss is on vacation in Europe. His assistant is drinking branch water and chasing around a little white ball in Myrtle Beach—why the hell else do you think they hold those meetings there. And the *real* reason why the Toronto Maple Leafs hasn't signed any free agents is because they don't intend to part with the dough! And why should they?" he concluded.

"What are you talking about?" Ron interrupted.

"I mean the Sally Ann owns the team, and in order to get the most value for it they don't want to be saddled with any big contracts that would devalue the team, and make it less attractive to prospective buyers, don't you agree?"

Ron couldn't contain himself. "No, I don't agree. Nothing could be further from the truth. If we signed a Joe Sakic or a Paul Kariya then it would make us a better hockey team. And who *wouldn't* want to own a team that is closer to a Stanley Cup than a team that finished 23rd overall!" Ron reasoned.

The reporter had to laugh again, "My poor naïve friend. Do you really think that whoever buys this team gives a damn about winning the Stanley Cup?"

The silence that followed Billy Sinfield's charge made Ron take a sip of his beer, and want to listen to the rest of the veteran reporter's theory. "I don't have to remind you that this team of yours hasn't won a Stanley Cup since this country's one-hundredth birthday. And since that time, the previous owner of the team took great pride in ringing up the cash register while dragging the team's reputation for winning through the mud—all for the gain of a buck."

Ron couldn't argue with history. The Leafs *had* gone from owning a lifetime winning record to holding a lifetime *under* .500 record, and all within the last forty years. "I don't dispute that," he conceded, "but since Ken Butler took over this team things have been different. We came within one goal of making it to the Stanley Cup final three years ago. And we did it by spending the money to acquire players that could get us there."

The reporter smiled. "You can't milk that 'we made it to the final four two years in a row thing' any longer, my friend," he reasoned.

Ron tried *not* to let a grin escape. "I just want to remind you that Toronto is not the only original-six team that isn't exactly shining these days. Look at Montreal—it isn't what it used to be, and everybody considers *them* to be the most successful team in history. Yes, they have won the most Stanley Cups; twenty-three to Toronto's thirteen. But *nine* of those Stanley Cups came while the Leafs were owned by the guy you chastised a minute ago. If it wasn't for him I suspect the numbers would be a little closer!"

The reporter wasn't willing to concede that. "We'll never know about that, my friend. But you have to admit that your fans have seen the Rangers and the Red Wings sip champagne from the Stanley Cup, and when those original six teams win the cup it only rubs salt in the wounds."

"What difference does that make?" Ron asked.

"Those are the teams that the Leafs used to compete with and beat—but not anymore. I think that it bothers most long-time fans when the Leafs lose to the Mighty Ducks or the Coyotes—but it really hurts to see them lose to an original six team. Don't you think it kills your fans to see them lose to the Montreal Canadiens you just compared them to?"

Ron had finished just enough large *Creemore Springs* drafts to let this one out of the bag.

"What if I told you that the real reason why the Leafs haven't won the Stanley Cup since 1967 has nothing to do with the previous owner's reluctance to spend money on players, or poor drafting or because of mismanagement, or whatever."

The reporter wasn't putting away his note pad just yet. "What are you getting at?" Billy Sinfield asked.

Ron noticed that the sun was beginning to set, although he had no idea what time it was. The bar did seem to have filled up since he had arrived there.

"Do you believe in superstition when it comes to sports teams?" Ron asked.

Billy Sinfield had been a reporter for over fifty years. He had covered everything from stock car races at the CNE to Cricket matches at Centre Island. He had seen the Canadian Grand Prix of just about *any* sport that *had* a Canadian Grand Prix. He had seen just about all there was to see, and then some. "Superstition, good luck, bad luck; it's as much a part of winning and losing as playing the game, I suppose," he philosophized.

"That's my point," Ron argued.

Sinfield didn't get the picture. "You mean that bad luck has kept the Leafs from winning for forty years? What did they do, break a dozen mirrors?" he scoffed.

Ron continued his theorizing, "Not exactly. I mean you've seen teams win titles that had no business winning a championship. They weren't the best statistically, or even the most talented. They weren't any better coached or managed than their competition. Yet they found a way to win."

Instantly the Old Goat offered up some examples. "You mean like the 'Miracle Mets of '69 or the Oakland Raiders 'team of destiny' in 1980. But those are teams that *won* with *good* luck on their side. Your team *hasn't* won," he countered.

"Exactly," Ron concluded. "But why *haven't* they won. A lot of good hockey players have come and gone in the last forty years; Sittler, Salming, McDonald, but they had nothing to show for it, no Stanley Cups."

The reporter was following the lead. "Are you trying to say that something has kept them from winning in spite of the talent they had?"

"That's right," Ron stated firmly.

Billy Sinfield thought about it for a moment. "You mean it's something like the curse of Bill Stewart and the Chicago Black Hawks."

Ron agreed, and considered something he had remembered hearing. "I thought they called it 'The curse of Muldoon'? I remember something about a curse of Muldoon," he speculated.

The Old Goat quickly corrected him, "The 'Curse of Muldoon'. It wasn't as big a deal as they made it up to be. You see, aaah, Pete Muldoon was the Chicago Black Hawks first ever coach, in 1926, and he was fired after they finished in third place, but lost out in the quarterfinal that year. Muldoon vowed that the Black Hawks would never again finish first, and they didn't for almost twenty years. But they did go on to win the Stanley Cup seven years later and again four years after that. The *real* curse came during the 1938-39 season, when, after Bill Stewart had coached them to a Stanley Cup the previous year, he was fired part way through the next season. *He* placed a curse on them, although it wasn't publicized like the Curse of Muldoon, and they didn't win another Stanley Cup until 1960-61; twenty-two seasons later!"

"How do you *remember* all of this stuff?" Ron asked in amazement.

The old goat just laughed. "So who placed a curse on the Maple Leafs and why?" He demanded.

Ron wanted to be careful here; he wasn't about to divulge any names. He proceeded to tell Billy Sinfield about his visit to Doug McCaine in Cobourg.

"This is *great!*" the Old Goat exclaimed. "And I thought this was going to be a slow news day. My boy you've just given me my column for Wednesday," he bristled, while slapping Ron on the back.

Ron was astonished. "You're not *really* going to write that are you?"

"This is marvellous! Don't you see? Why, now all of the GM's that have come and gone since 1967 are off the hook; they couldn't possibly have won a Stanley Cup because the deck was stacked against them." the reporter declared.

Ron was beginning to think the whole thing was in bad taste. After all, Doug McCaine had just passed on. He had to tell Billy Sinfield about that. "You can't print that. The man who placed the curse is just died! It would be in bad taste!"

"It makes no difference. I can do it respectfully. 'Here's to the man who kept the Maple Leafs from winning the Stanley Cup for almost forty years'," Billy Sinfield said as he raised his glass in a toast.

Ron Bailey declined to join him. "I don't think that's funny, Billy," he protested, "The man was sincere."

Billy Sinfield could sense that he had genuinely upset Ron. "My boy, there's something you have to understand in this business of sport. Good guys don't always win; in fact some, Casey Stengel for example, have said that 'nice guys finish last'. There are so many reasons *why* a team doesn't win a championship. The Chicago Cubs haven't won a World Series since 1908! The Boston Red Sox haven't won a championship since 1912! And even *if* you believe in the curse of the Bambino, that still doesn't explain why they are winless in 91 years. There are so many things involved with winning; trades, injuries, travel, scheduling, weather—hell, for all I know even astrology, if you believe in that."

The Old Goat lowered his glass to the bar. "There are so many reasons. Fans seem to think that their team should win at all costs. Well that's fine. Maybe they *should* make championships like a contest; once you have a winner they are ineligible until everyone *else* has had a chance to win. O' course that flies in the face of everything that sportsmanship stands for; the ideas that may the best man win—but maybe you've hit on something."

Ron felt that, as usual, Billy Sinfield had gone too far with his sarcasm. "I was only trying to point out that this fellow felt strongly about what had happened to his son, strong enough to place a curse on them."

"That's all right, Ron. The poor Maple Leaf fans have enough to worry themselves about without having to believe that they are cursed. I'll save that column for the day *after* they win their next Stanley Cup, presuming o' course that I live that long," he promised.

"You make a lot of sense about winning. Luck *has* a great deal to do with it. I don't really believe that something as mysterious as curse has anything to do with winning a Stanley Cup," Ron deduced.

The reporter nodded and stared at his reflection in the mirror behind the bar.

"That's right," the Old Goat agreed, "Unless o' course you consider something like the ghosts in the Montreal Forum."

Ron was uneasy. He turned to Billy Sinfield. "The what?" he asked.

"You know, surely you've heard about the ghosts in the Montreal Forum?"

Ron *had* heard of it, but he didn't know *exactly* what it meant. "What does it mean? Why is that always mentioned about Montreal?"

The Old Goat went to take another sip from his gin and tonic before he realized it was all gone.

"A couple more here!" he barked to the bartender, who he didn't realize was out of earshot. "Many people believe that the Montreal Forum is home to the ghosts of players who have passed on. It's a historic building, probably *the* most historic hockey building in existence. And that includes Maple Leaf Gardens, I'm sorry to say. Howie Morenz was one of the greatest players ever to wear the red, white and blue. When he died in 1937 they laid his body in state at centre ice. Thousands of people passed through the Forum to pay their respects to their lost hero. Can you imagine that happening to a player *today*? Why, you go in that famous dressing room and see the faces of those great former players emblazoned on the wall staring down at you. And there's that motto on the wall, you know from John McCrae's epic 'In Flanders's Fields', 'To yours with failing hands we pass the torch, be it yours to hold on high'. It's like they are *challenging* you, to be as successful as they were. It's eerie. Just ask anyone who has ever played for the Canadiens. It's positively spooky, I tell you!"

Ron knew all about what was spooky.

"The fans believe that many of those Canadiens Stanley Cup team were inspired, I dare say *aided* by those old players. You take a team like the 1971 Canadiens. Sure, they were loaded with stars; Beliveau, Cournoyer, Henri Richard, *both* Mahovliches, Savard, Lapointe. It was Dryden's rookie year."

"Sounds like a team of Hall-of-Famers!" Ron agreed.

"Yes, but they only finished third in the regular season. What was it that made them able to beat the mighty Boston Bruins, with Orr, Esposito, Hodge, Cashman, Bucyk, a team that had a league record 399 goals and 57 wins!"

"You think the *ghosts* helped them to win the cup?" Ron inferred.

"It's one explanation," the reporter claimed.

Ron thought about it for a moment and then asked Billy Sinfield the obvious question.

"Well what *about* Maple Leaf Gardens. Isn't *it* every bit as legendary as the Montreal Forum?

Doesn't *it* have it share of Hall-of-Famers, players from the past who would challenge the ones' of today to be as great?"

Billy Sinfield was trembling with excitement. Ron expected a great oration to follow, until he realized that it was only Billy's reaction to the arrival of the drinks.

"Ahhh but here's the difference," The reporter began, "the Leaf players from the past were all alienated by the management. They were no longer welcome, after a time. You do your homework my friend, and see how many of those former players were dumped at the twilight of their careers."

Ron was bewildered. "You mean like Sittler?" he enquired.

The Old Goat had to brace himself to keep from toppling off of the bar stool.

"I forget how young you are, Ronnie. No, I'm talking about players who are no longer with us. You look back at how the career of Charlie Conacher ended. He was the greatest Leaf right wing of all time. The Big Bomber would swashbuckle his way down the rink like nobody else. He scored 200 goals in nine years; he was an all-star four times. And he was sold to Detroit for $16,000! Or Busher Jackson—dealt to the New York Americans for Sweeney Schreiner. Busher was a partier. He drank his way out of the league ended up selling the *Globe and Mail* outside the Gardens for years after he hit the skids. And what about Tim Horton, who was dealt to save a few bucks in 1970? He played another four years after the Leafs let him go. Hell, he'd probably *still* be playing today if he hadn't been in that car accident."

And what about Dale McCaine, Ron wondered—the Ghosts in the Montreal Forum indeed. What about ghosts in Maple Leaf Gardens?

"So, you think that because these former players were treated so badly that they would never come down from the rafters and help the Leafs of today to win the Stanley Cup? You think that they would hold a grudge. Well what about all that pride that I hear you talk about? What about all of that pride I hear you say that they played for. It must have been pride. You are always telling me that they weren't doing it just for the money."

The old goat just smiled. "O'course they had pride in the way they played. They weren't doing it just for pride though. Let's face it—they were well paid for the time—though not in comparison to today!"

"But they loved to play the game. That's what *made* them. They loved to play the game. I know that young kids today still play the game for the love of it. But I suspect that somewhere along the line, the fame or celebrity status, or whatever takes over and the love of the game takes a back seat to the love of the buck."

Ron's outlook was not as cynical as that of Billy Sinfield. He agreed that the pressures that money brought with it were enough to outweigh the love for the game at times. But the average career of a hockey player is so short that the love of the game can be as motivational as the money. The finality of having your career come to an end, through an injury or some other circumstance he knew only too well. When the reality of a swollen knee that throbs even when it is iced down takes over, one soon remembers all too quickly what they really miss about the game. "You don't know what you've got 'till it's gone', Ron said.

"What?" the old goat asked.

"I was just thinking, like that saying. When you can't play anymore, when you have to retire for whatever reason, that is when you remember that you played the game because you loved it. That's when you start to really miss it."

"I thought we were talking about young kids today?" Billy Sinfield wondered.

Ron was through daydreaming. "I was remembering how it felt when I realized that I'd never be able to play hockey again. That's when I really understood what I loved about hockey. Yes, I was chasing an unrealistic dream about playing professional hockey. But I realized then how much I loved to play. I loved to feel of air rushing past your face when you skated down that white ice, and hearing that crack when the puck hit your stick as you took a perfect pass. To see the mesh of the net ripple like it was pushed by a ghost when you ripped a blistering shot past a goalie. I would never be able to do any of it again."

Ron realized that Dale McCaine must have felt the same way when he realized that his dream was coming to an end, when he embarked on that lonely drive home from Tulsa.

Perhaps fate would intervene and provide a new ending to Dale McCaine's dream

The men in black

R on Bailey loved to play the game but he had also developed an affinity for coaching it.

He longed to coach a team of kids because he hoped to be able to instil in them at a young age a respect for the game.

His position at the Gardens, and its heavy travel schedule prevented that. Instead he was able to get his coaching fix satisfied through summer hockey. He coached the Burger Hut Flyers, who played out of the Scarborough Ice Sports league. The team consisted of a group of minor league players, who punched their time cards in places like the Colonial, East Coast or Southern Hockey leagues. These guys were unlikely to ever make it to the American league—let alone the NHL. Ron was coaching them almost as a public service. He believed that his position as director of player personnel would give the guys some hope that they still had a chance of being discovered by a National Hockey League scout. And while scouts were unlikely to be found anywhere but a golf course or fishing boat in the summer time there was reason for optimism. If players in the league could impress a player personnel director then perhaps a chance to try out with a minor league affiliate was possible. Ron never made any promises of that sort. This was only his third season of coaching in the summer, and the assistant coach of the St. Johns' Maple Leafs would join him. This year he was being sent an almost entirely new crop of 'suspects', as he called them, for they were one notch below 'prospects.'

While the Toronto Maple Leafs did not have a working agreement with any teams below the American Hockey League,

Ron was campaigning to have the General Manager agree to place several minor-leaguers in either the Colonial or Eastern league so that they would be available to St. Johns', for evaluation purposes. He had it in his mind that there somewhere existed an undiscovered talent—a diamond in the rough who was over-looked by all of the scouting staffs of all of the other NHL teams. He actually dreamed of discovering such a player, of being the one credited for uncovering the prized archaeological dig. It would be the ultimate testimonial to the organization's skill in appraising talent.

It did not deter Ron that such fantasies were exactly that—*no* player in modern history had reached the NHL by failing to come under the collective microscope of NHLs' central scouting.

On this particular summers' day he was heading home from the Gardens when he got a call from the General Manager of the Macon Whoopee, of the Southern Hockey League. They had agreed to 'enrol' several young players in Ron's 'Summer School for the NHL' as they players referred to it.

"Ron, its Brock Anderson, from Macon—how ya doin?" the muffled voice on the phone asked.

Ron was expecting the worst; why else would the GM be calling except to say that they were *not* going to supply any living players? "I'm well, Brock, and you?" he asked. Just get to it, he said impatiently to himself.

"Ron, we were going to send you some fellas for your summer team, you remember? Well I have to apologize, but the four kids have decided to go back to Europe for the summer. But I'm not going to let you down. I spoke to the GM of the Ice Gators, and he has a line on a couple or three kids who are dying to come up there and play for the summer."

Ron was shuddering at the thought. It was bad enough to consider players who barely had enough talent to make the roster of the Macon Whoopee, but *replacement* players!

"Brock, I don't think we'd be interested. The idea of this team is to help players benefit from NHL style coaching, and to give the guys a chance to show their stuff to a NHL scout. I don't really..."

"They come highly recommended, Ron. Believe me these guys were given a great recommendation by our amateur scout. He saw them at a tryout camp. They're really eager, and when we mentioned Toronto, well—"

Ron knew that it would be hard to find enough warm bodies this late in the summer. If there were three or four of them to fill out the roster, well so be it, he thought.

"All right," he conceded, "just have them show up at Scarborough Ice Sports. The first practice is a week from Sunday night, seven o'clock."

"Great Ron, you won't be sorry, I promise you." That comment didn't leave Ron with a warm and fuzzy feeling.

"You won't be sorry" was a phrase he recalled hearing when he made a trade for a junior overage goaltender at the conclusion of the deal. As it turned out the player had committed some indiscretion with the local house league convenor's teenage daughter, and it was just a matter of time before the kid was going to be escorted to the city limits by the police. Had Ron known about the situation he probably could have had the kid in exchange for a copy of the *Hockey News*.

As a result of the news about the replacement players, Ron was less than enthusiastic as he approached the first practice for the summer team. The Burger Hut Flyers were certainly going to be a project. Ron had spent the previous evening going over the roster with the St. Johns' assistant coach, Al Swartz. Between them they had pencilled in line match ups and defense pairings based on the fact that some of these guys had played together before. The practices (there would be only two of them before the start of the brief sixteen-game schedule) would determine the set-ups as well as the power play and penalty killing units.

As Ron crossed the parking lot into the huge complex he was surprised to find a sudden chill in the air. After all it was still July; it shouldn't be this cool. A steady rain had been falling all day, ruining yet another weekend. Once inside the lobby he checked the board for the dressing room assignments. He found that the Flyers were assigned to room 3 on rink two, so he headed off to find the room, his equipment bag and sticks in hand. He was not afraid to test his knee again. He had been doing stretching exercises for an hour before he climbed into his car for the thirty-minute drive. Another fifteen more minutes of stretching would be required to properly be warmed up before he headed onto the ice. His knee would always hurt when he skated, but he would not be going at full tilt in a practice anymore. When he began his duties as director of player personnel he had been invited by Spencer Smith to participate in some of the game day skates at the Gardens, but he had declined. He told himself that he did not have the confidence in his knee to be on the ice with National Hockey League players, but in reality it had nothing to do with the knee. He honestly felt that because he had never played in the NHL that he had no right to be on the ice with them. Ron felt that there was a big difference between assistant coaching in junior or in the minors—the jump to the NHL was a quantum leap.

Ron arrived early to have his warm up exercises done before the other players showed up. He was startled at finding five guys already in the room when he walked in.

The five players were all standing as he entered, and Ron couldn't help notice that they were all dressed in a similar fashion. They all were wearing long, dark overcoats, dark blue or black slacks and dress shoes; even their shirts were dark. All except one of them wore ties, and two of them had on hats—one wore a black fedora and the other an English driving cap.

The one without a tie wore a New York Yankees baseball cap, of the 1951 style.

All of the players were about the same height, six feet or under, and with the exception of one were all of only a medium build.

"You must be the coach!" the husky one said, offering up his hand to shake.

"Yes, I'm Ron Bailey," he said, expecting the players to introduce each other as a return gesture. Instead the players exchanged glances among themselves, as if they were satisfied with the situation.

The peculiarity of the player's style of dress confused Ron a little, until he remembered where he had seen it before. Inside the *Leaf sport* store at Maple Leaf Gardens was a promotional photo series that was done to salute the team's beginnings in the thirties, sort of a link between the past and the present. The black and white photographs were a series of three, the second of which had the players in a garage around an old car, and dressed as thirties-style gangsters. These guys looked as if they had walked right off of that photograph. He felt a sudden uneasiness, but at the same time the familiarity of the player's faces was comforting to him. It was as if he had seen them before, but he couldn't recall where.

"I'm sorry if I'm staring, but I can't help but think that I've met some of you before. Any of you guys play for me in Rochester or Windsor?"

The group muttered amongst themselves, and this time the tallest one of the group seemed to be elected spokesman.

"We were sent here to help you out," he said, his words sounding like a prepared statement.

"Right," Ron agreed. "Brock Anderson of Macon explained to me that he couldn't provide the European kids. You guys are from the *Ice Gators*. So how do you like playing hockey in Louisiana?"

The group had an uneasiness pass from one face to the other. Ron was taken by how *pale* they all looked. They didn't answer right away, and Ron began to nervously fidget with his clipboard, as he searched for the roster sheet that listed the player's names and where they had played.

"Let's see whom we've got here," he said as if he was talking to a group of six-year-olds that were too shy to say their names. "I've got, Bachmann, Hansky, Bodine, Mouton, and, am I pronouncing this right, Is-bister?" he asked. Ron was greeted with blank stares.

"What's the matter guys, he asked, "Have I got the names wrong?"

Ron was about to raise his voice, as if they hadn't heard him, but finally the tall one responded.

"We're not the players from the Ice, whatever you said," he answered, "we're here to help win you a Stanley Cup, if you give us the chance."

Ron laughed, and dropped his clipboard in the process. "I'm sorry fellas, but they don't hand out the Stanley Cup for winning the Scarborough Ice Sports summer league!" he snorted, as he wiped a tear from his eye. The players were not laughing, so Ron felt he needed to set the record straight.

"Guys, I don't know what Brock Anderson told you but this is *not* a tryout for the Leafs. Yes, I promised that scouts would see you play, myself included, but there are no guarantees. And as far as the Stanley Cup goes—"

They were not sharing his laughter. They were conducting themselves as if this was a business meeting instead of the first practice of a summer hockey league team.

"Has someone told you that this was a tryout?" Ron wondered. The oldest looking one of the group spoke for the first time, but not to Ron.

"Maybe you better tell him who we are, Charlie."

The one he called Charlie nodded. For the first time Ron realized that these guys were *not* who they seemed to be.

"I guess I should have mentioned Dale McCaine right from the start," the one called Charlie said.

Ron dropped his clipboard. He sat down, and nearly missed the bench. "How do *you* know about Dale McCaine?" he asked.

The one called Charlie looked at the others and was given the vote of confidence, so he continued.

"We know that you offered Dale McCaine a chance to play. We're here to ensure that he when he gets his chance he'll make the most of it."

"Sort of an insurance policy," the tallest one added.

The husky one chipped in. "You see we know what it takes to win a Stanley Cup, we've all been there before!"

Ron's jaw dropped open like a pelican gathering fish. "You have all been there before. You have all won a Stanley Cup, and now you're in the Scarborough Ice Sports league?"

The situation was too bewildering to comprehend.

"I reckon we've won more than *one* Stanley. I'd say that between the five of us we've played on, let me see now—one, two, three, Billy has four, and Superman here has four. That makes *eleven* between us! Whattya know about that?" The one called Charlie said.

Ron was losing his grip on the situation. "Who *are* you guys?" he demanded.

The one called Charlie responded. "Yeah, we haven't introduced ourselves," he continued, directing his hand at the others, one at a time. "This here is Frank McCool, that's Bashin Bill Barilko, the ugly one there is Busher Jackson, the kid there's Timmy Horton, and I'm Charlie Conacher."

Ron nodded in agreement. "Of course you are. Why wouldn't you be? I mean, if Dale McCaine can materialize through the mirror in the dressing room at Maple Leaf Gardens, why can't you guys'?"

The one they called Charlie didn't readily pick up on sarcasm. "I take it you don't believe we are who we say we are?"

"Oh, but I *do* believe you, and I bet you can walk through walls to prove it!" Ron challenged.

"We didn't think we'd have trouble convincing you! You accepted Dale McCaine right away," the one supposed to be Barilko added, while jerking on his Yankee cap.

101

"Not right away. I saw a man move *through* a mirror! I would have believed he was *Elvis*

If that's who he said he was!"

The five of them whispered about it among themselves and then broke the huddle.

"Okay," said the one they called Charlie. "It seems as if you need to see things for yourself. I can't say as I blame a man that has to 'believe it when he sees it ', you'll want to see what we can do on the ice."

Ron remained unconvinced. "No—I want to see the five of you go through that door!" He dared.

"You give us a chance to show you what we can do on the ice first. You watch us practice and then we'll do whatever you want," the one called Charlie offered, as the five of them began unpacking their hockey bags.

Ron didn't respond right away, but instead noticed how *new* the bags looked, like they had just come out of a sporting goods store window, and the equipment looked as if it had rarely been used. The style of it was *another* thing. The skates, shin pads, pants and athletic supporters he saw come out of the bags were like antiques. 'Chico Resch would *die* to have this stuff in his collection' he thought. It was just like the stuff that Dale McCaine wore; only some of this equipment seemed even older. Everything about these five guys seemed genuine, but Ron could not help but be sceptical.

As he laced up his skates and started his stretching, he thought about how he *wanted* to believe that Dale McCaine was real. What he had *seen* could not convince him otherwise. But he thought that *anybody* could show up in a room with old equipment and claim to *be* anybody. He would need a lot more than that to believe that five old time hockey players had showed up to play for his summer hockey league team.

The players continued to go about dressing themselves, keeping their banter to a minimum, and talking only to themselves. Ron began to wonder where the other players were, until he glanced at his watch and realized it was still too early for anyone else to show up. He took charge of the situation.

"You guys really want to show me on the ice. Well okay, until the others show up. I mean, since the ice is free, and you guys are ready, well follow me out onto the ice," he ordered.

The five of them followed like a real coach giving orders to his real players. The only thing unreal about it was who they said they were. Ron walked out of the room and the door closed behind him. He heard the door creak and shut as it hit the jamb, but the next sound he heard was that of skates padding along the rubber walkway. He turned around quickly to see the last of them walking through the dressing room doorway, with their heads down, and the door to the room still closed. They passed by Ron, as he stood motionless, with his back to the rink bulletin board. He watched as the five of them lined up to the open door in the boards, and they skated onto the newly scraped sheet of ice.

"They would even go through a closed door for their coach!" Ron thought, "Just like old time hockey players!"

He watched them circle the rink, single file, like a precision skating team. There was no doubt about their skating ability. The fluidity of their movement was genuine—no one can fake the ability to skate. The five of them wore no helmets, and Ron didn't seem to care until he realized that the goalie had no mask.

"Hold it a minute fellas!" he shouted, as he stepped onto the rink. "We can't let you out here without proper equipment. You four have to wear helmets, and the goalie has to have a mask!"

Ron may as well have been speaking to them in Russian. They had no idea what he was talking about.

"Awww, c'mon coach. Nobody's sissy enough to have to wear headgear," Conacher answered for the group.

103

"Yeah," added Jackson, "next thing you'll tell us we have to wear dresses!"

The comments heralded a round of laughter. They group awaited the coach's first real direction, but Ron insisted that the league had its rules, and for insurance purposes they would all have to comply.

"What for?" Barilko asked, "What difference does it make? We're all dead!"

Ron was skating towards the group but suddenly stopped. He considered the absurdity of the statement, but then made this suggestion.

"You guys really want me to believe that you're who you say you are—but no one is going to give you the chance to play unless you play by the rules. None of you have played hockey since, when, thirty, even fifty years? Don't you think in all of that time that the rules could change? Players have to wear helmets, goalies have to wear masks; hey, for that matter do you guys all know that there is a red line at centre? And what it's for?" Conacher and Jackson looked at each other, and nodded their heads in agreement.

"We heard!" they said in unison.

Ron continued to amaze them, "Do you know that when a player is serving a penalty, and his team gives up a goal, he gets to return to the ice?"

This one was too much for Barilko. "What?" he bellowed. Jackson skated over to him.

"He's right Billy, ask the kid over there. The rule came in *after* you went fishing!"

Barilko went red in the face, and began to chase Jackson around the boards. The old captain was faster though, and Barilko never did catch him. Finally Horton stepped in, grabbing Barilko around the waist with a bear hug.

"Let go of me kid!" he fumed at Horton.

"The coach was talking!" Horton responded, wrestling Bashing Bill over to where Ron Bailey stood.

Ron did what any coach would do when he was losing control of his players; he blew his whistle. The five of them instantly responded. They understand respect for the coach, I'll give them that, he said to himself.

He ordered the players off the ice and into the dressing room. The practice would not continue until Ron had visited the pro shop to round up some essentials. He charged four black CCM pro helmets, one KOHO goalie mask, and five fibreglass-reinforced shaft, curved blade Easton sticks to his VISA card; $975.00 later (not including tax) he returned to the room. It'll be interesting trying to explain *this* one on my expenses, he thought as he handed out the equipment.

He returned to the room with the equipment and was greeted with disbelief by 'Busher' Jackson.

"What the hell is this? The sticks got a wow in it!" he exclaimed.

"A *what*?" Ron demanded.

"Well look at the blade. Here Charlie, grab and end of this and we'll straighten her out," he instructed the former captain. Conacher looked on, until Horton put an end to it.

"It's *supposed* to be curved, Busher! It lets you raise it easier!" the big defenseman said.

Jackson was sceptical.

"I reckon I *know* how to raise a puck, kid. I been doing it since before you was in diapers! I don't need a wow in my stick to do it."

Ron shook his head. He watched, bewildered, as the five of them struggled with their new headgear, sort of like kids trying on new clothes at back-to-school time.

He was about to jump in and help when a group of *real* players entered the room. Ron instantly recognized the group, most of who had played for him the year before. Al Swartz, his assistant coach followed the group into the room.

"Ronnie, good to see ya boy!" the assistant coach said as he shook Ron's hand violently, and slapped him on the back so hard that Ron's teeth chattered.

"Hey, Al," he said, forcing a smile. Ron didn't appreciate Swartz's gruff style at times. Behind the bench was a different story. When games were on the line he knew he could count on Al Swartz to deliver just the right injection of surliness to motivate the team.

"These the '*Louisiana* Ice *Gators*'? Al Swartz from St. Johns'," said, introducing himself to Charlie Conacher while offering to shake his hand.

The surprised player still had his hand stuck between his head and the helmet as he attempted to free himself, or remove the helmet; whichever was easier. Ron realized that the player was about to announce himself as Charlie Conacher, so he had to act fast.

"Al!" he shouted, getting the attention of the assistant momentarily, "I want you to meet Bachmann, Bodine, Mouton, Hansky and uhhh, I hope I'm pronouncing this right. *Is-biszter.*"

The five of them stood mouths gaping open as Ron introduced them. Swartz was confused as he tried to attach names to the five blank staring faces that stood before him.

"So you're Bodine?" the assistant asked Conacher.

"No," replied Conacher, "I'm—"

"That's right, he's Bachmann. Bodine is over *there,*" Ron said, directing Schwartz's attention to Busher Jackson. He wasn't about to let any of the rest of them say who they were. He decided to give them their *Cajun* names.

"And this is Mouton," he said, introducing Tim Horton, "and here is Hansky, *David* Hansky."

Barilko stared as if he was lost in the wilderness. That left only Frank McCool to be introduced. The goalie was still trying to figure out just how to wear the mask. He had it sitting so far back on his head that only his forehead was protected.

"So you must be...Is-bizter?" the assistant concluded.

"Yeah," the goalie replied, as he attempted to fasten the rear strap to the front of the helmet. "Except I think you pronounce it Iss-Bisster."

Ron's eyes went wide, and the goalie winked at him. He struggled to remember the first names of the rest of the players but it was no use. He would have to consult the roster sheet.

Ron was afraid that the old players would have difficulty mixing in with the new, so he asked Swartz to take the rest of the group onto the ice while he stayed behind to have a talk with the *Ice Gators*, as Swartz had called them.

"Guys, listen up," he said forgetting for a moment that he was addressing a group that included three Hall-of-Famers, a goalie who held the NHL record for most consecutive shutouts in the Stanley Cup final, and one of only two Leafs to have their sweater retired. "I think that it's going to be a little more difficult for you guys to fit in than maybe you thought—I mean except for maybe Horton there, I mean *Mouton*." The first shot of dissidence was heard.

"What's with the names?" Conacher asked.

"Mouton?" Horton griped, "That means *Sheep*! Tabernac, if I have to have a French name why does it have to be that?" he laughed.

"I don't speak it *that* good. And I don't have an accent!"

Ron continued his speech. "I wouldn't worry about that. I had to use the names, *any* other names. I can't, *you* can't be yourselves. How will it look—Tim Horton playing for the Leafs again? How am I supposed to explain *that*—you guys can't even explain it?" The players had to agree with him on this one, although they did not say so.

"You'll *have* to go along with the names, and you'll have to remember them. My god, I'll have to remember them. And I'll have to explain where you came from!"

"Just *how* are you gonna do that, coach?" Horton asked, with a deadpan expression.

Ron had remembered reading that Horton was very much a practical joker, so he wasn't about to give him ammunition.

107

"We'll cross that one when we have to," he replied. "If you want to come on board and help Dale McCaine, then you'll have to do it my way; the league has changed since you guys played. Just follow my lead," he ordered. The five of them agreed, and Conacher summed it up for them.

"Remember what your old coach said? It was Red Garrett who said 'Hockey is the simplest game on the face of the earth; you put this old rubber cookie past the goalie at the other end of the rink more times than they do to us, and we win!'"

"How do *you* know what Garrett used to say?" Ron asked. Conacher just smiled.

"You can learn a thing or two from us too, I suspect, coach."

Ron agreed that he could. That reminded him of what Billy Sinfield had said when he wondered why there were no ghosts in Maple Leaf Gardens.

The Ex-Leafs were a sharp contrast in style to the other wanna-bees that showed up for the practice. It was clear that they would take time to fit in with the modern style of hockey. Ron felt that both styles could complement each other, and that was precisely what the summer league could offer.

After practice Ron returned to the dressing room to find the ex-Leaf players still there, after all of the others had gone. "You guys aren't planning on camping out here until the next practice, are you?" Ron asked.

Charlie Conacher laughed. "Hell no, we were just wondering if you'd like to join us?"

"For a couple of 'pops'," Busher Jackson added.

"Gonna go down to the *Conroy*," Conacher said.

Ron had never heard of the *Conroy*, and had no idea where it was. He wasted no time in agreeing but at the same time suggested someplace closer. Had he realized that Charlie Conacher and Roy Worters formerly owned the Conroy Hotel he probably would have shuddered at the possibility of the former Leaf captain being recognized by some old bar fly. The group headed to the *Don Cherry's* lounge inside the complex. When it came time to order the round, the waitress approached Conacher first to ask him what he wanted.

"I'll have a *Dow*", he answered. The befuddled girl had no idea what he was talking about.

"I don't think we have *that*," she apologized. Conacher shook his head.

"Then I'll have a *Bradding's Ale*," he replied.

The poor girl simply shrugged, until Ron realized that he had better take charge, instead of letting Conacher consider any other beers that had not been produced for over forty years.

"A round of *Canadians*, please," he ordered. "I have to ask you this," Ron enquired after the beers came. "A sportswriter friend of mine told me all about the so-called 'Ghosts in the Montreal Forum', and I asked him why the same sentiment was not true about Maple Leaf Gardens. He told me it was because players like you were so badly treated at the end of their careers that they felt no loyalty to the organization; that they were more likely to want to help out the teams that they were traded to. Yet here you are, and you say you want to help the Toronto Maple Leafs win a Stanley Cup? I have to wonder *why?*"

The former captain was the one who answered for all of them. "What you say is right," Conacher started.

But it's not the Maple Leafs we're doing this for, not entirely. It's *Dale McCaine* we're doing this for. It wasn't his fault that he never got the chance. He *should* have gotten the chance to play for a Stanley Cup winner. It was supposed to happen. We're here to make sure it does."

There was finality, a sense of destiny in the statement that frightened Ron—he wondered what the motivating force behind these five *really* was. If they were really there to ensure that Dale McCaine got his chance, he was sure that they would do whatever it would take to win. And he was sure that they would listen to him to let them help to make it happen. But as with Dale McCaine, Ron considered the logistics of these apparitions. Ghosts in the Montreal Forum were one thing, Ron thought. But these guys seemed *real*. They certainly drank like hockey players.

Ron paid the tab and left them with one round on the table. He decided to take a cab home. Where the players would go when left, and what they would do until the next practice, he could not imagine. And how would he get in touch with them? These considerations were too taxing for him. He was content for now to take it one day at a time, and wait and see what developed.

Coach's corner

Ron had never enjoyed coaching as much as the sixteen games that comprised the Burger Hut Flyers schedule. From the first practice there was no question that the five old-timers were the class of the league. Ron marvelled at their dedication, and their appreciation for the team style of play that he found it so difficult to get across to young players. He was amazed by the simple skills they possessed—like their collective ability to headman the puck with a pass so crisp it whacked the stick with a sound that could be heard in the dressing room.

And Ron wasn't the only one who was taken aback by these relics. Al Swartz could barely contain himself when he sent the forwards Conacher and Jackson out with the defense pair of Horton and Barilko as a unit.

"The biggest problem," Swartz said, "is finding somebody that can play with these four."

As the short summer schedule drew to a close the Burger Hut Flyers had only a single tie to blemish their record; they had won every other game they had played. McCool was like a wall out there. His reflexes and stand up style were something that these minor leaguers had never seen.

As their first of two playoff games drew near it was already the end of August, and the start of training camp was looming larger in the minds of both Ron Bailey and Al Swartz.

"Have you decided to sign them?" was the question Ron was popped on the morning of their first playoff game.

Ron had been so enthralled with watching the newcomers play that he had neglected his duties as a member of the Leafs management group; if these guys were going to be invited to training camp their rights would have to be secured. Ron would have to sign each of them to a standard player contract, and register it with the league to make it official. If he failed to do that then the players would be ineligible to attend camp or play in exhibition games.

Ron was getting ahead of himself. He had neglected to mention any of these new findings to his boss. Ken Butler was on the last leg of his European vacation, and was due back in Toronto after the Labour Day weekend. He would have to prepare a story. He would have to invent a back story for finding these players, not to mention Dale McCaine.

Ron thought back to the question that Al Swartz had asked him, and answered truthfully.

"No. I *haven't* decided to sign them."

Swartz was ecstatic. "Yes!" he said, in Marv Albert fashion. "That means we have a chance to have them on the rock."

Ron decided he should nip this idea in the bud. "Al, it doesn't automatically follow that you'll be getting these guys with St. Johns'!" The assistant coach's bubble had burst.

"If you aren't going to sign them to the Leafs roster, then *of course* I want them with me. What am I, crazy?"

"There is a fine line between genius and crazy," Ron professed, "Fortunately with you Al; the line is not so fine."

Signing anyone to anything was premature. The procedure manual set down by the Leafs hierarchy had a very distinct and clear set of guidelines that must be followed in securing any player's rights. The league by-laws had to be followed to the letter—that was the first order of business. The second was that while technically Ron, Walt Fisher and Ken Butler all had the empowerment to sign players, it was always done as a collective task. Ron would present the recommendation, Walt Fisher would handle the contract negotiations, and Ken Butler would rubber-stamp the process. But the decision to offer contracts to free agent prospects was always decided at organizational meetings, or at least a session that included a minimum of Ron, the GM and his assistant. Like bringing Dale McCaine to practice, Ron had not followed the procedures in suggesting that the five *Ice Gators* would be offered a contract by the Leafs. Ron knew that he would have to get a scouting report in Ken Butler's hands as soon as possible.

While he had already filed his *own* reports, Ron was convinced that the opinion he would need most in convincing Ken Butler would be that of Fred Crowe, the chief scout and former drinking buddy of the GM. Ron proceeded to place the call.

"Fred!" he said, in his best butt-kissing tone, "its Ron Bailey. Are you having a good summer so far?" Actually, he could care *less* if Fred Crowe was having a shitty summer—he just wanted the old coot to warm up to the idea of seeing five ex-Leafs in action.

Fred Crowe was like an old woman on the phone. He was always complaining about his aches and pains. Ron would usually listen for a few minutes, sympathize for a few seconds, and then quickly change the subject so that the day would not be entirely wasted.

"Fred, we have some kids here I'd like to have you take a look at," Ron pleaded.

"Take a look at? Where? Why I'm still on my vacation!" he whined.

"I know, Fred, but you see we have to be on the ball on this one. There are some other clubs interested," Ron lied, "and you are the only one in town, I mean, that can file a report that I can present to Ken. What do you say?"

Ron pulled the phone away from his ear for a few seconds. Fred Crowes' initial response would have nothing to do with Ron's question. He would continue to gripe about having to go watch a game during his vacation time, and he would say that in the old days everyone took the summer off, or would be working at their off season jobs. No one would be playing hockey or watching it during the summer.

"Where are you talking, in Tronta?"

"Yeah, right here in Scarborough, only half an hour from your home," Ron added.

"Well, when is it? I can't be there this afternoon you know," he snapped.

"That's fine Fred. The game is at 8:30 tonight, at Scarborough Ice Sports."

Fred shrieked, "A GAME? Say, what league is this that you've got prospects playing in anyway?"

Ron explained the summer development team, but he didn't really think Fred Crowe understood.

"Well all right, but I doubt very much if it will be worth it—these guys never are, you know!"

"That was the right attitude," Ron thought. This was from the same guy who said the Leafs should draft a couple of 'can't miss' prospects: Lorne Graham and Dave Moore.

"They were 'can't miss' all right," Walt Fisher once said, "They can't miss last call at every peeler joint in the city."

Ron informed Al Swartz of his decision to have Fred Crowe attend the playoff game that night. Schwartz's reaction was that of scepticism.

"I don't know what good it will do. If you want him to read a scouting report it had better be in Braille. Now if you could get *Walt Fisher's* opinion, that would be something," he commented.

Ron agreed, but he had to go through the proper channels. The idea about getting Walt Fisher to look at these guys was a good one, but Ron knew that again he would have to go through Ken Butler to ask Walt Fisher to attend a tryout.

Before the game Ron was careful to tell Fred Crowe which players to concentrate his attentions on. Ron was ready to deliver a pep talk to the troops but when he entered the dressing room before the game he was shocked to find the four ex-Leaf skaters crowded around their goaltender. They were visibly concerned about Frank McCool, who sat slumped in the corner, his face pasty-white.

"What's the matter with him?" Ron demanded.

"Ulcers is having one of his attacks is all," Busher Jackson replied.

Ron took a better look at the goalie, which held a cup full of milk in his hand. Ron reached inside his pocket and produced an antacid tablet. He had always kept them when he coached, whether he needed them or not. Ron had developed the habit of keeping them in his pocket when he was an assistant coach in Windsor.

"I can get you some more if you need them," Ron offered.

The goalie was sceptical. "It won't help, but I'll take it—I usually only get like this before the big games."

Ron was concerned for his goalie, but he felt that if the team played the way they had in the past few games even an empty net would not keep them from winning the championship. The game itself was uninspiring, but it did serve to showcase the talent of the five former Leafs. Barilko and Horton took turns rushing the puck from end to end, resulting in a goal for each. Busher Jackson was content to feed the puck to Conacher for a pair of goals, while McCool had recovered enough to turn aside every shot but one. The quality of the competition was about what would exist in the East Coast Hockey League, but even factoring that into the equation it was obvious to anyone with an eye for talent that these players possessed skills that would let them compete at a higher level. It was obvious even to Fred Crowe.

After the game, Ron cornered him near the concession area where the old coot was dining out one of his staples—a Coffee Crisp.

"So, what do you think?" Ron asked.

"Well," he hesitated while munching on the chocolate bar and sipping his coffee, "you have to consider the guys they're playing against," he said, effectively dampening Ron's enthusiasm.

"Of course, Fred," Ron conceded, "but overall—the skating, passing—what do you think of their skills, their ability to work as a unit?"

Crowe was not about to concede much, but he did offer an overall favourable impression.

"It wasn't a *complete* waste of my time." For a moment, Ron thought he was going to say it was because he got to have the Coffee Crisp.

"I think there is some raw talent there," Crowe continued. "Maybe after a year or two on the farm these guys could compete for maybe the fourth line; the defenseman for the sixth or seventh spot. As for the goalkeeper, well I think he needs a great deal of work. His style has some serious flaws."

Ron was able to contain his disgust for the man's inability to see the obvious. He needed to get the concession that mattered.

"Fred, I agree completely, so don't you think the *next* step is to give these guys an evaluation at camp, you know, so they can be re-assigned to get the development on the 'farm' that you, and I, feel they need?"

Fred Crowe hesitated for a moment. Ron hoped he was considering his question, but suspected he was stalling so he could have another bite of the Coffee Crisp.

"Yes. Yes I believe so. I'll have a report for you to give to Ken," he agreed.

Fred Crowe always referred to his work in that way. His reports were always for Ron to give to Ken. He had been on the job for nine years before Ron was on the scene, and there was still some resentment of Ron's appointment. Fred Crowe felt that he should have been promoted to the position of director of player personnel. But because Ken Butler decided to bring some much-needed youth into the organization the old coot was afraid of losing his meal ticket, the close association he had with the General Manager.

Fred Crowe played out that resentment by refusing to acknowledge that Ron was his boss, and acted as if Ron was simply a go between that ferried information from himself to the GM. That, Ron knew, exemplified everything that was wrong with the *old* Leaf regime.

Despite Ron's frustration in dealing with Fred Crowe, he was happy that he was getting the desired result. By tabling a report filed by the Chief Scout it would confirm that Ron had done his 'due diligence', a corporate term that was all the rage, and one that he despised. He was a firm believer in doing his homework on every player. He liked to trace a player's development back as far as it would go, and eliminate every unknown about a prospect makeup and history. In bringing the former Leafs to a tryout, he felt that he had served up prospects with qualifications that scouts would only dream of—a history of performance at the NHL level that was beyond question!

Ron returned to the dressing room to inform the players of their chance to attend the training camp. They still had one playoff game to go in the summer season, but the real training camp was less than a week away.

"I'll get all of the paper work done," he promised, as he informed them of where and when to show up.

Just as before they gave him no indication of *where* they would be until then. And Ron did not want to even try to comprehend the answer.

The second playoff game resulted in the Burger Hut Flyers being crowned the champions of the Scarborough Ice Sports summer league 'A' division. Compared to the accomplishments the five ex-Leafs had when they were alive it was nothing. But it proved to Ron that they were good on their word. They had put up with the relative humiliation of playing in a summer league in order to secure a chance at a Leaf training camp, and hopefully help Dale McCaine live his dream.

The Leafs I Knew

When Ron returned to work on the day after Labour Day he had rehearsed his speech carefully. The story he would tell Ken Butler was only half a fabrication. He would tell his bosses the five ex-Leafs were in fact *Louisiana Ice Gators*, but he would add the discovery of Dale McCaine in Australia as a sidebar. He would take no credit for the discovery of either. He would, however be credited with their development, as he would make it his project to campaign for their inclusion on the opening night roster.

Ken Butler called an organizational meeting for ten o'clock the next morning. He needed the first few hours that day to get adjusted to his post-vacation agenda and review his mail of the last few weeks.

The usual group, consisting of Walt Fisher, Ron, Spencer Smith, and Fred Crowe, attended the meeting. The assistant coaches, Ralph Newton and Brian Ridley joined them too, as did the St. Johns' head coach, Dan Cameron and his assistant Al Swartz. Before the meeting came to order, Spencer Smith put the spotlight directly on Ron, probably without meaning to do so.

"You guys really missed out on the best scrimmage we've had around here in years," he began, referring to the rookie camp.

Walt Fisher was not going to bite on this one so he made no comment until Ken Butler had.

"I take it you're happy with the group we've assembled Spencer?"

The coach rubbed his hands over his two-day growth of beard as he fired himself up.

"I think our young director of player personnel deserves a pat on the back for uncovering a gem, Ken. This kid he brought in could be a real find. I'm dying to see what he can do against NHL hitting," he continued, glancing in Ron's direction.

Ron sunk a little further down in his seat without meaning to. Normally being in the limelight would not embarrass him in this way, but these circumstances were extraordinary. Since the subject of Dale McCaine was out in the open he was reluctant to bring forward his news about the five *Louisiana Ice Gators*. This bulletin would have to wait until later.

"Ron, it seems you've done the impossible!" the GM said, leaning forward. "You've managed to impress Spence with a young player; I didn't think it could be done!"

Ron said nothing, but made kind of a gurgling sound as if root beer had travelled up his nose while wondering, "If he likes Dale McCaine, imagine what he's going to do when he gets a look at the other five."

"I can't say that I approve of you going this far with a prospect without informing anyone," the GM scolded. "But no one will argue with your result. A diamond in the rough doesn't come along very often."

"Give me his agents' name and we'll get him to sign the 'A' form," he said, referring to the standard two-way players' contract that let teams send players to the minors without having to place them on waivers.

Ron would have to stall on this one as well. "He doesn't have an agent, but I'll have him sign," Ron assured.

Walt Fisher continued his examination of discovery. "And I see that we'll have a record number of invitees to camp; I believe the number is 75!" he said, raising his voice.

Ken Butler grimaced as if his haemorrhoids were bothering him. "Gentlemen," he reminded everyone, while removing his glasses, "I realize that we have to leave no stone unturned in trying to unearth talent, but SEVENTY-FIVE!" he continued. "I hope we have enough jerseys to go around."

The members of the group exchanged sheepish glances, as if someone might explain *why* there were seventy-five invitees. It was as if seventy-five wedding invitations had been sent out for a church that only held fifty.

Walt Fisher was ready to jump in because no one else was. "I'm sure that Spence will have it pruned down to a much more manageable number by the time the first scrimmage is over," he mused.

The GM wanted to resume business so he concluded the topic by saying to Ron, "This kid sounds like an interesting project. I'd like to see the scouting report on him when we've finished up here today."

Ron felt a shock wave of fear run through the pit of his stomach. He didn't *have* a scouting report on Dale McCaine, other than his observations at the rookie camp. Ken Butler would want background information. He would want to hear from the kid's coach in Australia, and see scoring statistics. He would even have to be satisfied that the kid's rights had been secured and registered with the league. In other words, he would have to be assured that Ron had done his 'due diligence', and of course, Ron had not.

The meeting continued, covering such areas as the timetable for the start of camp next week, the pre-season schedule and the procedure for breaking camp. Ron's attention began to wander to what information he would have to provide to the GM. He would have to stall his boss on this one until he could invent a past for Dale McCaine, other than the real one. One thing was too late to change; he had already introduced the kid to the coaches as Dale McCaine. He would have to stick handle around this one in his best Marcel Dionne style. He began to anticipate his boss's reaction to hearing that name again.

"He's the son of that guy you played against in the 'A', he thought about offering as an explanation. That one might be difficult to disprove. Or he could suggest that he was the same player that Ken Butler had faced, and wasn't the guy in remarkable shape for, say…a fifty-eight year old? Or Ron could simply tell his boss the truth, and show him the mirror in the Leafs dressing room, and maybe together they could look there for a second line centre like the great Syl Apps. Ron was going to have to do some creative thinking on this one.

"A real co-incidence his name being Dale McCaine," he told the GM.

"Excuse me Ron?" his boss, asked, conjuring up a look that took Ron by surprise.

"I mean, wasn't that the name of that kid we talked about last spring—you know, that you faced when you were with the Montreal Voyageurs?" he continued.

His boss began searching for his glass of water, but it appeared that he was really looking for something to take with it. "Really, is he related to the other Dale McCaine?"

Ron gave a sheepish grin. "It's possible, I guess—I can't say for sure!" he replied innocently.

Ken Butler suspected that Ron was not being totally honest here.

"So, you don't know if they're related, but if they were it would make an interesting fact in the media guide. Maybe we can play that up?"

"Not really," Ron shrugged, "His background isn't that remarkable. I understand he only played at the high school level. He played some pickup league seasons before going 'down under', but that was all."

Ken Butler was amazed. "And you got a tip on this kid—from where?"

Ron was on a roll. He thought about a player that he knew his boss would have no knowledge of. "Do you remember a centre man in the 'A'—Louie Rancourt? He played in the Flyers system—Hershey Bears?"

Ken said that he did not.

"Well, he played one year for us in Rochester, and then he moved to Australia. He called to tell me about this kid. He said that he couldn't believe that he hadn't been drafted by anyone." Ron was wishing that he could run home right then and write all of this stuff down in case he ever had to repeat it.

"If the kid pans out you'll have to send this Rancourt a finder's fee," the GM suggested.

"Yeah," Ron agreed, if *he* could find Rancourt.

Ron had exhausted his creative thinking skills. He realized that he would have to go all through this again with the five ex-Leafs, but he decided to let Ken Butler digest the Dale McCaine story first. He hadn't yet thought out the saga of the five former stars and how *they* had come to play for his summer hockey league team. He still had almost a week until the players would report to a hotel near the airport for medicals and fitness evaluations.

Ken Butler called another meeting for the day before camp opened. He suggested that everyone assemble in the 'war room' at the Gardens before collectively heading off to the Kitchener Memorial Auditorium, which would be their temporary home for the next ten days.

It was a gorgeous autumn morning, but it was just a bit too mild to give it the feeling of a classic fall day. Ron likened the first crispy fall morning with a touch of frost on the ground to the start of training camp. Ken Butler echoed those feelings.

"What a great morning!" he bristled as he entered the corridor of the executive offices.

"I love this time of year," he said to no one in particular. "It's like a painter with a fresh new canvas," he smiled, "The promise of creating a new masterpiece; the start of a new season with a chance to meet our goals. It's exciting!"

Ron found Ken Butler's optimism refreshing when he accepted his present position. But when exposed first hand to the acridly cynical Toronto media and their relentless second-guessing of management, his enthusiasm had been all but bled dry. He recalled what his mentor, Red Garrett had once said about second-guessers.

"Second guesses are for people that need *two* guesses because they can't get the *first* one right."

The meeting was short, and Ken Butler reminded everyone that the media would once again be at their posts. They would be covering the annual medicals, trying to snap a formula picture of some beefy player dressed only in a towel, wincing as a doctor in a white lab coat delivered a needle to the arm. And the quotes would be stock as well, with players providing their insight into what this season might hold.

Ron was particularly anxious about attending the medicals. He rushed to the Airport hotel to make sure that Dale McCaine and the others actually showed up. He felt like a kid running downstairs on Christmas morning to see if there were any presents for him under the tree, as he headed into the ballroom that served as the clinic.

He quickly checked the list of sign-ins to see if the names were there. Sure enough, Hansky, Mouton, Bachmann, Bodine and Isbister were all present as well as Dale McCaine. Ron sighed in relief, but had to satisfy himself that everything was going to go smoothly. He cautiously approached Charlie Conacher and asked, "Just exactly what are these doctors going to find when they examine you?" The big winger winked at him.

"Don't worry about it chief, we've got 'er covered. They'll never suspect that I've been dead since '67."

The first day in Kitchener was like beginning of a new school year. The surroundings were familiar, but some of the faces had changed from the year before. Ron shared his boss's enthusiasm for the start of camp feeling. There *was* a certain feeling about the start of camp—he had felt it every year since he finished school at

Massena College. It signified the end of summer vacation and the resumption of acquaintances. It was a chance to renew contact with players, coaches and team staff that had not seen each other since the end of the previous season.

The camp would be a hectic one. There would only be ten days in Kitchener, which really wasn't enough time for the coaching staff to evaluate *all* seventy-five players.

But as Ken Buttler had advised Ron when the organization drew up the list of invitees "The numbers usually shrink by attrition. There is a core of fifteen to eighteen of those seventy-five that we are counting on, that *have* to make the team," he continued. "Then there are another ten who are on the bubble even to stay in the league; guys with their last chance, who are too old to do one more stint in the minors. Then we have about six to ten who are career minor-leaguers who are here for another shot at making it a courtesy before they head off for their regular positions with St. Johns'. And then you have the juniors who are here for a taste of it before they head back, probably five or six of them, and then it gets interesting," he grinned.

"And there's the group of maybe five young bucks who are chomping for that fist real shot, either the top draft picks or the kids who have been ripening down on the farm and are ready for the big smoke. After that, it is the collection of fifteen or sixteen no-names that are here because their college coach was the best man at the assistant coach's wedding, or because a favour is owed to some scout or player agent. These guys won't get a real shot, but they can say they were at a real NHL camp before they head back to Barry's Bay to bring in the feed corn for the winter."

Spencer Smith knew what it took to win a job in training camp. His career as a journeyman NHL defenseman had lasted an amazing eighteen seasons, all of it with Detroit. He was participating in his twenty-seventh NHL camp, twenty of those as a player. He knew the routine better than he knew any other in his life.

Ron had never seen a man whose life revolved so completely around the game of hockey. When he wasn't coaching he was talking about coaching; he was forever sitting at coffee shops in hotels or airports drawing up plays on paper napkins. He never got tired of talking to the media as long as it was about what happened on the ice. He would never analyze the game from the player's point of view. He would never single out a player on either team, for either good play or bad. To him, everything that happened on the ice was a direct result of what the coaches had directed would happen. The coach took the blame when they lost, and when they won it was because the players had worked hard to execute the game plan.

Ken Butler looked at his coach this way: "We are a team without many star players, and therefore Spencer's greatest challenge is to take these youngsters and make them believe in the system, their collective goals instead of challenging each of them to improve their individual skills, and he has succeeded in doing exactly that."

Ron thought that the term 'succeeded' was being used bit too liberally by his boss—after all this team had only finished 23rd in a 30 team league.

Spencer Smith was largely responsible for the new structure that this years' training camp would take. He wanted to get away from the obvious scenario that divided the camp into two groups, the best players in one group and the second best in the other. He looked at it this way 'If the second group *knows* that they have already been labelled as the second group then they feel they are already targeted for the 'farm.' I don't want the guys in the second group to know if they are impressing or not. I want them to keep up the intensity. If a guy measures himself against one of the better players and shows he can do the job, then he has impressed me. And he will get his chance to show it in a pre-season game.'

The theory was not necessarily a mutual agreement among the management group. Walt Fisher thought the groups should be organized in the opposite fashion, but this year Ken Butler was willing to let the coach have it his way. Ron was caught in the middle—he felt the coach bore most of the responsibility for selecting the group that would fill out the twenty-five-man roster, though Ron's opinion would be weighed in helping to decide the final roster. And *because* the coach had that responsibility he should be the one to decide on the format.

"Did you see the column in today's *SUN*?" Spencer Smith asked Ron as they sat across from each other at a table at the Tim Horton's in Kitchener.

"I try not to read the hockey items," Ron snickered, "I'm surprised that you do."

Spencer laughed a throaty laugh. "Thick skin, and head to match!" he chuckled. He reached inside the pocket of his blue Toronto Maple Leaf windbreaker and produced the crinkled up copy of the column torn from the newspaper.

"The column said, 'someone in this camp needs to surprise—this team needs someone to emerge—someone unexpected—someone who will jump up and bite somebody on the rear end!' What do you think of that?" he asked.

Ron stopped slurping his searing hot coffee. "That's amazing. I wonder if that guy heard what you said after rookie camp?"

Spencer Smith smiled. "I have a feeling that this McCaine kid could be the one."

Ron shuddered at the thought. He *wanted* Dale McCaine to be the one, but he wondered how would it play out if he were? Ron was not ready to deal with that, but he would if he had to. "It's a big camp, Spence—there are maybe a few guys that could surprise!"

The coach read right through the director of player personnel's lead. "Now you're lobbying for those Ice Gators," he chuckled.

Ron was shocked. "You *know* about them?"

"Damn right! I read all of the scouting reports, even the ones the old Crowe puts in, mostly so I can pick 'em apart; tell him how full of shit he is!"

Ron got the picture. He conceded that he *was* lobbying for them.

"They'll get a chance if they deserve one. Don't worry. I know what the old Crowe wrote about them. I never trusted that old fart when I played with him in Detroit, or when he coached me, so I'm not about to trust his scouting reports now!"

Most of Ron's work was now ahead of him. Over the next ten days he would be putting more hours in than anyone else, even the coach. His day would begin with breakfast with the coaching staff, which was usually an excuse to compare notes on the previous day's workouts over bacon and eggs and coffee. He would attend the morning workouts of the 'B' group, which normally was composed entirely of junior-age St. Johns' and players, with perhaps a few minor league or fringe major leaguers thrown in to fill out the numbers. But since Spencer Smith wanted to give this camp a different flavour, he had grouped in a couple of big leaguers that were fighting for jobs. They were there to give the kids an idea of what they had to aspire to, and what it meant to earn a position.

After the workout, Ron would have to file reports, condensing the information compiled by the scouts who took in the workout and getting the opinion of the minor league coaches during a lunch break. After lunch he headed over to the main rink where the 'A' group would scrimmage. Ron compiled statistics from the scorer and impressions of each player from the scouts in attendance. It would usually take Ron until the dinner hour to condense all of the data, and after dinner the brain trust would gather to discuss that day's action and compare notes. This was the part of the day that Ron enjoyed the most. He could sit back and relax once his notes were passed around to the group. He *lived* to hear Ken Butler, Walt Fisher and Spencer Smith debate the relative virtues and inequities of the prospects, and of the veterans.

The discussion on the second evening of camp was a classic. During the afternoon session the Leafs number two enforcer, Lorne Graham, was heading into open ice while carrying the puck. This was a something that normally Lorne Graham would only dream of, but in training camp it is critical to try and impress. As Graham neared centre ice he put down his head, only for a second, as if to see if that black rubber thing was still with him. Suddenly he heard the sound 'BEEP BEEP', like the roadrunner makes in the cartoons. Before Lorne Grahams' heart could make its next beat he was met by Bill Barilko, who leaned into him while gliding at full speed. The defenseman braced himself, and directed his body upwards, and aimed his shoulder directly into the solar plexus of Lorne Graham. The collision reminded Spencer Smith of a mid-air crash between two 747's he had seen on an air disaster video, except that Barilko continued to skate forward, even scooping up the puck as Graham lay writhing on the ice. Lorne Graham was surrounded by a couple of his formerly embedded teeth that lay in a circle looking like a shark's necklace.

The Leaf enforcer wasn't about to let this one pass. After a trip to the bench to remind him what his name was, he returned to the ice on Barilko's next shift. Everyone knew what was coming next and everyone including Barilko couldn't wait for it to happen. Graham bided his time, and when Barilko attempted to clear a rebound from behind the net, Graham elbowed him in the face. Barilko was carried into the boards, but managed to turn around after making a clearing pass and just stood there, his arms hanging motionless at his sides. Graham dropped his gloves, and in two rapid shots, Barilko dropped Graham.

Spencer Smith laughed so hard that he had to take off his glasses and wipe the tears from his eyes. The assistant coaches, Ralph Newton and Brian Ridley, went in quickly to separate the two but the excitement was over. Barilko skated away while Newton and Ridley assessed the damage.

"Remember that number, Ralph, Fifty-Five," Ridley said to Newton.

"No, remember that name, Hansky!" Newton said to Ridley. Rookie defenseman David Hansky, alias Bill Barilko had made a lasting impression on Lorne Graham, and a favourable one with the Leaf coaching staff.

"You have to love what that kid Hansky did to Graham," Walt Fisher observed, as he took a sip from a bottle of St. Anne's spring water.

Spencer Smith leaned back in his chair, his hand firmly gripped around a bottle of Molson Export.

"I thought I was going to wet my pants!" the coach laughed. "Old Lornie's been asking for it for a long time. He's been getting away with those elbows in camp for too long."

"It was a *clean* check that the kid gave him?" Ken Butler asked.

"You could eat off of it, it was so clean," Walt Fisher answered.

Ken Butler smiled. "Well Spencer, it has been awhile since you've had to consider so many young guys at once."

Ron felt that he could finally intercede. "Wait till you take a look at what's been going on with the 'B' group," he smiled, as he handed out copies of the days' activity.

The group pored over the report. It wasn't long before the GM made a decision.

"I think you'll agree Spencer that there are some kids in this group that deserve your attention. Look at these numbers—this kid Bachmann, four goals! He put them all past Lars Rodgers!" Ron mused, referring to the Leafs backup goalie, "and this kid Bodine set up all four of them," he added. "Spence, I'd like you to take in the prospects game with the Red Wings' kids, tomorrow night in Windsor. You don't have a practice the next day until the afternoon."

The coach swallowed a big gulp of beer, and added, "I'd love to. I want to see these guys up close."

The next night in Windsor he got his chance. Detroit's prospects were among the best in the league, and this was largely responsible for the team's status as a perennial contender. The prospects were eager to show everything they could, as they tried to make it on the best team in the league. The Leafs prospects were coached by the St. Johns' duo of Dan Cameron and Al Swartz. Spencer Smith had a word with them before the game, asking what their impression was so far of Dale McCaine.

"I don't see what Ron Bailey sees in him," Cameron confessed.

Spencer Smith was surprised. "Well, he was the best player by far in the summer camp!" he countered.

Al Swartz interjected, "I know he has the skills; you can see it in his skating and the way he handles the puck. But he hasn't shown any drive, any grit. I'm just hoping that he's one of those 'bad practice' players," he concluded.

The game was the answer. If the Red Wing's prospects were the best there were then the Leafs had measured up quite nicely. Dale McCaine ended up with a goal and three assists in Toronto's 5-3 win, and if there was a first star in the game he would have earned it.

Ron Bailey had to miss the game in order to prepare for a weekend junior showcase tournament. He would have been thrilled with what he would have seen. The man whose opinion really mattered *had* seen it for himself. Spencer Smith phoned Ken Butler to tell the GM of his observation.

"We've got him playing in the wrong god dam group!" he claimed.

The GM was pleasantly surprised. "It's your call Spence. I guess I'll have to get out and see this kid for myself. I plan to take in the scrimmage tomorrow afternoon. I'll get a hold of Dan Cameron and tell him what we're doing. It'll make his life a little easier. By Wednesday we'll be down to most of the group he'll have with St. Johns' anyway. We have two more of the prospects games to get through, before we send part of the 'B' group back to their junior clubs."

Spencer Smith had not yet finished his requests. "There's one more thing Ken. I understand that the goalie young Ronnie signed has been playing very well in the 'B' group. How about sending him over to the 'A' side for a spell in the afternoon?"

Ken Butler went silent for a moment. "We may have a problem there," he said solemnly.

"It seems the result of his medical tests show that he has a significant duodenal ulcer."

The coach was astounded. "Can't they do anything for him?"

"Well fortunately, yes. The medication the doctors have him on will control it, and he should be completely healed in a few weeks."

The coach needed to know, as he was about to spring another surprise on his boss.

"From what I've heard Ken he's the best of the number three goalies. I was thinking, based upon what he shows with the 'B' group of course, that maybe it would be an idea to have him push Rogers a bit for the backup—maybe even give him a start in one of the exhibitions!"

Ken Butler was not prepared to agree to that just yet, "Perhaps, if the doctor okays it. I'd like to see us get a win under our belt, just to take the monkey off of our back a bit." The GM was referring to the fact that during the pre-season a year ago the Leafs finished with the league's worst exhibition record.

"I agree," the coach said. "We need to get a confidence lifter early. I'd like a lot of the veterans in Montreal on Saturday. We need a win early."

The coach was itching to get his troops into some real game action. Saturday could not come too soon for him. The next day following light morning and afternoon scrimmages, the 'A' team split into two groups for the annual Blue-White game that evening. Dale McCaine was assigned to the Blue group which, like the White squad was evenly sprinkled with veterans, borderline big leaguers and a couple of top rookies. Spencer Smith hoped that because the game was to be played before a charity-fund raising sell-out crowd of 6,000 at the Memorial arena that the guys would view the game as more than a scrimmage. He made it clear that he expected to see real hitting, and the kind of hustle that would show him that guys were going to battle to earn their spots. And he would not object to seeing a few scraps if it so developed.

Spencer Smith and the assistant coaches selected the line-ups carefully, so as to match players who were competing head to head on opposing sides. And just to spice thing up they included the prospects McCaine, Hansky, Mouton, Bachmann and Bodine (the latter aliases Barilko, Horton, Conacher and Bodine.)

"They've all showed something in the scrimmages, so they've earned a look in the intra-squad," the coach said. Frank McCool was absent from the list; partially because of his recovering ulcer condition and partially to give the Leafs' top two net minders a real good work out under game conditions.

This game was different than the scrimmages for another reason. While the media had been covering camp since it opened, they had concerned themselves up to now with interviewing the coaches and a few of the veteran players. But like the *Toronto Sun* column said: 'Somehow this team needs someone to emerge, someone unexpected.'

This game was going to give the media exactly what they had been looking for. Spencer Smith invited Ron Bailey to join him behind the bench of the Blue squad. Ron was flattered, and felt he should decline and offer the job instead to one of the two St. Johns' coaches, Dan Cameron or Al Swartz. But Spencer Smith was insistent.

"You have to help evaluate these guys too Ronnie. You can't do it from behind a desk! Get your ass out here and see what it's like in the trenches. Get your hands dirty!" he ordered.

The Blue squad featured the Leafs number one goalie, John Dennis, who would play the entire game, as would his backup from a year ago, Lars Rogers. To make the game a little more exciting, the teams would exchange goalies halfway through the second period.

The Blues also featured the team captain Floyd Shoniker, right-winger/enforcer Randy Rettig and the three players picked up in the Vaclav Artis deal, Ian Moriarty, Tobin West and Greg Sawchuck. On defense, they had the Leafs' oldest blue liner, Terry Oddy and their brightest defense prospect, Christian Andersson.

The White team had the Leafs leading goal scorer, Joel Kent, the player who led the team in points, winger Serge Moit, and the team leader in power play goals, Chuck Andrew. It also included their leading penalty-killer Lou Zanardo, their best offensive defenseman David Burks, so-called tough guy Lorne Graham and perhaps the two most disliked players on the team forward David Eagleson and defenseman David 'Shithead' Moore.

The crowd that filled the Kitchener Memorial Auditorium that night was comprised mostly of kids, who were anxious to get a close look at the Leafs for perhaps the first time. Holding the training camp in Kitchener rather than Maple Leaf Gardens was a promotional vehicle that could not be underestimated. It pumped some money into the local economy, helped to drum up support for the Leafs in the Kitchener-Waterloo area, and gave the players some much-needed experience in their role as community icons. For many of the younger players it was crucial in developing their roles as off-ice ambassadors for the team and for the game of hockey.

"It will be looked at on a yearly basis," the GM said. "Back in the sixties the Leafs used to train anywhere from St. Catherines to Peterborough to Kingston. It was a great way to gain exposure in those areas in the days before television."

Nowadays television provides so much exposure to the players that they cease to become real. They appear more as characters than as real people—for that reason, and to direct attention to the player's responsibility as role models Ken Butler decreed that his team would have more community involvement than any team in the past.

"I remember when I was younger you would see players from time to time signing autographs at the opening of a new car wash, or at a sporting goods store that their uncle owned. But as players started to get the big contracts that all died off—they didn't't need the public appearance money that these little attractions offered, and so the chance to meet a player in person started to disappear as well. I want our players *accessible* to the community, except for their private lives of course."

For the Leaf players the idea of attending countless charity functions was one they would have to get used to. The Blue-White game was more than just a charity fundraiser. Spencer Smith was anxious to see if his players would take their game up a level if they were organized into a match that was at least played under game conditions, with officials, time stoppages and a crowd. The game would also allow Ron Bailey to get a look at four of the ex-Leafs in real game competition. Dale McCaine along with Horton and Barilko would skate for the Blues while Conacher and Busher Jackson would line up with the Whites.

"The play of a few of these guys will determine who we take to Montreal with us on Saturday," the coach said, referring to the Leaf's first pre-season game.

From the opening face-off it was clear that many of the kids were willing to do whatever it took to stand out, whether it was finishing each and every check or delivering a hit after the whistle. The tempo was really set early when Chuck Andrew attempted to dig the puck out from under the pads of John Dennis. Tim Horton thought the winger was double-parked in the crease. He spotted the veteran about thirty-five pounds and five inches as he proceeded to knock the big lug out of the crease and into the net with such force that it became dislodged. And he did all this without raising a stick or delivering an elbow. Andrew had never been hit so hard or so cleanly. Dave "Shithead" Moore did not take to having a veteran treated like this by a rookie, so he jumped into the fray, and charged into Horton, knocking his helmet off with a vicious cross check. Horton was stunned, but only because he had lost the helmet. He reached over the bigger defenseman and proceeded to give him a bear hug before Shithead could even drop his gloves. Moore struggled to get free but it was obvious that he was having difficulty breathing, never mind getting his arms free.

"Let go of me you faggot!" Shithead screamed.

Horton only laughed. "I'll let you go when I'm ready, you lumberjack," he chuckled.

The more Shithead struggled the sillier he looked, and the redder his face became. The linesmen did not know exactly what to make of this, and it was doubtful if they could have broken the grip that Horton had on Moore anyway.

It was Barilko who finally skated over, still with his dancing partner and said, "You showed him who's boss kid, now throw him back—he's not big enough to keep!"

Horton agreed, and hurled the humiliated defenseman into the corner. The referee signalled offsetting minor penalties and the game resumed, but not before many of the crowd began checking their programs to see who number 57 was.

Ken Butler sat watching in the director's lounge and turned to Walt Fisher and asked that very question.

"Gilbert Mouton," was the answer.

"He's one of those kids Ron Bailey recruited from the East Coast League, isn't he?" the GM asked.

Walt Fisher leaned back in his seat and quipped, "We've seen this before, when one of these guys from the minors tries to make a name early in camp by taking on one of the veterans."

The GM sipped his water and added, "Yes, but Andrew does spend too much time in the crease. The kid has already exposed one of his weaknesses. And if he's not afraid to take on Moore, well I think we should keep an eye on this one tonight."

Spencer Smith also liked what he saw. He turned to Ron and said, "When will Moore learn? He can't keep doing that same tired old routine. Even the rookies are making fun of him now."

Ron was getting ready to observe Dale McCaine for the first time in a real game. He watched the coach tap the kid on the shoulder and over the boards McCaine went like he was high jumping. The change was made on the fly, and when the puck came near Dale McCaine he acted as if it was his own. He carried it as far into the White zone as he could, and when it looked like he could go no further without turning it over he did the right thing; he took a quick look and passed it to a teammate who wasn't covered. He threaded a pass between the legs of an astonished David Eagleson and onto the stick of Captain Floyd Shoniker who directed in past Lars Rogers and into the net for the Blues' first goal.

McCaine was so ecstatic that he nearly forgot to do the traditional embrace, and instead skated towards the net as if to catch the rebound. Shoniker caught up with him and gave him the compulsory 'rub of the head' to celebrate.

When the lines were changed Conacher and Busher Jackson decided it was time for them to show something.

"Work the give and go, Busher!" Charlie Conacher directed as they lined up for the face off.

"If you win the draw, just get it back to the point," Terry Oddy ordered the former Leaf, as if he was instructing a rookie.

Conacher just smiled, and when he won the draw he pushed the puck forward, past the surprised White team centre man, and Jackson quickly scooped it up. Busher streaked down the wing and waited for Conacher to appear, and he did just like an incoming flight. Jackson faked a shot and put the pass on Conacher's stick with a healthy crack. Conacher started to make his move on the defender, and looked him squarely in the eyes. Just when the defenseman was

136

ready to line him up, he backhanded the pass over to Jackson, still looking the defender in the eyes. Jackson beamed a wrist shot into the top corner of the net past John Dennis to even the score.

Ken Butler stood up and, for a moment, looked as if he might applaud. Instead he turned to Walt Fisher again and said, "There's a couple more numbers to watch Walt!"

Walt Fisher had to agree. He made a note in his personal planner to review the contracts of the players in the morning.

The period ended in a draw, and during the intermission Spencer Smith saluted his squad.

"I have to tell you guys—that's just the kind of effort we're looking for; what we've been missing around here. That's the kind of period I need to see to get you in the line-up for Montreal!" He bristled. His comments were made to the whole team, but he was really directing them at McCaine, Horton and Barilko.

In the other dressing room the mood was also up beat (except for 'Shithead' Moore, who was still steamed about being harnessed by Horton.) Dave Burks was the only one with enough balls to rub Moore about it—he was the only player who was feared by Moore, and therefore respected.

"That kid had some kind of hold on you Dave," Burks laughed.

Moore grimaced, "I've got his number. We still have 40 minutes!"

Burks wouldn't let it pass. "It won't do any good if he gets a hold of you again. You looked like you were wearing a strait-jacket the way you were twisting and turning out there!"

Moore was about to take up the challenge when a voice of reason stepped in. Joel Kent was not the Leafs captain. He was not the biggest or most physical player on the team, but he was the most respected, outside of the captain. Kent was the only player on the team that was capable of scoring the big goal when it was needed. He was the closest thing the Leafs had to a franchise player since they had dealt Vaclav Artis. Kent's nickname was the 'Man of Steel', and was sometimes called 'Clark' or 'Superman' by his teammates.

"Let it go!" he ordered.

Moore looked up immediately, but withdrew slightly when he realized that it was Kent who spoke. "Why should I?" Shithead demanded.

Kent did not even bother to look at Moore when he spoke. "Because this is a charity game, mostly kids here, and they want to see a game and the kid showed some life. He's not gonna make this team, but he's shown more spark than I've seen from a lot of us, me included."

The last part of the wingers' statement was not entirely accurate. Kent, on most nights was the Leafs *only* spark plug.

For the remainder of the game the fans were treated to some old-fashioned pond hockey, with end-to-end rushers capped by either spectacular goal tending or some very pretty goals. The suddenly elevated level of play was not lost on Spencer Smith.

"You see what's happening, don't you Ron?" he asked his makeshift assistant. Ron saw the same thing occurring. "Those new kids are making the veterans play," the coach beamed. "This is gonna make for some interesting choices for jobs," he concluded.

Get your tickets early for the media circus

The fans were sent home having got their money's worth, as far as entertainment went. And as far as a showcase for the talents of the newcomers it was a success as well. After the game the management and coaching staff were invited to a reception hosted by the Kitchener Rangers junior club and the mayor. Ron chose instead to accept an unusual invitation to join some of the players for a few 'pops' at a local watering hole owned in part by David Burks. The invitation came from the captain, Floyd Shoniker. The invitation was unusual because the players didn't normally invite members of management or the coaching staff and since Ron was unaware of this he was not suspicious about the player's motives. It was not his nature to be suspicious anyway. Ron assumed that the invite had something to do with his being a coach for a day, but after he had settled in at the table between the captain, and veteran Terry Oddy he began to realize why he had been included. Floyd Shoniker wasted little time in getting down to business.

"Ron, I understand that five of the rookies out there tonight played for a summer beer league team you coached, is that right?"

Just as he was getting ready to answer, the band that had been warming up quietly on the darkened stage began their first set. Although they were seated at the back of the bar, Ron had to raise his voice almost to a shout to be heard. Ron suddenly felt a little on the defensive. He didn't even stop to wonder *where* the players had gotten that information.

"Not exactly," Ron corrected, "the league is better calibre than *that*. There is lots of NHLers playing—guys coming off injury, free agents, and a lot of minor pros from the 'A'."

Floyd Shoniker was diplomatic to a point, and acknowledged the slight. He nodded before shouting. "Okay, so the competition isn't exactly a beer league. But these guys were playing in the East Coast League, Ice Gazers, or something," he added.

Ron tried not to smile. "*Ice Gators, Louisiana Ice Gators*", he repeated, almost in the captain's ear.

"Whatever! But you see Ron it makes the rest of us look bad. Show him the paper Terry."

The defenseman scowled and then after an almost sign language like exchange he produced a copy of the *Globe*. He directed Ron's attention to the piece by Neil Powers, the same columnist who had ripped the Leafs over their handling of the Vaclav Artis trade. Ron held the paper up to the light so he could read it. The headline said, "LEAFS BEATING THE BEER BUSHES FOR HELP." Ron figured that he had drawn the gist of the column's tone but the players insisted that he read it, out loud. He tried to shout it but it was no use. Instead he read

From the 'breaking news department', the Leafs have beaten every other NHL team to the punch with their latest scouting coup—director of player personnel Ron Baily (how about that, Ron thought—they had spelled his name wrong) has signed five players from the Scarborough Ice Sports summer league (sponsored by a brewery) to training camp offer sheets. That's right, the same league you or I or fifteen friends can play in by paying $250 for individual or $2500 per team entry (pro weight jerseys and socks included!) Here's your chance to make good on the bet that you and five of your friends could beat the Leafs, well maybe not anymore because now your five friends are playing for the Leafs. No word from camp yet if these guys have beaten out any veterans for a job but stay tuned to this column for *updates. PS—the scouting staffs were also reportedly seen approaching players at the Barrie Old-Timers tournament. More signings expected.*

Ron picked up his beer to get rid of the dry mouth, and to get rid of the bad taste that the column had left him with.

"What's the matter Ron? You look as if you've seen a ghost!" David Burks asked.

Ron wanted to crawl inside the bottle of Molson Canadian and hide, but it was no use.

"Now you see how this makes us, and the organization look Ron?" Shoniker cautioned.

"Guys," Ron began, as he noticed the players crowding in to hear his every word. They moved like a pack of wolves getting a little closer to their prey before the kill. He sized this up quickly. It wasn't the organization that was or could be made to look bad here. What would it say about the skills of one of the current Leafs if a guy that played for the Burger Hut Flyers beat them out? "You guys aren't really afraid of a little competition. You're not really afraid of what this clown Powers might write if by some remote chance you got beaten out for a job by one of these guys, are you?"

The countenances turned to scowls. "You're missing the point Ron," the captain continued. "You've made it look like our camp is a joke, like anybody can be invited! What does that say for the players you have drafted, and traded for? It looks to me like you're admitting that you haven't done a very good job at either, if you think guys from the East Coast League are good enough to bring to camp."

Ron had never seen it in that light. His boss had never mentioned that to him either, although he had conveniently neglected to tell his boss about the five players being on his summer league team; he had made sure that there were no references to it on the scouting report that Fred Crowe had turned in. Now he was going to have to deal with *that* as well as this new problem of the players concerns.

"I think you guys are making too much out of this. We need some more bodies on the 'farm'. Last year we finished with only fifteen skaters down there. We have to have more. So we bring in a few guys from the East Coast League. They play an exhibition—we've given them their chance. It's up to the coaching staff to decide whom to keep."

Ron hoped that he had appealed to the player's greatest weakness (or strength, depending on how you were looking at it), their ego. He wasn't going to snow these guys, but he could convince them that if it was up to the coaches, well who would they choose; the veterans of a bunch of guys from the *Ice Gazers*?

The players talked amongst themselves for a little while. Ron had only planted a seed. He had not really convinced them of *anything*. He was more concerned that there was going to be a rift between the veterans and these outcasts from Louisiana than he was about how his boss would react to the column. For the moment he was beginning to feel uncomfortable in the company of the players; after all, he really wasn't one of them. He thanked them for the invitation, and headed for the motel across the street. Before he made it to the front door David Burks stopped him.

"Ron! Wait up!" the big defenseman yelled. Ron turned to see all six foot four and two hundred and five pounds bearing down on him, like Ron was trying to steal the puck at the Leaf blue line. Burks was thirty-four years old but he still had some speed when he really needed it. "I need to talk to you. Come on up to my room," he suggested.

Inside the motel room Burks reached inside his shaving kit and produced a bottle of Maalox, and took a healthy swig.

"I can't have more than a couple of beers anymore without it bothering my stomach," he explained.

"Then why have any beer at all?" Ron asked.

Burks sighed, and it sounded more like a growl. "In a few years I won't be able to. You're right, but at this stage of my career I still need to fit in. It's a small price to pay."

Ron wondered if it was.

"I wanted to talk to you alone about these new guys. Some of the guys are a little concerned that management is doing this to prove a point. When you finish 23rd out of 30, well I've been around long enough to know that sometimes anything is an improvement."

Ron had to agree, but he didn't interrupt.

"I guess what I'm trying to say is, and this is just between you and me. I mean we haven't known each other that long but I've been around this team for seven years now, and believe it or not that makes me the longest current Leaf."

Ron had never stopped to consider it in those terms, but David Burks *was* the longest serving Leaf. That didn't say much about the team's record of player development.

"I just need to know. Were these guys brought in to prove a point, or because you thought they deserved a chance? This won't go any further than this room."

Ron could tell that Burks was genuine in his concern. And he didn't doubt that their conversation would not be repeated, despite the fact that they had not known each other for long.

"Dave, believe me, these guys are *not* here to embarrass you, or to prove a point, other than maybe that there are some guys out there who still believe that if you work hard enough then anything is possible."

Burks nodded his head. He was one player who did understand the meaning of hard work. Although he had never taken as much as a shift in the minors he did know quite a bit about it. His father had spent years bussing around in the old Eastern Professional League with Sudbury, and had ended up as a player-coach in the OHA Senior loop with Orillia.

"I want you to know that it was just by accident. I wish I could tell you the entire story. I wish I could tell someone."

David Burks could tell that something was upsetting Ron, and now his curiosity was peaked. "What is it you're trying to say?" he asked, as he kicked off a very expensive pair of cowboy boots and stretched out on the bed.

"I just mean that these five guys came to us under somewhat *unusual* circumstances; they aren't exactly like the young players you find coming out of junior or college." Burks thought about it for a minute and added, "I've noticed a few things."

Now it was Ron who was curious. "You *have*?" he asked. "You mean about how they play?"

"Not so much that—more like how they talk, even *what* they talk about. It's like they're from somewhere else."

"Somewhere *else*?" Ron asked, "Like where?"

Burks leaned up on one elbow and though about it for a moment. "I mean, like somewhere isolated. I went fishing with Joel Kent one summer. We chartered a plane and flew up to Ellesmere Island; took us two whole days to get there. The guys who ran the lodge, hell you couldn't even call it a lodge, the shack. Well, they probably only had contact with the outside world when fishermen came up. They had kinda a funny way of talking. They remind me of that."

For a moment Ron was beginning to wonder if Ellesmere Island was the centre of the universe. Ron had also been working on his 'history' of the five players; the one he would have to fabricate for the media guide should the five actually make the team. He hated to try this lie out on a nice guy like David Burks, but away he went.

"I understand that the goalie, Isbister, played a few years in Iceland, and that the defenseman, Gil Mouton played for a company team in Northern Quebec."

Burks nodded his head, as if it all made sense now. Ron was on a roll. He thought he should check in the mirror to see if his nose was growing longer.

"And Bodine and Bachmann, I believe they played together in Louisiana, but before that they played on some tier-three junior team in Northern Ontario—a real small mining town that's not even on the map anymore, since the mine closed."

"And what about that kid who clocked Lornie Graham, and Hansky?"

"Yeah" Ron wondered, "Hansky—I think he came from, I mean he's a bit of a mystery. I know he played some minor pro in California. *Northern* California, but I'm not sure where he played junior, if he did at all."

David Burks needed a bit more to complete the fuzzy picture. "So how'd *you* find them?"

Ron thought about it and decided to inject *some* truth.

"Completely by accident—I was supposed to get five guys from a team in Macon to help fill out my summer team—Europeans, and then went back home for the summer instead of coming to Canada. The GM in Macon heard about these guys who had a tryout with the *Ice Gators,* and he sent them to me."

"I'll be honest with you Ron," Burks began (this was more than *Ron* was being with *him)* "I think a few of those guys can play. I've seen very few defensemen that can deliver a check like that Hansky."

Ron wanted to do some more damage control. "Even so Dave, these guys are a long shot to make the team. Sure, they played very well tonight, but it was more like a controlled scrimmage than a real game. I know that Spence is leaning toward playing them in at least one exhibition game. But remember this: the better they play, the better it is for the team. Nobody, not you, not Joel Kent, have to worry about getting beaten out by one of *them*—only the guys who are on the bubble anyway have to be concerned about that. And whom would you rather have lining up beside you on the blue line—a guy who can deliver a hit like Hansky? Or like 'Shithead' Moore?"

Ron had made his point, and Dave Burks had to agree. He bid the defenseman good night and returned to his motel room.

It was only a little after eleven o'clock, and he realized that it was still early evening on the West Coast. He dialled the number of his fiancée, Kelly Garrett. The two had not seen each other since their brief vacation when last season ended. Ron was not as good as Kelly was about phoning. She would call him at least twice a week. When he was travelling he usually found more time to talk. Before she picked up the phone, he had made up his mind that he was going to tell her about the entire Dale McCaine story.

A 'Three Pipe' problem

Since the whole Dale McCaine episode had transpired Ron had been dying to tell someone—*anyone* about it. He thought about telling Spencer Smith, or Billy Sinfield, and he had even wanted to try it out on David Burks. He was not only afraid of the obvious disbelief, but he was somehow unsure that if he breathed a word about it that it could somehow affect the out-come of it all, even though he wasn't sure *what* that outcome would be.

He knew there was one person he could confide in, and who would tell him he was right to trust his judgement even though the facts were suspect. He could trust Kelly, so when he placed the call, he prepared to tell her everything, right from the beginning. When she answered the phone her surprise at hearing from him was quickly diffused, as he wanted to get right to the secondary purpose of his call.

"Kell, I have something to tell you, and your initial reaction is going to be disbelief, so I want you to just accept it first—and then tell me why it *isn't* possible!"

Ron's emotional state was as easy for her to read as a bottle of prescription drugs.

"Sweetie, I have no idea what you're talking about. I *hate* it when you start a conversation this way. This has to do with the wedding, doesn't it?" She sounded upset, and Ron realized that maybe he *wasn't* making any sense.

"Hell no, everything's fine. I'm talking about the *team!*"

147

She sighed, and gave him the obligatory reprimand for worrying her. He knew that she regarded his work a little more than a glorified hobby, like an adult video game. And compared to her pursuit of a medical degree in the study of viruses, it was.

"Kell, I want you to look at this from a scientific point of view," he prepared her. Ron proceeded to tell her everything, and she did not interrupt as he recalled every detail including the result of that night's game.

She started on him slowly, trying not to burst his bubble right away. Her pragmatic approach was always a contrast his emotional one. "If you look at it, as you say, to tell you why it *isn't* possible, consider this—you said that this Dale McCaine guy, passed through a mirror, and the other ones walked right through a door that was closed. You *have* to consider that perhaps this was some kind of illusion, like an elaborately staged trick. Remember when we were in the Bahamas, we saw that magician make the elephant disappear— you have to consider that it was some kind of special effect!"

"Kelly, nobody is going to go to that length to get an invitation to try out for a hockey team!"

"All right, she agreed. "Then you have to remember your *Sherlock Holmes*—you remember what he said, 'When you have eliminated the impossible, then whatever else remains, no matter how improbable, must be the answer.'"

Ron *had* remembered his Sherlock Holmes. But even Conan-Doyle would be the first to try and debunk this mystery.

"There are other possibilities I'm sure you've considered," Kelly continued, "It sounds to me Ronnie, that you really don't *want* to know if it's real or not. You don't really want to know that it's not real because you want to believe that it is real—you just want someone to confirm your belief."

"OK, maybe that's true." Ron agreed. "So if it is true, I mean that I just want someone *else* to believe, then how do I go about getting someone else to?" he asked.

She paused for a moment. "Well you know *I* believe you," she added.

Ron didn't need the patronization. "Thanks," he offered, "I love you too."

"You know what I mean!" she shot back, "I *love* you. *I* know you well enough to know that if you truly believe it then it must be something that is real to you. And if you have *eliminated* the impossible—"

"Yeah, yeah, I remember. Well thanks honey bunch. Now all I have left to consider is, was it an illusion, or am I delusional? Thanks for the time on your "couch". It's good just to hear your voice."

"So when are you coming out here?" she demanded.

"Our west coast swing isn't until December, but it's a beauty— five cities in ten days. The Vancouver stop is on the 18th".

"Well then, you can introduce me to these ghosts, and I can give you my opinion," she offered. Ron thanked her for the moral support.

The next morning, Ron and Al Swartz were on their way to breakfast when Walt Fisher intercepted them. The assistant general manager was flushed, and seemed to breathing heavily, which was unusual for a man who was always the epitome of cool calm and collected.

"Ken has called a meeting. Right away, in the boardroom at the arena," he said, sounding like a reporter.

Ron and Al Swartz looked at each other, exchanging the kind of glance that meant they each hoped that the other one knew what this was all about. Walt Fisher would not enlighten them when Ron asked.

"Ken will fill us in," Walt snapped back.

They walked into the Kitchener Ranger directors' room. Ron noticed Ken Butler slumped at the head of the table. His reading glasses were pushed way down on his nose, as he appeared to be pouring over a newspaper that was spread out on the table before him. Spence Smith was seated across from him. Dan Cameron sat beside him, and Fred Crowe was there also, though from the worried expression on the old Crowes' face he had no idea why he was there.

"Close the door," was the first thing that came out of Ken Butler's mouth.

Ron and Al Swartz sat down without being asked to, and Walt Fisher took up a seat beside Ken Butler. The General Manager looked up from the newspaper, at no one in particular and began to speak.

"We have some damage control to do concerning this article," he said, as he held up the infamous Neil Powers column, "I trust we've all read it."

Al Swartz confessed that he had not. Ken Butler tossed it across the table, and as Al Schwartz's eyes began to glow like an LED, the General Manager continued.

"This kind of thing strikes as the usual 'poison pen' journalism we've come to expect from this paper—the *last* thing we need to do is to give this clown any ammunition."

Ken Butler took off his glasses, and almost instinctively reached for his glass of water, which of course was not there. Unperturbed, he continued. This time he focused directly on Ron. "Why was I not told of the fact that these players had played for you in the Scarborough Ice Sports league, Ron?"

Ron knew that this was going to catch up with him eventually. He could feel the finality of the executioner's axe about to strike.

"I didn't think it was important, to mention that we had a look at these guys before inviting them to camp. I thought I was just doing my 'due diligence'."

It was fortunate for Ron that Ken Butler chose to ignore the sarcasm by his use of those words. Ken Butler leaned back in his chair.

"We have certainly made things difficult for ourselves. Here we are fortunate enough to have uncovered a few players with some obvious skill, but because of *how* we introduced them, we have a media bonanza on our hands."

Ron was silent, as was everyone else in the room. Walt Fisher took it upon himself to come up with a solution.

"We have an obvious, easy out; send the five of them to the 'rock'. If and when they return it will be after they've had some seasoning in the minors. Then they'll no longer be beer league bums, but instead polished prospects ready for a shot at prime time." Ron believed that Walt Fisher had missed his life's calling—he should have been a politician.

"I hate to lose the bastards!" Spencer Smith summed it up.

Ron had to agree. Al Swartz on the other hand was drooling at the thought of getting to coach the guys on the farm.

Ken Butler slumped a little further in his chair, and pressed his fingers together as if he was going to play 'Cat's Cradle' while pondering this one. "We'll have to issue a statement debunking Porter's column. The truth has hurt us, and we'll have to mention that they are targeted for St. Johns'. We have no choice." Ron in particular was devastated.

"We do have a choice. We don't have to give in to the media on this one. Do we really want to let the media decide whom we put on our roster?" he asked, "Why can't we give our own side of it, the truth and explain that we were only giving these guys a workout for the summer?"

Walt Fisher was ready to respond. "You have to understand Ron, that there is *more* to this. The *Globe* has conducted a vendetta against this hockey club for years, dating back to the previous administration—all because one of its writers was once barred from the Gardens over a particularly critical piece. It's time to mend some fences."

As usual Ron was less concerned with image than he was with substance. *He* knew why those players should remain with the big club. And the entire coaching staff knew it as well.

Ken Butler was ready to take action. He had allowed the discussion to take place to make sure that everyone understood the situation. He garnered input from anyone who had any to give, and now he was about to render his decision.

"We'll have to start them in the A," he said while clearing his throat, as if it was difficult to say.

Ron shrugged, and wondered how the guys would take the news. He even wondered *if* they would report to the 'rock'.

"I suppose there is a chance that they won't report," Ron guessed.

"They have a contract; they'll be there," Walt Fisher assured everyone.

Ron was visibly upset by all of this and Ken Butler decided it was time to grab the reins of this thing.

"The situation is unfortunate. I'm not finished with the *Globe* either. I'm going to drop a bug in the ear of the reporters collectively about the facts that were left out of the *Globe* story and ask why we haven't seen any ink on the players we acquired in the Artis trade; we should be reading about Sawchuck and Ian Moriarty and Tobin West."

Ken Butler called an end to the meeting, and offered to buy breakfast for the group. As they left the directors' room he took Ron aside.

"I don't want this to dampen your enthusiasm. Hell, I'm not even mad that you didn't tell me about the five of them playing for you this summer. You found us some good prospects—who knows what kind of players they'll develop into?" Ron was relieved.

"There is one more thing I'm curious about—how did the media know they played for my Summer team? The only people that were aware of it were Al Swartz, Fred Crowe and me. I didn't even tell Spence."

Ken Butler looked off into space. "I know that Fred would never say anything. And I can't believe that Al Swartz would talk to the media without talking to me first. You have to assume that the players were not interviewed, because their names were never mentioned in the column. I think you and I both know *who* the only person that could have knowledge about this that would talk to the media."

Ken did not want to even *mention* Tommy Stukko's name out loud, but it was clear that was whom he was talking about. Ron did not have to guess either—he just wanted to make sure that his boss also knew who the most likely culprit was. It was surprising, since Tommy Stukko had not been seen around training camp yet. He was reportedly still working at the Gardens preparing media information about the upcoming regular season.

At breakfast, Spencer Smith expressed his regret about not being able to have some of the ex-Leafs in the line-up for the upcoming pre-season opener in Montreal.

"You weren't really serious about that, were you Spence?" Walt Fisher asked him.

"Damn right I was!" the coach bellowed.

"But you said earlier in the week that you wanted mostly a *veteran* line-up, because you'd like to win early in camp to establish some confidence."

Spencer Smith didn't disagree. "That's right, but that was before I had seen those guys in a game. I promised them in the room between periods that if they showed that kind of effort it would get them in the line-up against Montreal. And now it looks like I'm going back on my word."

"But don't you have to ice at least seven regulars from last year's line-up, a league rule?" the assistant GM added.

Spencer Smith wasn't easily derailed. "So we leave a few guys at home instead. Hell, with those guys in the line-up I think we *could* beat the Habs."

Lost in all of the talk about the five ex-Leafs was the progress of Dale McCaine. Although he only totalled one assist in the Blue-White game he did impress the coach enough to be on the list for the Montreal trip.

After practice that morning the line-up for Montreal was announced, and so was the list of first assignments to St. Johns'. Ron asked to be with Spencer Smith when he delivered the news to Barilko, Horton, Jackson and Conacher. For the time being Frank McCool was in limbo while he recovered from his ulcer treatment.

"I just want to be there because it's mostly my fault that they are being sent down when they don't deserve to be," Ron pleaded.

Spencer Smith thought it was unusual, but the unflappable coach did not object. "Maybe you can learn how to send someone down, and make them feel almost grateful?" the coach suggested. "It's some talent, believe me."

Ron met with all five of the ex-Leafs after practice, just to be sure how they all were with the decision.

"I don't get it!" was the conclusion reached by Busher Jackson as he pulled down another Molson Canadian.

"Easy Busher, we're still in training," Charlie Conacher cautioned him.

"I know, I know, but I'm beginning to like these beers with the maple leaf on the label. It makes me feel patriotic."

Ron needed to know what this was going to do to Dale McCaine's, and ultimately the team's chances.

"I can't answer that," Conacher responded, "No one can. I can't tell you who's going to win the Stanley Cup."

"We told you that before," Barilko added.

"We're here because we're supposed to see that the kid gets his chance. I don't think it's important that *we* actually get to play on the team with him. At least not until—"

Ron was intrigued by the way that one stern glance from Charlie Conacher had stopped Bill Barilko in his tracks, the way that no single player on the ice could.

"Until what? Look you guys—I understand if you can't tell me everything. Only, at least tell me when something is wrong, okay?"

They nodded in agreement, but it did not seem if they knew *what* it was Ron Bailey wanted them to agree to.

"The important thing is that the kid is getting his chance!" Horton concluded.

"That's right," Busher Jackson, agreed, "It seems like you're so caught up about us that you've forgotten about the kid. *He's* the one this whole thing is supposed to happen for!"

"Thanks, guys," Ron offered, "At least I know that you guys are all for this. And it wouldn't surprise me if you guys all get early call ups."

Ron happened to be looking at Frank McCool when he said this. It was no coincidence that the goaltender was perhaps the most overlooked of the five, and the one who was least likely to welcome a stint in the minors. After all, Frank McCool had retired rather than accept a demotion before. And oddly enough, the job he would likely win if he were promoted was that of *backup* goalie.

"The weather today in Montreal is..."

When Dale McCaine returned to the team's motel he checked his messages and was informed of a team meeting scheduled for six o'clock that evening. The purpose, he was told when he arrived at the conference room, was to go over the game plan for the exhibition game in Montreal. The team itinerary was to take a bus to London where they would catch a plane to Montreal that would arrive in the city in time for them to be bussed to the Molson Centre to participate in a morning skate. Ron approached Dale McCaine after the meeting.

"I know it's only the first exhibition, but are you feeling any more a part of things? Do you feel like you're really getting a chance this time?" The kid's eyes went as wide as a cat's in the dark.

"This is great!" he said, "I've never played against the Canadiens in the Montreal Forum before!" he bubbled.

"Dale, they don't play in the *Forum* anymore. They play in the Molson Centre now. Anyway, the important thing is to make the most of your opportunity."

"And I really want to thank you for all of this, Mr. Bailey," the kid said. Ron was not going to grab any credit.

"You earned it. All I did was make good on a promise. Well, good luck Dale," he said as he got up to leave.

The kid suddenly had a worried look on his face. "Aren't you coming to Montreal too?" he asked.

"As a matter of fact I am. The General Manager has invited the entire scouting and coaching staff to be his guests. We'll be watching the game from one of the private boxes."

Dale McCaine had no idea what he was talking about. As far as he knew, a private box was something you sat in at the theatre.

Ron did not attend the morning skate in Montreal the next day. Instead he spent the early part of the day sightseeing. He even got his cab to stop at the old Forum site on St. Catherine Street West.

The building was devoid of life, or signs. The familiar marquee held only the words 'FERMEE' to indicate that it was closed. Although the building was slated for demolition, it had been delayed, the cab driver informed him, because it was being used for a movie shoot. Ron remembered seeing the closing ceremonies, with the symbolic 'passing of the torch.'

"It was a sad day when they closed this place, let me tell you!" the cab driver added.

"For the Habs sake, I can only hope that the ghosts have moved over to the Molson Centre with the team." he added.

There was that term again—the 'ghosts'. Well maybe someday the hockey world would talk about the ghosts in Maple Leaf Gardens. Of course, for that to happen, the ghosts would have to help them win a Stanley Cup. And how was *that* supposed to happen when five of them would be playing with St. Johns'?

That evening Ron was absorbed in the ultimate luxury of the Molson Centre and its plush suites. Compared to his red seats at Maple Leaf Gardens this was as far removed from sitting in an arena as a Lamborghini was from a Chevy Malibu. But as he looked around the place he had to wonder about what the cab driver had said. This place was nothing like the old Forum. Why would the ghosts want to take up residence here? There was nothing historic about the place.

The Leafs were a team trying to show some improvement over last year, and it wouldn't take much to do that. The Canadiens on the other hand, were a team that had disappointed fans with their early exit from the playoffs, and with a new coach, were anxiously anticipating that next giant step up to contender.

After the first fifteen seconds the Leafs trailed 1-0 as Michael Ryder redirected a shot from the point over the shoulder of a shocked John Dennis. And things got even worse. Although the score remained the same after the first period, the Leafs had just two shots on goal, despite the fact that they had two power plays.

In the dressing room, Spencer Smith was livid, "Two shots! TWO god damn shots! Where the hell was all of that drive I saw back in Kitchener this week? Did we leave it there? God dam it, there are jobs open on this team. And I don't care if you played in the A, the E, or the god dam Z last year. If you can take the body and beat somebody to the puck, or get a god dam shot on net then you can't play for this team—period!"

Spencer Smith fumbled in his pocket for a cigarette. It was always a sign that things were going wrong when he wanted to light up. He had quit smoking more times than Howie Meeker had 'Golly Gees', but he always started up again when things went really sour. The coach had made his point or so he thought.

At the end of the second, it was 2-0, the Canadiens having scored while the Leafs had a man advantage. Their shot total was up to a whopping twelve, though they were now 0-for-5 on the power play. And to make matters worse, Craig Rivet had flattened Tommy Rettig in a fight.

"When *your* toughest guy gets decked by *their* toughest guy, the entire bench seems to lose five inches in height and fifty pounds in weight," Spencer Smith was fond of saying.

Between the second and third the coach was silent. He left the room and stood in the corridor having a smoke. Assistant coach Brian Ridley stuck his head out of the dressing room door to see what the coach was up to. When he returned, Rettig, who sat with an ice pack on his dented skull, asked Ridley if the coach was smoking.

"He is," Ridley answered, "and I don't see any sign of a cigarette!"

The third period was more of the same. Though the Leafs managed a more respectable twenty-two shots by the games' end, they still had no goals to show for it. Jose Theodore had robbed them on the only three good scoring chances they had. And all three of those were from Dale McCaine. He was not named one of the 'Molson Cup Three Stars' but the coaching staff, including the Canadiens scouting staff noticed his play. And his play caused the many Leaf fans in attendance to check their 'Soiree Du Hockey Montreal' programs to see who number 16 was.

Spencer Smith left the dressing room early after the game, choosing not to confront the reporters right away. He waited until after the players had left, and then held court in the empty dressing room. The Montreal media were usually more thorough and in depth than their counterparts from Toronto, but slightly more tactful. Some members of the Toronto media attacked the lack of productivity of the power play while others expressed concern for the low number of shots on goal and subsequent scoring chances. And one radio head was most concerned with the fact that Tommy Rettig had been taken out so easily by Craig Rivet.

Spencer Smith was not in his usual jovial mood. He was still chastising himself for sneaking that cigarette. "Guys, it's only the first exhibition game; give it a rest. Of course the power play is going to struggle! Of course we had very few shots on net. These guys are experimenting, and so am I. Geeez, do you guys ever look on the bright side of *anything*. Look at the game John Dennis played— stopped thirty-nine of forty-two shots! Hell, one of the shots that beat him was from his own teammate!"

The shot was actually taken by Tomas Plekanec of the Canadiens and re-directed past Dennis by Dave Moore, who was trying to clear the rebound. But the coach had a point. The media were already questioning the coach and the players, after only sixty minutes of pre-season hockey.

The mood in the suite had been much less sombre, perhaps due to the seemingly endless flow of canapés, brandy, parfait, Cuban cigars, and Bailey's Irish cream. The thought of stale *Maple Leaf Gardens'* popcorn and warm syrupy-sweet soft drinks was enough to make one retch in comparison. Ron had enjoyed the game from a spectator's point of view. He was, however dismayed by the performance of the hockey team in such a showcase setting—the first (albeit, pre-season) Saturday night hockey game of the year.

"Some expose' of our camp so far, wouldn't you say Ron?" Walt Fisher said as he returned a particularly large Cuban cigar to his mouth.

"I thought there were some positives," he replied.

"Really–like the fact that we doubled our shots on goal from eleven to twenty-two in the third period perhaps?"

"No," Ron disagreed, as he downed the last of his Bailey's, now seeming somewhat ashamed that he had been drinking it. "I though the club had a lot of scoring chances, in the third especially, but we just couldn't finish them off. It didn't seem to me like a game that we were out of entirely."

It was as if Ron had only been watching the play of Dale McCaine; and perhaps he had.

New York, New York

After the game with the Canadiens, the Leafs remained in Montreal, as they would travel on Monday to New York where they would meet the Rangers that evening.

A limited practice was held on Sunday afternoon. Only those players who had dressed against the Canadiens were excused, with the exception of the backup goalie, Lars Rogers. Spencer Smith did not work the guys too hard, as he had already selected his line-up for the Ranger game. In New York, a decidedly tougher line-up faced off against the Rangers. Tommy Rettig (the 'baggage-smasher' as he was called by Stan Fishler) was out as Lorne Graham and David Eagleson were all inserted in the line-up to provide some toughness.

In the case of Eagleson it was to provide some stick work. He was the only player in the NHL who had received a spearing major against Wayne Gretzky, and was perhaps the most despised player in the league (behind of course, Ulf Samuelsson.) And as such he was often the subject of trade rumours. Eagleson ingratiated himself even less to the opposition with his endless 'trash talk' of the obscene variety.

Ron continued to accompany the team on the road, and would also catch the rematch against the Canadiens at the Gardens the next night before embarking on a tour of OHL cities. On this occasion he watched the game from the Madison Square Garden press box, and chose to sit with Dale McCaine and veteran defenseman Frank Maleki. The game was almost a replay of the disaster in Montreal— another shutout after the first two periods as the Leafs surrendered two power play goals (on ten attempts) as Eagleson and Graham each picked up double minors on separate occasions. And on all three of the penalties the Leaf players had been suckered into it by the same Ranger, ex-Leaf Cliff Rafray. Between the second and third periods Frank Maleki, who was on his third cup of coffee, could no longer contain himself.

"Why doesn't somebody, *anybody,* go out there and schmuck that little pest!" he screamed. "Jeezus, can't they see what's going on?"

As usual, Cliff Rafray was getting away with murder. He was the *first* to start something, and as that turned into a melee involving everyone on the ice (often including the goalies) he would emerge from the pile unscathed, and while the battle continued he would position himself beside the bewildered referee and remark on what a mess had developed.

Dale McCaine sat silent as he watched the Leafs unravel before his eyes. "We have no spark out there. No one is willing to go to the wall for the team."

Both Ron and Frank Maleki were surprised that they heard this coming from a rookie.

"It's great to hear you say that Dale," Ron commented, "You'd really like to be out there tonight, wouldn't you."

The kid's eyes glowed like embers re-establishing themselves in a fire thought to be out.

"Yes Sir Mr. Bailey," he answered.

Ron had been embarrassed again. He repeatedly asked the kid to address him as Ron, but the player always forgot and formalized his speech.

Frank Maleki was ready to jump down onto the ice as the referee signalled another Ranger power play to start the third period.

"Are those zebras watching a different game? They sure as hell ain't watching *this* one!" he yelled.

During the two minutes that David Eagleson spent in the box, the Leafs overworked goalie Lars Rogers had faced six shots, and the seventh found its way home as defenseman Christian Andersson failed to clear Steve Rucchin from in front of the net, and it was 3-0 Rangers. The Leafs got a little lift on the ensuing shift when it appeared that Floyd Shoniker had broken the shutout, with a blast from inside the face-off circle. It was too good to be true however, as winger Serge Moit was inexplicably parked with foot in the crease, and after a video review the goal was disallowed. Match point.

"Nothin left to do but down a few cold ones," Frank Maleki sighed, as he readied himself to take up with his teammates who would be heading to some local watering hole to drown the memory of this frustrating loss. He looked back at Dale McCaine and Ron Bailey who were still in shock at the fact that this team had not yet managed goal in six periods of play. "Are ya's goin, or no?" he asked.

Ron indicated that he was not, and Dale McCaine also declined and Maleki was off to partake in the ritual. "I'm heading back to the hotel...do you want to share a cab?" Ron asked.

Dale said he would, and both of them were silent on the drive to the hotel. When they arrived, Dale headed directly to the coffee shop, and invited Ron to join him.

"I'm kind of tired, Dale," he said, but the kid was insistent. They sat silent at a booth until the kid broke the silence.

"This is a lot different than I thought it would be," he began his head down as if he was timing the revolutions a blob of cream took in his coffee cup as he stirred it. Ron was concerned, at this first hint of disappointment.

"I mean it is a little like the last camp I was at, you know, in '68. That team didn't look like it was going to be very good either. Most of the veterans were getting too old to go all out in camp. And the coach really hated that."

Ron wondered what it must have been like to be coached by a legend like Punch Imlach, but he didn't interrupt the kid.

"I think that a lot of *these* guys aren't really going all out," he said sheepishly, as if he was blaspheming.

Ron almost had to laugh. The average NHL salary when Dale had attended that camp was thirty-five thousand dollars—the average salary in *this* camp was *nine hundred* and thirty-five thousand dollars. If that was not reason enough to not be motivated, he thought. Ron wasn't about to defend the actions of the current Leafs, but instead asked the kid if *he* knew *why* it was that way.

"I don't. Except I've heard things, you know, in the room," he replied.

Ron and Dale both knew that a very sacred taboo was being broached. The real motto of the dressing room was not what was emblazoned on the walls for visitors to read, to be impressed with as part of a tour of the building. No, the real motto was more like *'What you see here, what you hear here, let it stay here when you leave here'* Ron decided not to caution the kid, but instead to hear him out.

"I hear a lot of the guys talking like the coach won't be here for long. Some say it's because when the team is eventually sold, everybody in the front office will be let go!"

Ron raised his eyebrows a little, as Dale McCaine continued. "And others say that he is gone if we get off to a bad start this season. Either way they say it doesn't matter because he won't be around for very long." He continued to stir his coffee instead of drinking it.

"I don't like to hear that because I think he's a good coach. The things he tells us make sense. He's always talking about the right and wrong way to do things. He says we can take the easy way out—and that, of course, is wrong. Or do it the right way, which involves hard work. But already I've had a couple of guys tell me to take it easier in practice—not to knock myself out, or I'll never last very long in this game."

Ron had to bite his lip to keep from jumping in ahead of time. "The way I look at it, if you think that you can just get by without giving it your best—well you'll always be the kind of player who settles for second best. And a coach like Mr. Smith, well, he won't accept anything but our best. I know he likes working with the young guys better than the veterans when it comes to this."

"Dale, do you think that he likes working with younger players more than the veterans?"

"No, I didn't mean that. He is always using what they do as an example when we make mistakes. I know he is very loyal to the older guys, and most of them are loyal to him."

They should be, Ron thought.

Spencer Smith had taken a collection of mostly fourth line players and taken them to within one goal of reaching the Stanley Cup finals three years ago. And while it only seemed like thirty years ago, most of those veterans were still with the team. Spencer Smith was not willing to admit that half a dozen of those players were neither worth what they were being paid nor earning it. He was sticking to his belief that this roster only needed fine-tuning, and not a major overhaul. Ken Butler trusted his coach's instincts, while having to listen to the whispering in his ear that came from Walt Fisher, who suggested that trades had to be made, and that maybe even a coaching change was necessary if things did not continue to improve. This was how they finished last season, and two games into training camp nothing seemed to have changed. Nothing except that a rookie had already sized up the most glaring needs, and seemed to know what it would take to fix them. Still one player does not make a team, unless his name is Richard, Orr, Gretzky or Lemieux. And Ron was not ready to concede that Dale McCaine was in that class.

The last cuts are the deepest

The team flight home to Toronto was typically solemn, as they had been for most of the previous few seasons. The reporters would meet them after the morning skate and ask the same kind of questions that they asked after the last loss. And although Spencer Smith would use a slightly different line-up for the rematch with the Canadiens the result would be the same—another loss. But while the result was different, the way it came about was not. The tying goal came late in the third period.

Newcomer Tobin West, who had scored the Leafs second goal, found Dale McCaine all alone near the far boards, and fed him a nice pass that took a great deal of skill to thread through the legs of the Canadiens' defender. Just when it looked like McCaine would not be able to get past the Montreal player, he twisted his body in the air like a ballet dancer's pirouette, moved past the defenseman and collected the puck as if he had expected to. Without losing a stride he broke in on the goalie and fired a rising backhand that made the water bottle on top of the net dance like a puppet as he scored to tie the game. The ovation that ensued was like nothing that had been heard in the Gardens in years. And it was McCaine's third point of the game. Even the veteran reporters had to do a double take to convince them of what they had seen. It was a goal that would make all of the highlight tapes that night.

The celebration was short lived however. In the dressing room before the overtime Spencer Smith had only a few words.

"Make it happen right away! If we charge right out of the gate, get a good chance early. We can do this, guys!"

The veterans weren't really buying it. This was their third game in four nights, and this was only the pre-season. But the rookies were listening. When they faced off in overtime, Benoit Marlet won the draw and sent the puck over to Dale McCaine, who quickly set up on a two-on-one. He drew the defenseman to his side of the rink and fed the puck onto the stick of Serge Moit like it had eyes. The winger let go a beautiful wrist shot to the top corner of the net, but Jose Theodore snagged it, and dropped it to the ice. The goaltender steered the puck ahead to Andre Markov, who found the Leafs caught up ice. He sent the puck ahead to Michael Ryder who found himself in alone on John Dennis and beat the goalie cleanly with a low slap shot to the stick side—game over.

Shithead Moore, one of the two defenseman that needlessly joined the rush, cracked his stick on the cross bar. A subtle but still noticeable rumbling of boos descended on the players as they left the ice.

Inside the dressing room, the usual serenade of obscenities erupted, except from the players who said nothing at all. The coach entered quickly, and on this occasion chose not to lash out at his troops. Instead he offered encouragement.

"Great effort guys, we almost had them!" he bristled. Joel Kent looked up from his chair and towelled the sweat from his eyes as if he didn't believe that it was Spencer Smith who was talking.

"Sure, we lost, but that's the best effort we've had so far. And the next one we're gonna take, god dam it!" he shouted. That would take some doing.

The next game was not until Friday, but it was in Detroit against the Red Wings. The team would get a chance to sleep in their own beds tonight but would return to Kitchener the next morning, where camp still had a couple of days to run. Tomorrow the first real cuts would take place.

The coaching staff met early that Wednesday to plan their cuts. The day would begin by calling in all of the players who were ticketed for the 'rock'. The meeting would consist only of the player being sent down, the GM and the coach. They would explain why the player was being sent down, outline just exactly what was expected of him in the minors and offer the usual encouragement while listing all of the players' weaknesses that had to be worked on in order to spell their return to the big club.

The afternoon was reserved for the more upbeat task of the coach's 'One-on-One' chats with the players. They would review the players' progress so far and let each player know exactly where they stood at that point in camp. They would not be told that they had made the club (even if it was obvious that they had) but only what they had to do or continue to do in order to win a job. There were certain veterans, like team captain Floyd Shoniker and defenseman David Burks that the coach would question regarding their observation of other players. The player that Spencer Smith was most interested in getting a read on from his veterans was Dale McCaine.

"I don't really know what to say about him. You know I've only played on a line with him in practice," the captain replied.

Spencer Smith had to spell out what he was looking for. "I'm not talking about that, Shonker," he said pounding his fist on his desk. "I want to know what kind of character you think he has—you are the best judge of character of anybody I know, outside of myself of course," he laughed.

Shoniker didn't really know how to answer the question. "I know that he doesn't seem to be a great practice player. He seems to focus only on the games."

The coach smiled and leaned forward as if he was going to share a secret. "Can't for the life of me understand where he could have picked up a habit like that?"

Floyd Shoniker rolled his eyes upward.

"The kid seems a bit timid to me, Shonker. I know part of its nerves, first camp and all."

"No, I don't think that's it," the player answered. "I don't think he's nervous about the camp—he seems like he's out of place, not skill wise or anything. Hell, we've all seen what the kid can do with the puck. No, to me he seems like he's out of his element, period!"

The coach thought about it for a minute and then wondered "Do you think it would help if, say, a veteran such as yourself, took an interest in the kid—sort of made him a project?"

"You mean take him under my wing?"

"Exactly!" the coach agreed.

"Spence, if I had royalties on every rookie I've done that for, I could retire *now!*" The coach didn't disagree.

"I'm not sure if I should be the one—he might relate better to someone younger. He seems to get along better with the younger guys like West or Sawchuck."

"Maybe, but a veteran should be able to keep the work habits up—set an example and all that. Don't you agree?"

The captain thought about it for a moment. His entire life had been about taking youngsters under his wing.

Floyd Shoniker grew up in Goderich, Ontario, on the shores of Lake Huron. His father was a captain of a lake freighter, and was away from home more than he was there. It was one of young Floyds' duties to help raise his sister and six brothers. And to keep the whole brood out of trouble, his father insisted they all play hockey—Floyd even ended up coaching a few of his siblings.

Shoniker had been around this team for almost seven years, the same as the coach. He was there before they made a run at two straight semi-final appearances and he was still there as the roller coaster had continued its descent. More than anyone this team was going to need a rejuvenated captain in order to make any kind of a run at a playoff spot. He realized exactly what the coach was proposing. He didn't need the captain to try and bring the rookie along—no, he needed the rookie to try and make the captain pull his game back out of the garbage can. Spencer Smith had too much respect even now for the players that had stuck by him for the past seven years, to suggest that this is what it was going to take to inspire them—especially the captain. So Floyd Shoniker would make no comment on the coach's suggestion. He would agree to it, and that was all. No one else on the team would have to know about it.

"I'll give it a try coach," he said, though he never addressed the coach that way.

"Great!" Spencer Smith exclaimed, as he rubbed his hands together as if they had just embarked on a five-minute power play. "To make it easier maybe we could arrange for you to room with the kid on the road—who are you rooming with now?"

Floyd Shoniker just laughed. "Burks," he replied, "but I don't mind you breaking us up. He snores like an aardvark and he always has to have control of the remote."

The meetings continued and by the end of the day were completed. There were still five cuts to be made in order to get down to the twenty-two players they would carry into the season opener. Spencer Smith did not like any more than two standees in the press box during the regular season, as he knew that with the compressed schedule and the amount of travelling that the team did the injury list would average three bodies.

The following day they would break camp in Kitchener and head to Detroit for the weekend home and home series with the Red Wings. Management believed that a series with an original six rival (even half way through camp) would kindle some of the competitive fires and go a long way in seeing who would step up and try and grab a roster spot for them. The Friday game was played in Detroit, and as usual there were a fair number of Leaf supporters over from Windsor.

It was apparent from the start that the Red Wings were not taking this game as seriously as were the Leafs. Detroit was without a few big guns, while Toronto countered with the same line-up that had almost earned them the victory over Montreal. Spencer Smith had become more and more focused on the idea that the team needed a victory badly. The media were already comparing this year's edition to last years—the one that went through the entire exhibition schedule without a single victory. The coach knew that morale would take a quantum leap if they could just beat somebody, anybody. The idea that it would come against a perennial playoff team was a little far-fetched though.

As the team bus drove across the Detroit River and under the familiar sign in red lights that announced 'Ambassador Bridge', the coach could not help but feel that something on their side greeted them. When he was writing out the line-up to hand in to the referee he decided to play a hunch and placed Dale McCaine alongside Floyd Shoniker and Joel Kent on the first line. McCaine was a natural centre, but was also a left-handed shot and that would perhaps throw the defenders off a bit—to see a right-winger that shoots left. Chuck Andrew was normally on Shoniker's right side, but he had yet to score in pre-season and the coach was becoming impatient. The big winger had once scored over forty goals in three straight seasons, but the last one was three years ago, and since then his goal output had decreased exponentially.

From the opening face-off, the Leafs came out hitting and Spencer Smith had to pinch himself to believe what he was seeing. The tempo of the game was quickly established when David Burks was trying to bring the puck out of his own end and was nailed in the corner by Donald MacLean. Another Detroit player, Kirk Maltby rushed in to steal the puck and nearly ran into MacLean. Burks caught Maltby with his head down and as he moved to check him into the boards he met MacLean first and rammed him into Maltby knocking both Red Wings to the ice. Burks found himself still on his feet and scooped up the puck and fed a pass up ice to Floyd Shoniker who had a great scoring chance robbed by the Detroit goalie. From that point on the Toronto bench seemed to rise to the occasion, and took delight in delivering the body at every opportunity.

The physical play, combined with some great goal tending and the shift away from the club's tendency to give up the puck in their own end resulted in a 2-1 victory, the first one in the pre-season.

As Spencer Smith congratulated them all for a much-welcomed team effort he began to think about the inevitable letdown that would follow when the two clubs met back in Toronto the next night. He hoped for a carry over, and other than going with Lars Rogers in net, the line-up was the same as the night before. The result however was nowhere near the same. The two teams that went at it again in Toronto the next night bore no resemblance to the ones that had played just twenty-four hours earlier. Detroit iced a team heavy with youngsters and it was hard for the Leafs veterans to keep up.

Toronto fell behind early, thanks to some stupid penalties by David Eagleson and Randy Rettig. The score was 3-0 for Detroit before the Leafs got on the board. David Moore was halfway through his slashing penalty on Mikael Samuelsson when Spencer Smith sent Shoniker out on the penalty-killing unit with Dale McCaine. The two had never killed penalties together, but after the captain won the face-off he fed a blind pass to the rookie who took it like he knew it was coming. As they raced up ice it became clear that they had a good scoring chance, even though Niklas Lidstrom was positioning himself nicely to play the two-on-one.

Shoniker yelled, "Go to the net!" and McCaine did just that. Instead of feeding the pass that Lidstrom knew was coming, Shoniker elected to fire a wrist shot that rang off the cross bar. Before the big defenseman could handle the rebound it was in the net. McCaine had positioned himself exactly where the puck had deflected off the net, and had banged it in almost before anyone could move.

"Way to go kid! That's what happens when you go to the net," Shoniker gasped. McCaine was all smiles as he passed by the bench and got high-fived by the entire team. The celebration was short lived however. Before the period had ended the Red Wings had restored their three-goal lead, and the game ended a disappointing 5-2 loss.

On Sunday afternoon the coaching staff met for lunch at *Tim Riley's* bar and then returned to the Gardens to make the second to last cuts. As many as five or as few as two players would be designated for St. Johns', though they would not be going to the minors until Tuesday. The farm club was currently touring northern Ontario as sort of a mini PR campaign to drum up interest in the big club—St. Johns' were playing a three game series against the Hamilton Bulldogs, with games in New Liskeard, Timmins and Noranda, Quebec.

Ron Bailey accompanied the team to get a better read on the players who had been assigned there. With more cuts coming from the big club it was up to Ron and the coaching staff of Dan Cameron and Al Swartz to decide which players from the St. Johns' group would be going elsewhere. Ron was still trying to reach an agreement with a team in the United League, formerly the Colonial League, to place a few players for the coming season.

While the St. Johns' roster had not been decided on there were four players who had already earned a spot, based on their performance on this three game series alone. Barilko and Horton seemed inspired by the tour of their northern homeland, as they each scored a pair of goals in the first two games, which were both victories. Conacher and Busher Jackson accounted for all of the goals in the 4-3 overtime loss in Royun-Noranda.

Ron was treated to the biggest laugh of the tour. As the team was entering the arena in Noranda, Tim Horton happened to notice the name on the outside of the building. "Dave Keon Arena, what the hell is this? How come they named the rink after that little bugger?"

Ron replied, "Because he's the best player ever to come out of here, and he played on four Stanley Cup winners."

"Well goody for him. So did I, and you don't see a rink in Cochrane named after me do ya?"

Ron didn't tell him that there *was* a rink named after him, in fact an entire community centre—*that* would have to wait until if and when they travelled to Cochrane.

As the Leafs prepared for their sixth pre-season game, a home date against Buffalo the tedium of the schedule of meaningless games was beginning to grate on the players. The crowd was about half of what it would be for a regular season game, as many season's subscribers simply didn't go or gave their tickets away.

The media picked up on this as well. Training camp was also an opportunity for the fifth estate to get their hockey writing skills in shape for the coming season. Billy Sinfield noted in his 'Sin Bin' column that these games would be played before empty houses if it weren't for the fact that season ticket holders had to pay for the games as part of their package.

If the games have to be played, he wrote, *and I suppose they must to give the owners the kind of dough they need to feed those hefty payrolls, then at least they should pass out clothespins at the door so the patrons don't have to hold their noses for the entire sixty minutes of exhibition hockey.*

On this particular evening, he was wrong however. For the first time in this training camp the Blue and White looked as if they cared who won a game. The Leafs got a couple of early goals from some veterans who hadn't shown much so far in camp—winger Joel Kent and defenseman Mike McKenna. And for the first time in camp goalie John Dennis came up with an effort that made it look like he was ready to start the season. The Sabres were not to be denied for their good effort either. They scored once shorthanded, and another on a power play that caught the Leafs all rookie line of McCaine, West and Sawchuck on a line change. The final was a 2-2 tie that overtime would not settle.

Spencer Smith was elated with the effort, but instead of offering congratulations he elected to emphasize how close this was to a win, and how with some better concentration and effort the one point gained was really one point lost for a win.

The Leafs had a day off before the return visit to Buffalo and the media were really beginning their suppositions as to what three players would be cut, and what the teams' chances were based on their showing through six games of the exhibition schedule.

For the first time Dale McCaine's name appeared in the paper for something other than a game summary or account. The article was by none other than Neil Porters, the same reporter who had ridiculed the organization for their recruitment of East Coast Hockey League players. He was speculating on the makeup of the Leaf roster based on the results of camp to date. His most glowing praise came for a couple of rookies, notably Greg Sawchuck and Dale McCaine. And Tobin West was given honourable mention.

Ron Bailey took great pride in the fact that the youngsters were mentioned so prominently. West and Sawchuck were two of the three players that he participated in selecting from Pittsburgh in the Vaclav Atris trade, while Dale McCaine was quietly becoming the biggest surprise in camp.

The return match in Buffalo saw the Leafs use a somewhat experimental line-up. This was their penultimate game, and since the last game against Florida was basically a tune-up for the opener, this game was going to be the last chance for several guys to prove that they belonged.

Spencer Smith elected to sit out several veterans that had obviously made the club, and so Floyd Shoniker and David Burks were both allowed to remain in Toronto. And so was Dale McCaine, though he accompanied the team to Buffalo anyway. The Leafs were bombed 7-1, but it at least gave the coaching staff the necessary read on the final cuts.

And so, as the Leafs returned to Toronto for their final pre-season game the roster was set. The goalies would be the incumbents; John Dennis as number one and Lars Rogers as his backup, though the split in games was more likely to be 50-32 than the 65-17 of the previous season, as Rogers was gaining experience and Dennis had showed less reason to be burdened with the bulk of the work. The defense would consist of David Burks, Mike McKenna, Terry Oddy, Dave Moore, Christian Andersson, Frank Maleki and rookie Ian Moriarty. Up front the lines that would start the season were Joel Kent-Floyd Shoniker-Chuck Andrew as #1; David Eagleson-Serge Moit-Benoit Marlet as #2; Rookies Tobin West-Dale McCaine and veteran Lou Zanardo as # 3, and the fourth line would be Randy Rettig—John Hill—Lorne Graham (the enforcer line). The extra forward was rookie Greg Sawchuck, who the coaching staff deemed too valuable to be in St. Johns' although he had not yet unseated one of the veterans for a position. Sawchuck would get his chance when the first injury came, and when that would be was anybody's guess. Until then he would watch the games from the press box with the 'seventh defenseman', who would be Andersson, Moriarty or Moore depending on their play in the previous game.

The Florida Panthers arrived in town fresh from their Peterborough training camp. They did not want to risk injuries to any key players this close to the season opener, and that said a lot about what they thought about the Leafs; that they should be able to beat this struggling unit without their best players.

Spencer Smith viewed this game somewhat differently. With only one victory in pre-season, he was desperate another, and not to have the team read the headline that they were entering the season on a losing note, even if they had lost more exhibition games than they had won. He tried to pump the team up before the game by ranting about his favourite subject—the neutral zone trap.

"These guys think they're so damned good that they can walk in here and beat us without a full line-up. Well let's show them how mistaken they are. This is a team that loves to play the trap. Well we can beat the trap by not falling into it. Our defenseman are gonna move up with the play, and if it means the odd two-on-one, so be it. We're gonna see a lot of the neutral zone taken away this year, so we better get used to it now."

The Leafs got off to a good start by staying out of the penalty box for the entire period, while Florida gave them three power plays. The Leafs finally cashed in on one when David Burks grabbed a flying pass at the point and dropped the puck to his stick. He teed off on it and the hesitation seemed to catch the Florida goalie, Jamie McLennan by surprise, and the low shot drifted into the net to make it 1-0.

In the second, their persistence paid off as Dale McCaine stole a loose puck at the Florida blue line and went in alone on the goalie. As he brought his stick back for the expected wrist shot he noticed Joel Kent streaking in on the right side. He was still looking at the net however, and he drew the blade back to wrist the shot that the goalie expected would be rising up at him. Instead the puck travelled in a perpendicular streak across the ice and lay in front of Kent for a split second until he lifted it into the top corner of the goal to the amazement of McLennan who was well out of position.

Even Ken Butler, watching from the director's box had to do a double take on that play.

"You don't see that kind of thing every day now do you," he said smiling to no one in particular.

Only Walt Fisher picked up on the unmistakable satisfaction in the General Manager's tone. Ken Butler had found just the kind of player he had been looking for.

The period ended with the Leafs up by one. Spencer Smith was ecstatic as he tried to get the club whipped up into regular-season between-periods frenzy.

"We're skating man-for-man with a pretty good hockey club! Keep it up. It says a lot if we can out work a team like them. Don't let up or they'll come back on you!" he preached.

The period ended that way, as Spencer Smith continued to uplift his troops, while cautioning them not to let up in the final period.

"Let's win this one god dammit!" he screamed as they headed back on the ice for the third.

And win it they did. Shithead Moore of all people let go a shot from the point that had to have changed direction three times by hitting various player's sticks before taking an improbable bounce in off of the post. He was credited with the goal even though the replay showed otherwise, his first score of the pre-season. And to no one's surprise there was little cheering on the bench when he did score.

With the game almost out of reach the Leafs scored again, this time on the power play as Benoit Marlet was sent in on a breakaway by a nice pass from Serge Moit. It was a spectacular goal, and even with the score 5-1 it still brought most of the Leaf faithful to their feet. This was the kind of goal the fans had been promised by management when they chose the former all-time leading scorer in the history of the Chicoutimi Saugeneens of the Quebec League. Marlet had rarely delivered, but when he did it was always a goal of the highlight reel variety. Maybe, just maybe this was going to be the year that he made that long awaited breakthrough. Though he was only twenty-five years old, Marlet seemed to have been around forever. He seemed to have been a disappointment for a long time.

The end result was a 5-2 home victory—at least they would not be starting the season with the stigma of having lost their last game.

In the dressing room the mood was upbeat, as if the win had actually counted for something. John Dennis was congratulated by almost everyone. To a man they knew that even with the same amount of goal scoring they managed last year this team was only going as far as John Dennis could carry them. If he was capable of repeating the success of his first three seasons, then there was room for some optimism—if not, well perhaps Lars Rogers would be the answer.

Ron Bailey left the Gardens immediately after the game, choosing not to go for a post-game drink with the coaching staff. Instead, he had arranged to meet Dale McCaine at Fran's restaurant on College Street.

He arrived well before the hockey player, who would still be towelling off and dressing. Ron sat near the window, watching the post-game traffic dispersing. He didn't usually eat this late, because he was susceptible to heartburn if he ate after 9:00 PM. But Ron was hungry and he loved the hamburgers at Fran's. He liked a burger that was charbroiled, and even though these were lightly fried they were still better than the overly lubricated beef-like substance that fast food joints were flogging. He also loved the coffee at Fran's, but he couldn't drink a coffee with a burger; it simply wasn't done. No, with a burger it had to be a Coke, or occasionally a milk shake, unless of course it was the burger was served at an outdoor barbecue, such as a friend's cottage—*then* it would be acceptable to have a beer. Ron didn't wait for Dale McCaine to arrive before he ordered his burger. He chose a Coke, even though he was going to order a coffee later. He thought about the consequences or taking in this much caffeine so late in the evening, but he shrugged it off. So what if he had trouble sleeping, he thought. Maybe there was a good movie on television. Or maybe he could get a head start on updating his database to include the current Leaf roster and St. Johns'.

He had almost finished the burger when Dale McCaine walked through the door, his hair still slicked down as if he had not taken the time to properly dry it. He flopped down in the booth across the table from Ron.

179

"Great game tonight Dale!" Ron smiled as he rapped the kid on the shoulder with his fist.

Dale returned a half smile. "That was a great play you made with Joel," he said referring to the setup of the second goal.

Dale looked around to catch the attention of a waitress. "I'd love to play on his line," the kid said, his eyes lighting up like it was Christmas morning. "The coach pretty much has me pencilled in with Toby West and Lou Zanardo, but if I work hard, he tells me that it's possible I can get moved up. Whattya think of that?"

To Ron it was refreshing to hear a kid talk on those terms, rather than bitching about ice time, the lack of a spot on the power play or his contract.

Ron took a sip of his coffee to test the temperature. "I think that anything is possible on a team that was 21st in scoring a year ago," he said.

The kid tore into his plate of spaghetti when it arrived. "You know what the coach told me when we had our one on one in Kitchener?" he said as he went into a passable imitation of Spencer Smith. "He said, 'kid, you keep your mouth shut and your ears open and you just might learn something around here'!"

Ron wondered if he also got the other Spencer Smith work ethic euphemism 'Keep your head down and your ass up', but maybe that one had worn too thin by now. "Spence is a good coach," Ron professed, "but sometimes I wonder sometimes how long he will be here."

Dale looked genuinely surprised. "Don't they think he's doing a good job?" he asked.

Ron took a long sip from his coffee, which was now colder than he liked it.

"It's not even a question of that anymore. He could be the greatest coach in the history of the game—but if the players won't play for him anymore, and if the media and the fans are convinced that he can't do the job anymore, then the result is, either he quits or he gets fired. It's like you told me before about the talk in the room. Sometimes there's truth behind the rumours."

The grim reality of coaching was not lost on Ron, though he had never experienced being fired.

"But what is it about him that makes the players quit on him or the reporters and fans feel the way they do?" Dale asked as he twirled his spaghetti into his spoon.

"I don't have the answer. The players today are different than when *you* started out I suspect. Things are more in favour of the players than they are of management. And the players know it. There are some big name guys in this league that have had coaches fired because they couldn't get along with them. And with salaries rising like they are—the owners have so much money invested in some players that they feel they have to protect it. It's easier to fire a coach making a million to appease a player making three million dollars, I guess."

Dale was still bewildered by the state of the modern game. "I hear the guys talk about this stuff, but I don't let it bother me. I just want to see us win," he confessed.

Dale McCaine's attitude and his ethics continually amazed Ron. He was, as out of place in the twenty-first century as a player as Maple Leaf Gardens was as a building.

"I'm glad to hear you say that," Ron agreed. "Winning is sometimes secondary to guys making a good living. Life in Toronto as a hockey player can be pretty good even when the team isn't winning. The thing about winning is the attitude, and how contagious it can be. People, in every sport are always talking about needing players who know what it takes to win—it sounds like such a cliché after a while. But the truth is it's mostly attitude. A guy who knows what it takes to win, a guy who has played on a winning team in the past knows it's all about dedication and busting your butt—wanting to win each and every night more than the guy in the other colour sweater."

181

"And I think the same way. All it takes is hard work," Dale agreed.

Ron almost had to laugh. "You make it sound so simple—like it's easy. But there are a lot of guys on this team that think they are working hard each shift and when they come to the bench they tell themselves they're spent. But the only people they are fooling are themselves. That's why I think you can be so valuable to this team. Sure you've shown that you've got some skill around the net—and this team is not exactly knee deep in scoring. But the thing I think has most impressed the management is your attitude, especially for a young guy."

Ron thought he saw the kid blush, but it was probably just the degree of spice in the spaghetti sauce.

"I tell you where it is gonna show up Dale—take a kid like Benoit Marlet. He's one of the highest rated forwards ever to come out of the Quebec league. But in the AHL and up here

He's been a stiff to put it mildly. The only reason he's still on the roster is because the club doesn't want to admit they made such a huge mistake in drafting him so high. But I noticed something tonight. That kid, hell he's 25 now—he played like the game mattered for a change, and do you know why? Because for the first time, there is somebody younger around showing more hustle—he's being shown up by a rookie. And it's just what this team needs!"

"I'm still getting to know some of the guys," Dale responded, "I really don't know Marlet. There do seem to be some guys on the team who are what you said about fooling themselves. But I think that it will be hard for them to keep that up if the guys who are really trying start to get some results. I can't wait for Saturday night!"

"Hello out there...we're on the air"

Saturday night was the opener of the Leafs 88th season (including the years they were known as Arenas and later St. Patrick's). As Ron Bailey drove to the Gardens late on the afternoon of October the 16th, he was reminded that the club had lost last season's home opener and that by the third period fans had begun to boo the club—those that were still left in the building that is.

As an organization Ron felt they were on the right track. They had good management in place, including scouting, player development and coaching though they did lack the sometimes-important ingredient of ownership. The talent on the ice was mediocre, but the youth movement was supposed to bear fruit in the not-too-distant future. The party line that this team could, with a little luck, make the playoffs. If they did not, however there would be no wholesale changes of personnel simply for the sake of change. The factor that divided management was this—the coaching staff believed that they could get a few more miles out of such shell-shocked veterans as Chuck Andrew, David Burks, Floyd Shoniker and Joel Kent. They also believed that grinders such as Randy Rettig and David Eagleson still had the desire to do the kind of dirty work and be the kind of role players that every club needed. Sitting on the fence on this issue was Ken Butler, and Ron Bailey. Firmly convinced that a talent transfusion was the only answer was Walt Fisher, who made it his personal quest (when things turned sour) to point the finger at the veterans and the coach, because he supported them.

Ron could see one of two scenarios developing; either Spencer Smith would be right, and the team would qualify for the playoffs, and perhaps 'do some damage' as the coach referred to it. Or, as Walt Fisher predicted, suffer through another underachieving season of disappointment and miss the playoffs by light years.

Ron (and only Ron) knew that there was one factor that was likely to change all of this, and that was Dale McCaine. Ron had unconsciously forgotten at times just *where* the player came from. It was easier at times for him to simply close his eyes and pretend that the player had been discovered in Australia, and that his presence was not like some divine intervention in the team's fortunes.

Tonight, the curtain was going up on this one. From now until the end of the season, the media would seemingly be writing about every shift. All of the games would be televised, and the entire province would finally get a look at the rookie who had been getting headlines in *small* print. From now on, when Ron picked up the paper to read a summary, or looked at the standings on the 'net, every stat would count.

Ron stayed away from the coaches' room and dressing room on this night. He knew from experience that although the players were less likely to be distracted by his presence for the opening game, he also knew that there would be enough distractions, such as the extra media coverage that went with the shiny newness of the season opener.

The electric feeling was enhanced by the very building itself, which had been given a sparkling new coat of paint to the interior. The visual stimulation was invigorating, like looking at a bright sunrise. The players had been issued brand new white uniforms, fresh out of their wrapping. And the 48th Highlanders treated the fans with a taste of tradition as they piped the team onto the ice for the opening face-off. The building was darkened, as the requisite nuance, the laser light show, beamed a florescent blue Maple Leaf logo onto the ice and shot coloured beams around the darkened building to temporarily give it the impression of a rock concert. That image vanished with the rendition of 'O Canada' and the fans did their part giving the club a standing ovation at the end of it.

The obligatory ceremonial face off was staged, and there to drop the puck was none other than the last living member of the Leafs' first Stanley Cup in Maple Leaf Gardens, Red Horner.

As he watched from the GM's box, Ron could only wonder what Charlie Conacher and Busher Jackson would say if they had been there. Instead, they were getting ready to face off for St. Johns', who would be taking to the road against the Portland Pirates.

Toronto's opponent that night was the Ottawa Senators, at team that had the Leafs number during the past couple of seasons, but which had difficulty with them in the playoffs. The battle of Ontario was now one of the Leafs bitterest rivalries.

On the ice the Senators were superior in most areas to the Leafs. They had more firepower in the likes of Dany Heatley, Daniel Alfredsson, Mike Fisher, Jason Spezza, Antione Vermette, and Patrick Eaves. They had more grit in Chris Neil than the Leafs had on their entire roster. Their defense of Wade Redden, Zdeno Chara, Chris Phillips, Brad Norton and Brian Pothier was more solid, and the goal tending of Dominik Hasek and Ray Emery was more reliable. And Chara was capable of outscoring some of the Leaf forwards on any given night. This night was not to be a given, however.

Like their pre-season victory over Detroit, the Leafs came out of the gate hitting, a tactic that seemed to keep the crowd in the game early. The difference in this game was that the home team fell behind as a result of a power play goal given up because the hitting became *too* aggressive at times.

They trailed 1-0 after one, but in the second period they obviously became inspired by Spencer Smith's positive dressing room challenge that there were two points to be stolen here because the Senators were not exactly stepping up to the physical challenge. If the Leafs could keep up the physical play while staying out of the penalty box, then they had a chance for the upset. And so it began to unfold. Floyd Shoniker started it with an even strength goal, the result of a great effort by David Burks to keep the puck inside the Senators zone after a poor attempt at a clearing pass by Ottawa. On a power play that happened soon after John Hill positioned himself in front of the Senators net, Dale McCaine brought the puck in over the blue line. McCaine was nailed by Wade Redden, but not before he directed the puck right onto the stick of Tobin West, who fed Zanardo for the goal. McCaine did most of the work, but wasn't credited with an assist. His effort did not go un-noticed by the coaching staff, however. Before the fans had settled back into their seats the Senators caught the Leafs backed into their own zone, and banged in a goalmouth scramble to tie it at 2-2.

The second period ended that way, as the Senators were clearly becoming frustrated by the clutching and grabbing of the Leafs leaden foot soldiers such as Randy Rettig, David Eagleson and Lorne Graham. It paid off early in the third as Ottawa took a retaliatory penalty and Eagleson, left on ice for the power play because the coach was late in making his line change, deflected in a point shot from Frank Maleki to give the Leafs the lead.

Just when overtime appeared likely, rookie Greg Sawchuk, (a late addition to the line-up after a hamstring pull scratched Serge Moit), made the play of the game. He collected a pin-point pass from Dale McCaine and taxied in on the Senators net. Dominik Hasek in the Ottawa net anticipated his awkward attempt at a move to the backhand easily, but the goalie was unable to gather up the rebound, and Sawchuck banged it home as the fallen goalie looked on in disbelief. There was only one problem. Dale McCaine was double-parked in the crease, his left skate clearly outlined on the blue crease. He was in no way involved in the shot that entered the net but a rule is a rule—when it's called, that is.

Much to the amazement of the Ottawa bench and the crowd, the goal stood. Referee Scott Aberdeen didn't even request a video review, though he did briefly consult with the linesmen, who missed the call as well. The Senators coach was furious, and Chris Neil argued the call so poignantly that he was assessed a ten minute misconduct. The goal and the penalty came at the 19:27 mark, and it appeared as if the Leafs had indeed stolen this one.

After the face off, Ottawa had other ideas. They quickly pulled the goalie after winning the draw, and Daniel Alfredsson streaked by the wheezing Terry Oddy and let go a soft, low, stick side shot that even a peewee goalie could have stopped—but not John Dennis. He was transfixed, in a mode that former Blue Jay pitcher Mike Flanagan used to call 'vapour lock', when a batter was frozen by a called third strike. The Senators celebrated wildly, and eagerly got ready for the face off at centre ice, though there were now only 16 seconds remaining.

The Leafs checked their pants for messes, while they tried in vain to contain their panic. They lost the face off, and with time running out all the clutching and grabbing in the world was not going to keep Ottawa from rushing the net like a Green Bay Packers blitz. Both of the Leaf defensemen fell down on the play as they were pushed into the goalie. Just when it appeared that a shot was going to find the net, John Dennis managed to get to his feet as the shot came from in close, and he stuck out his outreached arm and grabbed the puck. The buzzer sounded, but it was all for nought anyway as the puck was actually wide of the net anyway. The Leafs had literally stolen a victory.

Ron wanted to go down to the dressing room and get in on the jubilation but he sensed it was not his place, at this time. Instead he quietly celebrated with Walt Fisher and Ken Butler.

On the way home he clicked on the car radio and got a completely different read on the game courtesy of 'Gil the Thrill' Baines. The caller was bubbling with the fact that the Leafs had beaten Ottawa. The Thrill had a different spin on it, however.

"Wait a minute—are you going to sit there and tell me what a great start this is to the season after witnessing a piece of crap like that? Were we watching the same game? The referee HANDED them the victory on a silver platter!" The Thrill screamed.

The caller tried to get a word in. "But they beat a good team. They scored four goals on one of the best defenses in the NHL—"

"Sir, they scored three, and Scott Aberdeen and his Seeing Eye dog gave them the other one. He was the only person in the building—hell in all of CANADA, that didn't see the foot in the crease. They called the damn penalty all during the pre-season. Every goal was a damned video replay! Soon they'll have to call it *Blockbuster Night in Canada!* But like it or hate it, it is the rule. And the only and I mean only reason they got the damned two points tonight was because the referee was too blind to see it. When are you people going to get it? This team is *never* going to win a Stanley Cup with the line-up they have...with the stupid management group they have. End of story. We go to David somewhere in Etobicoke." The Thrill was on a roll.

"Yeah Gil, I agree with what you said about the goal, Man!"

"Ahhh, at long last an honest man,"

"Yeah, but you have to agree Gil, that the Leafs did play a good sixty minutes with a playoff quality team!" The Thrill was not thrilled with this caller either.

"Now let's get something straight before we peel each-others' bananas—the Senators may be light years above the Leafs in talent, they are not, the last time I looked, the Stanley Cup Champions! And what you saw tonight was another example of a team doing so much holding, and hooking, and interference, and whatever the hell else you call that 'trap crap", that no referee, especially not the visually-challenged Scott Aberdeen is going to call everything! And do you think for a moment that the Leafs are going to get away with this *nonsense* for an entire season? And get two points out of it each time? Well my friend you better use that phone of yours to book a room in the Clarke Institute, because it ain't gonna happen! We'll take a break and take more of your calls—hopefully from some of you who actually have an idea of what you're talking about!"

Ron turned off the radio.

It was going to take more than an opening night victory against Ottawa to convince the media, especially the critics like Gil 'the thrill' Baines that this team could win games by something other than accident.

The Leafs next game was against Florida. The opposition was not exactly the Stanley Cup champions either. When it came right down to comparisons, the Panthers were just the kind of team that the Leafs were even with on the mediocrity scale when it came to the evaluation of talent. And this was the kind of winnable game that the Leafs would usually find a way to lose, especially at home.

Spencer Smith was in the habit of not naming his starting goaltender until after the morning skate. His choice had less to do with how the goalie performed in that days practice however and more to do with the coach's gut feeling for that particular opponent. He sometimes would considered the goalie's record against the individual team, and go with who had success in the past—or sometimes on a whim pick whoever he thought would do the job that night. On this particular occasion he chose Lars Rogers for no particular reason. He looked like a genius.

The Panthers were in a sleepwalking mood, despite the fact that this was their season opener. With all the talk of the Florida team changing ownership, perhaps the players were distracted.

Whatever the reason it was a surprisingly easy two points for the Leafs—a 3-0 shutout, which saw Lars Rogers have to make only 25 saves, though there were fewer than a half-dozen real scoring opportunities.

On his way home from the game Ron Bailey again tuned in to hear Gil the Thrill Baines' take on things. And not surprisingly, nothing had changed.

"IT'S THE FLORIDA PANTHERS FOR CRYING OUT LOUD!" he screamed at a caller who made the mistake of asking what the Thrill thought of the Leafs now. As he switched to the next caller, the Thrill paused to deliver a diatribe.

"I can understand how this city is starving for a winner, how the fans in this town would love *nothing more* than a team that is at least competitive. But two wins do not a winning streak make. Let's be real here."

Ron Bailey had to agree with one part of the thrill's philosophy. He agreed that consecutive victories hardly constituted a streak. And he reluctantly had to admit that Florida was not the kind of team that you could really be proud about beating, though in today's NHL the parity was becoming a parody of competition, as the majority of teams were at a common level of mediocrity as the thrill so scathingly complained.

The team continued to face eastern conference opponents with their first road game against the Bruins in Boston. Most of the media horde expected Spencer Smith to continue with Lars Rogers in goal, as he was fresh off a shutout. But in the kind of move that fuelled the second guessers in every sports bar, shipping dock and job site from Mississauga to Oshawa, he didn't. The coach nominated John Dennis to start in Boston.

"I have a feeling about this one," He told Ron Bailey as he dropped by the morning skate.

Ron accompanied the club on this trip only because it was to New England—he simply couldn't get enough of the area. It was among the most popular spots on road trips with Ron Bailey, even more so when they occured in the fall. He loved to travel in the area when it came time to look at high school prospects. There were so many little towns in Massachusetts, Rhode Island and Connecticut that had great bed and breakfasts, home style bakeries or quaint antique shops that he hated to leave the area and return home.

Ron liked Boston, but it was the surrounding area that really captured his heart. He really missed the trips to Connecticut now that the Whalers were gone.

On the bus from the hotel to the arena, Chuck Andrew agreed, "It's a damn shame. I played in Hartford for four years and the fans always supported us—we made only the playoffs twice, but they still loved the game. Now, well this team has been shitty for so long—I can't see how moving them is the answer."

The truth was that the Bruins-Whalers rivalry never developed the way it should have, but that was mostly due to poor management decisions by the Whalers that kept them an un-competitive team for the most part.

Ken Butler summed up the demise of the Whalers in one sentence. "The biggest mistake they ever made (from a public relations viewpoint and from a hockey viewpoint) was when they traded Ron Francis." He decreed. "That move took out the fans and cut the heart and soul out of the team all at once. And they've never recovered."

The game in Boston would be the first of many tests for the power play and penalty killing which had not been particularly sharp. Before the game the team was uncharacteristically loose. To a man, they seemed genuinely pleased to be playing away from Maple Leaf Gardens, though the start of this season did not constitute their typical 'home ice disadvantage' as Floyd Shoniker referred to it. Between the relentless criticism that the players took from the fans when the club was losing and the cheering that would erupt for players from the Toronto area on the opposing team, the club often felt like it was playing in an enemy building. Coupled with this was the fact that Toronto, hockey town that it was, also was home to large groups of fans of every other team in the league, and could be counted on for huge numbers in attendance that would cheer for the opposition. This was a sharp contrast, especially to American rinks where the home team was backed, no matter how bad they were.

The team's relief at being away from the Gardens scrutiny defined the game. The Leafs made an aggressive start to the game, pouncing on loose pucks, chasing down errant passes to prevent offside and icing calls, hustling because the shifts were kept short, and following the puck carrier whenever he tried to take a break behind the net. Before the first period was five minutes old Serge Moit, back in the line-up after his injury sojourn, had intercepted a pass and fired a wrist shot past a surpassed Tim Thomas in the Boston net. The Leafs increased their lead when Benoit Marlet took the pass from Dale McCaine and drew Thomas too far out of the net before stuffing the puck behind him on the backhand. It got worse from there for Boston. All this Leaf team needed was some confidence furled by a two-goal lead.

Spencer Smith was practically foaming at the mouth with enthusiasm as they made it 3-0 when Joel Kent un-wrapped a wrist shot that he had seemingly been saving since last season, and lifted a shot over Thomas' shoulder that the goalie never really saw.

The bizarre result was that the club earned back-to-back shutouts for the first time in twelve years.

Ron Bailey made a rare visit to the dressing room after the game, primarily to find out where the coaching staff planned to go for a drink after the game. He ventured down to ice level just after the rink had emptied. He found Spencer Smith leaning against the open doorway of the dressing room, answering questions for a *Hockey News* reporter while scraping his back against the doorjamb in an attempt to satisfy a spot that itched. The way he twisted his huge frame writhed made him look like a bear rubbing its back on a tree after hibernation. The toothy grin on his face may have been from finding the itch, but it was just as likely from the fact that the club had stretched its record to 3-0 for the first time in five years. And the way the players saw it, they could shoot for 4-0 because the next game was on the road as well.

The coaching staff, Smith, Ridley and Newton, and Ron agreed to get together for a nightcap. Spencer Smith decided on the '*Skylight Lounge*' at the Prudential Building, primarily because it was quiet, but also because it featured good jazz. Ron would have liked to check out the '*Bull and Finch*', but he told himself no. Each time he returned there he was more disappointed to find that it had become more of a tourist stop than the time before. Whatever ambiance it had once had, as the 'Cheers' stand in was now dead and buried like the TV show itself.

At the '*Skylight Lounge*' Spencer Smith could barely contain his euphoria. "This is like a dream!" he admitted, as he took a huge swallow of his Captain Morgan Dark Rum and Coke.

"I mean I know it's only the third game, but there's a kind of presence on the bench—I can't really describe it—only I can *feel* it!"

Ron felt a shiver, as if the window beside him had suddenly opened. Just exactly what was the coach referring to?

"I mean, why all of a sudden?" Spencer Smith asked.

Brian Ridley put down his beer long enough to ask, "What do you mean?"

"We've got practically the same god dam roster as last year, but they're playing like all of a sudden they're doing what I tell them to!"

Ralph Newton almost passed his entire mouthful of soda water through his nose at this suggestion.

Ron Bailey tried to get more information from the coach. "So, you feel like these guys are playing above their heads?" he asked.

The coach began to chew on his swizzle stick. "More like they're playing above the ozome layer," he answered.

"*Ozone* layer" Ron added automatically. He tried not to remember that he had heard that Spencer Smith didn't complete the ninth grade before beginning his hockey career.

"Like way up there!" the coach boomed, "we've had good starts before. We went 10 and 0 three years ago, remember, and finished only eight games over five hundred. So *without* that great start we would have been *below* five hundred for the entire year."

The coach was right, but no one was foolish enough to compare this team to the one that was one bad call away from going to the Stanley Cup final.

"I can't account for it," Spencer Smith continued. "Ask Newt here—he says it's because we cut out the cancer," The coach said, referring to the trading of the unpopular Vaclav Artis.

"I think it's more than that," Ralph Newton added "But it may be part of the answer."

Ron decided to fish for his own catch. "You said you were surprised because we're doing it with much the same bunch as last year—but what about the new guys—Sawchuck, West, and McCaine?"

Spencer Smith laughed the great belly laugh of his that could rattle glass. "I's wondering when you'd get around to tryin' to grab some credit for it Ronnie," He laughed, as did the other coaches, as if on cue.

Ron probably blushed, but in the darkened bar no one noticed. "I was only asking if they were making a contribution," he said, defending himself.

The coach grinned, helplessly. "As I said before, some of the young guys are putting pressure on the old guys to play up to their game. I said that at the end of last year—you remember me tryin to tell that to Fisher—that I didn't think we needed a wholesale change. We have a good core, but sometimes it takes a young horse pushing for an old one to start moving."

"So if the core was as good as you say," Ron prompted, "Why did the team rank so badly last year?"

"I wish I had the answer to that kid," the coach answered as he gulped his rum.

A 'Le Mans' start

The previous season was beginning to become thought of as a bad dream. In their next game, also on the road, the Leafs walked into the Molson Centre and promptly stole a 2-0 win from the Canadiens.

Toronto scored a second period power play goal, and it held up until the third. In the dying minutes the Habs pulled Jose Theodore, and with the extra attacker surrendered an empty netter courtesy of David Burks. The team came home to a media hug so tight that the players could hardly breathe.

Everyone in the media, with the exception of Gil the thrill Baines, was awarding the Stanley Cup to the Leafs in October, the same way they used to give the Grey Cup to the Argos in June. And the feeling got stronger, as the Leafs eked out a 1-1 tie with Los Angeles on their return home.

"The Leafs find themselves at the lofty heights at the top of the league, behind only the Vancouver Canucks who are a perfect 5 and 0" wrote Billy Sinfield in his Sin Bin column

"The result can only be vertigo for the Leafs who will likely find the heights dizzying at the top of the league. By Christmas, or even American Thanksgiving they should see themselves nearer their familiar roost in the league ground floor, if not the cellar" He continued. Others in the media were not so kind. Even play-by-play man Jim Gerber saw the realism in it.

"The feeling around Maple Leaf Gardens is 'Let's enjoy this little upswing while we can, because we have all seen too many indications that this hockey club cannot continue a stretch like this for any length of time,'" He quietly professed on his pre-game broadcast before the Leafs home date with the Carolina Hurricanes.

Gil the thrill was predictably less in agreement as he teed up the pre-game show on the rival CHIL radio, the non-broadcast rights station.

"For all of you out here who are lining up Bay Street for the ticker tape parade I submit this to you; tonight the Leafs will actually play a team that has a chance—mind you not a lead pipe cinch chance, to actually challenge for the Stanley Cup. That, my friends, is something this Leaf team is light years away from claiming, and I suspect that the result at Maple Leaf Gardens tonight will reflect that."

What the game did reflect was that this Leaf team was at least respectable. The Hurricanes were clearly the better team all night as far as controlling the play was concerned. Controlling the outcome of the game was another matter. The score at the end of the first period actually favoured Toronto by 1-0, on a power play goal that came as a result of a disputed high sticking major to Cory Stillman.

The Leafs were outplayed and out-shot. Martin Gerber was something less than his spectacular self while John Dennis stopped everything but the wind. The Hurricanes were visibly frustrated by their inability to get at least one past Dennis, with a games worth of shots in the second. In the third, the dam began to break when Carolina got an early goal when Terry Oddy attempted a clearing pass that Dave Moore turned his back on. Dennis barely had time to position himself before the puck was in the net. The crowd descended on Oddy like a curtain going down on a Broadway opening night flop. And to make matters worse he was called for hooking later in the period when beaten to the puck, just after the Leafs had restored their one goal lead. Of course the Hurricanes scored on the power play to tie it. If the fans were angry at Oddy before, they were ready to lynch him now. Spencer Smith mercifully moved him to the end of the defensive rotation, and did not send Oddy out for the five-minute overtime that settled nothing.

The Leafs kept their unbeaten string intact, but it was clear that they had only dodged a bullet.

After the game Spencer Smith would not acknowledge the media questions targeted at him regarding Terry Oddy. "What are you trying to get me to say? That he cost us the game? Hell, we wouldn't be in the damn game unless John Dennis does his magic act! Go ahead and write what you want about Oddy, but the guy knows how to play defense. He didn't win a Norris trophy with the Flyers by being stupid!"

That the coach backed his veterans was admirable. But it was one of the things that irked his critics the most. Gil 'the thrill' Baines was one of them. He purposely delayed the phone-in segment of his post-game show until the excitement of the Leafs moral victory had subsided. And when the first callers praised the team for its credible showing against the Hurricanes, the 'Thrill' went to work.

"Let me get this straight," he told the caller, "you are *ecstatic* because this team was out shot a gazillion to one, because they played the entire game in their end of the rink—at home I might add, and to cap off this momentous occasion, blew a lead in the third? Well, I agree—let's get out the Dom Perignon and get shit faced—we go to Larry in his car on the 401!"

"Gil, I agree when you put it that way," the caller began, "but there are some positives Leaf fans can get from this. The club still hasn't lost a game yet. The defense hasn't given up more than two goals in a game since opening night, and one of the big question marks going into this season was whether or not John Dennis was going to be able to return to the form he showed a few years ago when he almost single-handedly carried this team to a berth in the Stanley Cup semi-finals."

"Larry, I think you're missing the point. Yes, the guy stopped everything but the exit sign, but the play in their own end was putrid. And if that stench continues, how may more points can they expect to steal, even *with* a hot goaltender. And while we're on the subject, what about scoring? This team is third from the bottom in goal *scoring!* And how many points do you think *that* is going to get them?"

As usual the 'Thrill' was not thrilled with the team's performance. As Ken Butler explained it 'He is not simply content with criticizing the team but revels in ridiculing the organization. While I can sympathize with the frustration of fans I cannot let our players be held accountable for the mistakes of the past.'

Still, Gil 'the thrill' considered himself to be the barometer of the feelings of the real hockey fans in Toronto, not simply those who supported the team win or lose. His argument though was beginning to lose water as the club was actually showing signs of respectability. The talk in office coffee rooms was about how the Leafs were doing for a change, and not about what was wrong with them.

And the talk in the dressing room was more about what was going right on the ice rather than what needed to be changed. And just when it appeared that Gil 'the thrill' was no longer going to have an audience for his whining, in came the New York Rangers to fix everything.

The Leafs had always had great difficulty beating this club, no matter who was coaching it or who the players were. Over the last couple of seasons the Rangers were the team with the best record against Toronto, including seven straight wins. And try as he might, Spencer Smith could not get his troops to muster even a mild hate for these guys. The Rangers had done little over the years to piss off the Leafs; no cheap hits, mouthy media quotes or high scoring embarrassments. It seemed as if the Leafs always caught New York at home when the Rangers were rested but the Leafs had been on the road the night before. And the result was usually a two goal uneventful loss.

This night however was not uneventful. For the first time this season the Leafs played a first period so good that it appeared it would be unnecessary to play the other two. The score was 3-0 after twenty minutes, and New York had neither registered a hit or a scoring chance, while Toronto scored one goal of each variety; even-strength, power play and short-handed. So dominant were the Leafs that, as the coach said in his post-game press conference.

"They felt they'd already done a days' work, so they decided that it was okay to go home early."

The Rangers on the other hand sensed this, and proceeded to get goals from three different defensemen in the second and tied it up. Their third goal was so soft that it appeared to awaken John Dennis as he stumbled in the goal crease as the puck almost fell into the net. At this point Spence Smith had no choice but to replace Dennis with Lars Rogers. The media on press row were clicking their keyboards at ward speed. To them it appeared as if it was 'Midnight for Cinderella' as Billy Sinfield stated in his column the next day.

In the third the Leafs actually went ahead 4-3 on a disputed goal that required the dreaded video replay, which failed to show conclusively whether or not Chuck Andrew's skate was in the crease. The goal stood, and it appeared as if Toronto was about to register another win when, with the goalie pulled the Rangers tied it with 3.6 seconds left when Terry Oddy of all people, left Jaromir Jagr alone at the side of the net. It took the sniper something less than 3.6 milliseconds to fire a shot past the shocked Lars Rogers and force overtime.

Spencer Smith had nothing to say to the guys as he stood behind them while the brief intermission ticked down. The virulent shades of red that his face had become said it all.

"Look at Smith!" Neil Powers called to a rival columnist as he watched from the press box "His head looks like the bottom of a thermometer."

When the period began, the Leafs sent out their checking line of Lou Zanardo, Lorne Graham and Randy Rettig. The Rangers countered with Jagr, Nylander and Rucinsky, their best scoring unit. The fans probably knew what the likely outcome was but they stayed to witness it anyway. Before there was time for Spencer Smith to change lines the Rangers had the Leafs bottled up in their end and when Jagr's rebound made it all the way to the point, Tom Poti drilled a low shot past Rogers that the goalie never even saw. The streak was over, and in the minds of those like Gil the thrill Baines, the season had finally begun for the Toronto Maple Leafs. The dream as they say, was over.

The team got a much-needed break in the next few days after having played four games in seven nights. Spencer Smith hoped it was only fatigue that had cost them victory in their last game. He sensed that, and gave the club the next day off. He was an unorthodox coach in many ways but the way he practised the team was perhaps his biggest departure from the norm. He didn't believe in hard practices, but rather preferred to work on tactics and special teams. He feared injuries, and didn't want to risk them for something as meaningless as a scrimmage.

"If they practice what I want them too, and listen to me when I talk, then I don't care how hard they work in practice. But when the game starts I don't want any excuses for not giving me everything they have until the bell goes," Spencer Smith decreed.

The veterans praised the coach for this routine. Floyd Shoniker, who had played for Smith for seven years, felt that it had prolonged his career by at least three years.

"The day after a game I am so sore," he once told Ron Bailey, "that it's all I can do to get up and have a crap. If it wasn't for Spence I may not have the energy to be here today."

"God...I love Florida!"

Though it was only the first week of November the players were actually getting anxious to get out on the road, though this was usually felt more by the younger players. And the destination was the most desired of the whole schedule; back to back games in Florida.

"Why the hell can't it be in January though?" Frank Maleki whined as several of the players gathered at the Pearson Airport departure lounge coffee shop.

Chuck Andrew didn't care about what time of year it was—to him Florida meant only one thing. "Boca Za!" he told Ron Bailey.

"Boca what?" Ron asked.

Frank Maleki rubbed his hands together, and licked his lips almost up to his moustache.

"I can taste it now," he slobbered.

Ron had to know. "What is 'Boca Za'?"

Chuck Andrew stared off into space. "Only the best pizza in the Eastern Hemisphere, East Coast, East whatever—you haven't lived until you've had Boca pizza."

Ron had to wait until the team was in Florida, actually Boca Raton, until he could say that he had lived, according to Chuck Andrew. But first there was a little matter of a game to be played with the Florida Panthers in Miami.

The Leafs were somewhat refreshed from their light work schedule over the past couple of days and they showed more spark in the first period of a road game than usual. Overall though, the game was a resounding bore, like many others in the early part of a season that was deemed to be too long, even by the most avid hockey fans. The final score was 1-1, and even *that* total flattered the numbers.

The tropical distraction of Florida proved to be too much for many teams and the Leafs were no exception, though they did earn a point. After the game the team was scheduled to remain in the area and catch a mid-morning flight to Tampa. The players took advantage of this and chartered a fleet of stretch limousines to take them to the famous 'Boca Za.' The excursion had been organized by Messrs. Maleki and Andrew, and although the entire team was invited only a select group, mostly veterans were partaking.

"So how did you hear about this place?" Ron Bailey asked as the limo pulled away from the Miami Sports Arena for the forty-five minute drive north.

Before Ron could get anyone to answer he was cautioned to remain quiet by Floyd Shoniker. Four of the players in the car, the captain, Chuck Andrew, David Burks, Joel Kent and Ron watched as John Hill attempted to pop open the can of Busch Beer that was handed to him. As he pulled on the tab the entire contents shot straight into his face and sprayed all over his Tommy Hilfiger sweater.

"Andrew!" he screamed, as he tried in vain to contain the spill, and tried even harder to salvage some of the remaining beer by sucking on his sweater.

As it turned out, John Hill was targeted because he was a 'non-believer' as Frank Maleki put it. Hill was not with the Leafs last season, and therefore was not apprised of the ritual of 'Boca Za.'

Ron Bailey too was classified as a heathen, for he had never tasted the pizza of the gods either, as Chuck Andrew referred to it. As the limo pulled to a halt Ron Bailey was at last able to get a glimpse of the Mecca of the pizza world according to Frank Maleki. Ron stepped out of the glistening white limo onto the pavement of a grungy strip mall, where nestled between the '60 Minute Cleaners' and the 'Paint City' discount decorating store stood a straw hut facade that looked like something out of *Gilligan's Island*.

And crowning this monument was a faded red neon sign that was supposed to read 'Boca pizza' but because the P, I and first Z in the word pizza were burned out, it read simply, 'Boca za'

As they entered the darkened restaurant Ron searched for some sign that the place was worthy of the praise that the players had heaped on it. His initial reaction was that he was the butt of some elaborate practical joke. But as Frank Maleki organized a bunch of smaller tables to be pushed together to form a grouping with all of the determination of a settler making a circle of covered wagons he realized that this was for real.

"We'll start with some of them Brush-etta things," he ordered. Ron was impressed. He had never seen Frank Maleki start a meal by ordering any food before he ordered a beer.

"And a round of draft...better drop a couple of jugs," Mike McKenna added.

"So how did you guys discover this place anyway?" Ron asked as the waitress handed out some menus. Ron noticed that the players largely ignored them, because they already knew what they wanted.

"It's a great story Ronnie," Joel Kent began.

"We had a game here the first year Florida was in the league. Mikey's outlaws have a winter place just north of here and a bunch of us were goin up for a visit. Anyway, the rental car gets a flat about a block from here, and after we changed the tire Burks starts whinin that he's gotta eat or else his ulcer's gonna give him trouble. So we asked a guy in the gas station where was a good place to eat?"

"And so he sent you here," Ron assumed, as he took a glass of the draft that John Hill had poured for him.

"Nope," Joel Kent continued. "He sent us to a burger joint—*The Burger Meister* it was called—anyway we pull up to the place just as two guys come running out of the place, and they fire a round into the front window. So we're sitting there, not moving, watching all of this like it's that show *Cops* or whatever, and a cruiser pulls up. So the two guys take a shot at the cruiser, and the cruiser fires back. Well, by this time we're all on the floor of the rental, and the cops chase the guys when they peel out of the parking lot. So by this time a few cruisers show up, and when Mikey lifts his head and takes a peek out the window he's looking down the barrel of this magnum—"

Mike McKenna added, "I swear that when I saw that barrel pointing me in the beak, it looked as big around as a donut!"

Kent continued the story. "Anyway, they get us out of the car, and don't believe us right away when we say who were are, until this one cop gets us to say 'house' and 'boot' and 'have', and after a few of us do, he says 'Okay, these here are Canadians all right.'"

Ron had to know—how did this lead to the Boca Za?

"The cops were due for their code-7 or whatever they call it, and they invited us here. But the best part of the story is—"

But before Joel Kent could finish, the Bruscetta came. Ron was anxious to see a menu after he tasted the lightly toasted bread covered in mildly cooked tomatoes simmered in olive oil and onion. If the pizza was *half* as good as this, he thought, it would be worthwhile.

"Okay, we have a virgin Za'er here tonight!" Frank Maleki announced to the table as he raised his glass of draft. "We are going to break with tradition and let him sample the best."

Joel Kent pretended to be aghast. "No! You mean he gets to experience the 'Fifth Wonder of the World'?"

"He does," the defenseman concluded.

"Feel honoured, Ronnie," David Burks added, "Not everyone gets to taste the best they have to offer their first time here."

"The 'fifth' is like nothing you've ever had. We didn't get to the fifth until we got to be a second or third timer! How does that make you feel?"

Ron felt honoured. In fact he still felt somewhat honoured even to be included in such a typically players-only outing. He wondered if the meeting that took place back in training camp when

Floyd Shoniker approached him about the five guys from the Ice Gators had changed the player's mind about him. Conversely, he also wondered if they still viewed him with some suspicion. If the latter were true, then why was he invited to tag along tonight?

When the pizza came his attention turned to it. The fifth was so named because it was comprised of five kinds of cheese, and it was the most delectable recipe imaginable for a pizza lover who craved extra cheese.

"It's the ultimate! Just taste it!" commanded Frank Maleki, "Mozzarella, Parmesan, White Cheddar, Monterey Jack, and Swiss."

Ron could not argue. It was the best pizza he had ever tasted. It was that simple. For years others gave him grief when he requested extra cheese on his pizza because non-cheese junkies thought it made the pie too gooey. But despite the presence of five cheeses, it was a perfect consistency.

"The secret," Frank Maleki professed, "is in the proportion of them. It has to be just right, and it is!"

"And even better is the way they deal with you freaks that like anchovies," Floyd Shoniker added. "They put them on the side."

And as Ron had long professed, pizza without anchovies was like beer without a head, a hot dog without the mustard, or popcorn without the butter; they simply belonged together.

"I have to tell you Floyd," Ron began, as the beer was beginning to have its effect on him, "That the only reason that God created anchovies was so that we could have them on pizza. I mean, what else are they good for?"

Floyd Shoniker could not answer, but he could also not care. He didn't like anchovies, and for him that was the end of the story.

As the beer began to flow more freely, and the slices of pizza began to disappear, Ron seemed to be more at ease with the situation. He wasn't one of the players, but they were treating him like he was one of their own. At one point, Chuck Andrew leaned over to him and asked "Ronnie, I know I probably shouldn't be asking you this, but just how much do you *really* have to do with the trades?"

The question took Ron by surprise. Up until then the conversation centred on everything *but* hockey, but now he was faced with a serious question. His honesty got the better of him.

"I guess I have a little bit of input—not as much as you might think though." His response did nothing but pique the players' curiosity.

"Really—you mean to tell me," Chuck Andrew slurred. "That they don't even ask your opinion if say, well like *me* for instance, if tomorrow Dallas came calling for a scorer, and Ken Butler says, 'Ronnie, I think we can get Arnott for Andrew, whattya think?' He's not gonna ask you?"

"If Dallas wanted a scorer Andy, why the hell would they ask for *you*?" John Hill added.

The table erupted in laughter. Hill was trying to get even for the loaded can of Busch. Andrew though stayed focused, despite the oncoming intoxication. "What would you say?"

Ron raised his eyebrows momentarily and sighed. "I get asked for my input, but it doesn't quite work *that* way, at least not in our organization. We only discuss trades as a group. Ken Butler and Walt Fisher have the final say. I mean, I get asked about players on other teams or in junior all the time. When it comes to keeping a file on our own players—well, I keep the files but the coaches are the ones who really do all of the paper work."

The topic was beginning to gain interest from the others. John Hill had suddenly lost his sense of humour. "You mean they have files on all of us? What the hell kind of things do they say about us?" he demanded.

The blank expressions on the other player's faces told Ron that he had better tread carefully. "It's not like that. Nobody's keeping a file about you that *says* anything about you! They're just statistical files, about goals scored at even strength, points scored on the power play, plus-minus, that kind of stuff."

John Hill was clearly not satisfied with the answer. "Why the hell do they have to keep a file on that? It's all in the paper everyday—or they can just pick up a copy of *the Hockey News* and get it!"

"You know Butler," David Burks interrupted, "he's too cheap to spring for a copy of the *Hockey News*."

There was some laughter at this, but there was also some lingering doubt in the mind of John Hill, and even one or two of the others. Floyd Shoniker sensed this, and leader that he was he stepped in. "Hill—you've got nothing to worry about other than what you do on the ice. Nobody does—every teams' the same."

John Hill was not as understanding. "That's easy for *you* to say Shonny. You've never been traded."

The captain did not get his back up easily, even when challenged. Joel Kent had to put his two cents worth in. "Hilly, there's no sense worrying about it! It's part of the game. I've been traded twice. Most times you see it coming but not always. Don't go fishing with Ronnie here for it. If you've read it in the paper then most likely it's gonna happen. If not, well it's probably nothin to lose sleep over. Anyway, today it's more often about contracts than it is about the player, ain't that right Ronnie?"

Ron knew that Joel Kent had a point. At after this many beers the truth was the most likely thing to come out of his mouth. "Well—" he waffled.

"I mean take Artis," Kent continued.

"Yeah, if you could find somebody to take him!" Mike McKenna interrupted.

"The little asshole!" Chuck Andrew added.

Joel Kent was not fazed by the interruption. "The reason it took so long to deal him was because of his contract. Not many teams could afford him. They *all* wanted to have the little bastard, but why is anybody's guess considering what a selfish little—"

207

"You're right!" Ron shouted, not realizing that he was shouting. "He was tough to deal, I mean we wanted to. We were under a lot of pressure to get something good in return, but we were limited in where we could deal him because of his contract."

"Another advantage of making a good buck!" Mike McKenna concluded.

There was silence for a second, and then Floyd Shoniker added, "Until they don't want you anymore, or until you can't cut it. Then the *contract* is the big road block all of a sudden."

Chuck Andrew almost slammed his empty beer glass on the table. "What the hell do you mean by that?"

"I mean when your contract is up, or they decide to move you, if you're commanding a good buck, you're not so attractive to a lot of teams. The budgets are getting tighter—teams are not so willing to eat a part of a guy's contract when they trade him."

These words could easily have come from Ron Bailey's mouth, because he knew them to be true. He did not want to rock the boat however. Better to let the captain steer the ship. He was the one the players respected, not Ron.

"Is that really the way it is Ronnie?" John Hill demanded.

"Pretty much," he responded, staring into the empty glass as he answered. Ron's words continued to ring in the air of the quiet that followed. The sound of a vacuum cleaner being turned on by one of the waitresses cleaning up a spill finally broke the silence.

For Frank Maleki all of this shoptalk had been too much. His parade was being rained on.

"Well never mind all of this horseshit—let's get some paper cups and see some peelers!"

The cheque came and each of the players dug deep in their pockets and a pile of cash was quickly deposited on the table.

"Never mind Ronnie," Mike McKenna ordered him. "You're money's no good here."

Ron was alarmed at first, until Floyd Shoniker explained, "Our treat, just for being a good sport."

As they were leaving, the players all stopped by the cash register. David Burks grabbed Ron by the arm to prevent him from going out the door yet.

"Have to get some paper cups first," he said.

Ron was confused. "Paper cups—what for?" Joel Kent filled him in.

"Yeah, Ronnie, I didn't get to finish my story from before. When we came here the first time, when the cops invited us here, we paid their bill, to thank them. Anyway, on the way out, the older cop says to the owner, 'we'll have some paper cups, and we don't know what they mean. Well Marco, the owner gets out some paper cups from behind the bar, and he fills them with draft! And he hands two of them to the cops, and away they go back on duty! They're driving around back on duty with these paper cups full of beer!"

And the tradition continued. The owner, Marco, thanked the players for coming and produced a paper cup of draft for each one of them as they left.

"God, I love Florida!" John Hill proclaimed. Hill avowed his love the next night in Tampa by scoring the Leafs only goal in a 1-1 snore fest in the building they called the 'Thunderdome'. The only curiosity about the game was that Leafs had earned their first point against a defending cup champion in three seasons.

On the road again

The road trip continued in New York, where the team was anxious to avenge its only loss so far, to their conference rival. Spencer Smith stressed the importance of a victory over the Rangers, even at this early stage of the season.

"If we meet them in the playoffs it's gonna be the season record that gives them the confidence going in. We have to show them that we can beat them. Now's the time to stick it to them, in their own building just like they did it to us," the coach said.

The game was monumental for more than that. At the 5:05 mark of the second period, NHL history was made, Ron Bailey would recall later. For the first time in league history, a player who had been dead for thirty-six years scored a goal—his *first* NHL goal at that. Dale McCaine accomplished the feat—even if he and Ron were the only ones who knew the significance. And what a goal it was, coming just after the Rangers had killed a five minute major when Darius Kasparitis high-sticked David Burks.

With the Rangers pumped up by their excellent penalty killing, which limited the Leafs to just two shots in the five-minute span, McCaine took the wind out of their sails by scoring the game's first goal. He stole the puck from inside of centre and raced in on Henrik Lundqvist with only one defenseman to beat. And beat him he did with a head fake, and then twisting his body the other way. The defenseman tried to wrap his stick around the small Leaf forward but McCaine was too quick. He darted in on Lundqvist and raised a wrist shot to the top of the goalie's stick side that Lundqvist thought he had, but the red light signalled otherwise.

In the jubilation, McCaine forgot to retrieve the puck. David Burks, still with the freshly gashed face courtesy of the high stick collected the puck, and patted the kid on the helmet as he handed it to him.

"Go give it to Nev—he'll keep it for you!" Floyd Shoniker ordered.

With the momentum shifted the Leafs pressed ahead. Whether it was the sudden move into the limelight by a rookie, or some other motivation, the Leaf captain decided he must take control of the game himself. And just after the Rangers had tied the score he did. Shoniker scored his first goal on a power play to put the Leafs up by one. And when New York scored again on a shot by Jaromir Jagr that only he could take, Shoniker recorded his second to put the Leafs up by one again, just before the second period ended.

The Rangers were not to be outdone, however as shortly after the teams returned to the ice for the third Michael Nylander tied it once again. And Shoniker pulled up his socks, gritted his teeth and told his young winger, Benoit Marlet, to 'Find him in front of the net again.'

And find him the kid did. With less than three minutes left in regulation Marlet racked up his third assist as he fed Shoniker in the slot, where he was wearing the stick of the Ranger defender around his neck. Despite that he turned around quickly and fed the puck under Lundqvist's pads as the crosscheck met with his face. Shoniker did not even flinch, even as the bruise began to develop. Instead he took the congratulation offered to him by Marlet and Chuck Andrew and the rest of his teammates that poured off of the bench to congratulate him. Madison Square Garden was suddenly subdued, and some fans even began to file for the exit. The game was not over however. Just minutes later the Leafs were caught on a much-needed line change as some of their wheezing elder statesmen were heading to the bench. Martin Straka sensed an opportunity and quickly orchestrated a two-on-one that Terry Oddy couldn't even dream of breaking up. The defenseman fell down while Straka faked a shot and fired it right at the head of John Dennis who reached up and snagged the puck at an almost impossible angle.

The victory was preserved, when Spencer Smith sent his checking unit out for the last two minutes of the game, and the Rangers rarely saw the puck again; 4-3 was the final, another complete team victory—the kind that put a smile on even old sourpuss Spencer Smith's face.

On the bus to Long Island the coach got up to answer the call of nature and was stuck waiting in line for the head behind Ron Bailey.

"I've never seen you smile this much coach...at least not without Captain Morgans's help."

The coach showed even more teeth, though most of them were false, a badge of courage of his eighteen years in the league.

"Ten games Ronnie and we're 5-1-4. Even in my wildest dreams I didn't expect it. You remember that I told everyone who'd listen that this team was *capable* of it, mind you, I never thought I'd see it!"

Ron checked the door to see if the 'OCCUPIED' sign had moved to 'VACANT' yet but it had not. His bladder was telling him that the sign better move soon.

"I've seen every game so far, and I don't see the same team that finished off last year, but I see mostly the same guys. What is it coach?"

"I'd be lyin to ya if I told you I knew! Like I said in Boston, it's un-explainable, if that's a word. I honestly don't know, and what's more I don't care. As long as we keep playing this way, it's gonna be good enough to get us in the playoffs. And that, you remember was what we were tryin for at the start of the season."

"I'm really gonna miss travelling with you guys the next little while," Ron said while still eyeing the bathroom door.

"Whattya mean? You're our good luck charm—ya can't walk out on us now!" the coach quipped.

"Yeah, but I have to start looking at a few other teams, junior teams, college teams—I have to start working on next year," he answered.

"Yep, go out there and draft us a Gretzky, only one that'll be ready in three years."

"Three Years!" Ron gasped, "why not now?"

"Because," the coach drawled, "this team is gonna win the god dam Stanley Cup *this* year—but in three years we'll have to start replacing the vets who are gonna be gone!"

Optimism, Ron recalled was one of Spencer Smith's more endearing qualities.

'Same old Leafs'

After the Leafs took care of the Islanders on "Lon Guy land", Ron Bailey was forced to keep track of the teams next few games via television and the internet. He started his mini-tour of eastern Ontario and western Quebec to see how some of the higher rated prospects were starting off the season. He managed to catch the Leafs demolishing Boston at the Gardens, in a game that Dale McCaine score three times and record two assists.

He picked up the *Montreal Star,* the only English-language daily available where he was in Quebec, and got shivers down his spine as he read the small lead line *'Leafs continue win unbeaten streak as rookie nets hat trick'* How he wished he could have been there. How he wished he could have seen his boss's reaction when Dale McCaine tied a rookie record with five points, and was named the game's first star.

Ron would have loved to have seen the post-game interview, Dale's first, when the Global TV interviewer asked him what it was like playing hockey in Australia. Dale looked as if he had no idea what the guy was talking about, which of course, *he didn't.* The fans were beginning to notice that this rookie was tied with Floyd Shoniker for the team lead in scoring.

The club was experiencing something of an oddity in their schedule, as they were to play their second consecutive Saturday game on the road, this one an *afternoon* game in Ottawa.

It was an oddity for another reason as well; it would be the first game of the season *not* televised in to the Toronto market.

And as a result, 1430 CKFH let everyone know it. And there was considerable interest in such an early season contest, considering that the Raptors regular season had not started and the Argonauts were winding down their first place season and getting ready for the playoffs.

Before the game, Floyd Shoniker sat by himself in the dressing room reading the latest copy of *The Hockey News*.

"Lookit this!" he exclaimed to no one in particular. Because he was the captain, other players tended to listen. "It says here we're fifth in the league in scoring—first in goals against average, first in penalty killing—people are gonna start to notice this team!"

Mike McKenna added from across the room while he taped the knob on a new stick, "And it also says we're sixteenth on the power play."

"Yeah, leave it for a defenseman to point that out!" the captain responded.

On the ice the Senators line of Heatley, Spezza and Alfredsson, exposed that weakness. Each one of them scored, while the Leafs could manage only one even strength goal (and went 0 for seven on the power play) as Ottawa skated to a rather easy 3-1 win.

The club's next game was in Buffalo, where, like Florida, a lot of recent attention had been on whether the club was about to go through an ownership change.

The city was also getting a good 'hate on' for Toronto, as the crowd was usually split 50-50 between Leaf and Sabre supporters.

The Leafs made Buffalo wish the Toronto club had stayed home, as Toronto escaped with a 4-1 victory.

Ron returned home from his scouting trip to find the Leafs in second place in their division, with twenty-one points, only three points behind Ottawa. And the schedule could not have called for a stronger test—the Leafs were about to play the league-leading Red Wings in Detroit.

Ron tuned in to the all-sports radio station, hoping to hear Gil 'the thrill' Baines backtracking now that the Leafs were on a roll, having lost just once in their past seven games. Instead he heard the opposite.

"We have Mike from Mississauga on the line—what's on your mind besides your hat?" the Thrill asked.

"Gil, you've been riding the Leafs pretty good so far this year, but they're showing they're for real, now—don't you think?"

"Mike, let me correct your grammar. I've been riding them very well. And let me tell you, they are showing nothing so far! Yes they've lost only a couple of games, but look at whom they've lost *to*! They've only lost to the Rangers and Ottawa, two of the teams they are going to have to measure themselves against, and while we're at it they only tied two of the *worst* teams in the league, and could only score one goal in the games to boot! Now you tell me that that is a team ready to challenge for the Stanley Cup, and if you do I'll send the narcotics squad from the OPP over to your house to do some search and discovery on whatever it is you are growing and smoking—we go to Dave on a car phone in Thornhill!"

Ron was glad to see that some things never change. The thrill went on to pontificate about how if the Leafs were for real the results of the game with the Red Wings would show just how far this team has to go to be taken seriously. And he predicted that the Leafs would come up on the short end of the stick, and would be lucky to score more than a goal.

The game was played at Joe Louis Arena, and Spencer Smith had already determined which goalie he wanted, courtesy of a coin flip, which determined that Lars Rogers would play in Detroit, so he told John Dennis to stay home and rest, and a call was placed to St. Johns' for a backup. Ron was invited in on the selection, though it really wasn't anything of a decision making process. The only way the goalie called up would get into the game would be if there was an injury to Rogers. Ron was hoping to see Frank Isbister called up, just to see what the 'old veteran' would look like playing against the franchise that he had beaten so regularly. The decision was made to call up rookie Denis Lemieux.

"Isbister has been playing well; they need him for their game Saturday night," Walt Fisher dictated. As usual, the St. Johns' general manager liked to flex his managerial muscles once in a while on occasions such as this.

And so the stage was set—a trip to 'Hockey town' as the banners decking out the city declared. The moniker always bothered Ron, who felt that the word 'USA' should be added. *If* there was a hockey town, then how could Toronto be overlooked, or Montreal, or Windsor NS, or Kingston, for that matter. And try telling the folks in Edmonton or Regina that *they* are not 'Hockey town'.

Nickname or not the Red Wings did play like they were worthy of the title. The game was not even seven minutes old before they had taken a 2-0 lead, and the score was 3-0 at the end of the first period. Spencer Smith unleashed a tirade on his players between periods. Indeed the Leafs seemed afraid of the puck, and the Red Wings. The only hitting going on was the players' sticks against the boards as their frustration mounted.

Midway through the second, Floyd Shoniker scored for Toronto to give them some hope, but it was quickly dashed as the Red Wings scored on a power play. In the third Toronto closed to within 4-2, and Spencer Smith even tried pulling the goalie with just under two minutes remaining, but Brendan Shanahan made that move look ridiculous as he scored into the empty net to ice a 5-2 victory. The ride back to Toronto was a sombre one as players took turns cursing their personal shortcomings and those of the team. And the coach told his assistants that this kind of 'gutless effort' would not be tolerated in front of the home fans.

The next morning, prior to the pre-game skate Spencer Smith decided to call several players into his office, on an individual basis. He chastised Randy Rettig, Lorne Graham and David Moore for their collective lack of effort, and even for their suspected lack of courage. He told them on no uncertain terms that things would be different the next night against New Jersey.

The start of the game was the antithesis of the last, as the Leafs took a quick 2-0 lead courtesy of Joel Kent, who scored the first one, and then set up Chuck Andrew for the second. Early in the second period the game seemed to take a different turn. Kent, who had been the source of the Leafs energy on this evening, became embattled with Cam Janssen along the boards. Words were exchanged, and gloves were dropped and the players and fans alike expected to be treated to an old-fashioned slug fest between an old gunslinger, Kent and the relative new gunslinger, Janssen. Instead they experienced the embarrassment that sometimes goes with fighting in hockey— the knockout punch. Kent was hardly able to position himself before Janssen decked him with a right, and the Leaf player fell to his knees. Janssen seemed stunned by it all, and didn't even attempt to go in for the kill. As the linesmen rushed in to break up what was already over, the fans sensed that something was wrong. In addition the Leafs were assessed a minor on the play; Brian Rafalski found the net on a power play with a screened shot from the point.

New Jersey tied it shortly thereafter when the Leafs, with the man advantage, took an inordinate amount of time trying to get the puck out of their end. Alexander Mogilny made the play for them, as he intercepted a weak clearing pass by Terry Oddy and lifted a rather harmless looking wrist shot over the shoulder of John Dennis, who may have gone down too early on the shot.

The Leafs had not given up entirely, however. Floyd Shoniker tied the score on a beautiful two-on-one. He passed the puck to Benoit Marlet and then using the winger as a screen when he got the return pass, put the puck by Scott Clemmensen to restore the lead.

The second period ended that way, with the Leafs up 3-2. Joel Kent was done for the night; having taken a pretty good cut to the left eye that made it swollen shut. The Devils then seemed to want to go for the kill. The Leafs got a break at the start of the third when Scott Clemmensen was called for a delay of game penalty when he nonchalantly lifted a clearing pass over the glass. On the power play Terry Oddy was deciding whether to pass the puck in or shoot from the point. Brian Gionta of New Jersey made the decision for him, as he picked the pocket of the veteran defenseman and broke in all alone over centre with the gasping Oddy the only Leaf who took up chase. John Dennis was so surprised that he made his move uncharacteristically early. Gionta went to the backhand as the goalie expected, but while Dennis was stacking the pads, Gionta deftly brought the puck to his forehand and slid it under the goalie that was expecting it to be delivered upstairs. The Gardens' crowd was stunned.

Spencer Smith tried to institute some damage control, as he called a time out. The crescendo of boos came down from the crowd as the play ensued, and Spencer Smith bravely sent Terry Oddy out to finish the power play. The defenseman was greeted with suggestions about his personal life, including comments about his sexual preferences. And he was resoundingly booed every time he touched the puck or stepped onto the ice for the rest of the game. Off the record this kind of treatment hurt the sensitive player deeply, but he made no reaction to it and refused to comment on it to the media.

The game was still not out of reach for the Leafs, but just when overtime appeared inevitable they got an apparent break. Mike McKenna was hauled down in front of the Leaf net, and it appeared as if Toronto would go on the power play. The referee failed to raise his arm, however and as McKenna filled the referee's ear with superlatives, Alexander Mogilny filled the Leaf net with the puck. The result was a 4-3 loss that added new meaning to the phrase that fans would repeat to themselves on their way out of the Gardens that night—'Same old Leafs.'

After the game Spencer Smith was outraged when asked about Terry Oddy's miscue.

"There's no call for that kind of crap. That's no way to treat a player, a seven-time all-star in this league! The fans in this town—they have no idea what kind of a quality person they're doing that to."

The coach was almost shaking as he delivered this, and for a man of Spencer Smith's size, it almost seemed to make the ground underneath him shake as well. When one of the beat reporters Commented that Oddy's seven all-star selections happened in Philadelphia, and perhaps the Leaf fans didn't see him as an all-star because the last one occurred four years ago the coach flipped.

"What the hell difference does that make!" he fumed, "The man's played in the Canada Cup, he's played for his country in the Olympics—he's probably going to the hall of fame someday. He deserves to be respected, and not treated with that bullshit!"

Ron Bailey was fortunate enough not to have to see this latest down slide. Before the game with Detroit he had departed for St. Johns' to have his first look at the 'baby Leafs'.

He accompanied Walt Fisher, who was similarly being exposed to the farm club for the first time that season. On the plane, Walt Fisher remarked that if the season continued to progress as it had then there would be little likelihood of any call-ups to the big club, barring injury.

"Al Swartz should be content to work with what he has," the St. Johns' GM commented.

This would be a vivid contrast to the previous year, when no fewer than a dozen players were called up to the big club. Ron was still concerned for the mindset of the ex-Leafs, and asked the players to meet him for coffee after the morning skate the next day.

As the players crossed the street from the arena and headed for the coffee shop, Busher Jackson remarked when he saw the red scripted name on the outside of the building.

"Since when do they name restaurants after rookie defensemen in this league?"

Tim Horton only shrugged his shoulders as they entered the store, but Jackson would not leave it alone.

"And these damn things are everywhere! In Fredericton, in Hamilton—they even have the damn name of them painted on the board in the rink!"

"I don't remember there being this many of them," Horton exclaimed.

As they sat sipping coffee, Ron again asked them if they were content to be there, informing them of what the GM had said regarding their chances of being called up.

"That's okay—and it may change," Charlie Conacher commented.

Ron was startled. "What may change? Are you guys thinking of leaving?" Ron panicked.

"Relax Ronnie!" Conacher said as he placed a big hand on Ron's shoulder. "I mean the need for us to be called up may change. Guys're re always getting hurt in this game."

Ron wondered aloud, "What do you guys know that I don't?"

"Nothing—why do you always ask that—why it's as if you think we could tell fortunes or something," Busher Jackson said.

"We don't mind it down here Ron," Bill Barilko added. "It's just kinda hard to take. What I mean is—well, Charlie here is third in the league in scoring. And Busher, well he's doing okay for himself too. And the kid here doesn't look too far outta place on the blue line. Even old McCool there is settling in—he's even got a couple of shutouts in his last few games."

Ron glanced over at the goalie that was genuinely enjoying the cup of coffee he was sipping. "You're not saying much, Frank. Is everything okay?"

"Just fine!" the goalie exclaimed. "I'm just enjoying the coffee—it's a real treat for me!"

"Yeah," Barilko added, "Ulcers' gonna need a new moniker. He gets to drink coffee now. Since the doc fixed him up with some new meds, why he can even have a beer now and then!"

"Well, you guys are taking it well," Ron, said.

"That's no small feat," Horton added, "We saw the game against Detroit. What we wouldn't love to do to those Red Wings! I mean the way we used to play them—it's pretty sad to see."

"Yeah, what is it with those guys? Is it just me or do those guys in Tronta have trouble passing the puck over the red line?" Busher Jackson added.

"They do seem to like to just flick it or shoot it into the other teams end an awful lot—same as in this league."

Ron was amazed. And that night before the game he conferred with the St. Johns' coach, and Walt Fisher.

"Those guys from the East Coast league, the five of them; they're far and away the best we've got here Walt," the coach commented. Ron tried to hide his smile.

"I don't really have to coach them. I let them do whatever the hell they want in the offensive zone. And when the puck gets back in our end, hell I don't even have to remind them to come back. Imagine—rookies who know how to play in both ends of the rink! What a concept." Walt Fisher raised his brow a little and fidgeted in his chair.

"Of course I knew they could play! They did the same thing all summer," Al Swartz added.

"You know you two really should have exalted their virtues a little more in training camp. Maybe they would have made the big club. I mean, even though our decisions are made collectively, sometimes it's necessary for one man to try and sway the group if he feels that he's—that *it's* right. Ronnie sometimes you have to be a little more vocal about your beliefs."

Ron and Al Swartz exchanged glances. Al Swartz popped his mouth open for a second, as if a great idea had just occurred to him. All Ron could remember was the newspaper article during training camp that led to the players being sent down in the first place. And he knew that it was exactly Walt Fisher's style to try and sway the group into seeing things his way, especially when it came to personnel decisions.

The game that night against the Albany River Rats was typical of the St. Johns' contests of late. Frank McCool delivered good solid goal tending, even if he was reluctant to come out of his net to handle the puck.

"Every time he does it's an adventure," Tim Horton remarked.

For his part Horton was a very steadying influence on the blue line. And Bill Barilko relished his role as the physical defenseman, delivering the body at every opportunity. It was such an anomaly, as his determination belied his size. It didn't matter how big the forward was—Barilko would meet him with the well—timed hit. And after it was delivered at the very *least* both players would go down, and the baby Leafs would end up with the puck.

Conacher was third in league scoring though on this night his powerful shot would only rattle off of the goal post a couple of times. Busher Jackson was the games' first star, collecting a goal and a pair of assists.

"Just remember us at call up time," Jackson told Ron in the dressing room after the game. "We'll show those guys in Tronta a thing or two about how to pass the puck."

The next evening Ron was back home, preparing a scouting report for the clubs first quarter organizational meeting which would be held on the following Monday. He sat at his computer with the radio tuned into CHIL, the station that featured Gil 'the thrill' Baines. Ron wanted to hear the latest take on the Leafs recent downward swing, and no one could slant it like the Thrill could.

"We have Enzo on the car phone, somewhere in the GTA— Enzo how's the driving out there this evening?"

"Not bad Gil."

"Whereabouts are you?"

"I'm on the westbound Gardiner, just west of the 427, things are moving well, but eastbound it's a different story—it's down to one lane just east of me"

"Ladies and gentlemen, Enzo and the traffic are brought to you by Mr. Submarine—for all you want in a sub, it's Mr. Submarine."

"Gil, I wanted to ask you about the Leafs. You were right when you said wait until they meet a club like Detroit or Philadelphia."

"And I do take all of the credit for that, Enzo."

"Yeah, but despite that I think you have to agree that they are playing better this year. The goal tending—it's like the John Dennis of old. They're getting scoring again from Shoniker and Andrew. Even this new kid McCaine—it's not like it was last year."

"Enzo, that's fine, but you're missing the point. This team still can't score goals, and that was painfully obvious against Detroit. Their power play is a joke. The Detroit game again... and as for John Dennis, well he got a couple of shutouts early this year, but so did every other starting goalie in the league."

The thrill was on a roll. "The problem is you have some fossils on defense like Burks, and Oddy and Maleki, and some tough guys who aren't so tough. And to top it all off you have a coach who's stuck in the eighties, who thinks that the rink consists of only one end. And if his players *should* venture into the other team's zone it better be to take the puck away from the other team. I mean if Spencer Smith were awarded a penalty shot he would instruct Chuck Andrew to dump the puck in and chase it—end of story.

The coach will be gone once they get a new GM, who will be in place when they get a new owner. And with them will go the bunch of stiffs in the scouting department who drafted such gems as David Eagleson and Lorne Graham!"

"But Gil, I think they are improving. Take this kid McCaine—"

"Ah, yes the rookie! Well now maybe there is some hope for the *future,* and with that who best to be coming to town this weekend for a little 'original six' nostalgia than Les Canadiens, a chance to see a historic hockey team that is actually moving forward."

Winter wonderland

Before the home encounter with the Habs, the Leafs were on the road in Washington for a Friday night game with the Capitals. The club arrived on Thursday at Delles airport about 9:00 AM, and the weather was typical for an autumn day, clear, but very cool.

By noon Thursday, a storm front had moved in from the Midwest, and it met with a warm front from the south. The result was one of the biggest snowstorms that the Washington area had ever seen; ten inches in all fell between noon and midnight, Friday.

The Leafs afternoon skate was cancelled, and it was doubtful that they would get to Landover for the game on time, no matter *how* early they left. The team bus made it to the rink after plodding its way through bumper-to-bumper traffic. The normal fifteen-minute drive from the airport hotel to the arena took a record-breaking ninety minutes, with the Leafs getting to the rink twenty minutes before the warm-up was scheduled. The Capitals did not fare much better. They had played the night before in Chicago, where the storm originated, and although the weather there was not as bad it did delay the plane from taking off. Upon approach, they were re-directed away from DC, and ended up landing in Baltimore, and took an Amtrak train that got them home in the wee hours of the morning.

The Capitals were a team that epitomized all that was wrong with the NHL circa 2004-05. They had never won a Stanley Cup, had no great moments in history save for once holding the league's single season futility record. They usually made the playoffs but never seemed to advance past the first round. They had never developed a player who could truly be called a superstar. They played in a city where hockey was firmly established as 'sport #4' on the pecking order. Even their uniforms were uninspiring, though they had recently joined the bandwagon of league corporate marketing and redesigned their colours and logo as they joined the league's rebranding trend.

The game had about as many spectators as players and coaches—unfortunate for the locals who witnessed their team shut out the Leafs 2-0, on a decidedly un-physical game, or a 'no-hitter' as Mike McKenna called it. Lars Rogers was somewhat of an undeserving loser, though it was the kind of game that he could have stolen if his team mates had not decided, like many of the fans, to not bother to show up.

The team had planned to leave for home right after the game, as they were scheduled to meet the Canadiens the following night. With the airport closed, they wisely decided to stay another night in their hotel, which had fortuitously been booked for two nights instead of one by Walt Fisher.

"It happened once to us in Quebec City—had to sleep at the airport, and it probably cost us the game in New York the next night. Ever since then, we double—book!" he once said.

Still at the hotel, Ron Bailey was in the lobby awaiting news on the whereabouts of some luggage belonging to Benoit Marlet. He could not help noticing how appropriate the snowfall looked, even though it was only November, and very unseasonable for the DC area. It looked appropriate to Ron because the entire lobby had been decked out in Christmas decorations, as the American thanksgiving was only two days away. He was reminded of this from his stints in Massena and Rochester. Thanksgiving was *the* biggest holiday on the American calendar, and since Christmas came along not so very far behind it, the decorations were set out at the same time.

He stood near the hotel front desk and watched as a snow covered man slipped inside the revolving door and shook himself off like a Labrador retriever.

"You should see it out there!" John Hill laughed as he stood in the lobby of the Landover Mariott. "It looks like Petawawa on a Friday night in January!" He brushed the snow from his fall weight coat, before it could melt and really soak in. He had ventured out into the storm on a mission, 'to find some brown buddies' as he put it. Unlike many of his teammates he was particular about what brand of beer he drank. And when the best that room service could offer was a few cans of Bud, well John Hill just had to have beer in a bottle. So he bravely ventured out into the storm, reminiscent of a Stroh's commercial.

And true to form, when Joel Kent asked him where he was going, and Hill replied, "To get a two-four!" Kent deadpanned, "John, if you think of it—get two!"

With the town practically shut down because of the weather, the team had to find something to do after the game. It was left to the club's unofficial social director, Frank Maleki, to organize a party.

Word quickly spread from room to room that the adjoining suites occupied by Messrs. Maleki and Oddy and Kent and Burks were designated as 'party central.'

The garbage pails had been ceremoniously filled with ice, as had the bathtub, and beer cans had been separated from their plastic collars and were buried in the ice. The music was left to Chuck Andrew, who had brought along his personal 'boom box' for the trip. The tune collection consisted entirely of the Rolling Stones.

Frank Maleki was busy organizing the game of password. He had two of the rookies (non-participants because of their status) busy writing out selections on the hotel stationery. The choice of words to use in the game was critical, Maleki reasoned, because they had had to be fair for both teams, and the selection of teams had to be fair as well. The standard groupings were Maleki, Kent and Andrew versus Burks, Oddy and Shoniker.

Ron Bailey was invited to watch the grudge match, and as the participants were readying themselves Ron was treated to the tradition behind the game.

"We used to play charades—TV shows," Frank Maleki explained, "but one time Andrew and Kent got into a real argument over some old show. Kent says there never was a show called that, and Andy tells him he doesn't know the name of every TV show that's ever been made. Anyway, it goes back to one time we were up at Burks' cottage, and we got snowed in—even the TV wouldn't work. There was nothing to do, and Shonny finds a box with the game Password in it. We had to pick teams that were fair—we had to have a braniac on each side. So that's why Oddy and Kent are on different teams, and we had to have somebody that really knows how to play the game on each team so that's why me and Burks are on different teams, and—"

"And we have to have somebody who knows how to win! And that's why me and Andrew are on different teams," Floyd Shoniker added.

"In a pigs' arse!" Frank Maleki responded, "Anyway, we had a few pops and played it. And now every time we go up there to fish or whatever we have a return of the grudge match."

And so the lines were drawn in the sand. The game started with the Maleki team getting the word 'Suspicion.'

Frank Maleki had to give the clues to his teammates, and he said the word 'Question' but he said it with an almost *musical* intonation. Right away, Chuck Andrew responded 'Sus-pic-ion', with the same musical intonation.

Frank Maleki jumped to his feet, and made a waving motion with his hand. "Wavelength!" he shouted.

Chuck Andrew returned the motion, as if it were the secret greeting of a mystic loyal order.

"You can't do THAT!" Floyd Shoniker objected.

"What's the matter?" Joel Kent asked.

"You can't use a word like that…he sang it just like in the Elvis song; 'Suspicion' you can't *do* that!"

"It's not *Elvis's* song—it's Terry Clark!" Frank Maleki responded, "and you can kiss my bum, chum!" he said as he marked up the score for the first word.

The Shoniker team appealed to Ron Bailey as an impartial judge, but Ron didn't want to be involved.

As the evening progressed, and the score seemed to be a stalemate, the room eventually began to clear. Even Dale McCaine complained that he was tired, and was heading off to bed. Ron secretly wondered how it was possible that Dale was tired.

As a spectator, Ron found himself paying less attention to the game and more to the music that was coming from the boom box—since he had been there that evening, nothing but Rolling Stones music had been played.

"What's with the Stones?" Ron asked.

"It's Andy's favourite, but you have to ask him why. I mean why just the *old* stuff."

So Ron took the lead and asked Chuck Andrew why he only played *old* Rolling Stones songs. While they took a beer break, Andrew responded. "I don't like any of their stuff after '*Exile on Main Street*'. They've never sounded good after that. A couple of more mediocre albums, and then they got into all that disco sounding shit with Mick singing in that stupid falsetto crap. I think what *really* happened was that the albums since then are just out takes, that the *real* Stones were killed in a plane crash in 1973, and that these guys are just impostors, you know, like one of those tribute bands."

Ron couldn't believe what he was hearing from a man revered by thousands of people. Did he actually believe this? It was like meeting the kind of person who actually believed that Elvis was still alive, and working at a K–Mart in Ypsilanti, Michigan. But here was Chuck Andrew in the flesh. His name would have appeared on the list of hundreds of hockey pool enthusiasts, who were gambling that he could once again find his forty goal scoring touch. Would they still have selected him if they knew that, to him, some of the most important things concerning the game revolved around the music that was played in the dressing room, or on road trips?

Two solitudes

The resumption of the Montreal–Toronto rivalry was always good for getting the collective blood flowing in the veins of Leaf fans that bled blue and white. Some people could not care less if the Leafs won a game all *year*, as long as they beat the dreaded Habs.

No team in any sport was as disliked by Toronto sports fans as were the Montreal Canadiens, their arrogant 'Habs fans', possessing an ingratiating swagger that burned deeply into the soul of any Leaf supporter. Yes Montreal has won more Stanley Cups than any other organization, but until the Leafs were saddled with ownership that better suited a travelling sideshow than a professional sports organization, this was barely the case. From 1967 on, when the Leafs last won the cup, Montreal has taken home the prize a remarkable eleven times. And during that period the Maple Leafs, whose descent into mediocrity was rapid, never challenged them. Before 1967 the comparative Stanley Cup score favoured the Montrealers by only 13-11. And Ron wondered how much of that lopsided 11 against zero run had to do with the curse placed on them by Doug McCaine?

Or was there really a curse? The reality of it was that the team, despite their recent slide was playing better hockey than they had in years. And this was *despite* a roster that, while experienced, seemed to be getting it done on desire alone. And fans and management were looking at the recent slide alike as something of a defining moment. If the club could break out of it, especially against a high-profile opponent (never mind a bitter rival like the Habs) then perhaps the pendulum could once again swing up.

For his part, Ron was excited by the prospect. He had been showered with requests for tickets, and his prized pair of reds was receiving monetary offers and promises unprecedented in his short stay with the organization. Ron felt personally nostalgic about the Montreal games. The first time his father took him to the Gardens it was for an afternoon game against these Canadiens. It was a season that Canadian hockey fans would rather forget, as it was the one and only time that a Canadian franchise did not qualify to play for the Stanley Cup. The Leafs were pretty much out of the playoffs by the time the middle of March rolled around, but the Canadiens were still fighting a historic battle that would take them to the last day of the season. For Ron, it was his first time inside the Gardens, and he had never been in a building so large. He had seen the historic facade so many times—it was as familiar to him as the exterior of his parents' home. The building always seemed to be photographed looking northward from the corner of Carlton and Church streets. The lines of the white mortar interrupting the layers of golden brick made the building seem larger than it was, as it appeared to extend to infinity, like the palace at the top of Mount Olympus.

The only view he had ever seen of the interior of the building was the one he would take in every Saturday night on *Hockey Night in Canada*. In person however, the picture was so vivid it seemed almost surreal. When the television lights were turned on the ice became whiter than any ice could possibly be. The glistening sheet seemed to be perfect, and impervious to melting, or any ravages that could befall ordinary ice.

Ron's view of the game was also near perfection. The seats were excellent; low row blues at centre ice, and the players were so close, closer in fact than he could see them on television. He was entranced by the colour of it, the swarm of blue jerseys all skating in a circle at once during the warm-up, looking like the precision drill of an army. And at the other end of the rink, the enemy force regaled in their white uniforms with the striking red and blue trim.

And the frozen battlefield, the player's skates scraping the ice, making a sound that was never detected on television. The whole spectacle was much bigger and bolder than he had ever seen before.

He was thrilled to be in the same room with his heroes! Bower, Keon, Ellis, Pulford, Armstrong; still some of the core of the Stanley Cup teams, and some of the younger guys who would eventually take the place of the veterans, and keep the tradition, Walton, Ley, Glennie, Dorey, Selby, and Ron's favourite new Leaf, Jim McKenny.

And when the game started, he couldn't believe the hush of the crowd. There was no screaming and yelling from those around him like when he watched the game with the family at home. There were no announcers booming 'There's a pass that fails to click,' or 'He shoots...He scores!' like on TV or radio. Instead it was like being at a live theatre—the only crowd sound would be when a player made a break out with the puck, or when a close scoring chance was missed and the crowd let out a huge '*Oh!*' in an almost rehearsed unison chant.

The game itself went so fast. And the huge crowds made it almost impossible to venture out of your seat and into the hallways to stretch your legs.

Ron's father could not sit for any length of time beyond the end of a period, and this gave Ron the opportunity to be treated to an ice cream bar during intermission. He also browsed the souvenir stands for any item that had the famous Leafs' logo, or for a picture of one of his heroes. His dad however sneered at the souvenirs, which he thought were overpriced. Ron didn't even get a program to remember this momentous occasion. But the memory of that first game would remain with him forever, and it was even better that the Leafs were able to manage a 3–3 tie with a team that was clearly superior.

On Saturday night the stage was set for a resumption of this oldest rivalry in Canadian sports.

And the number of red Montreal jerseys in the Gardens that night was a testimony to that. On the ice the game was the same to the players as any other on in the standings, but the electricity surrounding the game had transferred to the players.

There was no question that Spencer Smith had pushed all of the right buttons in preparing the team for this one. After the morning skate he showed a video to the players, a Molson Stanley Cup highlight film from the 1967 final; Leafs versus Canadiens. It seemed to do the trick early, as Toronto jumped out to an early 1-0 lead on a goal by Captain Floyd Shoniker. Just minutes later his protégé Dale McCaine scored, and the period almost ended that way, until Alexei Kovalev broke the shutout.

In the second the shots were flying furiously as both teams were drawn up in the spectacle, and seeming to enjoy the atmosphere that saw every successful pass cheered as if this were a playoff game. John Hill of all people put the Leafs up 3-1, but Kovalev closed the gap to 3-2, on the kind of offensive play that the Leafs could have used in those losses to Detroit and New Jersey.

On the ice the Leafs were taking advantage of being let off of their leash. The defensive game plan was torn up, and the end-to-end action had the fans positively feverish. The Leafs restored their two-goal lead when Chuck Andrew bravely stood in front of the net, taking hack after slash from goaltender Jose Theodore and defenseman Sheldon Souray. But the big winger stood his ground, when Shithead Moore wisely delivered a shot at the net that Andrew skillfully directed down and to the left past the goalie's blocker. It was a goal that few men could have scored, because few had the guts to take that kind of physical abuse for as long as Andrew was willing to take it.

On the bench Spencer Smith was ecstatic, not just because of the goal but also because of how it was scored. He frantically rushed up and down the bench, almost taking out a surprised Brian Ridley who almost strangled himself with the cord from his headset while trying to get out of the way of the charging coach. Smith was trying to get the collective attention of his younger forwards, Marlet, Sawchuck and West, to demonstrate to them the value of what Andrew had just done, and the dividends of having the balls to do it. Indeed, if it were a practice he would have blown the whistle. The game went on and at the end of the second the score remained 4-2 for the Leafs, with the shots on goal an amazing 38-34 in favour of Toronto.

In the room, Smith was still raving about the goal, while Andrew shrugged it off. He knew that it was the kind of thing that while was admirable; it could not be delivered on a regular basis. Even *he* knew that he could not take that kind of pounding every game. The coach said nothing about abandoning the defensive game plan—he seemed more concerned with the win. And with the team's psyche still bruised by their recent losses, a two-goal lead against the hated Habs going into the third was a better confidence builder than any shrink could prescribe.

The third period was much like the second. The Leafs went ahead 5-2 courtesy of Floyd Shoniker's second of the game, and the Habs drew closer when Alexei Kovalev, who had been rumoured to be coming to Toronto in a deal for Joel Kent, closed the gap. The irony increased when, moments later, Joel Kent scored his first goal in ages, as if to say 'don't deal me; I can give you what he can.'

The final was 6-3, and the fans loved it, being able to hold their head high against their Montreal rivals as they left the building. The importance of this morale building victory was not lost on the coach either. Spencer Smith declared it a holiday, and cancelled the practice for the following morning.

Montreal coach Claude Julien was not drawn in to the romance of the game, preferring to criticize his team for a sub-par effort in a very winnable game. He did praise the effort of the opposition, noting that he was impressed by the play of young number 16, Dale McCaine. Indeed, the rookie's goal was the most skilful move of the night, which was a compliment considering the prowess demonstrated by Kovalev.

The good old hockey game

The Leafs were approaching their 20th game of the season, and with that came the first quarterly organization review. The meeting was to be held at the Gardens directors' room the morning after their game against Boston, a game in which the Leafs exploded offensively for the first time.

Maybe, Neil Porters wrote in his *Globe and Mail* column the morning following the game,

The Leafs have come to the realization that dull defensive hockey may win games but it does not win fans. Of course, winning fans has never been a problem for this organization, but keeping them awake is another matter. The Leafs may have accidentally discovered caffeine in the form of rookie Dale McCaine, who seems to single-handedly be able to rouse his sleeping teammates and generate some excitement around the opposition net.

Against the Bruins, Dale had scored once and assisted on a power play goal by Joel Kent, who had re-discovered his offensive touch around the net. Floyd Shoniker again led the scoring with a pair of goals, but it seemed that the media were suddenly focusing on Dale McCaine as something of a catalyst for the sudden chemical reaction that was transforming this Leaf team into something unusual.

The quarterly meeting was much more upbeat than the one held at the three—quarter mark of the previous season.

"Well, for once I don't have to listen to Walt bitch about what trades we should be making in order to turn this thing around!" Spencer Smith roared, as he reached into the box of Tim Horton's donuts that had been anonymously placed on the boardroom table.

He chose a powdered sugar, filled with some unknown flavour. Ken Butler tried not to laugh, partially because he was chewing on a Maple Dip donut, and was also trying not to let small pieces of glazed sugar fall onto his new suit.

For his part Walt Fisher was ignoring the donuts, and instead was finding a napkin to place under the oat bran muffin someone had thoughtfully included for the health-conscious assistant GM. The assistant coaches, Brian Ridley and Ralph Newton were taking turns going for the sprinkle donuts, while Ron Bailey was busy flipping through his notes, looking for the scouting report he had compiled about his recent trip to St. Johns'.

"Let's get started," Ken Butler directed, as he had now finished enough of his donut to prevent him from being distracted.

"Ron is going to give us a report on the St. Johns' club," he nodded in Ron's direction, and Ron nervously began to realize that he could not find the page where he wanted to begin.

"Here it is," he said to no one in particular. He enthusiastically began to read the report, which extolled the virtues of Conacher, Jackson, Horton, Barilko and McCool.

"Jesus—don't we have anyone else down there?" Spencer Smith laughed.

Walt Fisher was wondering the same thing. "I was just going to ask. We have two former first round picks playing down there, and a defenseman we picked up in a trade who was the WHL most valuable player last season, and you have nothing to report on them?"

All of the eyes around the table were locked on Ron, and he could feel the heat.

"I'm just reporting what I saw, and what our scouts tell me. These guys are the best prospects we have, and if someone had to be called up tomorrow, that's whom I would recommend!"

Ken Butler leaned back in his chair, and brought his chin down on his chest, as if disappointed. "Well, the good news I suspect is that these kids are doing well. The bad news is that they aren't the ones we were expecting to be progressing so well. However, that's the luck of the draft. We monitor the situation, and we judge who gets called up if and when the need arises."

"And it shouldn't," Spencer Smith concluded, while failing to wipe some of the residual powdered sugar from around his mouth.

"Well, you have to admit Spence, that we've been lucky so far as the injury situation goes, only Sawchuck has missed any games," Walt Fisher said.

The coach became enraged. "Don't go jinxing us like that Walt! Jesus Christ! That's the last thing we need. Man, we have no depth on this club as it is. We lose anybody and you better have your ear to that waiver wire the next day."

Ron was surprised by the coach's sudden lack of faith in the players in the system. "You don't want to see any of those guys from the rock get a chance up here?" he asked.

Spencer Smith made his point. "It isn't that—they'll get their turn eventually. I said that in camp, but if we are gonna make a run, a *real* run at the playoffs we'll have to do it with some experience."

That was when Walt Fisher lost it. "Spencer, we've had this discussion before, and I for one am not going to sit here and say nothing while this comes up again. We've tried it *your* way with the veterans, and granted it got us to the semi-final two years in a row. But it didn't get us over the top. And now that we're trying to rebuild with a younger team, I'll be damned if I'll see us take a step backwards. Sooner or later you are going to have to learn to relate to the younger players."

The room was like an acoustic vacuum for a second. The loudest sound seemed to come from the ticking of everyone's wristwatches. Spencer Smith was getting ready to stage his rebuttal, but yielded the floor to the General Manager. Ken Butler was the first one to break the silence.

"Let's not everyone forget that this is a team effort…things are going well for us so far, so there is no need to turn on each other.

I'm sure what Spencer said was taken out of context. And as for your statement Walt, I fell that's unfair. I see Spencer making a great deal of progress with our younger players, Marlet, and McCaine—I for one am happy with the results we have achieved after twenty games—we're the ninth ranked team in the league so far, and everyone in this room has contributed to that."

The two adversaries glanced suspiciously at each other from across the table, but said nothing to each other. Their mutual lack of respect for one another was telling, but it did not, at least yet, get in the way of their duties. And Ken Butler aimed to keep it that way.

"I think it's fair to say that we have maybe overachieved a bit, if that's possible. But I feel that twenty games into the season is a reasonable barometer. Enough time has passed for us to see what this team really is about. And where we take it from here is up to us. We'll continue with an evaluation of the season so far, our personnel, and a look forward at the remainder of our schedule," the GM continued, as the meeting took a more civil tone.

The examination of the club's weaknesses, most notably lack of scoring depth, was discussed. And potential trades were also tabled with the idea that the club could afford to give up some toughness and some defensive strength at the forward position. The GM informed his staff of some recent interest in the suddenly struggling defenseman, Terry Oddy. The performance of the various players was reviewed, and those who were considered to be underachieving were duly noted.

The meeting concluded with the assignment of scouting duties, managerial meetings, and team charitable and marketing commitments, and at the conclusion Ron remembered an errand he had to run.

He accompanied assistant coach Ralph Newton down to the dressing room where the players were just preparing to take to the ice for practice. As they entered the room, the unmistakable sound of 'Green Day' could be heard blaring from a boom box that was placed above someone's stall.

Chuck Andrew came around the corner from the washroom, and when he realized that the sound was coming from the stall of Ian Moriarty, a rookie, he took control of the situation. He strolled over to the spot, reached up and slammed the stop button.

He looked down at the surprised defenseman, who was tying his skates and said, "When you are a *veteran,* you get to choose the music. Until then, WE do!"

The surprised kid had no idea what to say and just sat there as Andrew reached for his helmet and passed through the doorway in the direction of the ice.

"Just a rite of passage—don't worry about it," Terry Oddy said to the confused youngster. Oddy stood up and turned the boom box back on, but also adjusted the volume down, ever so slightly.

Ron remembered his mission. He caught up with the trainer, Nevell Carpenter, and asked him, "I need a favour. I promised the mechanic that looks after my car that I would get him a team signed stick. Who do I have to see about that?"

The trainer looked at him suspiciously. "All requests for that kind of thing are supposed to go through Mr. Fisher," he said. Ron could practically hear the red tape being wound around the situation.

Just as he was about to answer, Spencer Smith stuck his head in the door, and when he noticed Ron he said "So, what do I owe the honour of this visit? Come to sell me on some more of your St. Johns' Maple Leafs?"

Ron explained his predicament, and the coach got right to the bottom of it.

"Hell, we don't need the assistant GM to okay a lousy hockey stick. Nev, grab one of those team sticks, the blue and white jobs— leave it in the trainer's room and make sure all of the guys sign it, will ya?"

The trainer did exactly as he was told; after all it was the coach who was asking. After Ron had left, with instructions to return later that afternoon to pick up the stick, Joel Kent was approaching the trainer's table to get some therapy on his shoulder. He saw the stick laying on the table, already with a bunch of signatures on it.

"Team stick—who's it for?" he asked Nevell Carpenter.

"Ron Bailey," he mumbled.

"Oh yeah—where's the pen?"

The trainer was holding the pen, and handed it to the player, who held the stick awkwardly while trying to write his name on it. When he was done Kent put the stick back on the table, and the trainer picked it up. He tried to conceal what he was doing while Kent sat down and began removing his practice jersey and shoulder pads. Just then Kent noticed that Nevell Carpenter was writing on the stick.

"Hey, don't tell me you're signing it *too*, Nev."

The trainer blushed, and as Joel Kent stood up to see for himself, he noticed the spot where the trainer had signed. It read a scripted signature of David Moore.

"What the hell is this?" Joel Kent asked.

Nevell Carpenter began to blush the colour of a plum. "He doesn't like to sign," the trainer responded in a hushed tone.

Joel Kent turned and stormed out of the room and into the player's lounge where he saw David Moore slouched against a bench beside the refrigerator, gripping a coke in his hand, while enjoying a laugh with some of the rookies.

"Hey Shithead—the next time Ron Bailey asks you for a favour you better damn well do it!" Joel Kent fumed.

Moore instantly lost the smile on his face and gave Kent his attention. "What the hell are you talking about?" the defenseman asked.

"He wanted a team stick signed—though why the hell he wanted *your* god dam signature on it is anybody's guess. But the next time

243

somebody asks you to sign a team stick you better sign it yourself, and don't suck out and get the trainer to sign it."

Kent's outburst would have provoked a fight in some dressing rooms, but not in the Leaf's. David Moore was supposed to be a tough guy, but these days he wouldn't even do his fighting on the ice, never mind in the dressing room. He was no longer respected by his teammates because of it. When he was the fighter, he was respected, because it was a thankless job that had to be done, and none of the others wanted to do it—now he was making big money to be the enforcer, though he was no longer sticking up for his teammates. And as a result, the Leafs had to replace his role by acquiring Randy Rettig from the Flames—even though it had cost them a first round draft pick.

Joel Kent was not afraid to take on anyone, but he was paid primarily to score goals. And Kent resented the fact that he had to do some of the fighting for the team now that Moore was turtling. His shoulder had taken one beating too many by being stretched out while trying to break his arm free in fights. As a result his goal scoring was down and that was not good, since he was becoming a free agent at the end of the year. The resentment showed, but so did Moore's cowardice, as he did not even respond to Kent's accusation. And the younger players could see it as well.

Off the ice the team was not totally a divided group. There were so called cliques of players that preferred to hang together after the games, but it was more a division of age and years of service with one team than anything else.

The Bomber returns to Toronto

T he Leafs had an off day prior to their next road stop in Carolina. It ended up costing them as they delivered a listless effort as the steadily improving Hurricanes disposed of them quite easily, 2-0. The club rebounded in Nashville with a win, but came home to a deliver their poorest defensive performances of the schedule so far, a 7-5 home loss to Boston. Offensively it was one of their brightest outings, but the coach was furious at giving up so many goals, especially at home, and to a divisional team that he expected to steal two points from.

The coach punished the team with a workout the next morning at 8:00 AM, two full hours earlier than their usual start. Many of the players complained bitterly, especially those that lived in Mississauga, and were not used to fighting the early-morning rush hour traffic.

"Welcome to the *real* working world." Spencer Smith responded to the grumbling.

The game result gave the media more propaganda for their party line that the Leafs were an improved team but not one ready to challenge for anything significant.

Following the game, which Ron watched from his hotel room in Halifax, he got a phone call from Ken Butler.

"I want you to fly down to Worcester, Mass and have a look at a kid that the Blues have. They've made us a very interesting offer. And check the schedule to see where the Blues are playing next. I want you to get the pro scouts to have a look at Jim Campbell."

Ron was surprised that St. Louis would be looking at giving up a rookie who had scored 23 goals last year. "Who are the Blues after?" he asked.

"They want Terry Oddy, but we're going to offer David Moore and maybe something else—maybe a draft pick or two."

Ron was shocked that his boss would even propose such a ridiculous counter offer. "You really think that they'll go for David Moore and some picks for Campbell?"

"No, but I want to hear their counter. They seem to be desperate for a defenseman, especially an *offensive* defenseman. And Oddy has the credentials. It would be nice to move him out of here. It really pains me to see the way the fans have been treating him."

It hurt almost *everyone* in the organization to see the way Oddy was being booed. True, he could no longer move up and down the ice like he used to, but his point shot was still one of the most reliable in the entire league. And he was the team's highest scoring defenseman.

"If they don't go for it then we'll offer Oddy but ask them to sweeten their offer. We may have to add something to the mix. I've told them about some of the guys we have on the rock. They mentioned Mouton—one of your guys from the East Coast league I think."

A shock ripple of fear spread through the pit of Ron's stomach. He hoped that the Blues would not end up with Tim Horton, of all people. "Are you serious?" Ron shrieked.

"I think we have to do whatever we can to improve our offense. Our third line is really not getting the job done. And as for our fourth line..."

Ron had to agree. He had heard it all before.

"Let me tell you what I see when I get to Worcester. Who is the kid they have?"

"Jamie Masters, you remember him—we wanted to take him a few years ago, the year the draft was in Quebec City, the year we didn't have a pick between the first and fifth round. He went about two rounds before we could get him."

Ron's memory was experiencing gridlock. He thought that his boss was confused. Ron was not with the team then—was his boss a bit confused? And the name Jamie Masters—it sounded familiar. It sounded like the name he had read on a hockey card when he was a kid. While he kept Ken Butler waiting on the other end of the phone he called up the entry draft stats on his computer and there it was—just as Ken Butler had stated; Selected 63rd overall, by the St. Louis Blues defenseman Jamie *Rivers*.

"You mean Jamie *Rivers*," Ron responded.

"Yes, that's what I said," his boss confirmed.

"No, you said Jamie *Masters*," Ron repeated.

Ken Butler thought about it for a moment. "Yes, yes I guess I did. At any rate, he's the one I want you to look at—Jamie Masters. I mean Jamie Rivers. Just get on the damn plane and have a look at him. I hope he's a better hockey player than *Masters* was."

And with that, the conversation was over. Ron wondered if memory loss was an indication of anything other than memory loss. On the other hand, Ken Butler was able to recall vividly where the draft had been held and exactly how many rounds Jamie Rivers had been taken ahead of the Leafs next pick.

Toronto followed up its disappointing showing against the Bruins with a road win, even if it was against the Columbus Blue Jackets. And after dropping a home-and home series with the Sabres, the club had now played exactly .500 hockey since the game in Washington. They had only one remaining home date, a Saturday night meeting with the Calgary, before embarking on their longest road trip of the season. The westward swing would see stops in Vancouver, Calgary, Edmonton, Colorado and St. Louis—five games in ten nights.

"What the hell did the schedule maker *eat* before he went to bed and dreamed up this nightmare?" John Hill asked, as the players awaited the face off with Calgary.

"Think of it as a chance to visit a whole new set of bars on the West Coast, Hilly!" Floyd Shoniker yelled from across the room.

"And peeler bars," Frank Maleki added, as he drew the blue and white number 2 sweater over his head.

Lorne Graham had a keen insight on this aspect of the trip. "The peeler bars *suck* in Colorado! Don't you remember when we were in the 'I', Frankie? We went to that hole in Denver, what was it called—*the Shotgun Lounge*? The damn broads didn't even take off their G-strings," he broadcast.

Lou Zanardo was amazed. "No!" he gasped, in mock anger.

Frank Maleki put his coffee down long enough to set the record straight. "That wasn't Denver, Horny," he said referring to Graham, "It was Salt Lake, and unless they move a team there we ain't going to Salt Lake on this trip."

The Leafs did dispose of the Flames quite easily though. Late in the game a seemingly harmless play, turned out not to be. With Toronto ahead comfortably by a 4-1 score, the Leafs went on the power play when Floyd Shoniker was hauled down while trying to break in alone on the Flames goal. He was slowed just enough that he was unable to regain his balance when he tried to plant his left leg—had he been travelling faster the momentum of pushing off would have sent him upright almost immediately—instead when he tried to push up, the leg was now carrying almost all of his two hundred and twelve-pound frame. When he pushed his groin took all of the strain, and it not only pulled the muscle away from the tendon, it tore it as well. When Shoniker tried to get up he collapsed at once, as if he had been shot, and the veteran knew better than to try to move on his own. David Burks and Mike McKenna were the ones who had to help raise their fallen captain and help lift him gingerly off the ice under the watchful eye of trainer Nevell Carpenter. Spencer Smith stood motionless for the longest time, obviously concerned for the player but also doing a slow burn internally. His usual swagger was missing, and he did not stand with his hands folded across his barrel shaped chest as if he was getting ready to direct traffic. Instead he held onto the stairway leading up to the gold seats, as if he needed it for support.

When it came time to change the lines up, he did nothing, except stare in the direction of the painted Maple Leaf logo at centre ice. When Ralph Newton tried to get his attention, the coach did not respond. When Newton saw that they were about to lose the last change, and would be forced to go again with the line that was already in need of a break, he tapped Benoit Marlet on the shoulder, who hopped over the boards, followed by wingers, David Eagleson and Serge Moit.

The Leafs seemed to play the remainder of the game while looking over their shoulder. They were not glancing backward to see if the Flames were gaining; in fact, the game was all but in the bag. They were collectively hoping that their captain would pass through the dressing room corridor and take up a place on the bench until it was time to return for his regular shift. But it was not to be. Just as Chuck Andrew was being post-game interviewed as the Molson first star, Shoniker was being wheeled on a stretcher to Wellesley Hospital for further examination.

The initial exam by the team physician Dr. Jahaul was inconclusive, and so the doctor and Nevell Carpenter accompanied the player to the hospital for more conclusive tests. Before Ken Butler made his way down from the director's box, he called down to the director of media relations, Tommy Stukko, to get an urgent message to Nevell Carpenter. He wanted to be informed once even an *initial* diagnosis had been reached, and instructed him not to discuss the injury with anyone, not even the coach. As usual, Tommy Stukko took the message, but decided for himself how best to address the situation. The first reporter that caught his attention, Mike Howell from *The Toronto Sun*, thought he had the scoop, when he grabbed Stukko by the arm to get the mole's attention.

"So what's the news on Shoniker?" the scribe asked.

Stukko glibly responded, with a look as if he had the answer to everything.

"Looks like the same knee he tore up three years ago when he was out for ten weeks—probably the same, but you didn't hear that from me."

Of course he didn't hear it from Tommy Stukko; no one ever did, officially. A colour picture of Shoniker wincing in pain, and being cradled by his team mates would appear on the cover of *The Sunday Sun,* with the caption *'Leaf captain expected out ten weeks.'*

Ken Butler was livid when he saw the paper the next morning, and immediately called Stukko at home. The mole was too chicken to answer his phone, and instead took the brunt of the GM's blast as a voice message.

When he finally had the guts to call his boss back in the afternoon, the GM had time to cool off by then, which was fortunate for Stukko. The team issued a formal statement Monday morning after the doctors had reviewed the MRI, and the diagnosis was a torn groin muscle, and the prognosis was rest, followed by physiotherapy. He was expected to be out between six and ten weeks. At Shoniker's age the healing process could take all of the ten weeks. And not factored in the equation would be the team's propensity to rush him back, especially if they were still in the hunt for a playoff spot.

Now the decision about who to bring in as a roster replacement had to be made. The meeting was done by conference call, as Walt Fisher was off to an AHL general manager's meeting in Portland, Maine, Ron Bailey was scouting in Windsor, and the team was getting ready to leave for Vancouver.

"You bastards—you jinxed me," was how Spencer Smith began the meeting.

Ken Butler wasn't ready to acknowledge that, but Ron Bailey secretly wondered if it was not fate that was intervening on behalf of the *Dead Leafs Society.* "Well, Sawchuck should be back any day now, but we will still need a spot to be filled. One of the youngsters— one, who have earned the chance, will come up. Who's it going to be Ron?"

All of the other lines were silent. Ron was paying attention, but he was trying to call up a file on his laptop, and it was taking a while. As he clicked on the scoring file for St. Johns', the name stood out as if he had already spoken it.

"Charlie Conacher!" Ron said aloud.

Spencer Smith roared one of his belly laughs of seismic magnitude. "I'll take him, if you can get him. But you better get yourself a shovel," the coach chuckled.

Ron tried to compose himself. Walt Fisher did not even bother to make a remark. "We should call up Bachmann," he responded. "He's leading the team in scoring, fourth in the league—he's 6'1", 205. And fast, has a great shot, good power play man."

"If I remember, he'll even go to the net," the coach agreed.

Ken Butler was ready to close the deal. "So it's settled then. Walt, if you can do the honours. Notify Al Swartz. Have the player catch a flight to the coast. Ron, send the necessary paper into the office and have the league notified."

Ron though about the media announcement, "Do you want me to call Stukko and have him announce it to the media?"

"Hell, let him find out about it in *The Toronto Sun,*" the GM fumed.

And it was done. Charlie Conacher, the bomber, would once again be patrolling the right wing for the Toronto Maple Leafs. Ron was gripped with anxiety, the chance to see a Hall-of-Famer skating on this team. It would almost take a back seat to the other reason he was anticipating the trip that would take him to Vancouver—the chance to be with his fiancée. He was catching an early afternoon flight out of Detroit that would have him in Vancouver by dinnertime on Monday.

Ron wanted to surprise Kelly, and didn't tell her he was arriving early. When he called her from the airport, he was the one who got the surprise—her answering machine picked up the call. He told her he would be at the hotel, and that he would call her again from there. With nothing to do, and no one to do it with, he took a cab to the teams' hotel, and he hoped to hook up with some of the players or coaches.

When he arrived to check in, he called Kelly again, but once again got voice mail. He quickly placed some calls to several of the rooms, starting with Ralph Newton and Brian Ridley, and gradually worked his way up and down the roster—no one was in, not even the trainer.

After checking in and dropping his suitcase in his room, Ron decided to go down to the lobby. He disliked spending time alone in hotel rooms, except when he was working. He never wanted to get into the habit of just crashing in front of the television when on the road—which was too easy to do. Instead he went in search of something to do, which, he thought, should not be too hard in a town like Vancouver. He tried to think of anyone he knew in town—players on the Canucks roster, or even ex-players that he was familiar with, but he drew a blank.

He had dinner alone at a *Swiss Chalet,* his only companion being the *Vancouver Sun,* which had a big spread on the upcoming Leafs-Canucks game. The Canucks were *the* story in town, and the Leafs were anxious to show well against a conference—leading team.

As Ron was turning the pages of the sports section he noticed a shadow appear over the paper. He looked up to see Dale McCaine and Charlie Conacher staring down at him, as if they were a couple of deputies that had just found their outlaw, holed up in some out of the way saloon.

"Whatcha doin here all by yerself?" Conacher bellowed, as he slid in the booth bench across from Ron. McCaine sat beside Conacher, as if directed to.

"How did you guys find me?" Ron asked, as his eyes widened in disbelief. "I was hoping to meet someone," he said, closing the paper.

Charlie Conacher winked at McCaine as he said, "The sweetheart stood you up!"

"How did you know-how did you know *who I* was supposed to meet?"

Conacher smiled. "It's written all over your face, kid. Why else would someone your age look so disappointed?"

Ron wanted to change the subject. "Pardon me for saying so, but I find it strange that you call me 'kid', I mean, you really don't look older than me! As a matter of fact—"

"As a matter of fact, I was born four years before the Great War, 1910, which makes me a sight older than you!"

Ron erroneously looked around to see if anyone had heard the comment. No one had. "I'm glad you two are here," Ron continued, as he remembered the conversation he had months ago with Kelly, about the existence of these very players. "There is someone I'd like you to meet. You guys wait here—I'm going to make a call and I'll be right back."

He got up to find a pay phone, remembering that he left his phone at the hotel. It didn't matter, as he got the answering machine again. This time he didn't leave a message. What would he have said, 'Hi, it's me, I'm at the downtown Swiss Chalet with a couple of dead hockey players I'd like you to meet—how soon can you get here?'

He shuffled back to the table, the look of disappointment still on his face. Ron's face was about as difficult to read as a ninety-foot billboard.

"Looks like we're all you have tonight, son," Conacher said, "C'mon, let's go find a drink somewhere. All of the old watering

253

holes can't be gone. There has to be one grand old hotel that's still standing."

Conacher was right. There was a grand old hotel still standing, but it was undergoing renovations. The Empire Hotel was closed, but the restaurant and west wing lounge was still open. The trio enjoyed the ambiance of the place, although it was new only to Ron.

"Stayed here when we went across the country—barnstorming." Conacher remarked. "We even used to play an exhibition series against the Blackhawks out here for the Totem trophy."

Dale McCaine too had seen the inside of the Empire before. "We played an exhibition game one season—Rochester and Vancouver," he said. "This is where we stayed. It looks almost the same."

Ron excused himself to phone Kelly again. This time he reached her. Within minutes she had joined them. Kelly Garrett was not the kind of girl who turned heads because of her good looks. The first thing men noticed about her was her height—she was just a half-inch less than six feet tall—the first impression she made with most women was how bright she was. It was impossible to have a conversation with her and touch on a topic she was entirely unfamiliar with. As intelligent as she was, however, she carried herself without a hint of arrogance or egotism. Ron was too accustomed to the first two virtues to let her radiance go unnoticed. To him, she was breathtakingly beautiful, and he assumed most other men saw her the same way. After taking Ron's lead and talking to the two ex-Leafs, she came to a conclusion.

"There's nothing ghostly about your players," she testified. "There is simply nothing to suggest that they are any less real than you or me."

That Ron already believed—what he had *seen* told him otherwise. But Kelly's opinion only reinforced his own—whether these players were ghosts come to life or not he really didn't care any longer. They were real hockey players as far as he was concerned. And more importantly, they were *good* hockey players.

And what the Leafs needed more than anything else were some good hockey players. Despite the fact that they were there until closing, the two dead players were the only ones who showed any signs of life the next night. The Canucks skated to an easy 4-2 win. Conacher saw only fourth line duty, and Ron knew that with such little ice time it would be hard for him to impress Spencer Smith.

The next game, a 6-4 loss in Calgary was much the same—little effort from the veterans, and only sporadic hustle from some of the kids.

When they reached Edmonton, things seemed to take a turn. Spencer Smith cancelled the planned off day and scheduled a practice. It was during this workout that the coach's eyes were opened wide as if propped up by toothpicks. Charlie Conacher took the opportunity to showcase himself. He skated every drill as if it was a game, swooping down the wing in the passing drill and rifling each shot at the net until John Dennis complained so loudly to Ralph Newton that the assistant had to come over and tell Conacher to take it easy—it was only a practice. Spencer Smith said nothing; his was too busy drooling at the sight of a player working his tail off in practice. The scrimmage was more of the same for Conacher, as he fired a pair of goals past the startled Lars Rogers.

In the game against the Oilers, Smith kept Conacher on the fourth line only because the other lines had suddenly picked up the pace. Dale McCaine was mostly the story, notching his second hat trick of the season, and counting a pair of assists. Chuck Andrew was the hero, however, scoring the last two goals of the game, including the overtime marker in the 6-5 victory.

While the team would continue to play on the road, they headed home for a brief Christmas break.

Ron Bailey was not looking forward to the break. When he was a kid, Christmas was his favourite time of the year, a time full of family get–togethers, celebration and traditions. But since he became involved in the business end of hockey it meant only a short time for family reunion. And for the last few years, not even that frequently, at least during the days immediately around Christmas.

"Merry Christmas, Mr. Potter!"

For the second year in a row, Ron was dispatched to the World Junior Hockey Championships in Europe. They always began with a Boxing Day game, and when the games were in Europe (as they almost always were) it involved catching a plane on or about December the 23rd, and travelling that entire day, arriving on Christmas Eve. Christmas day was a day of phone calls home for the players, and some gift opening and a team dinner, but also a practice for the all-important Boxing Day opener.

For Ron it was a chance to see the best juniors in the world, and the price to pay of being away from home seemed small. His family was spread around the continent anyway, his parents in Arizona, his brother in England and his fiancée in B.C.

This year the games were held in Zurich, and Ron caught a flight to London two days early in order to spend some time with his brother's family and Ron's two young nephews. The visit was over too soon and before long he exchanged the company of family for that of TV people, newspaper reporters and other scouts and player agents.

On Christmas night he was in the *Knosterberg Room* restaurant at the *Hotel Biezenbach*, seated at a table by an enormous fireplace. He shared the company of TSNs' play-by-play man Dave Erehart and Colin Thomas of the Hockey News.

Ron had patched up his differences with THN, since their inflammatory article 'Rating the Prospects' was published. And to further bury the hatchet Ron had accepted Thomas's offer to 'buy.'

To pass the time, and to celebrate the spirit of the holidays, they were taking turns ordering rounds of beers from around the world that they had never tried.

"After all, these are the *world* championships!" Dave Erehart observed.

"Here's one I have never even heard of, let alone tried!" Colin Thomas reported, "Santa Claus Beer—I guess you have to have it with a 'Rudolph' chaser!"

The round was ordered, and just as Ron began to take his turn proposing a toast the room went dark, but he could still feel the warmth of the fire and could smell the sweet smoke that the hardwood gave off. Someone had placed their hands over his eyes.

"No guesses who it is." the voice ordered.

Ron didn't need a guess. The voice belonged to Dennis MacDonald—Ron's former defense partner and the only Massena College alumni who had ever made it to the NHL.

"What in hell are you doing here?" the two of them said in unison. Ron attempted to stand up, but MacDonald grabbed him by the shoulders and with a powerful thrust lifted him right out of his chair, and gave the Leaf executive a bear hug.

"I can't believe I found you here." MacDonald bristled. Before Ron could respond, the big man was grabbing for Ron's beer bottle and proposed a toast.

"Here's to Massesna College—educators in the school of hard knocks—developers of great hockey players!"

"And where they have the best glazed donuts in the world!" Ron added.

Dennis MacDonald suddenly cocked his head to the side, like a wolf sizing up his prey to see who had the advantage. "Now you're not to mention *that*" he said, half seriously.

This was obviously an inside joke, because Colin Thomas and Dave Erehart glanced at each other and exchanged shoulder shrugs.

"I don't have to introduce this guy to you fellas, do I?" Ron asked.

Neither one of the media types recognized MacDonald at first, but then it came to Thomas as if he had discovered the legendary unicorn.

"Dennis MacDonald! Of course! I didn't recognize you without the beard—yes, you're playing here, somewhere!"

"Bern," the player answered.

Ron went to sit down, as if the excitement had somehow weakened him, but MacDonald had already stolen his chair.

"What was that about 'glazed donuts'?" Erehart asked.

Dennis MacDonald began to turn crimson, and Ron perked up as he readied himself to tell the story.

"You can't use *this* in your paper!" MacDonald warned Colin Thomas just as Ron began.

"When we were playing for Massena—we were on the road, in Boston. I was sharing a room with Mac here, and we had both been out after the game for a few pints. Anyway he picks up some 'local talent' as he calls it, and asks me not to come back to the room for a couple of hours. So I kill some time here and there and finally I'm getting tired. It's about 2:30 in the morning by now, and his two hours are more than up. So I listen at the door—not a sound coming from within, and I knock on the door and there's no answer. So I figure they're gone. So I unlock the door and there he is, going down on her, and he turns his head and there he is with a big grin on his face, his beard glistening like he'd eaten a box of glazed donuts. Well, I didn't know whether to laugh, sit down and watch, or get the hell out of there. But I did get the hell out of there!"

Thomas and Erehart were in tears, and MacDonald smiled a wistful smile at Ron, and added, "And the next day, in the dressing room, Ronnie comes in and presents me with a box of glazed donuts—sort of as a souvenir."

Dennis MacDonald took a sip of his beer. "He *lives* to tell that story! I'm surprised you found somebody else that hadn't heard it," he said. "By the way, some deal you have there Ronnie! They send you over here at Christmas—don't you have people to do that for you?"

Ron was somewhat embarrassed by the question, and suddenly felt the need to defend himself in front of the media types. "We have two scouts here as well," he answered, looking for his beer until he remembered that Dennis MacDonald had taken a drink from it— meaning he had lost it for good.

"We know why Ron's here," Colin Thomas interrupted "But what about you Dennis? What made you walk away from a $750,000 dollar a year contract to come to Switzerland—for what, maybe a quarter of that?"

MacDonald got serious for a moment. "I didn't like the way I was treated in St. Louis. I was promised some things that never came through. I have a good deal here, plus a car and a condo, and a chalet in St. Moritz, thirty game schedule, plus playoffs. And the competition isn't that bad."

"But that was the money then. Five years later you'd be making more like three times that now!" Erehart added.

"But having one third of the fun doing it!" MacDonald laughed.

Ron could sense that Dennis MacDonald wasn't telling the whole story. Colin Thomas ordered another round of beers they hadn't tried yet, and hoped that he could get a story out of the Dennis MacDonald meeting.

"So Dennis, have you considered coming back to the NHL?" Thomas asked.

"The truth is that nobody's asked me. My agent isn't soliciting any offers back home because I haven't asked him to. So, I don't really know if anybody's interested in a thirty-five year old thirty-five-goal scorer. But maybe when I'm fifty and I'm a fifty-goal scorer—" he laughed.

"Well now maybe we do have a story here after all," Colin Thomas announced. "Here, on Christmas night, perhaps we'll witness a deal being made. Perhaps we can report that the Toronto Maple Leafs have come to terms with former St. Louis leading scorer Dennis MacDonald." Thomas stood as if to propose a toast.

"Sit down, Colin," Ron directed. "We're not signing anybody."

Thomas was disappointed. "What's the matter Bailey—don't you have the authority to sign anybody?"

Ron rolled his eyes and sighed. "He does," Dave Erehart interrupted, "but it's those damn NHL by-laws. I'm surprised that you don't know that Thomas," he said while taking a sip of a beer that surprised him as bitter. "Our friend here can't sign with an NHL club until his contract with Bern is up at the end of their season—which coincides nicely with the NHL playoff run. So, just when Mr. Baileys Maple Leafs are struggling for the last playoff spot, along comes Dennis MacDonald to help them out—with a timely goal here and there, just like he did with the Blues."

Dennis MacDonald smiled; his eyes fixed firmly on the roaring fire in the cavernous fireplace. Ron watched his eyes dancing with every flicker of the flames. He could see that MacDonald was wondering if he still had the competitive edge that would allow him to still play at that level, especially after five years in Switzerland.

"It's a great story, but I can't see it happening," Ron concluded.

MacDonald did not react, but continued to gaze at the fire.

"Why the hell not?" Colin Thomas demanded.

"Because we're not willing to part with a player, or draft choice as compensation," Ron responded.

"Not necessary," MacDonald informed them. "The Blues held my rights when I left, but I'd be a free agent, now. Under the new agreement, as an old fart, my former club isn't entitled to any."

Ron though that he knew the rules better. "I think the league has that covered. You'd be 'Grandfathered in', that is to say the rules

261

were changed *after* you came here. But *before* you could become a free agent."

Colin Thomas perked up at this news. "This could still be a story, something the league hadn't considered, like the Bure compensation. They'd have to rule on it. MacDonald here may be the only case."

"But it doesn't matter if he doesn't want to play in the NHL anymore," Dave Erehart reasoned.

"What makes you think I'm still in such demand?" MacDonald said, sipping his beer.

"Hey now Mac—you forget the effect you had on fans! They may not have forgiven you in St. Louis for walking away, but you do have that reputation for scoring the big goals."

"*Had* the reputation—there are no *big* goals to be scored over here," MacDonald said.

For the first time Ron noticed the loneliness in the players voice. Dennis MacDonald hadn't been sentenced to serve five years in Switzerland—he went there of his own free will. Even if he hadn't been the victim of broken promises, he was such a free spirit that he was destined to eventually leave the structured world of the NHL. Ron knew him that well. But there did seem to be an interest in all this talk about him coming back.

MacDonald was ready to diffuse the talk. "Ronnie here doesn't have to worry. I've been following his team on the 'net. They're off to a pretty good start. They've got a good mix of vets—guys like Shoniker, Andrew, Oddy, Burks, McKenna, Maleki, Dennis—they can win a lot of games for you in the playoffs. Those guys don't make mistakes when the games are on the line. And some of the younger kids—that Swedish defenseman, Andersson, and the kid you got in the Artis deal, Sawchuck. And this McCaine kid seems like a find. Hell, even Benoit Marlet seems to have woken up."

MacDonald paused to wet his whistle, but Ron wished he would continue. He loved hearing his team being praised by someone's opinion he valued.

Colin Thomas had to pick his jaw up off of the table. "So exactly how much did this little testimonial cost you, Ron?" he asked.

But Ron wasn't the least bit embarrassed. He agreed with every word of it. Colin Thomas wasn't about to let the hall of fame induction speech go without bringing up last season. "So if this team is the second coming of the Montreal Canadiens dynasty of the fifties, then how come they finished 23rd overall last year?"

MacDonald wasn't at a loss for words yet. "They're a veteran team like I said. They can't get up for every game during the regular season. Those old muscles take longer to recover—trust me, I know. That team was out of contention early. I'm not going to say the guys tanked it. But they could see it was an early end to the season. But coaches like Spence Smith—he's the right personality for a playoff contender. He may not work well with a young team, but give him some vets; man—he'll bring out the best in 'em. He knows when to push the buttons."

The evening concluded with the swapping of a few Christmas stories from home, though nobody wanted to be reminded for too long of the fact that they were all away from their homes at Christmas.

When Ron shook hands with his old friend in the lobby before heading off to his room, he wished Dennis MacDonald a 'Merry Christmas,' and good luck.

"And say 'Hi' to Les when you see him! Tell him he owes me a call," Ron said, referring to Dennis' agent.

"I will!" he promised, "and don't you forget to give me a call when you get home!" he said before departing.

Team Canada was doing rather well in the tournament, and Ron was busily conferring with his scouts before and after every game. They were compiling reams of data on the three players whose draft rights they held, and were also keeping a close tabs on a dozen or so who could potentially represent their first pick in next Junes' draft.

Ron was also trying to keep abreast of what was going on at home. As the team resumed the road trip, Conacher finally stole the show, scoring the winner and setting up two more as the Leafs won 2-1 in Colorado, and 5-1 in St. Louis.

Conacher had earned a spot with his gritty play, and it paid off the next game in Anaheim where he got the Leafs first goal in their 2-1 win. The rest of the team seemed positively resurrected by the Bomber's performance. He was still on the fourth line, but every time he was on the ice something happened—whether it was breaking up a scoring chance by back checking, or intercepting an opposition pass, he was making his presence felt.

Spence Smith's new permanent grin could not have been removed, even with reconstructive surgery. But the coach was not ready to reward the newcomer with a promotion—at least not just yet. The stubborn coach believed that someone else would have to play himself out of a job before this kid could steal a spot. And that had not exactly happened—at least not yet.

The plane ride home was like a New Years' eve party. It was the most successful west coast journey in club history, and though the Leafs were still second in their division behind Ottawa, they were now fifth in the conference, and sixth overall in the league.

Spencer Smith was so high that it was doubtful if he really needed to be inside the plane in order to fly home. He sat beside Ken Butler on the flight back, which was indicative that all was well in the world. The coach would never sit beside the general manager—it wasn't superstition with Smith, but was almost protocol. He believed that he was a sergeant, and not an officer. And although he was management and not labour he still felt that his place was with the players, and not the suits. He would usually sit beside the trainer, an assistant coach, even the team's play-by-play man Jim Gerber—anyone but the GM. This flight was special, and so the seating arrangements had to be. The coach had to let the GM in on the secret of the club's success so far.

"You know why this team is 6th overall instead of 30th he slurred, as the effect of Captain Morgan and Coke was finally reaching him.

Ken Butler didn't look up as he sipped his soda water and lime, simply saying "No."

"Neither do I!" the coach confessed. "I said it when we were in Boston! Dammit we're not doing anything differently—same practice schedule, same personnel, and with a couple of additions, same training staff. The only injury was a big one, but we've kept on winning! I can't believe it."

Ken Butler could not help but detect a concern in the voice of the coach. "It almost seems like this is bothering you for some reason!" the GM added.

Smith stared at his drink as if his next words were written on the ice cubes like cue cards.

"It does bother me dammit! It bothers me because I don't know what the hell we can do to regain it if something goes wrong!"

"Spencer, if I didn't know you better I'd think that you were afraid of the success?"

The coach quickly brushed that aside. "I've never been afraid of anything, except losing," he barked. That was something the GM could not dispute.

In his time, Spencer Smith was perhaps the most fearless defenseman in the entire NHL. He began his career when the ashes of the six-team league were still warm—indeed he may only have got his chance because the league had expanded to twelve teams. He learned his craft in the minors when there were only six teams, and many of the players were simply too good not to be in the NHL. But when Smith got his chance he impressed right away, and played his hard-nosed style on a team loaded with highly respected veterans like Gordie Howe, Alex Delvecchio, Bill Gadsby and Roger Crozier.

Smith was like a Clydesdale; in fact his physique, including his enormous size eighteen neck, suggested that of a horse. On road trips he was forever tucking his shirttail into his pants, because he could not find tapered shirts, and the ones he bought that were sized to accommodate wearing a necktie flared out at the waist like a tent. He took a great deal of ridicule for this early in his career. But he was rarely made fun of on the ice. Smith did not have the reputation of a fighter, only because there were few courageous enough to challenge him. He was incredibly strong, yet he stood just over five foot ten. He had a mean streak too, but only when provoked. In his second year in the league he was playing in a game for the Red Wings in Chicago Stadium against the Black Hawks. He skated into the corner, to cover the puck carrier, none other than the notorious Howie Young. When Smith tried to strip him of the puck, Young delivered a vicious elbow to the temple, and a butt end to the cheek of the young defenseman. The blows were so direct that Smith was sent to the ice, where he lay unconscious for several minutes. He had to be helped from the ice, and no penalty was given on the play.

Smith sat in the dressing room with an ice packed strapped to his head as he struggled to remember where he was, and even who he was. He had no trouble remembering who had hit him. Smith returned to the game in the final period, and predictably went looking for Young.

As they lined up for a face off, Young began to taunt the young blue liner. "So ya come back for more did ya kid? Where wuz ya last period? Gone home to mommy to get a suckle?"

Smith dropped his gloves, but instead of landing a punch he grabbed the stick from the startled Young's hands and broke it in half across his knee, and tossed it at him. He then grabbed Young by the collar and belt buckle, lifted him off the ice and swung him around like a farm hand heaving a haystack onto a wagon. Young sailed through the air for about ten feet and landed heavily into the boards with a thud that even the fans in the rafters could feel. The action should have resulted in a bench-clearing brawl, but no one dared venture near the crazed Smith. He skated away from the still prone Young, not knowing where to go next, and meekly followed the linesman who directed him without objection to the penalty box. From that day onward Spencer Smith's reputation as someone not to mess with was engraved forever in the Ten Commandments of the game.

The General Manager studied the message that his coach was giving him. "All I can tell you Spence is just to enjoy the ride. Keep doing what you're doing, and the rest will take care of itself."

All was well at home, he thought as the club had just extended its unbeaten streak to ten. Ron stayed to watch Canada breeze through the medal round, and was thrilled to see Canada take the gold with an impressive 5-1 win over the Russians. He joined in the festivities as anyone with a Maple Leaf on their passport was instantly welcomed to join in the celebration. A bunch of the pro scouts and agents gathered to toast the victory at the *Auberge Profenna*.

When Ron had about enough of the celebrations, he returned to his hotel—he thought that if he heard the song '*Who the F is Alice?*' one more time, he was going to be sick.

At the front desk he was surprised to find an urgent message from Ken Butler. He noted the time difference and calculated that it must be 1:00 AM in Toronto by now but since the message was labelled urgent he decided to place the call to the GM's home. Ken Butler was obviously still awake, and was also close to the phone as he answered it with one ring.

"Ron, good of you to get back to me," he said sounding understandably tired. "We have a situation that needs addressing right away. We've lost Chuck Andrew, for at least eight weeks—tore up his knee against Atlanta tonight."

Ron was shocked. First it was their captain while he was leading the team in scoring, and now their leading goal scorer while he had just taken over the team lead in scoring.

"We'll have to promote someone from the rock, as a short term solution. But we have to get working on a long term one. The eight weeks I mentioned are at best. It's only a minor tear of the ACL, but he had a tear in it before, different place. He may take a lot longer than eight weeks—it's too early to tell."

Ron could tell that Ken Butler was deeply disturbed by the loss of another key veteran, and it was valid. Veteran goal scorers are not offered up for trade on a regular basis.

"I think that the best guy to promote from St. Johns' is Jack Bodine. He won't put the puck in the net like Andrew, but he is a tough winger and will go in the corners to set up his centre man."

"Well, I'll take your word on that. But more importantly, we'll have to do some serious shopping. Our surplus is on defense, so we'll have to see if we can fit our needs as well as someone else's. You'll have all kinds of time on your flight back to go over the rosters. See what you can come up with."

Ron had hoped that it would be a leisurely flight home, but that was now dashed. He thought that he had better get a spare battery for the laptop, if he could find one in Switzerland. "How did we do in the game?" he asked.

"We took care of them 3-1, and your kid did notch another hat-trick," he said, referring to Dale McCaine.

"So are you going to make any calls in the mean time?" Ron asked his boss.

"Well, there's still the interest that St. Louis has in Oddy," he replied, "but I think that their asking price may just have increased.

"Just about any GM in this league would make a deal with the devil if he thought it could improve his hockey team," Ken Butler used to say.

Ron spent the flight with his computer planted on his lap. He scoured the NHL and AHL rosters and made a file of potential candidates that would partially fill the void left by Andrews' injury.

Busher Jackson comes back

When he arrived back in Toronto he found that the mood around the club had changed significantly from the one that he had left before Christmas. Even though they had started another unbeaten streak, a frustrating 1-1 tie with New Jersey, and victories over Ottawa and Pittsburgh, some of the veterans, David Burks and Joel Kent in particular, were shaking their heads over the loss of Chuck Andrew. Ron dropped by the last practice before the team departed for Chicago, and chatted with a few of the guys.

"Couldn't have come at a worse time," Burks lamented.

"Yeah, it could have. It could have happened just before the playoffs," Kent disagreed.

Ron also wanted to greet Busher Jackson, and see how the latest member of the Leaf legends was acclimatizing to the NHL of the next century.

Busher had just completed his first practice with the big club, and was a little miffed that he didn't get to play on Conacher's line. "Can't believe that one," he complained. "But I guess your coach hasn't seen what we can do together."

Charlie Conacher, who was still getting only fourth line duty and had only a few goals added. "Don't mind Busher—he forgets what it's like to break into this league. I told him we have to earn our chance here, no matter what he thinks of the competition."

"I was just getting used to all of the travel down there in the A. Heck we fly to Cleveland, Albany, Hamilton—sure beats the old rails," Busher Jackson commented.

"Wait until he gets on a west coast junket," Ron thought.

The Leafs lost next games without Andrew and Shoniker, to struggling Dallas and the Islanders. It was time for the organizations' next quarterly meeting, and the tone had changed significantly from the last meeting. The think tank convened it the director's room at the Gardens, this time without the donuts.

Spencer Smith was the first to say anything. "I said it last time and I'll say it again: get on the damn waiver wire because we need somebody who can put the puck in the net. I warned you guys last time that we didn't have any depth, and look!" He fumed.

Ken Butler tried to calm his emotional coach. "Spencer, we're doing everything we can. There simply isn't a body out there that can fill the void at this time. We've had some good discussions with St. Louis regarding, what was his name—"

"Jim Campbell," Ron added, as he couldn't help noticing the size of the vein that bulged on the side Spencer Smith's neck.

"Yes," Ken Butler continued, "he's one possibility."

"What about Federov?" the coach asked, referring to the future hall of fame winger, who was reportedly asking to be traded from Columbus because of his lack of playing time.

"Well, I met with the GM when we were last month. The story in the paper was overblown as usual—something his agent had planted. The truth is Federov isn't going anywhere. The Jackets won't move him, at least not until they're out of it, or the trade deadline—whichever comes first."

"They certainly didn't look out of it when we played them," Walt Fisher interjected, noting that the Leafs had not played particularly well against a team so far below them in the standings.

"We'll look at some other options instead, Spence. Ron has been listing them and we'll have a look in a moment."

The GM removed his glasses for a second, and searched for his glass of water; as if what he was about to say would leave him with a bad taste in his mouth.

"I want to pass on some information that is going to be public by the end of the day," He said as his voice began to lower to the point where the others in the room had to strain to listen.

"I received a call, just this morning, from the lawyer for the trustees of the estate. The judge has handed down his decision over the claims against the will. To make a long story short, he has decided that the ownership of the hockey club will be decided by a public tender. Bids for the shares will be received by 4:00 PM a week from this Friday, which I believe is the 28th. At that time the successful bidder will have sixty days to deliver the full payment to the trustee, who will in turn transfer the funds to the Salvation Army."

Ron was listening to see if he could hear his own heartbeat, but he wasn't sure if it *was* still beating.

"So, we're all out of a job—or not until the end of the year?" Spencer Smith questioned.

Ken Butler was prepared for any and all questions. "After the tender is received, the trustee has to inform the league of its desire to transfer the ownership. The league will request a formal application for transfer, and once it has the required information it will begin its process to evaluate the applicant. I believe that process takes sixty days."

"So, in effect, it can take a minimum of 120 days before the ownership transfer is approved." Walt Fisher observed.

"That is my understanding," Ken Butler replied, as he took another sip of water.

Spencer Smith looked at the ceiling. "120 days—four months," he began to count on his fingers.

"January, February, March, April—hey, we should be safe until the end of the regular season!"

Ken Butler wanted to establish the setting of composure. "I don't anticipate any changes before the conclusion of the season. In any event we all have contracts until that time that must be fulfilled. The team will continue to operate just as it always has. There will undoubtedly be distractions from the media, wanting reactions and so on. Doubt will be cast over the future of the entire management structure, and it will filter down to the players. I'm not just talking about the contracts that are in place. Players will be asked if they think they are going to like working for so and so, who is rumoured to be taking over once the sale has gone through. There will be much speculation, and our job through all of this will be to concentrate on one thing and one thing alone—making the playoffs. Nothing else matters, distractions or no distractions."

Walt Fisher raised the obvious question. "When does this all become public?"

"I understand that there will be a press conference at noon today. We have not been asked to attend, so I have asked Tommy Stukko to call one for 3 o'clock at the Hot Stove Lounge. He will not call it until the Judge has notified the media. We will only answer questions at that time."

Ron sat back in his chair, and for the first time in a long time wondered if he was going to have a job for much longer. He had never been unemployed in his life—and fate had a good deal to do with that. For the life of him though he could not see how fate was intervening here. Could a new ownership group, and presumably a new management group, fare better than the group Ken Butler had assembled?

Though the meeting returned to the topic of player personnel, in the back of his mind Ron thought about the possibility of his tenure with the Leafs coming to an end. If he had to go somewhere, maybe Vancouver was a good choice. At least he would be close to Kelly.

Or would it be advisable to take a role with a junior club, maybe as GM? He didn't want to think any more about that. He directed his attention to the problem at hand; trying to land the Leafs a replacement for Chuck Andrew.

The Leafs were going through uncertainties on the ice as well. With Andrew out Spencer Smith was experimenting with Dale McCaine at centre between Joel Kent and rookie Tobin West. Randy Rettig had to be bumped up to a line where he was going to be asked to do more than just smash baggage. Charlie Conacher was moved up to the third line, and taking his place on the fourth line was Busher Jackson.

The first game under this experiment was at home against division-leading Ottawa, and the result was mixed—the Leafs battling back but still losing 6-5, despite another three goals by Dale McCaine. Just when it appeared that the city was going to be rocked by an earth tremor caused by the collective jumping off the bandwagon of thousands of Leaf fans, the unexpected happened. Toronto ended its' winless streak with a 3-2 win over the Canadiens at the Gardens, courtesy of a wicked slap shot from the blue line by Conacher that tied the game late in the third, and a nifty give and go between Benoit Marlet and Serge Moit for the winner.

The lines remained the same for the Leafs home encounter with surging Carolina, but the result was a 5-3 loss. It was during this game that the low light of the season was reached from the viewpoint of behaviour on the bench. David Eagleson well reputed shit disturber that he was, reached a new plateau in this game as he tried to bait Mike Commodore of the Hurricanes.

In the second period when Commodore took a run at Benoit Marlet (and missed) Eagleson called him a 'cream-filled testicle', and later in the period, a 'dick-faced moron.' The verbal barbs didn't end with Commodore however. The bespectacled Carolina forward

273

John Thomas was called a 'goggle-headed menace' while Aaron Ward got away easy, dubbed a 'bearded idiot'.

He even saved one for the referee, suggesting that he had 'scrotum-breath.'

What really incensed the Carolina players was that Eagleson did all of his trash talking from the bench, and followed none of it with action on the ice. Every time one of the insulted players was on the ice, Eagleson was nowhere to be found. Instead, it was up to the other Toronto players to have to deal with the physical results of the Hurricanes' frustration.

"He's not helping us with that shit!" Mike McKenna complained. That feeling was the club consensus.

You've always got time for Tim Horton

xcept for a surprising win over defending champion Tampa, they dropped two of their next three games to Ottawa, Pittsburgh and Washington. The loss to Ottawa was expected, and not only because the Leafs always found it a difficult place to play.

The loss to the Penguins was more upsetting, as several of the Leafs had been ready for this game for months. It was supposed to mark their first meeting with ex-teammate Vaclav Artis and many of the Leafs were foaming at the mouth to get a shot in at the man most of them blamed for the 23rd place finish a year ago. It wasn't to be though, as Artis declared himself unfit to play when he bruised his sternum during practice the day before the game.

"It's just like the little asshole," complained Joel Kent, who was among those who had suffered the most by Artis' drop off in play due to his demand to be traded the year before.

"He never gave a shit about anyone but himself. I used to scream inside when I'd see him at those charity events pretending to care about signing autographs and stuff like that. He was only there because he *had* to be. He would never volunteer to show up for *anything*."

The Leafs did manage to break the streak with a 5-2 home win over Washington. As it was the talk radio shows were buzzing over the recent seesaw behaviour of the 'blue and white'. Ron was out of town, scouting North Bay, Sudbury and the Soo when the Leafs were on their three game skid, but he could not drive out of the

275

earshot of Gil 'the thrill' Baines. Sometimes Ron wondered why he listened to Baines at all, except that it was like trying not to look at a car accident.

The loss to Washington was particularly tasty to the thrill, who earlier in the day called it gut-check time for the club. The loss set the stage for the first caller, as he gave Baines the platform he wanted.

"Gil, you've been pretty hard on the Leafs ever since they lost Shoniker, but now that Andrew's out you should cut them some slack, man. They're still in the playoff hunt."

"Yes they are. And the coyote is still in the hunt for the roadrunner, and I can see how that chase is going to end up too!"

Gil went to the next caller, but continued down the same road. "What you fail to understand, Rob is that this hockey club has no depth, and the reason that this hockey club has no depth is that they are managed by the same kind of deep thinkers that ran the Titanic. The management of this club is its' weakest link. And now that there is new ownership on the horizon, they will do the only sensible thing and *fire* the collective keysters of the bunch that are taking up all of the good air over at Maple Leaf Gardens."

Again it was time for Ron to turn 'the thrill' off.

Despite the fact that they defeated the league-leading Canucks in their next outing, the game was not so positively memorable. The Leafs skated away with a 4-1 win, but without defenseman Mike McKenna. During the third period, Terry Oddy was ridden hard into the boards by Todd Bertuzzi. As Oddy limped to the bench, someone had to spell him on the ice. McKenna was just on the shift before, and should have been resting, while David Moore had sat a shift and was due to go back on. Moore pretended not to see Oddy coming toward the bench, and when McKenna looked down the bench and saw no one ready, he jumped over the boards himself. Just when Ralph Newton was admonishing Moore for the oversight, play was called in the Toronto end. The entire Leaf team was caught off guard as the referee motioned for the trainer to come out. McKenna had taken only a few strides towards the Leaf net when he caught his skate in a rut and fell awkwardly to the ice. He landed hard on the shoulder that was operated on only a year earlier, and it was obvious by the way he winced in pain as he was helped from the ice that the shoulder was once again separated.

After the game, when Spencer Smith was informed of the circumstances of the mishap he demanded a closed door meeting with Moore. The team was already beginning to look upon 'Shithead' as something of a liability in team spirit, if not in on ice play. The severity of it was that the Leafs had lost another veteran for an undetermined time. Before the next game with San Jose, Spencer Smith met with Ken Butler and Ron Bailey over their latest setback.

The coach was so distraught that he forgot to put cream in his coffee. "What is it about the god dam third day of the month? We lose Shoniker on the third, Andrew on the third and now McKenna on the third. I'll be damned if I'm sending this team to Detroit on March the 3rd. Call the damn league and reschedule the game!" the coach ordered.

"Actually, we lost Andrew on the *sixth* of January," Brian Ridley corrected.

Spencer Smith looked at his assistant as if he had spit on him. Ridley quickly got up to fetch himself a bagel, before the coach's stare threatened to burn a hole in his retinas.

Ken Butler turned to Ron, "I have to ask you, but I'm afraid you'll tell me. Who is our best candidate for promotion?" he questioned referring to the St. Johns' farm team.

Ron sighed and responded. "Gilbert Mouton—just like I said at the last meeting."

Spencer Smith pounded the table so hard that the salt and pepper shakers hovered in mid-air before landing again intact. "GOD, you've got to bring me some *veterans* who can play this game!"

For a moment, those at the table didn't know if the coach was speaking to them or if he was in fact talking to his maker.

"You know Spence I can't help but notice the great strides that Ian Moriarty has been making over the last couple of games," Ralph Newton said, while trying to diffuse the bomb.

"Yeah," the coach conceded, as he appeared to cool down. "The kid's played well. He makes mistakes, but he has to learn. And right now that's not going to get us in the playoffs. Ken—we need some help out there," he said, appealing to the GM.

This was *not* the time, Ken Butler knew, to bring up the possibility of the trade with St. Louis and Boston that would see *another* veteran defenseman go the other way.

"We have talked about some deals Spence, but you're going to have to be patient with me on this one. We'll get you some help, but it may take a little more time than we'd like. You'll have to hang in there a little bit."

Spencer Smith went quiet for a moment and then added. "I was expecting that the sale going through might have something to do with any deals," he said as his voice trailed off.

"No, it hasn't. We've had no indication that the new ownership group will have anything to say as yet. Keep in mind that they are not officially the owners until it is approved by the league."

That seemed to ease the mind of the coach for now. But Ken Butler could see that even a token gesture towards the coach would show that at least the GM cared about the coach's predicament.

Spencer Smith did not feel any more confident as the club reeled off three straight losses, two of them shutouts. That drove home the point that, in addition to help on defense the club was still without its two best scorers.

The All Star *bleak*

The all-star break was something of a perk for members of the organization, as various junior executives, dubbed 'low men on the scrotum pole' by Spencer Smith, were treated to a trip to the game. This year's festivities were in Atlanta.

As Ron Bailey sat in the lounge of Pearson airport awaiting the 6:00 PM departure of Air Canada flight 505 to Atlanta, Billy Sinfield recognized him.

"Well hello Mr. Bailey—making the trip I see," he remarked as he pulled up a stool at the bar.

"One of the best perks we get," Ron answered.

"Well I'm here to congratulate you on the fact that a player you discovered is the Leafs representative at this years' all-star game," he remarked, as he ordered a gin and tonic, and motioned for the bartender to give Ron another of what he was drinking.

"That means a great deal coming from you Mr. Sinfield!"

"Seriously though, Dale McCaine is becoming quite a story. He's leading the team in scoring, now that Chuck Andrew and Floyd Shoniker are out. And last time I checked he was second, albeit a distant second to Denee Mercure in rookie scoring."

"Sometimes they just fall into your lap, Billy," Ron lamented.

"However there does seem to be more on your mind than the place your team occupies in the standings."

"We are doing well in the standings, if you care to write about that," Ron responded, trying not to sound like he was gloating. "If

I recall you wrote something a while ago about us returning to our familiar spot in or near the basement."

The old goat made no attempt to apologize for his column that slighted the Leafs. "It was merely an opinion, and was not stated as anything but. I take my hat off to the Leafs for the way they have played since. It seems to me though that your place in the standings is the least or your worries now."

"I don't know, as usual, what you are fishing for Billy."

The old goat took a generous sip from his drink, as if it were Gatorade. "I'm referring to a conversation we had a while ago, at Tim Riley's bar, when you mentioned that perhaps the sale of the team to AGM Communications was in the offing."

Ron put down his beer. "Did they call boarding for our flight?" he asked rhetorically.

"No, they did not," Billy Sinfield, replied.

"If I recall, Billy, it was *you* who mentioned AGM! I told you I had no idea, and if I did I wouldn't be allowed to discuss it— why don't you ask Tommy Stukko? He's the one with the inside information"

"You and I both know that he *won't* comment on anything, for free".

Ron laughed at this observation, while reading the label on his beer.

"So go and write this story. Here's a good one. The Toronto Maple Leafs have been sold by tender to the highest bidder. It was revealed today that the highest bidder was none other than Henry Potter, owner of the Toronto Raptors, radio station CHIL, television station CTOR, the Lake Rosseau Inn and Resort, Harewood Acres race track, and Buttonwood Fairways Golf and Country Club. Have I left anything out?" Ron said taking a large swallow of his beer.

Billy Sinfield was visibly salivating. "Can I quote you on this?" he asked.

"Only if you think I'm *serious*," he laughed.

Billy Sinfield shook his head. "You had me going there for a moment, you honestly did. It was better than the AGM story. Think of it—the Leafs and the Raptors playing under the same roof. Who would believe it?"

"Well then I guess you can print it, seeing as how no one *would* believe it. I guess you'll just have to wait until a week from tomorrow like everyone else until the public tendering period is over, and see who the highest bidder is," Ron smiled.

The plane was on time, and the conversation did not continue any longer. While Ron searched for his boarding pass, Billy Sinfield searched for a telephone. He calmly called the story in to the editor, quoting an unnamed source in the Leafs front office as the insider who broke the story that next Friday, H.F. Potter of Thornhill, Ontario was to be announced as the highest bidder for the tendered shares of Maple Leaf Gardens Ltd.

The next day at the arena, Ron was visiting the dressing rooms of the two all-star teams before the media had the chance to descend upon them. He was attempting to get a stick signed by the players, as a gift for trainer Nevell Carpenter. He was having very good luck, as the Leaf trainer was well known to most players from both his experiences at the world championships and the Canada cup. His success was thwarted though when the media began flowing in. As the lone member of the Leaf front office in the line of fire, he was immediately asked to comment on Billy Sinfield's column in that morning's *Toronto Star*, which broke the story of the change in Leaf ownership. He could hardly believe his eyes, as he was shown a copy of the *Sin Bin*, which by now had been picked up by the wire services. Although it did not name Ron as the source of the story, it did recount the conversation that was held at the airport lounge, sans the important qualifier 'only if you think I'm serious.'

The fact that Ron was *not* serious was a minor detail; it had often been said that Billy Sinfield was not one to let facts get in the way of a good story, like his often told tale about why the Canadiens traded Ralph Backstrom to Los Angeles.

"I have nothing to say. No comment, other than to my knowledge the results of the tender have not been given to our organization."

Ron should have left it at no comment. The media present in Atlanta took that to mean that only the results were not for public consumption, but the story was in fact true. This time Ron's name *did* appear in the papers.

When Ken Butler arrived at the Atlanta airport, the media immediately descended him upon while he attempted to retrieve his bag from the luggage carousel. He was not even given a copy of the story to read for himself, but was only asked to comment.

"I have no idea what you are talking about. I can only assume that Ron Bailey has been misquoted," he answered curtly, and then hurried to find a cab. When he was seated inside the car he reached for his phone.

As the car sped away from the airport, he contacted Ron at his hotel, and quickly took him to task. The worst part of the story was that it was true.

"What I said was off the record – I mean that I told Sinfield that I wasn't serious."

"Off the record or not, it is going to look very bad for us when the ownership is announced."

Ron agreed, and once his boss had finished the tongue-lashing he sheepishly asked, "How do you know the results of the tender process – isn't it supposed to be confidential until next week?"

His boss declined to answer over the phone, but instead instructed that they would continue the discussion when he got to the hotel.

Back in Toronto the story was receiving more ink than the all-star game. Representatives from the H.F. Potter group could not be reached for comment. Billy Sinfield was suddenly the toast of the

NHL media, as he unashamedly basked in his glory as the reporter of record.

Ron caught up with him at the hotel bar, where Billy was holding court with a group of young reporters (were there any older ones?) who were hanging on every word that the old goat uttered.

"O' course the all-star game was started by the Maple Leafs," he heard himself say, until he was arm locked by Ron Bailey and whisked away from his bar stool

"The story was a joke!" Ron fumed, as he failed to get the seriousness of his tone through to Sinfield.

"You told me to print it only if I thought you were serious; well I thought you *were* serious. In any event, you have nothing to worry about, my friend—unless o'course the story turns out to be *true*. Then there might be some questions asked, such as how did you know the result of a supposedly sealed tender—before the tenders had closed?"

Ron realized that he could only get in more trouble if he commented. "Billy, I thought that you were a friend. I guess in the future I'll have to be more careful whom I accept drinks from," Ron said, as he stormed away.

Ken Butler had left a message for Ron to meet him in his boss' suite. When Ron got there the GM was standing beside the phone, trying to keep his balance as he kicked off both of his shoes. The phone rang and Ken motioned for Ron to have a seat. The caller was obviously another GM, because whenever Ken Butler was talking to another of the brethren his whole tone of voice changed, as if he were the member of the 'Loyal Order of Water Buffaloes', and he had to speak in some secret dialect.

"I'll see you downstairs in about half an hour," he told the caller and hung up.

"Looks like we may have some interest in Terry Oddy," he said.
"Really?" Ron asked.

"Yeah, the Bruins need some help on the power play. He may be just the guy for them."

"But Boston doesn't have any scoring depth that can help us," Ron countered.

"Maybe not, but I'm thinking more of a three way deal. I'll fill you in later. We'll go down for a drink before dinner and see if we can find anybody who's interested."

Ron was beginning to wonder if his boss was even going to mention the story, and then all of a sudden, he did.

"This comment, quote or whatever you gave Sinfield for his story—where on earth did you hear that?" he asked as he began searching for one of the shoes he had kicked off.

"It was just the first name that came to mind. He mentioned AGM Communications, and when I think of them I think of Potter, because they had that big battle over, what was it, pay-per-view for the baseball games?"

Ken Butler found the left shoe, but was having trouble locating the right one. "Well the unfortunate thing is, the story will likely turn out to *be* true. It seems that Potter contacted *our* lawyer, the clubs' lawyer, and wanted to know about the possibility of the sale not going through if he is declared the highest bidder."

Ron did not understand. "But why *wouldn't* the sale go through if he is declared the highest bidder?"

Ken Butler smiled. "Potter wants the Leafs, but he also wants to make sure that the cable guy *doesn't* get them. He wants to be the highest bidder, but he also wants to make sure that he doesn't pay too much."

"Well how can he ensure that? Won't he just *lose out* if he isn't the highest bidder?"

"Not necessarily. If, let's say, he gets a couple of his corporate buddies to bid also, and their bids are sandwiched around his—one is higher and one is lower. If the friend's price above Potters' is declared the winner, he could withdraw his bid. Maybe he comes up with the financial shorts—then Potter would be the next highest, and get the team."

"But that can't be *legal!*" Ron argued.

"It isn't, if it is *proven*. Collusion is a hard thing to prove. But the guy who withdraws his bid doesn't get away 'scot free'. He has to forfeit a bond, which is probably a percentage of his bid price. The Sally Ann gets the bond money and the sale is completed to the next highest bidder."

"But that still might not be Potter."

"It could be, or it could be the cable guy. The only real way he can be sure that he gets the team is to outbid his competition."

"And he has," Ron concluded.

"Maybe—maybe Potter was just fishing for some inside information from our lawyers. We really won't know for sure."

As Ron and his boss got on to the elevator Ken was immediately greeted by Florida GM, Rudy Pavitch.

"How arwya, Kenny?" he asked, obviously having been into the potent potables by now. Ron had never before heard his boss referred to as 'Kenny.'

"Good, Rudy—good!" he replied.

"Kenny, there's a party going on up at the Nike suite! Better check it out."

"Can't Rudy," Ken Butler replied, watching the floor numbers countdown to 'L'

Suddenly Rudy appeared interested. "Oh, you have a deal in the works I can see. Meeting with Tampa maybe?"

Ken Butler smiled, as he saw that Rudy was still suspicious of any moves that his cross-state rivals made. The Florida GM was still taking heat over the fact that the Lightning had become a bigger success than the Panthers had become.

"No Rudy, nothing in the works with Tampa. But I think I saw Jay Feaster talking to Bobby Smith on the way up here," he said referring to the rival GM's. Rudy suddenly sobered up, and looked determined to find out what was going on.

"I better find a scribe," he said, as the elevator stopped at the lobby.

When they got off, Ron and Ken headed off to the lounge where it seemed that his boss had pre-arranged a meeting. They were directed to a table in the unnecessarily darkened bar, occupied only by Boston GM Doug Forster.

"Hello Ken," he said formally. Ken began by introducing Ron Bailey.

"So this is the kid who's going to be taking your job someday, is it?" he asked, as he eyed Ron up and down the way a cattle buyer gives the 'once-over' to a hoof of beef.

Ron felt slightly uncomfortable—both at the suggestion and by the way the short man with watery grey eyes examined him.

"I understand that Ron's the man that landed you Dale McCaine," Doug Forster continued.

"That's right," Ken answered, as he squinted to find a waitress.

After some idle chitchat, the Boston GM got down to business.

"I know that you've had some offers for Terry Oddy. I don't know if you've heard from Detroit or not but I think they're getting ready to make a deal for a veteran on the blue line. It might only get you a pick, but it would free up some money, wouldn't it?"

Ken Butler didn't comment one way or the other. "Thanks for the information Doug. St. Louis has put together an interesting proposal," Ron's boss bluffed. "They are willing to part with Jim Campbell."

Right away Ken Butler had pushed the Boston GM's button. Doug Forster made no hasty reaction, but it was obvious only to the trained observer by the way he started to run his finger around the rim of his glass, as if he was distracted. Jim Campbell was precisely the kind of player that the scoring-challenged Bruins were looking for. The Leafs were interested in the winger, but that had changed now that Toronto didn't have as much to offer as other teams did.

If the Leafs were going to move Oddy, then they would need help from someone else. And Boston could just be that someone, the GM surmised.

"I'd be surprised if the Blues are that willing to part with Campbell—I mean Terry Oddy is a good defenseman, and lord knows the Blues need help on defense." Doug Forster rambled.

"But Terry is no spring chicken."

"That's exactly what they like about him," Ken Butler continued. "They need some veteran steadying influence back there."

The conversation went on with some small talk until Doug Forster was ready to get down to business. "You really have to be careful dealing with the Blues—Ed Decker would sell his own mother if it would get him the price he was after." he said, referring to the St. Louis GM. Ken Butler reacted only by *not* reacting, instead preferring to stare into his Rye and Ginger Ale.

Doug Forster elaborated. "Do you remember the deal he made with the Islanders a few years ago, when Clare Francis was still the GM? He stiffed his own brother-in-law. He traded him a goalie he knew was damaged goods for a first rounder! Francis was crucified in the press for that—especially when the pick turned out to be third overall," he said while leaning forward on the table to make his point. "That deal cost Francis his job—and to have it done to you by your own brother-in-law!"

Ken Butler knew all about the story and knew also that there was more to it than that. And he also knew that Doug Forster had a personal axe to grind with the St. Louis Blues, and especially with Ed Decker. It was the Blues GM who had fired Forster as coach many years ago, and forced him out of the game by spreading rumours (which years later turned out to be true) that Forster was suffering from stress-related psychological problems. Forster did manage to claw his way back to the NHL, thanks to getting a few jobs along the way out of the compassion of his contemporaries, one of which was Ken Butler.

It was the Leaf GM who, when he was in Vancouver, offered Forster the coaching position with the Canucks' AHL affiliate; a Calder Cup win later, and Doug Forster was on his way back to 'the bigs.'

"Thanks for the concern Doug. I do have another deal for Oddy in the works, but if the deal for Campbell goes through, perhaps you'd be interested in him?"

Ron suddenly was brought to attention as if a drill sergeant had ordered it—he couldn't believe his ears.

Doug Forster was trying to remain calm but it was evident that he was bursting inside. "Well who wouldn't be," he understated, and then tried to backtrack. "I'm not sure we would have anything that would help you out, Ken."

Ron couldn't help but notice that the temperament of the two men had changed dramatically, as if they were now two kids trading hockey cards.

"We could use a blue liner like Valeri Ragulin," he said, as Doug Forster recoiled momentarily. Ken Butler acted like a dentist who had accidentally drilled too close to a nerve and caused his patient some discomfort. "I'm sorry. I didn't mean to bring up that name. I should've just said 'you-know-who' and left it at that."

Ron's boss was referring to the young Russian defenseman who made headlines in the *Hockey News* over a blow up with a Bruins assistant coach. During a practice Ragulin swung his stick at the coach when he was accused of not working hard enough. The Bruins had suspended the kid indefinitely, despite the fact that he was among the leading vote getters for the Calder trophy. He was a problem that Doug Forster was going to have to deal with sooner or later anyway. And there was no way that he could get anything approaching a scorer like Jim Campbell.

"Well, *Ken*—I mean Ragulin is a first rounder! Campbell isn't a first-rounder," Forster downplayed.

"More importantly Doug, he's *playing* like a first-rounder. He's already shown what he can do at this level over a whole season. Ragulin hasn't shown that he has the head for it yet."

Doug Forster smiled at the spectacle of Ken Butler pointing out the wormholes in his apples.

"Somehow I can't see Ragulin playing for Spencer Smith," he smiled, challenging Ken Butler to defend his coach.

"Maybe that's exactly what he needs," the Toronto GM returned, taking a mild shot at the Bruins' low-key approach to coaching. When the smoke had cleared it appeared to Ron as if nothing was close to being finalized. But as they adjourned to attend the all-star dinner in the main dining room, Ken Butler confided in his young protégé.

"We just have to bring St. Louis on board and it's a done deal," he proclaimed.

"I must have missed something," Ron confessed. "I didn't hear the words 'okay', or see a handshake or anything."

Ken Butler smiled. "That's not how Doug and I do business. We have an understanding that goes back a few years. It's not he as if he's indebted to me, but he trusts me to get things done. I guess he respects me. If I can pull off the deal with the Blues then he will make good. I can trust him."

Ron wasn't so sure; there was something about Doug Forster that didn't instil trust, at least not on a first impression.

The all-star dinner was a colossal bore as far as the media was concerned, and it was chiefly to stroke the sponsors. Colin Thomas of the *Hockey News* felt the same way about the game. He ran into Ron between periods of the game, outside of the private boxes.

"You guys will have to do *something* to liven up the format," he warned.

Ron agreed. "Why not go back to the way it was eons ago, the Stanley Cup champions versus the all-stars?"

"Better than what you have now," Thomas suggested.

"I was going to add that the all-star team would be more, *more* *stellar*. If you're choosing only one team, instead of two, then it's like you really are seeing *the* all-star team playing."

"Exactly!" Thomas concluded. "So now all you have to do is to bring that up at the next governors' meeting," he added sarcastically.

"It'll be my first action as Governor," Ron stated.

The game was an example of what shinny is all about—pond hockey at its' finest. There was skilful passing, and lots of shooting but not one open ice hit, body check, or example of anyone taking anyone else into the boards. But the fans seemed not to care. Ron couldn't help but wonder what this kind of game would play like in Maple Leaf Gardens, as opposed to the Phillips Arena. The fans at the Gardens were used to hitting, even if it came infrequently from the often-timid Leafs. He would have to imagine the reaction, because the game had inexplicably not been played in Maple Leafs Gardens since 1967, even though it had been played in every other rink, sometimes twice, since that time. And the game was not scheduled to be played there anytime soon. Ron thought about this as he looked on, and wondered if the only way to get the contest back to the Gardens was: a) win the Stanley Cup and b) return to the old format of the champs versus the all-stars. Either way he thought it would be a long time.

Ron spent the second week of February scouting in western Canada, and returned home as the Leafs prepared to meet the Carolina Hurricanes. He wondered how Spencer Smith would react if he knew that the help he was given from St. Johns' was in fact his boyhood idol, Tim Horton. Horton (Gilbert Mouton as far as everyone else knew) was prevented from joining the team right away. There was a little matter of serving a three game suspension he had incurred at a road game in Pittsburgh, where the St. Johns' Maple Leafs played the Penguins' farm club, the Cleveland Lumberjacks. Horton had been speared, not once but twice by a Cleveland player and had finally snapped. As they tussled in front of the net, Horton grabbed the offender in a wrestling lift and tossed the 190 pounder over the glass and into a row of empty seats.

"'Happens all the time to him here!" Bill Barilko remarked to a linesman.

Horton's first game back with the Leafs was ironically against the last team he had played for—the Buffalo Sabres. Spencer Smith was taking a calculated risk in dressing the kid against the speedy Sabres. The coach was second-guessing himself over his blue line corps. As usual Burks would be with Maleki, and Christian Andersson would normally be with be Terry Oddy.

The coach was reluctant to make the last pairing a couple of rookies, Mouton and Moriarty, so he switched them, putting Andersson with Moriarty and pairing Oddy with Mouton.

"The kid has some speed—maybe he can help Terry out," he told Newton and Ridley after the morning skate the day of the Buffalo game. The Leafs still trailed Ottawa in their division by an increasing margin, and were now only two points ahead of Montreal, though the Leafs held a game in hand.

The Sabres played a close checking game, and the Leafs spent much of it with the puck in their end of the rink. Terry Oddy was logging a lot of ice time, but rarely was he called to make the fast break back into his own end; he had the legs of a young Tim Horton to do that for him. As a result, Oddy was not caught up ice even once during the contest. He was able to do what he did best—work the power play from the point, and consequently he set up two goals with the man advantage. The Leafs were sharp, and skated away with a 4-3 win. The media overlooked Oddy, Spencer Smith thought, and said so after the game.

"He deserved one of the stars, he really did. I don't usually comment on such things, as you know," the coach stated, "but what else does a guy have to do to get recognized?"

Oddy got recognized the next game against the Oilers, where John Dennis had perhaps his finest game of the season, stopping all 33 shots Edmonton fired his way. Benoit Marlet got the Leafs only goal, set up by Terry Oddy, who joined the rush with confidence, knowing that Horton was behind him if the play suddenly shifted to the Leaf end.

Off the ice the Leafs gathered for one of their most popular charity events, the annual 'Have a Heart' dinner at *Alice Fazooli's* restaurant. The Leaf players turned waiters for the event, in support of the community Humewood House and Redwood Shelter for women.

Christian Andersson amazed everyone with his ability to memorize drink orders without writing anything down.

"I used to work at a resort near Goteborg in the off season," he said. "This is easy, compared to understanding where Spence Smith wants me to be in front of the net," he added.

Ron Bailey was sitting at a table with the Leafs' play-by-play man Jim Gerber, who also served as emcee for the evening. Two players, David Moore and John Hill served their table. Ron could not help but notice that there seemed to be a good deal of camaraderie among the players off the ice, but not much of it seemed to include Moore.

"He doesn't exactly seem to have the warm and fuzzy personality like a lot of the other guys," Ron said to Jim Gerber. Gerber's face lost most of its elasticity.

"There's a lot *more* to it than that," he said, leaving an uncomfortable silence. Jim Gerber did not want to leave it at that, especially for someone that obviously had not heard 'the story.' And the Leafs play-by-play man had just enough glasses of wine to elaborate.

"You didn't hear this from me," he started, not looking in Ron's direction. "A few years ago, before you joined the club, we had a young forward, who I'm not going to name but I'm sure that you'll soon figure out who I'm talking about."

Ron was all ears. He didn't want to be the *only* one who didn't know the dirt on David Moore.

"Anyway, this young former fourth pick overall in the draft. A kid who was likable in a sort of 'Lumpy Rutherford' way, not the sharpest knife in the drawer—always seemed to have a chocolate bar melting in his fingers, or a potato chip crumbs on his sweater. Anyway, one day the kid seems to get it all together. He meets a girl and gets married. And everyone thinks that this is great because maybe it's just what he needs, to help him grow up—have some responsibilities. Well just when everything seems to be going well the kid up and leaves the team. He goes home to Minnesota, and starts seeing a shrink. Well Ken Butler is beside himself. The media are told that the kid is injured. Meanwhile Butler is trying like Joe Friday to figure out what went wrong. And of course nobody on the club is saying anything. It's a veritable 'see no evil, speak no evil' in the room. Well, it turns out that David Moore has been doing the wild thing with 'Mrs. Kid' and the kid is devastated."

Ron was bewildered. "But, this 'kid'—he's still with the Leafs?"

Jim Gerber grimaced. "No, he's *not*. He was traded to try and diffuse the situation."

Ron felt that he was missing something. "But if *Moore* was the cause of the problem, why not trade…"

"Because," Jim Gerber said, gritting his teeth "The kid was never the same after it. His play dropped off so badly—again the media was told it was the injury. And Moore, well he is a veteran defenseman. He still has some value—but not to his teammates. There isn't one guy on this roster that was here when this happened that would give Moore the time of day. And what's worse, Moore doesn't care."

The story seemed to explain a lot of things about the kind of person that David 'Shithead' Moore was. Not that adultery was grounds for being ostracized in the dressing room. If it were there would be a lot of divided rooms all across North America. It was because the team felt a kind of kindred spirit with the kid, Ron was told. They treated him like he was their little brother. They tried to look out for him. They all knew he was immature, but he was a good hockey player. And he was a good teammate. And all Moore did was take advantage of someone who was weaker. On the ice or off the ice this was unacceptable in the player's eyes.

"It still bothers a lot of guys that Moore wasn't the one who was traded. They don't really blame anyone—not Ken Butler or Spencer Smith. They blame Moore."

Ron wondered if Moore's name was going to come up again as the trade deadline approached. He recalled that Ken Butler had mentioned Moore in a counter offer to St. Louis in their demands for Terry Oddy, and speculated that Moore would be moving anyway.

The NCAA season was now in full tilt and Ron had to get out and see some of it He followed the next few Leaf games over the internet and via the satellite dish of sports bars, as he travelled through Minnesota and Wisconsin while catching some of the college action. He was grateful that he didn't have to witness first hand some sloppy games as the Leafs registered another three game losing skid.

New York was the city the Leaf brass liked to visit most, for reasons other than hockey. After the game the Leaf brass met at the *Café on the Park*, the lounge in the Chrysler building that overlooked Central Park. The view was the reason they were there. It offered spectacular panorama of the Gotham skyline. The lights of the buildings looked like stars, and the concrete and glass were like the night sky.

Ken Butler had arrived earlier with Walt Fisher, and sat sipping a Manhattan when the coaches arrived. The view only kept the coach's mind off of hockey for so long, however.

"I don't know what it is about the number three," Spencer Smith declared, commenting on the Leafs third road loss in a row, to the Rangers at Madison Square Garden. As they sat chatting at a window table it became obvious to them all that the season was beginning to slip through their grasp.

"Do you remember me saying we better have a plan if something starts to go wrong, because I can't put my finger on what's gone *right* for us so far? Well, it's time for a plan." the coach decreed.

"I'm not concerned right now that we're going through streaks, especially when we don't lose more than three in succession," Ken Butler offered.

"I'm encouraged by the club's ability to end the losing streaks... it says a lot about your teams character," Walt Fisher added.

Spencer Smith took off his glasses and cleaned them, adjusted them, and returned them to his head.

"Something wrong, Spence?" Walt Fisher asked.

"Yeah, I had to see who said that!" He laughed. Walt Fisher had been right in his observation.

The next game in New Jersey the Leafs continued their tailspin. Terry Oddy again played well, although he didn't earn a game star this time. He did however draw the attention of the visiting St. Louis scouting staff. Blues' GM Ed Decker met personally with Ken Butler after the game 'for a chat' as he put it. It was obvious that the Blues' interest in Oddy was growing as they lost in New Jersey the next night to put them four points out of a playoff spot.

John Dennis was being saved for the Saturday night road game against the Canadiens at the Molson Centre. To Dennis, a native Montrealer, the chance to play in front of his hometown crowd was something more than money could buy. He was not a francophone, but in his final year of junior some scouts referred him to as 'Jean Dennee'—with the French pronunciation. It was widely rumoured that, once he became a free agent, he would jump at the chance to return to the city of his youth. And the Canadiens were biding their time until the opportunity presented itself.

For the struggling Montrealers the game with Toronto meant a chance to close within four points of the Leafs. The game featured the entire aura of a traditional Toronto-Montreal encounter, but with the speculation that these two teams could meet in the playoffs, a little spice was added.

In honour of this fact, Toronto had chosen to wear a sweater design from the thirties, which included the famous 35-point maple leaf. The sweaters seemed to inspire the younger players on the team, and it even lifted the spirits of some of the veterans. But for Conacher, Jackson and Horton, it just made them feel at home. In the 2-1 win the Leafs earned that night, it was the legends who stole the show, Horton scored the game's first goal, rushing the puck from outside his own blue line and muscling his way around both Canadiens defenders before depositing a backhand into the net. Even many of the Canadiens supporters agreed that they had not seen a defenseman score a goal that way—perhaps not since the days of Doug Harvey. And on the winning goal it was all Busher Jackson, who not once but *twice* worked a give and go with Conacher to move the puck through across the neutral zone, before Conacher blasted a shot over the goalies' shoulder.

The win was huge for the Leafs, because both Ottawa and New Jersey won on this night. The loss was a real blow to the Habs' playoff hopes, as they fell closer to the final playoff spot. And privately Spencer Smith was grinning inside. He thought that finally he had some kids that could give the veterans some rest.

The dead trade line

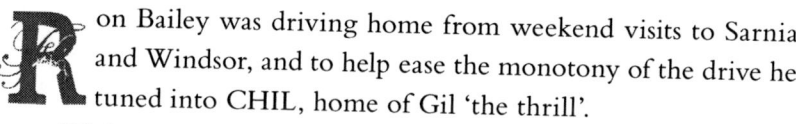

R on Bailey was driving home from weekend visits to Sarnia and Windsor, and to help ease the monotony of the drive he tuned into CHIL, home of Gil 'the thrill'.

"If there ever was a testimony to how mismanaged this hockey club is," the thrill began "it is the current state of affairs down at MLG. Here we have a club that had climbed as high as 4th overall in the standings, mostly with smoke and mirrors, but 4th nevertheless. And now they are sinking faster than loan shark's patsy in cement galoshes," he continued. Ron didn't turn the thrill off—he wanted to see where this was going.

"And to be fair, they have lost key veterans, Andrew, Shoniker, McKenna, but instead of trying to salvage this thing they are sitting on their big fat duffs feeling sorry for themselves. Well, Leafs, you have no one to blame, but yourselves! All of last summer, the Leafs were told by anyone who would listen, SIGN SOME FREE AGENTS, open the wallet, let out a few months and part with some cash. IMPROVE THE HOCKEY TEAM WITH SOME DEPTH!"

Ron would have loved to get through on the call in portion of the show that would follow, but he knew it would be useless. Agree with the thrill, and he lets you talk—disagree and it's on to the next caller that will agree.

"But instead of signing some free agents they scoop up four or five guys barely good enough to make the East Coast Hockey League. Well, Leafs. I'm sorry, but you brought this on yourselves!"

Ron knew that the criticism was valid—about the lack of free agent signings. But 'the thrill' should have mentioned that the impending sale of the hockey club did have an effect on that. There was no stated policy against signings. But Ken Butler was given definite budget to operate with. And that budget was used up signing existing players whose contracts were up for renewal. The rate at which salaries were escalating was something that even the most pessimistic budget could not possibly forecast. There was no question that salary room in the budget was a big factor in the Vaclav Artis trade.

"And now with the trade deadline quickly approaching, we hear nothing but silence from Maple Leaf Gardens. No rumours, not a bite. Well, the truth is that a playoff spot, while likely, is not a lock. Where the Leafs sit now, they'll be playing New Jersey or Ottawa, who are what, 25 points ahead in the standings? It'll be over after game 4 and then they're on the golf course *yelling* fore. The management of this hockey club has to, *has to* make some kind of a move at the trade deadline, and not just a token move like shipping out Terry Oddy, in order to save face with the fans." The great and powerful Oz had spoken.

Only hours before the Leafs took to the ice at the Corel Centre the official announcement of the public tender results were released. The Potter group was indeed declared the winner of the bidding, and understandably enough there was a protest filed, though not as expected, by the cable guy. The protest came from the brewery group that had put together a last minute proposal. The protest was only expected to delay the inevitable, and Billy Sinfield did not even mention it in his follow up column. The 'Old Goat' did his fair share of 'You heard it here first' in the column, but spent even more time speculating on how the Gardens' faithful would take to having their team play at the new Air Canada Centre. The players were predictably distracted by all of the media attention to the purchase, and it showed on the ice as they went down 5-3.

The funk that the club had found it in was not easily shaken. The club had gone from not being able to score goals to not being able to prevent them.

In the room, the tension was readily broken by one of John Hill's annual events. He was responsible for organizing (and more importantly collecting the money for) the Memorial Cup Pool.

"It works like this," he instructed the newcomers. "There are forty teams eligible for the tournament. We need twenty warm bodies to draw two teams each out of the hat. It costs a C-note per man, and the winner takes all two grand."

Right off the bat there were some objections from rookies over the entry fee, but Hill quickly pointed out that *their* participation was not an option—either they paid the fee or risked a team-levied fine of *two* hundred dollars. When the draft was completed there were some major complaints—especially among those players who were stuck with teams that had been their bitter rivals during their junior careers.

"I am not keeping Sherbrooke," Serge Moit groaned, "No god damn *Castors!*"

Joel Kent flipped a grin that highlighted the missing tooth at the corner of his mouth. He had selected Moit's alma mater, the Laval Titans. "It'll cost you a hundred to make a trade," Kent laughed.

"Tabernac!" Moit grumbled as he handed over the cash, and added, "No matter. It'll be worth it when they beat you in the next round."

Philadelphia came in to the Gardens next, with a chance to establish themselves as first in the conference, and that's exactly what they did, earning a relatively easy 6–3 victory. Spencer Smith, to his credit, stood there and took it from the media after the game. He was asked every obvious question, about the possibility that the Leafs were in danger of missing the playoffs for the third year in a row. Montreal had won on this night and was only four points back of the

Leafs. The coach chose to deflect the attention from his team's play to its injury plight. He preceded this by saying that he wasn't using injuries as an excuse for the club's streaky play of late.

The club remained at home for their 69th and 70th games, including the March 17th resurrection of the Toronto St. Patrick's jerseys. The coach continued his ritual of alternating goalies for back-to-back games, and therefore Lars Rogers was given the start. Spencer Smith wasn't concerned that Lars Rogers wasn't performing up to his capability. He *was* however concerned that Rogers' teammates would not have the same confidence in him that they had shown in John Dennis. This could be a concern if he had to rest John Dennis down the stretch. Lars Rogers would have to get at least three more starts in their remaining twelve games. And a victory in any one of those three starts could be the difference between making and missing the playoffs—.500 would not do it. Spencer Smith was spared the grief. It was as if the Leafs knew that their goalie would be rusty, and they did their best to keep shots to a minimum, earning an easy 6-2 decision over the tame Minnesota Wild.

Another home victory, courtesy of the Rangers, lifted their spirits even further but despite the fact that it was a Saturday night, Ken Butler ordered a special meeting of the team executive.

"The trade deadline is Monday," he began, "and I expect to be on the phone for the better part of tomorrow and Monday."

Ron Bailey knew that would mean that he would probably not leave his boss's side for that duration. They may even pull a rare 'all-nighter.'

"We are going to review all of our options before we leave here tonight," he continued.

A knock came to the door of the directors' room, and a waiter from the *Hot Stove Lounge* appeared with pots of coffee and tea, and a tray of some fancy dessert pastries. The refreshments were largely ignored, at least during the first hour of the meeting. Walt Fisher, Ron and Brian Ridley were all in favour of the three-way deal with

St. Louis and Boston for Terry Oddy, which would also include the Leafs second round draft, pick. Spencer Smith was unconvinced, and Ralph Newton was shuddering at the prospect of coaching a defenseman who liked to swing his stick at assistant coaches. Ron was having trouble staying alert as the meeting entered overtime, so he gave in and poured himself a black coffee. He was startled by how hot it still was.

Eventually the others began to sway Spencer Smith, which was not an easy task. Ron thought that it reminded him of a deadlocked jury trying to convince the one holdout.

Finally, Smith said. "I'll back you in public on this one Ken, but between us here I don't think this kid is the answer. I think we'll have another Artis on our hands. But bring him in here and we'll do our best."

The GM had gotten what he wanted to hear. "We agree on the deal then, Oddy for Ragulin," he stated.

"Now tonight, during the game, I had an enquiry from Lou Lamoierello, regarding David Moore. I don't think I have to say any more, no pun intended. The deal is for a fourth round pick. It will also free up some salary, and, well, I need to know what you all think."

No one said anything at first. Walt Fisher cleared his throat, and was about to speak, but instead just raised his eyebrows and looked over at Ron. He glanced at Ken Butler, who was looking for a reaction now from Ralph Newton, who just smiled. Brian Ridley was fixed on Spencer Smith's reaction.

The coach was stone faced, but when it became clear that no one was going to say anything, he said. "Get 'Shithead' the hell outta here. The no good dog fu..." he ranted; only the mouthful of plain donut left any question as to what he had meant to say.

The GM was mildly surprised by the coach's reaction, but was happy to get a unanimous vote. "We do have to address the changes to our defense. We will be losing two veterans, and gaining one kid, at a time when we also have an injury to Mike McKenna. Where does this leave us?"

The question was probably meant for the coach, but Walt Fisher was first to answer. "Well," he said, uncharacteristically giving in to the temptation of a cinnamon and raisin Danish that seemed to be calling his name, "I understand that McKenna will be out another week to ten days. So it leaves us with Burks, Maleki, Andersson, Moriarty, the new kid Ragulin, and the kid from the rock."

"Mouton," Ron inserted.

"Yes," Walt Fisher continued.

Spencer Smith started at the highly polished oak boardroom table. "It doesn't exactly fill me with confidence," the coach continued. "Ken, I think you have to see what else you can find out there—what about a guy like Sean O'Donnell or Adrian Aucoin?"

Walt Fisher almost choked on his Danish. "You mean someone you actually *played* with, Spence?" he said.

Spencer Smith was about to return the shot, when Ken Butler intervened and asked Ron "Down on the farm, Ron?"

"David Hansky," he responded, referring to Bill Barilko.

"He's the best plus-minus of all defensemen in the league—physical, steady, stay at home type. He won't be joining the rush when Spence doesn't want him to," Ron said while nodding to the coach.

Ken Butler wanted to leave the topic on a positive note. "I'll be on the phone, Gentlemen. We'll see what we can come up with in the way of blue line help."

The next item was the erratic goal scoring of late. Spencer Smith began. "Well, if there's no help on the horizon, we'll have to make do with what we have. The medical staff tells me that Shoniker is probably still out another ten games *minimum*—Andrew, at least the same. So we shouldn't expect any help until the playoffs. On the upside, I'm happy with the way some of the kids have picked up the slack—Marlet, West, and of course Ronnie's boy McCaine. And even those rubes you sent me from the rock—Bachmann and Bodine."

"The *Killer B's*," Brian Ridley added.

"Yeah," the coach continued, "they're fitting in nicely. I'm not as worried about that, Ken," he concluded.

The meeting ended early Sunday morning, but before noon all of the scouting staff, Ron and Walt Fisher were summoned back to the Gardens for one more session that concluded at around 11:00 PM. They fielded calls from half of the teams in the league. Walt even had an offer for John Dennis from Philadelphia that, had the Leafs *not* been in the playoff hunt, may have been entertained.

Just before they headed off to their respective homes Ron received a call from an unexpected source.

"Is this *the* man around the Gardens in charge of mergers and acquisitions?" The caller asked, his voice having an unmistakable trace English accent. It was the kind of language flavour that fades after having been in a foreign country for too long.

"Leslie, how are you old bean," Ron bubbled. "It's about time you returned a call!"

"I know, I know, I've been meaning to call you. I said to Joan just the other day, 'now I must get round to calling Ronnie Bailey,' but I've been so damn busy!"

It was the same old story with Leslie Winston. The two of them had worked together briefly, with the Windsor Spitfires. Ron was an assistant coach, and Leslie was the head scout. He had taught Ron *everything* he knew about scouting. Ron had tried to keep in touch with Les over the years, but the scout turned player agent was notorious for not returning calls.

"So what do I owe the honour of this call, or should I say 'what's the special today?'"

Ron was taking a jibe at his friend. On their many lunches together, Leslie Winston would routinely ask what the specials were before he would even consider a menu.

"Now Ronnie, don't make me regret that I called," he said, adopting a more serious tone.

"I was wondering if the Toronto Maple Leafs are the only team that isn't interested in Dennis MacDonald."

Ron went silent on his end of the phone. His memory raced back to Christmas and the unexpected meeting in Switzerland with his old teammate. He recalled that Dennis had asked him to call him once he got home.

"Are you telling me that he's interested in coming back to the NHL?"

Leslie laughed a throaty cackle, "For the right deal," he said.

Ron realized that he probably should have mentioned the chance encounter to Ken Butler.

"Really!" Ron muttered, "And what kind of deal might that be?"

Leslie was never one to get right to the point. "Dennis isn't interested in peddling his services to the highest bidder. He wants to play for a team, with the right fit," he said, dangling a carrot before Ron.

To his credit, Ron wasn't biting. He did form a mental picture of Dennis MacDonald in a Leaf uniform, and it was a picture worthy of a Beehive photo.

"We've talked to Ottawa, and Philadelphia, and the Rangers," Leslie went on "But Dennis isn't sure that's where he wants to be."

"What about Vancouver?" Ron asked, continuing to play the game.

"Nooooo," Les responded. Ron could picture the screwed up, forcibly contorted face on the other end of the phone.

"Oh!" Ron commented, still not sure why Vancouver was a 'noooo'.

"Dennis thinks you guys have the right idear. A veteran club, with just the right mix of some kids, and a coach that knows how to treat the older guys."

Leslie was obviously fishing. He didn't doubt for a moment that there was interest from those other clubs, and perhaps a few more. If the Rangers, for example, were seeking Dennis MacDonald, money was not going to be the roadblock. Ron needed to know more, before he got his boss involved.

"I'm surprised you haven't heard from the Canadiens!" Ron exclaimed, knowing full well that they were the kind of team that Dennis would never play for—a young coach with an equally young group. There, Dennis would be expected to be a leader—a veteran to set the example for the younger ones. And he knew that at this stage in Dennis' career that he didn't need that kind of pressure. He was content to worry only about himself. That was the kind of location he was looking for. And Toronto, it seemed, fit the bill.

'Maybe it wasn't so *coincidental* that I ran into him in Switzerland,' Ron thought.

"I was just calling to let you know our situation. Dennis informed me that you probably had your head too far up your behind, trying to make a deal for David Moore."

"That was like a sucker punch, Leslie," Ron warned.

The agent just laughed. "It's a credit to you if you can deal him. And I know where you can find a very, *very capable* replacement," he said.

Ron's response to the bait was laced with scepticism "Really?" he commented. He could tell that Leslie Winston was grinning a toothy grin from ear to ear.

"Two words—savvy veteran."

To Ron that could mean anything from a 'high mileage case' to a 'wheelchair jockey.'

"Which is it?" he asked.

Leslie continued the guessing game, "Russian captain, '91 Canada Cup."

Ron had to think so hard whom the Russian captain was in '91, so hard that it hurt.

"I give up!" he said.

"Alexi Gusarov." Leslie whispered.

"Are you for *real*?" Ron shrieked. "He must be fifty-five years old! I drafted him in our hockey pool when you and I were in Windsor! He was thirty-five then! That was *nine years* ago!"

Leslie only grinned a small grin now. "He's thirty-eight."

"In *dog* year's maybe!" Ron laughed, "Or does it work with Russians the way it does with some Latin American baseball players. You see them in the little league world series when they're supposed to be 13, only they're eighteen, and then you draft them five years later. And after six years in the minors when you go to sign them to a contract extension they show up with a birth certificate that says they're twenty. It's the climate down there; they don't age as fast. Or is it that Ponce DE Leon thing, you know, the fountain of—"

Leslie interrupted. "He would be a big improvement over what you have now."

Ron wasn't so sure. "Les, I'll mention this to Ken. But I can't see him going for it. Sure, we'd love to have Dennis MacDonald—we'd be foolish not to."

"If for no other reason than keeping Ottawa or Philadelphia from getting him," Les added.

"*Exactly,*" Ron agreed.

Leslie Winston was getting ready to close the sale. "Well, I really think you'd be doing yourself a great disservice if you didn't bring Gusarov to Ken's attention," he continued. "You have until noon tomorrow; the deadline for signing players that played this year in Europe is the same as the trade deadline."

Ron had almost forgotten *this* little detail. It had meant nothing to the Leafs in the past three years, but now that they were taking a run at a playoff spot, it could. Ron was more concerned about the lack of scouting reports that he had on Dennis MacDonald. And the fact that he had *no* information whatever on what Alexi Gusarov had been up to.

When he got off the phone with Leslie Winston, he immediately dialled the number of the team's European head scout, Jarmo Nuowanen, in Helsinki. Ron didn't even bother to calculate the time difference. Upon waking up the startled ex-NHL'er he was surprised to find that Nuowanen knew all about Alexi Gusarov and Dennis MacDonald.

"I'll fax you the reports, I can tell you that they had a great season in Bern though," he said before begging off for some more pillow time.

When Ron got off the phone he dialled Ken Butler. Now that he had started the 'due diligence' process in motion he would be able to answer his boss's first question: 'What do we know about how these guys are playing?'

Ron was surprised to find that his boss was not there when the Leaf executive reported to the Gardens for an eight o'clock resumption of their meeting.

"He's at Pearson Airport," the secretary informed Ron.

Ron's blood pressure began to rise. "Did he say *where* he was going?"

"Oh he's not going *away*. He's gone to meet some people."

The call that Ron received at 9:15 explained it all. Ken Butler had been on the phone almost since he spoke to Ron, at about 11:45 Sunday night. Since that time, Ken Butler had negotiated in principle a deal that would land the Leafs both Dennis MacDonald *and* Alexi Gusarov. In addition, he had almost finalized the deal with St. Louis for Terry Oddy. It was now to include underachieving winger David Eagleson.

As expected Ed Decker asked that the Leafs to sweeten the deal—Toronto would get Jim Campbell in return, whom they would send to Boston for rookie defenseman Valeri Ragulin.

307

"I've gone over it with Spence," the GM advised Ron," and we have his vote of confidence. He seems to think young Ragulin will be greatly influenced by Gusarov—the kid idolized him growing up. I found that out from Jarmo Nuowanen. The kid will be in heaven playing here with Gusarov. And Gusarov has always wanted to play in Canada."

Ron had to wonder what the sudden influx of Europeans; specifically Russians would do to the chemistry of the team that Spencer Smith was trying to mix. The Leafs currently had only one player on the roster from overseas, defenseman Christian Andersson.

"He thinks it's great to be having a couple more savvy vets along for the stretch run," Ken Butler commented.

"So, where do we go from here?" Ron asked.

The phone connection was not very good. It sounded to Ron as if his boss said 'no more.'

The cell phone cracking had distorted his words. What he had really said was 'and now, Moore.'

Ron had to hang up, hoping that his boss would call back right away. But it was close to half an hour before he could track Ken Butler down. The Leaf GM had been on the line to the Islanders, Detroit and Colorado in that span, and had managed to make a deal that would send David 'Shithead' Moore to the Avalanche for a fourth round draft pick.

"Get a hold of Stukko, and have him get the press release ready. And get the paperwork ready to fax into the league," Ken Butler ordered. "I'm going to meet Les Winston. He is coming in from New York any minute, with MacDonald and Gusarov," his boss said, enthusiastically.

"Did you get *any* sleep last night?" Ron asked.

"Plenty of time for that later—I love this time of year—nothing like a few deals to get the bloods moving. I'll call you later. I'll be bringing the three of them to the Gardens. We won't make it in time for practice, but we will for the press conference—*Hot Stove* lounge.

Remember also to ask Walt to let Moore and Eagleson know what's happening, before practice. Spencer is going to Oddy's home to tell him. He asked to. You might also want to let Newton and Ridley know. Spence will be a little late for the practice."

Ken Butler sounded like he was well fuelled by caffeine. Ron followed his boss's instructions to the letter. All of the phone calls took some time, and the practice was well underway before Eagleson and Moore were notified of the trade.

Ron was in his office helping to get material ready for the press conference, when his phone rang. It was Neil Porters of the Globe and Mail.

"Mr. Bailey—Neil Porters, Globe and Mail. How are you this morning?"

Ron's suspicion was not yet raised, but he was surprised at being contacted by the reporter. Usually only the coach, the GM or the assistant GM was called upon for quotes.

"I'm calling to ask you about the incident after practice this morning," the caller said.

Ron looked at the wall clock. It was 11:30. Yes indeed, practice was over. But what was the incident that Porters was referring to? "I'm afraid I don't know what you mean. What incident?" he asked.

"Can you comment on the details of the fight in the dressing room?"

"*What* fight in the dressing room?"

Neil Porters kept on Ron like a pit bull. "After the team found out about David Moore being dealt to St. Louis, there was an incident in the dressing room. Apparently several players, shall we say, gave Mr. Moore a less than affectionate send off. Can you comment?"

Ron momentarily chuckled at the media experience. The trade had not been formally announced, and therefore Porters had only heard about it second-hand. And of course, he got it wrong, as Moore was *not* going to St. Louis.

"I'm sorry Neil, but I have no idea what you are talking about. I guess, to be cliché about it, I have to say 'no comment' and leave it at that. I'm sorry I can't help you."

With that Ron abruptly ended the conversation. He wasted no time in getting down to the dressing room from his third floor office. There was a large congregation of media already mobilized around the entrance to the room. Nevell Carpenter was doing an admirable job of keeping them at bay. Ron was able to brush right past, only because most of the media types didn't recognize him.

Once inside, he sought out Spencer Smith, but the coach hadn't returned from his meeting with Terry Oddy. Before he could find any of the assistants, David Burks got hold of Ron, and filled him in.

"The man of steel clocked him," he said referring to Joel Kent.

"Why?" Ron asked.

"When we heard that Shithead had been traded, he wasn't even on the ice yet. Superman was on the ice with a bunch of us, and he headed straight for the room. You have to understand that this thing has been building for years. I don't know if you know the history of it. But this has been a long time in coming. Everyone would have stood in *line* to take a shot at Shithead."

"What did Kent do, just walk up to him and sucker punch him?"

David Burks seemed to take offence that his buddy would stoop to that. "Shithead knew exactly what was coming. They had words first, but then he turtled. It was just like the gutless wonder!"

Ron had seen this kind of thing before, but rarely among teammates.

"Just wait till he gets to Denver. Everybody went looking for the schedule to see if we play them again!" Fortunately for Moore the Leafs did not.

The practice resumed, but it took on a low-key mood. There was more talk than action, as the players buzzed about the deals that had been made. And the fact that a few of them had dodged a bullet as far as their status as Maple Leafs was concerned. On the ice the speculation began.

"MacDonald will be with me, and McCaine. You know Spence. He'll put all his eggs in one basket," Joel Kent observed. He was referring to the coaches' habit of putting all of his scoring ability on one line.

"Then he'll probably put a line of the rookies together; West, Sawchuck and that Bachmann kid," he continued.

Davis Burks joined in on the speculation. "I'm surprised about Ragulin. I heard from Leetch that the guys' a whiner. He has to do everything his way. Nobody can tell him anything."

Joel Kent laughed, "Can you see Spence putting up with that crap from a rookie?"

"Or from a vet," Burks added, "Lookit Shithead—he finally got the boot because of it."

Frank Maleki joined in on the conversation as he skated over. "I bet they picked up Gusarov just to baby sit the little comrade," he added.

Joel Kent couldn't help himself. "Nice to see them get somebody on the blue line older than you two farts," he said.

"You should be talking, Kent! You're so old your rookie card is actually *worth* something!" Maleki shot back.

After the practice ended Terry Oddy showed up to clean out his cubicle. There were a lot of congratulations going around, from the core of veterans. The rookies generally avoided this ritual, preferring to keep their place. Maleki, Burks, Dennis and Kent all said their good-byes. And Floyd Shoniker, Chuck Andrew and Mike McKenna came by from sickbay to offer their best wishes.

"See you in the playoffs," Andrew kidded Oddy, knowing that the only way the two clubs could meet would be in the final.

The press conference formally announced the trades and welcomed the new faces to the media. All three of the newcomers would be in the line-up against Montreal the next night.

The media reaction to the trades was surprisingly positive. On the afternoon talk show on CHIL, host Eddie LeBec was talking with the Globe's hockey beat writer, Grant Baker.

"Getting Dennis MacDonald could be a major move, *if* the Leafs make the playoffs. It was missed at the press conference...but the deal is only for this year. He is signed to an option for next year, but only if the Leafs make the playoffs *this* year. Otherwise he's free to go," Baker noted.

Eddie LeBec followed the party line to critique the Leaf organizations every move. Since they had lost the rights to broadcast the Leaf games they jumped at every opportunity to dump on them. "You really think it helps, getting a guy who has been out of the league for six years?"

"It's only five," Baker corrected, "but yes, I do. He was sought after by a few clubs, the Flyers, Senators, and Canucks—all clubs ahead of the Leafs in the standings. It's not as if he wasn't a hot commodity."

Le Bec was disappointed in the reaction, so he went in a different direction. "What about Gusarov?"

Baker backtracked a bit. "Well it's a bit different there. Here you have one of the few old Russians who have never had a taste of the NHL. He did go to training camp with New Jersey a few years ago."

"Well if he wasn't good enough for the New Jersey Red Devils," Le Bec jibed, "At that time, everybody with a hammer and sickle on their passport and a pulse was being signed by the Devils!"

"Yes, and as I recall they got a Stanley Cup out of it!" Baker observed.

Le Bec tried to save face. "But they didn't sign Gusarov, so I guess he wasn't good enough."

"From what I heard at the time, they offered him a contract, but just before they came to terms he decided he didn't want to come to North America after all—at least not to the US."

"So what changed since that time?"

"Well," Baker continued, "he hooked up in Bern with MacDonald, as the two imports allowed. I guess that MacDonald painted a pretty good picture of Canada, and here they are now together in Toronto."

"Well it remains to be seen, at age 35 and 38 respectively, if these two have anything left. The Leafs could be looking awfully foolish if this thing backfires," Le Bec bristled.

"Or awfully *smart* if it doesn't!" Baker countered.

The next obligatory controversial topic was the young Russian defenseman, Valeri Ragulin.

"Well I guess the Leafs figured it's better to have a pair of Russians on the blue line than just one," Le Bec laughed.

Again Baker looked at the flip side. "I think the Leafs had an interest in Ragulin at draft time last year, but went for help up front instead. The interesting thing about Ragulin is that his boyhood idol was Gusarov. And his father was the great Alexander 'Rags' Ragulin, who patrolled the blue line for some of those legendary Soviet teams of the sixties. He had trouble in Bean town where the word is that he wouldn't listen to anyone. But the thinking here is that the kid will listen to Gusarov."

Again, Le Bec could only see the risk involved. "Not a safe bet by any means," he concluded.

The media were all over the game day skate the next morning as they continued to milk the trade story for all it was worth. The dressing room incident between Moore and Kent was still receiving more than just sidebar status. None of the players would comment, though, even off the record. As usual, the media had to use the 'source close to the team' trump card. In this case it turned out to be Moore, who got back at the team the only way he could; a parting knife in the back.

Post season or post mortem

The game that night with the Rangers had almost the same kind of electricity for die-hard fans as opening night. Who would be lined up with whom, and the all-important question 'What number would they be wearing?' would take centre stage, and deflect attention from the Leafs struggle to fend off the suddenly competitive Carolina Hurricanes.

Jim Gerber began the broadcast that night in his inimitable, monologue style. "Welcome to the return to the NHL of Dennis MacDonald and Alexi Gusarov, former Swiss league team mates. And as you have probably heard by now, the Maple Leafs have parted company with the much maligned Terry Oddy, and have acquired rookie defenseman Valeri Ragulin from the Boston Bruins via the St. Louis Blues in one of those complicated three way deals that Ken Butler loves so much and that only he and 'the Amazing Carnac' can understand."

He continued to prevent the inept Bobby Swanson from interrupting, "And going the other way—David Eagleson. And to Colorado, David Moore, who had both probably worn out their welcomes in Toronto. The ironic thing about Terry Oddy is that he probably played his best hockey of the season over the last ten games. At any rate, in practice today the three newcomers looked a little tentative as expected. It appears that the lines will look something like this!" Jim Gerber continued, taking time to inform the listeners whom the starting line-up was brought to you by.

"It looks as if it will be rookie Dale McCaine, who has now dropped behind Joel Kent in the team scoring lead, at centre between Joel Kent and Dennis MacDonald, who will be wearing number 27. Tobin West will be alongside Serge Moit and Benoit Marlet. It'll be John Hill between Lou Zanardo and Lorne Graham, and we'll see the call-ups, Bachmann, Charlie Bachmann, and Jack Bodine flanking Greg Sawchuck."

For the first time, Charlie Conacher and Busher Jackson would be re-united, if only on the fourth line.

"On the blue line, Christian Andersson will be with rookie Ian Moriarty. David Burks will be alongside Gil Mouton, and the Russian tandem of Alexi Gusarov and Valeri Ragulin." Suddenly there was some surplus on the blue line, with Bill Barilko, a.k.a. David Hansky, and Frank Maleki, forced to the press box.

"And just to add, Gusarov will be 44 and, no, that's his number *not* his age."

Bobby Swanson thought it was time to add some wisdom. "And that will be Valeri Ragulin out there as number 24, not David Moore. I think we'll notice a difference. And interestingly Jim, this will be the first time that the Leafs have gone with any Europeans in the line-up, since they traded Vaclav Artis."

As usual, Swanson's observations were flawed. "Well the last time I looked, Christian Andersson's homeland of Sweden *is* in Europe, continental drift notwithstanding," Jim Gerber corrected.

The Leafs played their most energetic game in weeks, skating away with an impressive 3-2 win, though due largely to the goal tending of John Dennis.

"He *was* our team tonight," Spencer Smith said in the media interview after the game.

"We were out shot, something like 35-17. He stole this one for us, no doubt about it," the coach continued, rubbing perspiration from his brow. Having gone only 4-6 in their last ten games, this win was a must.

315

The Leafs got goals from Kent, Moit and Christian Andersson, only his third of the season, as if to remind everyone that he was the still the resident European on defense.

The Leafs headed out on the road for the last time, first to Atlanta, where Kent and Andersson scored but the Leafs, obviously having trouble adjusting to a 1 PM start, dropped a 4-2 decision. Montreal lost a home game to Ottawa, and still trailed the Leafs by two points.

Spencer Smith gave John Dennis the night off against Phoenix, as he told Ken Butler that he was concerned that the veteran had been facing too many shots of late. It was a good call; as the Leafs won 3-2 with Rogers only required to make one difficult save all night, albeit with less than a minute remaining. Joel Kent scored for the third straight game, and line mate Dale McCaine added one. Busher Jackson scored his first since being called up.

The atmosphere around the team was becoming more positive, as the Leafs increased their lead over the Habs to four points, and they were even in games played.

"Things are looking good!" the coach said, as he looked forward to that nights' game against the struggling Capitals

The game that evening gave him little to change his opinion. The Leafs did skate away with a relatively easy 3-1 win, on goals from McCaine, Busher Jackson and Marlet. But it was the third period that really hurt. John Dennis went behind his net to 'corral a loose puck' as Jim Gerber called it, when winger Bryan Muir of the Capitals, all six foot four and two hundred and twenty pounds of him went after the puck. Dennis took an excruciatingly long time to get control, and Muir couldn't stop. He ploughed into the goalie and sandwiched him between the boards and himself, toppling onto the Leaf net minder.

Muir got up as fast as he could, to try and get the puck. Dennis didn't move. John Hill didn't care that it was an accident. He sideswiped Muir, and had the gloves off before the Washington player knew what was happening. Frank Maleki joined in, and was awarded the third man in as a result. Miraculously, the benches didn't clear, though it took the mighty grip of Spencer Smith on Lorne Grahams' jersey to keep the Leaf winger on the bench.

When the fisticuffs were settled, Nevell Carpenter was shocked to find that John Dennis was unconscious. He had taken a hit that, even with the collective strength of equipment equivalent to body armour, had given him a concussion.

Lars Rogers had to come in to finish the game, but the real concern was John Dennis. He was hospitalized overnight, for observation it was said. The next morning he had trouble remembering the hit. He knew what city he was in, and what the date was. What he could *not* remember was the hit, or how he came to be in the hospital.

Ken Butler met with Spencer Smith at the Wellesley Hospital cafeteria the morning after the game.

"I've never seen anything like this Spencer. I've never seen a club lose four of its top players in succession like this."

The GM noticed that the coach was nervously rubbing his arm up and down. "What's the matter?" he asked.

The coach rolled up his sleeve to reveal not one, but *three* nicotine patches.

"What are you doing to yourself?" the GM asked in horror.

Spencer Smith looked him squarely in the eye and said, "It's the only god dam way I can get through this without having a lousy smoke. I promised Carol I would quit during training camp, and I haven't had one lousy butt since before our first game. But this is too much. I understand fate, and jinxes, and curses, and all the rest of it. But this time it wasn't even the god dam third of the month. What gives, Ken?"

The GM took a slow sip of his hot tea and lemon.

"A religious man would say 'these things are set to try us'."

Spencer Smith scowled at this. "I'm as god damn religious as the next coach, but this is too much! We're *past* the trade deadline. We've called up everybody from the rock except Pis Parsons, and we lose the goalie, the captain, the defenseman and the winger. And we're four points out of a playoff spot. It's like the bloody cards are stacked against us."

The GM reluctantly added some sugar to his tea. "Well, like I said, it may just be a test of our collective character, including you and me. I have faith in our organization. In our coaching, scouting. I feel that we've made the right moves this year. The proof is in the fact that we've come this close—all the way from 23rd last year to this. I just can't believe that we're supposed to go out like this. We still have eight games to go, and two of those are against the team four back of us. At least we have some control over our fate."

The coach wasn't so positive. "Don't get me wrong Ken. I'm not throwing in the towel. I know what we can do. I know this team; even what's left of it is good enough to make the playoffs. But the way we were playing before Shonker went down we were good enough to really *do* something in the playoffs."

The GM found it hard to disagree. "We'll just play the cards that have been dealt. On the bright side—we don't know how much longer Shoniker and Andrew will be out. They could be back sooner than thought. And McKenna should be back before the playoffs."

"Except that we're starting to get a little overstocked on the blue line," Spencer Smith pointed out. "I hate like hell to send those kids, Mouton and Hansky back to the rock. I think they've earned a chance to stay. But we can't carry nine defensemen!"

Ken Butler heard his cell phone ring. He had been willing it to for the last half-hour.

"Ken, I got him," the caller said, triumphantly.

"Good Ronnie, very good—so when can we get him there?"

Ron Bailey had given the good news first. He had tracked down the number one net minder in St. Johns', the incomparable Frank McCool, a.k.a. Frank Isbister. "I have him on a flight leaving in forty-five minutes; St. Johns' to Hamilton. Then he goes from Hamilton to the island airport."

Ken hung up and passed the news on to the coach. It was agreed that Frank McCool was the best goalie to call up to back up Lars Rogers. "I'm going to stay here tonight," the GM announced.

"But isn't Dennis' wife coming here tonight?" Spencer Smith asked.

"She is, but I want to stay close to it. I need to know how he is," the GM frowned, and added, "You know yourself, with concussions. It can be a long time before they can tell how long somebody's gonna be out. Or sometimes they can tell very soon if someone is going to be out for a long time. Either way I'd like to know as soon as possible."

At practice, when they were about three-quarters of the way in, Spencer Smith blew his whistle continuously until he got the attention of his assistants.

"Wrap it up!" he ordered them. "We're not getting anything useful done!" he grumbled as he skated off towards the dressing room. "Might as well get some rest if they're not gonna work," the coach called from over his shoulder as he left the ice.

Ron Bailey returned to Toronto after having seen St. Johns' one last time. The baby Leafs did not make the playoffs, and he wanted one last chance to view a couple of prospects that the Leafs were wavering on re-signing for next season.

He dropped by the Gardens on the morning before their game with Tampa, and as he walked the corridor between the rail seats and the golds he saw David Burks alone on the ice firing pucks at the net. Or more exactly he was firing them at the boards, to the left of the net. He was puzzled by what he saw. Surely Burks, who had once been one of the better point men in the league, could not be having *that* much trouble hitting the net?

"Burksie, what on earth are you doing?" he asked.

David Burks paid little attention until he was out of pucks. He then skated over to the boards where Ron was leaning over them.

"I'm trying a little trick that Gilly told me about," he said, referring to the former Leaf defenseman. Todd Gill.

As a former blue liner, Ron was all ears, "Oh yeah. What is it?"

David Burks pointed to the boards, to the left of the south goal. "You see that *Three Musketeers* ad on the boards—the two E's in three. Well Gilly told me that if you hit that spot with a shot from the point it bounces our right on the door step of the crease, right where Andy likes it!" He said referring to Chuck Andrew.

Ron was slightly sceptical. "Go on!" he shouted.

Burks rested his chin on his stick and continued; "Gilly said that it happened to him in a playoff game against the Sharks a few years ago. He hit the boards by accident. It came out in front and Andy, who was in his crease residence—banged her in."

Ron was still unconvinced.

"The next day at practice, Gilly tries it again. It didn't work at first, and then he skated over to the spot there to get the pucks, and he noticed this big dent in the plastic boards. I asked the maintenance guys about it. The say it happened when the guys doing the signs had trouble getting it back in place, and they just beat the crap out of it with a mallet."

"And you say you can hit that spot and it comes out in front?"

"Watch me!" the defenseman bragged, and skated off to the blue line.

Sure enough, when he nailed the spot with three of the five shots he took from the point, the puck caromed off the E's and landed about three feet in front of the crease.

"Amazing, eh?" Burks asked.

"Yeah," Ron added. "Now all we need in Andy back, to bang it home."

Oddly enough, Chuck Andrew was closer to returning than many had thought. He was completing the third week of rehabilitation, after the eight-week recovery period. Ron encountered the big winger working out on the stationary bicycle, under the watchful eye of the team's physician, Dr. Jahaul.

"Ronnie, you finally got that whole team of yours from the 'E' up here I see. Well get ready to send one of 'em back. I should be back for one of the games this weekend," he puffed.

"When are we gonna see you on skates?" Ron wondered.

"The doc says I can try it today!" Perhaps David Burks was even *closer* to trying out his experiment.

Lars Rogers seemed shaky during the warm-up for the game against the Lightning. Many of the players noticed it, the fact that he was letting almost every shot, even the softest get by him. Most of the players shrugged it off, though this was a sharp contrast to Rogers' serious work ethic during practices.

Only Frank Maleki mentioned it though, telling assistant coach Ralph Newton that Rogers,

'Didn't look as if he could stop a beach ball.'

Perhaps Rogers would have had more luck if the game *had* been played using a beach ball. All of the first three shots that the Sabres took on him made it past. After the third, David Burks asked him if he was okay.

"I'm fighting the puck. I don't know what's wrong. It looks like they're shooting marbles at me," the veteran goalie uttered.

Spencer Smith waited until the period was over. He had Brian Ridley confer with the goalie, and then tell him he wouldn't be starting the second period. Smith walked over to Frank McCool's stall and said, "Get ready Isbisser—you're going in!"

McCool looked the coach straight in the eye and said "It's Iz-Bister!"

"I don't care if it's Maholovitch—you're going in. Show me you can stop the puck, and I'll get the name right!" He said and stormed off.

McCool did exactly that. He faced 34 shots over the next two periods and stopped them all, giving the Leafs a much-needed win.

His style was unorthodox, compared to the current floppers who made up the leagues' goal tending brethren. Frank McCool stood on his feet the entire game, never venturing out of the next to grab a loose puck. He was impossible to beat along the ice, as the goal stick was always ready. The five-hole was the size of a grapefruit, and despite that Tampa repeatedly tried for it. And the top shelf was also out of reach because McCool's quick glove hand was not far from it.

Even though they were outshot so badly, the Leafs managed pairs of goals from Serge Moit and Busher Jackson, and a single from Denis MacDonald, his first as a Leaf.

Lars Rogers was the first to congratulate Frank McCool after the game. He realized that, in a time when the team needed him the most he had not come through. But more importantly he realized that it was the team that mattered, and the win was all that counted.

Spencer Smith had a difficult decision whom to start in goal the next night. He didn't make up his mind until the bus arrived at the Molson Centre for the morning skate.

He conferred with his assistants, before announcing that it would be McCool.

"I admit, I'm playing a hunch," he said, going against his hard and fast rule of alternating goalies on back-to-back games.

The decision seemed like genius, as Frank McCool and the Leafs stole a 1-0 nail-biter. In the press box Billy Sinfield said it was the "best effort by a Toronto goaltender in this building since Wayne Thomas came back to haunt his former team in the seventies!"

Sinfield recalled the memory correctly, even if he did mix up his buildings.

The next night in Toronto was more of the same. McCool stood on his head as the Leafs were assured of finishing ahead of Montreal.

During a break in play, Bill Barilko was parked beside young Ian Moriarty on the bench. The youngster was tapping his glove on the boards to the beat of *'Fifty Mission Cap'* which boomed over the Gardens' PA. When it came to the infamous opening line, Barilko suddenly sat straight up and asked the kid "WHAT THE HELL ARE THEY SINGING ABOUT?"

The surprised rookie answered, "It's about some old Leaf guy. He's on a hockey card after scoring a goal in overtime, and then he died in a plane crash."

Barilko slumped on the bench as if he'd been shot.

"I never thought they'd write a *song* about it!" he gasped.

Dale McCaine continued to impress the broadcasters on *Hockey Night in Canada*, as he notched a pair, and singles went to Tobin West, Greg Sawchuck, and Charlie Conacher.

"The young Leafs looked good out there tonight," Bob Cole of the CBC remarked "They could give some team a lot to handle in the playoffs!"

Frank McCool's name came up often in the broadcast as well, although this time he was forced to make only 21 saves.

"It was as if the rest of the club was either rewarding him for saving their bacon the night before or trying to protect the rookie by keeping the puck away from him," Harry Neale of HNIC remarked.

The word from the Leaf infirmary was still not encouraging. Floyd Shoniker's groin was still not healing well, and Mike McKenna was not ready to go either. John Dennis was still experiencing headaches, though they were lessening each day. He was evaluated every day, but the medical staffs were not able to predict a return date. That meant that the coach had to play his 'revolving goalies'.

It was particularly worrying as the Leafs dropped their next two, albeit while actually gaining ground in the playoff hunt.

"We've got to figure this thing out," he lamented, "the way it looks to everyone on the outside is 'the Leafs can't win without John Dennis'. That's the wrong kind of message we want out there, going into the playoffs."

Lars Rogers was clearly the number two man, and had played well enough this season to keep his job as the number two man, and to fill in capably when called on. The coach wondered if suddenly being thrust into the number one role had somehow upset the goalies fragile psyche.

"Net minders are a breed unto themselves," the coach often preached, "so much of their game is up here," he would say, touching his temple. "Confidence is everything with goalies sometimes, and I think we have to show some in Lars. I want to keep him in there as long as I can."

The truth was that Frank McCool had played better than Rogers, but two games against the young Canadiens wasn't much of a litmus test.

The dressing room was like a golf gallery after the game. Only David Burks broke the silence as he sat next to the stunned goalie.

"There's only one way I know to get over this, 'Lars Bar,'" the defenseman said. "Go back to being number two. If you tell yourself you're number two, and that you have to try harder to *be* number one, then you'll play like it."

Lars Rogers was too bright a person to listen to David Burks' advice without considering the real meaning behind it. Rogers had played in the NCAAs' Ivy League, graduating with a 3.9 grade point average and a degree in Physics. He had never even remotely considered turning professional until a player agent advised him that he had been heavily scouted by three teams, including the Leafs and could probably garner a $200,000 signing bonus. That went a long way to paying off student loans. Three years later Rogers was in the NHL, making $650,000 US per season on a three-year contract, or roughly ten times what he could have been making as a physicist. And he would still have plenty of time to devote to his true ambition, even if he retired after his contract was up.

"You're saying that if I consider Frank Isbister as the number one goalie, and consider myself the number two, and play as if I'm number two and have to compete and win the number one role, that my play will improve?"

David Burks thought about it for a second, and said, "Yeah!"

When the Leafs took to the ice for their next to last game, their fate was in their hands. They needed only one point in the next two games to earn a playoff spot, or to have the Islanders fail to win both their remaining games. And when the Sabres did the Leafs a favour by beating the New York club, Toronto literally backed into the playoffs, losing 3-1 at home to the Capitals.

No matter how they achieved it, the result was reason for celebration. Toronto had clinched their first playoff spot in two years!

Spencer Smith wanted to mark the occasion but didn't want it overplayed. "No Champagne in the room tonight," he decreed, "they can have pints, instead," he told the trainer.

David Burks was one of the first to douse him with beer, forcing Ron into an unwanted shower. He had to appeal to Nevell Carpenter for a Leaf track suit to wear home.

"You're a big part of this Ronnie!" Spencer Smith told him as he shouted to be heard above the cheers in the room. Normally the coach could be heard over anything slightly louder than a 747, but the noise level in the room was staggering.

"These guys wanted this badly, right from the first day of camp. I knew we had most of the horses, adding McCaine, Sawchuck, and Toby West, even Moriarty. Those young legs made a difference. And now old MacDonald and Gusarov—I'm more concerned about getting the mix right when we get Shonky and the Chief back," he said, referring to the captain and to McKenna.

It was one of the rare occasions when *anyone* made a reference to Mike McKenna's aboriginal status. McKenna was proud of his heritage, but didn't see why anyone around the team had to make a big deal out of it. Back on the Alderville First Nation he was just another kid with a hockey stick. He didn't flaunt his status but he did try his best to improve the quality of life by pumping money back in, leading to the founding of a new community centre. Right now McKenna was looking ahead to the Leafs first playoff date in just over a week. He told himself he would be in the line-up, no matter what the status of his shoulder.

Floyd Shoniker made the rounds of the room hugging and backslapping all of his teammates. It was important that the captain be there to show support. And it was important for the players to remember that the captain would almost certainly be on the ice with them when the puck was dropped on the playoff opener.

As they players continued to celebrate long into the night it appeared likely that the Leafs first round opponent would be the New Jersey Devils, who had passed the Leafs only the night before, earning them the 4th seed and home ice advantage.

The newspaper headline the next day was all about McCaine, how the rookie had capped a spectacular season by leading the team in goal scoring with 47, and establishing a new Leaf rookie record in both goals and points. And McCaine would be garnering some consideration for the Calder trophy, though he trailed on both offensive categories to the Sabres' Denee Mercur.

A little money riding on the Maple Leafs'

T he series with New Jersey would open on a Tuesday, and Spencer Smith requested that the team fly out on the Sunday morning following their last home game. He had booked the team into a facility resort in Newark, not far from a small practice rink. The team could practically walk from the hotel to the rink.

On the Monday leading up to the big game he kept the team sequestered from the media, and on that afternoon, following their practice, he adjourned the team to the hotel's conference room for a video showing. Instead of watching game films of the Devils, or a motivational type flick, he had the Leafs video guru, Mike Wardyz, (or 'Mr. Know-it-all' as Spencer Smith affectionately referred to him) prepare something a little different. He had him piece together the last two minutes of several series ending games, including the last two minutes of the Leafs last playoff appearance, which was three years ago against these same New Jersey Devils.

"I want you guys to remember the helpless feeling of those last few minutes, when you know that the series—that your season, that everything you prepared and worked for all year is about to end in two minutes. It's like staring down the barrel of a gun. I can't think of a worse feeling. I don't want any of you to forget it."

This type of negative motivational technique surprised several of the Leafs, particularly those who had not been playing for the coach for very long.

"One thing with Spencer," Ken Butler remarked, "You should always expect the unexpected."

Spencer Smith was a little more predictable with his line-up for the opening playoff game though. His first line would be the re-united Kent-Shoniker-Andrew combination that had not played together since the injuries to the captain and the right-winger. Dale McCaine would centre the second line with Denis MacDonald and Randy Rettig. The third line would have Serge Moit with Benoit Marlet and (surprise!) Charlie Conacher. And the fourth line (checking unit) would be John Hill with Lou Zanardo and Lorne Graham. It was a decidedly veteran group of forwards, with rookies Greg Sawchuck and Tobin West notable by their absence, as was hard working Busher Jackson. The media were all over Smith for his selection of older players, and the exclusion of the suddenly popular Jackson.

On defense it was much the same, with the pairings of Mike McKenna-Frank Maleki, David Burks-Christian Andersson and Alexi Gusarov and Valeri Ragulin. And in goal, John Dennis, who was given a clean bill of health only the day before the game.

"You dance with the girl that you brought to the party!" Spencer Smith declared to the media when asked to explain his line-up.

The Leafs were catching a huge break with Martin Brodeur out for at least the first round of the playoffs with a back injury. Before the game the coach was uncharacteristically nervous, even going so far as to place a cigarette between his lips, though he wisely discarded it before the period began.

After the obligatory opening ceremonies, designed to pump up the home crowd at the expense of the visitors, the game began. The Devils broke the scoreless tie with two quick goals at the end of the first, catching the Leafs in a mental vacuum. The first goal came on a giveaway by Frank Maleki, who tried do it all himself when trying to ice the puck instead of looking for someone to pass it to. Scott Gomez wasted no time in firing it past John Dennis, who reacted slowly to the shot.

Moments later the Leafs were caught on a line change that took too long to execute, and the resulting two-on-one found David Burks out of position. He tried to play the pass, but it never came. He looked handcuffed, as he stood motionless while Alexander Mogilny rifled a shot past Dennis that he again moved too late on.

Down 2-0 after the period the coach tried to inspire his troops, cautioning them not to dig themselves too deep a hole on the road, but at the same time reminding them that they were not out of the game yet.

In the second, the Leafs had few good scoring opportunities as the Devils played what in the NFL was called 'ball control offense'. The Leafs never seemed to have the puck, and as they grew increasingly frustrated by their attempts to gain control, the penalties began to mount. Holding, hooking and tripping calls were the result as the Toronto forwards were stymied in their attempts to slow down the speedy New Jersey lines.

The power play for the Devils worked like an army precision drill squad. They passed the puck, not shooting it until the ultimate shot opportunity opened up, and when it did they took advantage of it. Brian Gionta scored on the third extra man chance, and the Devils went easily ahead 3-0 before the end of the second. Mike McKenna was frustrated by his team mates' reluctance to take the body.

"Hiiiiiiiit!" he screamed from the bench, standing up as Lorne Graham and Randy Rettig skated by. He briefly caught their attention, and shouted, "Take him!" at the top of his lungs. McKenna's advice went unheeded, as the Toronto forwards largely tried in vain to skate with the New Jersey forwards.

The Leafs were not totally outplayed in the period. Just when the Devils should have been going in for the early kill, they appeared to take things just a bit too much for granted. With the puck deep in the Leaf zone, Patrik Elias tried to make one pass too many to Mogilny. Dale McCaine was back checking as usual, and he intercepted the pass like he knew it was coming. He skated between the Devils' defenders and went straight for the net, noticing, but disregarding the fact that the offensively challenged Randy Rettig trailed on his right side. McCaine swooped in alone on Scott Clemmensen and deposited the puck high in the top corner of the net with a slap shot that he rarely used.

The goal was timely, as it gave the Leafs something to build on going into the third period. He was praised by his teammates for providing some spark. But in the room as the players downed their orange slices, the coach went over what they had to do in the third to salvage this thing.

"Don't try to skate with them. Lay on the body—you *know* they don't like it!"

The advice was well intended but the coach seemingly forgot an old hockey adage, 'you can't hit what you can't catch.' And the Leafs veteran line-up could not keep up with the Devils' speedy forwards. Gionta scored his second of the game early in the third, and Lorne Graham took a needless roughing penalty after the whistle. With the Leafs attempting to kill the penalty, New Jersey quickly went ahead 5-1. Chuck Andrew's late power play goal made the final score slightly more respectable, but a loss was still a loss.

In the room after the game the loudest sounds seemed to be the panting and wheezing that came from the Leaf veterans. Spencer Smith had all ears turned to him as he stood by the chalkboard, his arms folded across his wide chest.

"We knew the first one would be tough, our record here, their speed, guys back from injury. Hell, you guys can think of more excuses if you try. But I'll be damned if we lose this series because they out-hustled us! If they are a better team than us, we'll make them show it. But don't hand the damn series to them because they beat you to the puck every time. Practice tomorrow as usual. The time will be posted at the hotel", he blared, as he went off to face the media conference.

It was only the first game of the series, so Floyd Shoniker was not ready for any inspirational speeches yet. Instead he quickly towelled off and offered, "The challenge for you guys is not to play as shitty as *I* did tonight. Play better than that and we'll take the god dam thing."

Of course the others knew that Floyd Shoniker had played a competent, if unspectacular game. This was only a mild reminder that they would collectively have to pick things up the next game.

Spencer Smith stubbornly decided to go with the same line-up in game two, despite the lacklustre result.

The game began as the first one had ended—the Leafs trying in vain to hit the speedy Devil forwards and drawing frustration penalties as a result. The difference was that the Leaf forwards had picked things up defensively, and New Jersey led only 1-0 after the first, courtesy of a Jamie Langenbrunner power play goal.

Langenbrunner scored again early in the second, and Dale McCaine matched it with a pair of goals to tie the game midway through the period. At that point momentum appeared to swing toward Toronto. For one brief moment the Leafs gained the upper hand, and got a great scoring opportunity from Benoit Marlet, only to have Scott Clemmensen make a spectacular glove save.

New Jersey sensed that this one was slipping away, and began to take the play up one level. Zach Parise was left alone briefly in front of the net, and he banged home his own rebound to make the score 3-2 just before the end of the second.

Spencer Smith tried to lift the Leafs spirits between periods, reminding the players of how close the game was, and how they could hang on and steal one and bring the series home all tied up.

Things seemed to be going the Leafs way in the third as they earned an early power play, courtesy of a gift penalty to Ken Klee. Instead of scoring with the man advantage, the Devils were awarded a scoring opportunity when Sergei Brylin relieved David Burks of the puck at the point, and skated in undisturbed on John Dennis.

Brylin made only a token move on the sleepwalking goalie, but it was enough to get the puck past for a 4–3 lead. The goal expectedly demoralized the Leafs, but the coach wasn't about to let things end that way.

To their credit the Leafs held their heads up, and battled to the end, though they did give up an empty net goal when the lifted Dennis with sixty-five seconds left in the third period. The mood in the room wasn't sombre like the last game. Four of the first five players that filed in after the game either threw or whacked their sticks against the wall—the only exception being Dale McCaine, who was remarkably calm.

"I'll be damned if the season's gonna end *this* way!" Chuck Andrew fumed.

David Burks leaned back heavy on his chair and slumped against the wall, making no attempt at moving. He stared off into space as if he was still seeing Brylin and Mogilny whiz around him like an old-fashioned table hockey game player; one that could only pivot.

Obscenities and silence were the alternating reactions by most of the players. Only Dale McCaine spoke anything else. And he was speaking to himself.

"We're going to beat these guys," he said softly.

Serge Moit sat at the chair next to his, and looked at Dale. "What did you say kid?"

Dale was reluctant to repeat it, but he did. "I said we're going to beat these guys. We just have to believe we can beat them!"

Serge Moit looked at the rookie like the kid was afflicted. But he considered that the kid had scored forty-seven goals that year and two more on that evening, and so he treated the kid with some respect.

"Sure we can kid! We just have to get the Russian Mafia to kidnap Brylin and Mogilny before we get back to Toronto, and we can beat these guys!"

Sarcasm was not something that Dale McCaine appeared to understand.

The coach made no appearance in the room—instead he was forced to meet with the media in the league-orchestrated post game conference. One player from each team was also required to be there, and the coach selected his captain, Floyd Shoniker. When the player was questioned about the Leafs lack of speed and their apparent lack of cohesiveness on the ice he became unsettled and reacted strongly with his answer.

"Well of *course* we are! We added three players down the stretch, and added five guys from 'the rock' over the past couple months. We get guys back from injury—hell the whole season has been a lack of playing together!"

The flight back to Toronto the next morning was the highlight of the Leafs stay in New Jersey. The media were understandably cautious in how they approached the players for interviews. The mood was down beat, but the chance to resume the series on home ice offered some optimism. The players would have to wait one extra day for that to happen. Due to television scheduling there would be an extra day off before the series would resume.

Ken Butler was concerned that the series could potentially get out of reach. He wanted to discuss this with Spencer Smith, but felt that the plane ride home was not the right place. He chose to meet with the coach at the Gardens' coffee shop the next morning before practice.

Spencer Smith was already seated at a table alone when the GM arrived. Ken sat across from him, and the GM couldn't help but notice that the coach looked like he still needed a good nights' sleep.

"I never sleep well the night after a road game," he complained, "and I don't have to remind you of the importance of a 'game three'." The coach was referring to the statistics that showed that a high percentage of teams that win the third game of a series go on to take the set.

"And don't forget the problem we've been having with the number *three*," he added, superstitiously.

The GM broached the touchy subject of the line-up for the game the next night. "Spence, you know I never interfere when it comes to coaching. We've never had any disagreements when it comes to this."

The coach looked up from his coffee as if he could see what was coming.

"No one knows better than me the loyalty you feel towards guys like Shoniker, McKenna, Burks, Kent, and some of the others that have played for you for a while."

Spencer Smith's huge frame shifted uneasily in his seat as if he was getting ready to bolt.

"But I want to remind you that there is no shame in realizing that there has come a time to pass the torch, so to speak, and give some of the younger guys a chance."

The coach squirmed, practically biting his tongue not to speak while the GM was still delivering his monologue.

"There are a few guys who haven't pulled their weight, for one reason or another, and there is no disrespect in sitting them down for a while and giving some of the kids a chance. I only want to remind you of that."

Now that the GM had placed it on the table, the coach could give his side of it. "No shit!" he said. "Ken—it's probably the hardest thing I've ever had to do."

With that, the coached reached inside of his blue Toronto Maple Leafs windbreaker and produced a line-up sheet for the GM's perusal. It listed lines as follows: Kent-Shoniker-Andrew were listed as #1; McCaine-Conacher-Jackson (or McCaine-Bachmann-Bodine as the coach had written it) as # 2; Marlet-Moit and MacDonald as # 3 and West-Sawchuck-Hill as # 4. On defense, it listed McKenna-

Moriarty as # 1, Ragulin and Gusarov as # 2, and Horton and Barilko (or Mouton and Hansky as the coach had written it) as # 3—and in goal, Frank McCool (alias Frank Isbister).

Ken Butler took out his glasses to read the list, and when he was done he cracked a subtle smile. "We've known each other a long time, Spence. I suppose I should have known better that to think that it was necessary to have to tell you what you could see for yourself."

The coach smiled as he sipped his coffee. "Hell, if you didn't, I'd think you didn't give a damn!" he said.

They drank their coffee in silence for a while, until Ken Butler broke it. "You feel confident with Isbister in there—I find that interesting."

The coach wasted no time in defending his choice. "Denny still looks like he's feeling something from that concussion. He doesn't seem a hundred per cent. And Rogers, well I don't know if he's up to it. I think he's psyched himself into this number one thing. And I don't think that a start will get him out of it. If worse comes to worst, we start Isbister, and go with Dennis as backup; give Rogers some time to think about it. I feel confident that we'll take the game tomorrow tonight. I know the guys are ready. I expect to see that in the practice today."

The coach was right about the practice. After that mornings session he wished that they could face off right away for game three. The players felt the same way. And the New Jersey side was bemoaning the fact that there was an extra day for them to lose their momentum.

Charlie Conacher got Ron's attention after practice and got him to stop in the dressing room.

"We're back together," he said referring to two thirds of the famous 'kid line', "and we've got McCaine along for the ride. We've got a few tricks planned for these New Jersey guys," he said with a wink.

Ron could hardly wait. Through the first two games of the series he was becoming concerned. He had yet to see any indication that this post-season had anything special about it.

"By the way, Ronnie, a bunch of us is goin over to Hamilton tonight, to see some lacrosse."

"*Lacrosse?*" Ron asked.

"Yeah, a great game—love to play it. We thought we'd take in a game, Busher, me, McCool, and the rest of us '*ghosts*' as you say."

Ron looked around uneasily to see if anyone was listening in on this. There was too much going on in the room for anyone else to care. "I don't think you should use words like that," Ron admonished. "But, if you don't mind, I'd like to tag along with you to Hamilton."

Conacher agreed. Ron suggested it would be a good idea if he drove, as he didn't want to consider how the players were going to get to Hamilton otherwise.

Copps Coliseum was practically deserted for the game. The upper level of seating was curtained off, as if to give the place less of an empty feeling.

"I guess it's not too popular a game here?" Conacher questioned, as the group watched the Hamilton Raiders and the visiting Baltimore Thunder warm up.

"This game may be a hard sell. I don't know. The area hasn't done too well supporting minor-league sports," Ron observed, noting that the Hamilton Dukes, Steelhawks, Canucks, Skyhawks and Cardinals had all failed to attract fans in their different sports over the past few years. And the AHL Bulldogs weren't fairing much better, despite their success.

"Even the Tiger-Cats are having some trouble," Ron added.

Horton and Barilko found this hard to believe, as they were used to the idea of a sold out Ivor Wynne Stadium for CFL games.

"What's the problem? How come it's not a good sports town anymore?" Busher Jackson asked.

"I don't know," Ron answered. "People have too much else to choose from I guess. But there's no question that this city would support an NHL team"

Those that chose not to come to Copps that evening missed a great night of entertainment. The home side led 9-8 going into the third period. Midway through the second period, a Baltimore player broke in on the Hamilton goal and carried the ball behind the net while trying to set up a pass in front. There was no one to pass it to, so he tried to carry the ball around by himself. The Hamilton goalie had another idea. He chased the player around the boards and delivered a vicious body check that cost the player the possession of the ball. The goalie picked it up and fired it up the floor to his defenseman. The fans loved it, and Barilko and Horton quickly turned to Frank McCool and rode him about it.

"See what you could do if you came out of the net like the other goalies, Frankie." Horton teased.

"Dammit Frankie, I hear there's a goalie that scored a goal in the league—fired the puck all the way the length of the ice into the empty net. Why can't you do that?"

Frank McCool burned slowly at the jibes he was getting. He had been reluctant to venture out of the net; despite the coaching he had received to do just that. On the rare occasions when he had left the net, he had difficulty in quickly regaining his position to be ready for an ensuing shot, and he had looked soft on a few goals. He vowed to change that soon.

The Leafs were pumped like an over-inflated tire for the third game of the series. The pre-game ceremonies took longer than for a regular season game, as the club was taking full advantage of all of the hype associated with the playoffs. The fans were eager to get the game underway, but the Leaf players acted as if it had already begun.

No sooner had the puck been dropped, the Leafs took charge as if the game was a controlled scrimmage.

All of the tentativeness that was part of their style during the first two games was gone. The change in the line-up did not affect Floyd Shoniker personally—his line had been kept intact. But Shoniker got the message more than anyone did that the play had to be fast and decisive. The Leafs were not going to react to what the Devils were doing—it was going to be the other way around.

Shoniker hooked up with Joel Kent on the first goal, as he simply out-muscled the New Jersey defender and loaded a pass onto Kent's stick that was wristed into goalie 'no man's land.'

With the Leafs quickly up 1-0, the crowd was invited to join the rush. The volume noise that descended had not been heard at the Gardens in five years. Before the period was over Kent found Shoniker behind the net, and he keenly directed what looked like a pass out to the waiting Chuck Andrew. When Shoniker looked at how the defenseman was positioned, he figured that he could bank the puck in off the player's skate, and it worked.

"Take 'em any way we can!" he told Andrew after the goal, though he did apologize for not passing the puck.

"That's it, that's it, that's the kind of period that will beat these guys!" Spencer Smith roared between periods. "They don't like it when they have to try and keep up with us!"

Though the Conacher-Jackson-McCaine line had not been awarded a goal, they were crucial in keeping Elias and Mogilny off the board. And when big Jamie Langenbrunner tried to stake a personal claim in front of the Leaf net, Tim Horton had something to say about it. Without even placing a stick on Langenbrunner he moved the forward around as if he was Fred Astaire leading Ginger Rogers.

The second period was more of the same. Benoit Marlet stole the puck from Brian Gionta during a New Jersey line change, and skated in alone on Scott Clemmensen. He made not one but two head fakes and deposited the puck along the ice just under the goalie's stacked pads.

The Leafs got another on a power play, as New Jersey was now the frustrated team that was resorting to holding and hooking to keep up. Dennis MacDonald scored his first playoff goal in six years to make it 4-0—the score at the end of the second.

"Don't let up for a second you guys!" Spencer Smith preached to his charges before they returned to the ice for the third period. "You give these guys an opening, they'll take it. Just like a shark smelling blood."

The opening the Devils were looking for came early. With Tim Horton off for a questionable interference call on Jamie Langenbrunner, the big Devil centre was free to take some liberties with Frank McCool. With the referee's attention up ice, he took the legs out from under McCool. The goalie was still down, having trouble regaining his position when the play returned to the front of the net. Langenbrunner had perhaps the softest goal of his career as he simply directed the puck around the still sprawled goaltender, which looked as if he'd been nailed to the ice.

Spencer Smith was furious with referee Bob Edwards, and had to be restrained by both Ralph Newton and Brian Ridley, to keep from going on the ice.

With the score 4-1, and plenty of time on the clock, the coach wisely signalled for a time out. During the break, the coach surprisingly said nothing to the team. Instead he used the break to calm down, and stood behind Joel Kent on the bench.

"I've never done this before, and I'll never do it again. Go take out Janssen!" He ordered.

Joel Kent was no longer the twenty-year-old winger who had earned such a great reputation with his fists that he no longer even used them. His reputation was still intact, though, and few but the greenest rookies would be stupid enough to test him, even at age thirty-three. For Spencer Smith to order his one-time tough guy to dust off the six-gun and venture out onto the dusty streets for one more gunfight was incredible. It was also too much to pass up.

Kent didn't say anything, but took a short swig from the water bottle and waited for his shift. When his turn came, the coach had matched lines so that New Jersey tough guy Cam Janssen would be on the ice still.

Kent was preparing mentally for the battle that would ensue. He watched Janssen take a couple of runs at Chuck Andrew, but they did no damage to the big winger.

When New Jersey dumped the puck into the Leaf end, and Janssen went to chase it, Kent knew that the opportunity had come. The puck rolled around the boards, and past the Leaf net. Janssen chased it, and Kent skated in to chase after him. Just as Janssen reached the puck in the corner, he was levelled by a devastating body check that came from—Frank McCool. The Leaf goalie, fresh from his puck-handling lesson at Copps Coliseum, had ventured out of the net for the first time in his NHL career. And he had done it in the most unorthodox way that had ever been seen at Maple Leaf Gardens.

Joel Kent stopped beside Janssen, as the linesmen rushed in to break up the potential donnybrook.

Janssen got up on one knee, and looked up at the smiling Kent and said, "What the hell is with your damn goalie?"

"You know those goalies kid, they're not all there. Just remember, though, hands off the goalie, or it'll be me you have to deal with."

Joel Kent's threat did not go unheeded. The play was a turning point for the Leafs. They got another goal from Kent, and their sixth and final one came from Dale McCaine, as they skated away with a rather easy 6-1 win.

The mood in the room was the antithesis of that of game two. Spencer Smith actually took turns congratulating the players as he walked around the room before heading off to the obligatory press conference.

"That's what happens when you play good team defense," he lectured.

The coach expected this message to be carried forward to game four. After giving up ten goals in the first two games of the series, Spencer Smith thought he had driven home the point about defense winning hockey games. And he broadcast that very message in the press conference after game three, declaring that the Leafs were 'not the kind of hockey team that ordinarily wins by 7-5 scores.'

But game four of the series was not an ordinary game. New Jersey came out as wired as the Leafs had been in game three, and took an early lead as Langenbrunner scored to get them going. The Leafs tied it near the end of the first, on a nifty give-and-go between Serge Moit and Benoit Marlet that saw the latter unselfishly deliver the puck back to Moit, rather than shooting.

Spencer Smith was adamant that the Leafs were not going to lose their edge in play. He sounded like a fight manager, pepping up a boxer while massaging the tired muscles of the heavyweight.

"Don't give them an opportunity to take the lead. We've got to get the next goal!"

Dale McCaine took that as an order, and before the second period was two minutes old he had outworked a Devil defender in the corner and whizzed around in front of the net, depositing a high backhand that, even from the replay, was hard to determine just how it went in the net.

The Devils battled back to their credit, an earned a hard-fought goal on a power play. Jamie Langenbrunner out-muscled young Ragulin in front of the Leaf net; winning a goalmouth scramble while Frank McCool was inexplicably down on the play.

The tempo seemed to suddenly pick up, as if videotape was being fast-forwarded. The Leafs went ahead when Chuck Andrew fired a shot from forty feet out that Scott Clemmensen, even if he had seen all of, could likely never have stopped. Less than a minute later, the play had moved to the Leaf end, with Mike McKenna still caught up ice on a rush.

341

Richard Matvichuk moved up into the play and took a drop pass from Grant Marshall, firing the puck in front just as Viktor Kozlov arrived to screen McCool on the shot that trailed easily between the stunned goalie's legs.

Spencer Smith was furious with the brand of pond hockey that was being played, and promptly called a time out.

"This ain't shinny! Somebody take their god damn man out of the play!" he ordered.

Before the period ended, however, the lead had changed hands yet again. New Jersey went up 4-3 when John Madden found some open ice when he stepped out of the penalty box, and he weaved his way around Gusarov and beat McCool cleanly on the stick side. But before the frame ended, Chuck Andrew evened it up with a power play goal, as he staked his claim in front of the net, taking several vicious swipes to the calf from Scott Clemmensen. It paid off though when he re-directed Mike McKenna's point shot past the goalie.

"All I can say is, they aren't taking the man any better than you assholes are!" the coach fumed.

He stood in front of the chalkboard that outlined several plays that were diagrammed before the game. He took the chalk and drew X's through the dots that were supposed to represent the Devils.

"When their man has the puck, skate up to him, and after you've asked him, 'how's it going,' you take the body. Steal the puck and pass it to the other guy in a Leaf sweater, or am I going too fast for you?"

It appeared that only Dale McCaine was paying attention.

In the third, New Jersey went ahead 5-4 when Chuck Andrew, who was supposed to be covering Viktor Kozlov, let the Devils' player get by, and watched helplessly as Kozlov worked a two-on-one for the goal.

Spencer Smith threw a water bottle to the ground, and when Andrew came to the bench, he just glared at him. Andrew had scored twice, and only that fact kept the coach from railing on the veteran. With only seven minutes left in the period, the coach was preparing to shorten the bench a little. Before he could, he sent out McCaine's line for the next shift against the Brylin—Mogilny line. So far, the trio had kept the Russians off of the board. As they readied for the face off, Charlie Conacher motioned to Dale McCaine that he wanted to take it. McCaine respectfully stood aside, while on the bench, Spencer Smiths eyebrows were raised as if being tugged on by a winch.

Conacher won the draw, and shovelled the puck forward to Busher Jackson, who took it like he had been expecting it to be there. McCaine kept pace with them and the trio worked the puck into New Jersey territory by passing the puck back and forth over the red line, each one of them managing to find the open man like ballet. Jackson was the last man to control the puck as they moved to the net, and he quickly faked the shot before depositing the puck momentarily on McCaine's stick. The shot rose fast into the top corner before Scott Clemmensen could react.

The score was tied at 5-5. There were just more than six minutes remaining when they faced off at centre. Spencer Smith kept the group out there, as the shift had been short. McCaine took the draw this time, and fed Conacher with it. The two of them burst quickly into the New Jersey end with Jackson trailing. McCaine dropped the pass, and went to the net. Conacher took the puck and moved far left of the face-off circle. Just when the Devils' defenseman realized that he could steal the puck, and moved in to take it, Conacher flipped it to Jackson who was now in front of the net. He moved in on Clemmensen and deked the goalie not once, but twice, before slamming the puck into the net.

The Leafs had the lead at 6-5, but there was still plenty of time left for dramatics. New Jersey got a break late in the third, going on the power play when Mike McKenna was given a questionable penalty for holding in front of the Leaf net. The Devils had some great scoring chances, but on one line change Dale McCaine separated Jamie Langenbrunner from the puck and sped in alone on Scott Clemmensen, and deposited a nifty wrist shot on the goalie's stick side to make the score 7-5.

The game finished as improbably as it started, and after the post-game press conference had concluded, Grant Baker of the Globe reminded Spencer Smith about his comment regarding the Leafs not being the kind of team that wins many 7-5 games.

"I guess even a blind squirrel can find an acorn once in a while, eh?" the coach commented.

The media attitude did an about-face after game four. Now that the series was tied, the obligatory 'it's anyone's series now' comments started to appear on all fronts.

Billy Sinfield wrote in his 'Sin Bin' column that 'Perhaps the Toronto Maple Leafs have finally been let off of their defensive leash by their coach, and have been given the green light to cross centre ice with the puck. All season long, Spencer Smith was so concerned with defense that actually held team practices using only one half of the rink. The high scores of the last two games may not be textbook hockey, but they are a hang more exciting for the fans than the 'Sominex on ice' that they have been forced to watch many nights at Maple Leaf Gardens this year.'

As the series returned to New Jersey for game five, Spencer Smith was again faced with a line-up dilemma.

Frank McCool was not exactly steady in his latest outing, though the Leafs did steal the victory. Smith was concerned that it would take a bigger effort in order for the Leafs to take the next game, and control of the series. After conferring with his assistants, he decided to go with the hot goalie (ironically McCool) in game five.

Jim Gerber, the radio voice of the Leafs, described it this way: "Spencer Smith rolled the dice before game three in deciding to replace John Dennis with the rookie Isbister, and if it worked once, and twice, well play the song until the audience gets tired of it.

Isbister looked strong in game two—a little less so in game three, albeit it was a loosely played affair defensively on both sides. And here in game five it will again be Isbister."

Bob Swanson had to lend his expert insight.

"The reason for changing goalies was to improve on the goals-against. And the Leafs have done that, allowing an average of five in the first two games, and five in the last game. But they did improve. But you have to count the game before that when they only allowed one, then it makes it an average of three in the last two games which is better than five."

As usual Swanson's colour commentary was abstract at best.

The game had the potential to be a series turning point, and both teams played it that way, approaching the play with caution. New Jersey predictably scored first, catching the Leafs snoozing it the Devils' end, and breaking out when the tandem of McKenna and Frank Maleki were caught pinching in a bit too far. Sergei Brylin raced in alone from centre and beat McCool with a stick side shot when the goalie failed to go down as expected.

Benoit Marlet tied the score midway through the first but the Devils reclaimed the lead before the period ended on Brylin's second of the game.

"We gotta stop the little comrade!" Frank Maleki yelled in the dressing room, before realizing that Valerie Ragulin and Alexi Gusarov were within earshot.

Mike McKenna just glared at him, and Maleki shrugged it off. "Well, even if he isn't a commie, we still have to stop the little bastard!"

Spencer Smith toyed with the idea of putting Dale McCaine's line on Elias' but with Dale having scored six times in the four games he was unwilling to trade off the offensive output. When the second was only three minutes old, he changed his mind, when Brylin beat Greg Sawchuck to the puck and worked a great two-on-one with Mogilny that saw Brylin complete the hat trick.

"Change it up!" the coach ordered. He stood behind McCaine just before he jumped over the boards. "You see that little number ten out there? Well you stick on him like shit on a blanket. If he reaches in his pocket for his wallet, I want him to find your hand there—got it?"

Dale McCaine got it. The Devils' followers were now pumped, and began to make the kind of noise that would swing momentum in their team's favour. Chuck Andrew had other ideas. The veteran knew that *this* was the time to take the crowd out of the game. He knew that anything more than a two-goal lead would be next to impossible to recover from.

On his next shift he was determined to be the one to do it. He had three goals in the series already, and was showing no effects of his season-shortening injury. Andrew stole the puck when New Jersey made a feeble attempt to clear the puck from the zone. He found Floyd Shoniker in front of the net, and fed him a pass along the ice that was so low it could have been an envelope being delivered under a door. Shoniker one timed it past Scott Clemmensen, and the Leafs had closed the gap and the crowd hushed all at once.

A sip from the water bottle later and the Leafs had tied it. On the same shift, Shoniker set up Andrew and the Devils were reeling. New Jersey called a time out, and the Leafs skated over to the bench to hear what Spencer Smith had to say during the stoppage.

"Bad time for us to stop—got to keep it going guys. Serge, switch sides with MacDonald—let him take Langenbrunner for a while. You're doing a great job on Brylin, kid. Ragulin, you gotta take Elias out in front of the net better than that. *Goose* him if you have to—so what if he thinks you're queer?"

Smith could always be counted on for blending the right mix of unflappability and earnestness to keep the player's spirits up.

The second period ended in a 3-3 tie. Between periods, Smith kept up his encouragement.

"Don't be afraid to play for the tie. They don't do well in OT," he professed.

What the coach was forgetting was that the Leafs were not exactly the second coming of the '92-93 Canadiens; their record was only 2-1 after regulation. In the third the play transpired much to the coach's liking, being scoreless until almost midway through the frame. Joel Kent recorded his fourth goal of the series, and the Leafs had a much-unexpected lead. Try as they might, the Devils were unable to mount an attack that could get by the Leafs furious back checking.

With only two minutes remaining in regulation, Spencer Smith was beginning to wonder when New Jersey was likely to pull the goalie. He no longer had to wonder when John Hill was beaten to the draw on a face off in the Leafs end. Brian Rafalski fired a point shot that Patrick Elias tipped low to the ice past Frank McCool, and the game was tied. Spencer Smith almost shattered the Plexiglas with his fist behind the Toronto bench.

"Change them up!" he ordered Ralph Newton, and the lines were exchanged. The players coming off the ice were cursing, while the unit going on the ice hung their heads at the prospect.

The score remained tied and overtime ensued for the first time in the series.

Up in the visiting director's box Ken Butler, Walt Fisher and Ron Bailey were decidedly upbeat considering the fact that the Leafs almost had this game won.

"It stands to reason that whoever can take this one has the leg up on the series," Walt Fisher pontificated. On the surface it sounded as if he was stating the obvious, but the statistics bore him out, almost as tellingly as the numbers concerning the third game of a series.

Ken Butler had a different observation on the series. "I think Spence has it under control. The guy who has been killing us in this series is Brylin. Have you noticed that since he put McCaine on the 'Russian Pocket Rocket' that he hasn't as much as registered a shot on goal?"

Ron fully expected the Devils to seize the momentum, considering that they had tied the score to force overtime. And he expected it to be over soon, noting the statistics that the average length of an overtime period is less than ten minutes.

When the period began, Spencer Smith decided to go with the McCaine unit—as expected the Devils started with the Brylin line. This piece of chess mastery paid off for Smith, because, as before the Russians were unable to make the big plays due to the Leafs close checking. The next group off the bench was the Shoniker line, and the coach held high hopes, as each member of the line had scored in the game so far. But the Devils countered with their checking line, and Shoniker, Andrew and Kent were held scoreless.

It was time for the third line, and the trio of Serge Moit, Benoit Marlet and Dennis MacDonald were ready for the task. There was a face-off inside the Leaf blue line, and Moit took the draw and fed it back to Gusarov. The cagey old Soviet carried the puck over centre and looked like he was going to shoot it in for the forwards to chase. Instead, he fired a rink wide pass to Marlet, who sped like a jet taxiing down the runway just before takeoff. He took the pass in full stride and fired a shot from about thirty feet out that Scott Clemmensen never really saw. The swamp denizens were stunned.

The Leaf players poured off the bench to mob the young francophone, who, as Serge Moit had predicted, would be a force in the playoffs. It was Marlet's third goal of the series, but by far his most important. For his effort he was also named first star of the game by *Hockey Night in Canada*.

The Leafs celebrated in the room after, but Spencer Smith put an end to that quickly.

"Get dressed, and let's get the hell out of here. We have a plane to catch in the morning, and a practice in the afternoon."

Even this news couldn't damper the enthusiasm. It wasn't usual for the coach to order a late afternoon scrimmage upon returning home. But it was even more unusual for the Leafs to be this close to winning a playoff series.

The next day's practice was held at Maple Leaf Gardens, and was scheduled for four o'clock in the afternoon. It gave the players exactly enough time to head straight for the Gardens when they got off the plane. By now the group was becoming discontent about the timing of the workout.

"We're coming back here tomorrow afternoon—why the need to have a skate today? Why not just give us the day off?" Mike McKenna complained.

But the coach had his reasons, one of which was the fact that he didn't want the players feeling as if they had *earned* a day off, at least not until they had actually won something. The practice was low key, even by Spencer Smith's standards, but he felt he got the point across.

Perhaps the coach's instincts were *not* sharp; perhaps it was the player's reaction to having a skate on a day that they felt they should be off. But the next afternoons' session was a waste of time; most players were more concerned about saving themselves for the game than about a game day skate. As a result, the group looked flat, and the coach expressed this concern to his assistants afterwards.

"Did you get the feeling that they tanked it on me because of yesterday?" Spencer Smith asked his assistants.

Neither could be described as 'yes men', but both of them felt that it was more likely they had just had enough and were saving something for the game.

"No," they both answered.

He looked them square in the eye, one after the other and said, "Your ass is a windmill!"

Spencer Smith tinkered slightly with the line-up, resting Frank Maleki and inserting David Burks in his place. He also gave John Hill the night off, and put Randy Rettig in his place. He knew that if the Leafs got ahead the Devils might decide to use some muscle to get even. He knew Hill was tough, but Rettig was tougher, even if it meant trading off some skill.

As it turned out neither move had any effect on the game—the Leafs, almost to a man were, as Spencer Smith said in his post-game media conference, "flatter than piss on a plate."

New Jersey led 1-0 after one, 2-0 after two, and was already up 3-0 when Floyd Shoniker broke Scott Clemmensen's bid for the shutout.

The game finished 4-1. The general consensus, (except for the most optimistic of fans) was that the Leafs had given this thing a good ride, but could not possibly take one more game on the road. Some of the blame was even falling on Frank McCool.

Ron burdened himself on his drive home from the Gardens that night by tuning in the soothing sound of CHILs' Gil 'the Thrill' Baines.

"It's beginning to sound a lot like the last time the Leafs made the playoffs—good enough to take a game or two; close, but no cigar."

The first caller in disagreed vehemently. "Gil, you've been on their case all year, and I for one want to say that this team has come a long way this year—from 23rd to 10th in one year. They made some good moves down the stretch, had a ton of injuries—brought in some kids from St. Johns' that didn't look out of place. I mean, what more could you ask for?"

More, it seemed.

"You're missing the point. All of this stuff was just to get here. Now that they are invited to the party, you have to do more than just sit in the corner by yourself. You have to have some life—this team had none tonight, nada, nil, doodley squat, donut, zilch!"

The caller pleaded, "They've won *three games* in the series, Gil!"

The Thrill had to resume control, because he was losing the point to a caller that made sense. "So let me get this straight—you think that this season will be a success even if they lose this series?"

The caller wasn't willing to put it in those words. "Well, they haven't lost it *yet!*"

"Ahhh, but if they lose this series, is this season still a *success*".

The caller had to ponder this for a second, and then boldly said, "Yes."

"Well then you sir, are an idiot! We go to Brampton."

As usual, Ron thought, getting the last word in for Gil was sometimes, all that mattered.

On the flight to New Jersey the mood of the team reflected the weather they were experiencing. The skies over the city were grey, and a light rain fell. Cloud cover obscured the usually picturesque seascape to the city. The view gave nothing to be excited about, but the prospect of playing in a series-clinching game seven did.

Spencer Smith had begun to second-guess himself. He had made the right move in replacing John Dennis with Frank McCool, but now he had to deal with the fact that the former Leaf great had given up thirteen goals in the last three games—even if he wasn't to blame on all of them. Lars Rogers probably still wasn't the answer Smith knew, as the goalie excelled at coming into games as a reliever. The alternative of course was John Dennis, the number one. He had been given the green light to play in the first game, but the coach wisely decided that he was not ready. A week had since transpired, and the coach had seen him working well in practice, and had not spoken a word about the chance to replace McCool.

Some coaches would question Dennis' competitive spirit over this. Spencer Smith however, was not like some coaches. He knew that the goalie had too much respect for him to treat him that way.

351

After the morning skate before the seventh game, he skated over to Dennis, who was the second last man off of the ice. He had been fooling around with Floyd Shoniker, who wanted one last goal before skating off for a shower. Dennis wasn't willing to have the last shot go in—he had to make a save before going off. The stalemate was finally broken when the coach ordered a penalty shot—a sort of 'winner-take-all' solution to the problem.

Shoniker took the puck to centre ice, while Dennis readied himself at the goal line. When they were both ready, the coach blew his whistle. Shoniker skated in at full speed, as if the goal counted towards winning a game. And Dennis reacted as if this was overtime, and the game was on the line. Shoniker drew a fake to his backhand that the goalie wouldn't fall for, but then faked to his forehand that Dennis did buy.

But just when Shoniker got control of it on the backhand and lifted the puck high into the top corner of the net, the goalie's leg came up to direct it away.

Shoniker whacked his stick on the boards in disgust, while Dennis told him that the captain 'would be buying', after the game.

It almost seemed as if the coach's news would be less important than what had just taken place on the ice. And when told about his starting assignment, Dennis reacted calmly.

"I'm ready," he said confidently.

Spencer Smith could tell. Before the game he reminded the players about the video that he had shown them before the series started, the one with clips of various teams just playing out the last helpless minutes of their seasons.

"We can do this, guys, but we have to do it together, otherwise our season ain't worth a piece of coon shit," the coach observed. It seemed that the coach agreed with Gil the 'Thrill.'

The game was full of promise and suspense at the start, but once the puck dropped, it moved at a snails' pace for the first ten minutes, as the teams were in a 'Mexican standoff' as the coach referred to it.

"We'll see who blinks first," he told Ralph Newton behind the bench.

Chuck Andrew was the first to get a good scoring chance, coming on the power play. He parked himself in front of the net and took all of the abuse that the Devils' defenseman could hurl at him. And when Mike McKenna's shot from the point came, he calmly directed it past Clemmensen.

Spencer Smith was whipping them into frenzy on the bench, and John Hill, reinstated instead of Rettig, was leading the cheers. On the ice he hit everything with a pulse, and although his contribution did not show up on the scoreboard, it did not go unnoticed.

Jim Gerber called it for the fans at home in Toronto. "Here's Langenbrunner bringing the puck over centre, the pass ahead, and he's hit by Hill! Oh my! John Hill has just schmucked Jamie Langenbrunner. The hit may have come a tad late, but in any event there is no penalty on the play."

For once Bob Swanson added something that didn't have to be discarded.

"Jim, I don't really think that hit was late. Langenbrunner had just completed the pass, and I don't think he saw John Hill lining him up. I don't think he *could* have."

"I think you're right," Gerber agreed, surprising him by what he had said.

The period ended 1-0, and John Dennis looked solid, turning all nine New Jersey shots aside. The second was less to the Leafs liking, as Patrik Elias evened it on the power play with Valeri Ragulin off for interference.

On the bench, Spencer Smith remarked, "I told him to *goose* Elias if he had too. I guess he took me liberally."

No one on the bench was willing to correct the coach's malapropism. The score was tied after two, but the Devils were ahead in the shots on goal category, 21-17.

"Don't let up out there. Don't hold anything back," Smith told his troops before the third "There aren't any guarantees in overtime," he added.

As he looked down his bench before the face off, he could see Floyd Shoniker with the kind of expression on his face that a player gets once in a while when he has the determination to make something happen. On his next shift, Floyd Shoniker did just that. After the Devils had dumped the puck into the Toronto end on a line change, Shoniker sped up ice with it before his winger could cross behind the net, as was usual. This seemed to catch the new Devils' line off guard, and the new group all converged on Shoniker. He found Joel Kent all alone on the left wing, and hit him easily with a great pass. Kent tried to make a move on Scott Clemmensen but the goalie made a sprawling save. The rebound went straight out to almost the centre ice circle—just where Shoniker was gliding. He took the puck and rifled it into the open top section of the net, and the tide had turned.

With a little over five minutes left in the third, it appeared as if the Devils were the ones who were running out of gas. Benoit Marlet took advantage of this, with his great speed and beat a New Jersey player to a loose puck, and headed for the net. He waited until the last possible second before depositing it in the five-hole, to give the Leafs a 3-1 lead. The Devils called a time out, and the expressions on their faces were the same ones that the Leafs had seen earlier in the video that Spencer Smith had shown.

When play resumed, the Leafs were determined not to let the noose slacken around the Devils. The New Jersey club was fighting for its life and with 1:33 left in the third, Viktor Kozlov shovelled in a puck at the goalmouth to bring the Devils within a goal. But New Jersey never again had control of the puck, and Toronto skated away with their first playoff series win in five years.

The players expectedly went wild in the dressing room, but the coach had warned the trainer earlier, "No Champagne, not until it matters." Instead, Nevell Carpenter substituted bottles of ginger ale, which served the purpose.

As the players doused each other with bottles of Canada Dry, John Hill broke into a rendition of 'Philadelphia Freedom' when the realization came that the Leafs next destination would be Philadelphia, to face the conference champion Flyers.

"In Philadelphia, it's worth fifty bucks!"

The Philadelphia Flyers disposed of the Carolina Hurricanes but it had taken them a surprising seven games to do so. When Ron Bailey had finally settled into his window seat on the air plane, and got as comfortable as he could, he unfolded the copy of the *Globe and Mail* that he'd been waiting to read since he bought it at the airport newsstand. He was anxious to read Grant Baker's piece on the Philadelphia-Toronto series match up.

Baker, he felt was one of the few journalists who had the proper insight into this kind of thing—only because he interviewed the right kind of people.

'*On paper it is an obvious mismatch*' Baker began '*When you consider that the Flyers finished twenty-five points ahead of the Leafs, and won their last two meetings by a combined score of 9-3 Philadelphia also featured one of the league' top goal scorers in Simon Gagne. Penetrating their defense, with Eric Desjardins and Derian Hatcher will be a formidable task.*'

Ron had to agree with every word. He read on.

'*Goal tending also favours Philadelphia, as Robert Esche and Antero Niittiymaki were a combined sixth in the league, compared to the Leafs triumvirate that finished twelfth. But if series were won on statistics alone there would be no point in playing the games, would there? For that reason we will explain in the next few sentences why Toronto will be competitive in this series, and with a few breaks could* even steal it in—*say, seven games*'

Baker went on to compliment the Leafs for having the foresight to acquire wily veterans like Dennis MacDonald and Alexi Gusarov and to have the guts to gamble on a kid like Valeri Ragulin.

"Those are the kind of dividends that will pay off more the longer this team goes in the playoffs. Two of those guys are still fresh, having just completed thirty game schedules. And Ragulin gives them some youth on defense. If Toronto has an Achilles' heel, it may be in their goal tending Though John Dennis looked sharper in the series clinching game in New Jersey, he still does not look completely recovered from the big bonk he took against Washington. And rookie Frank Isbiser (there...they still can't get that name right, Ron thought), who handles the puck the way most people handle a vial of nitro-glycerine, looks spectacular one night and shaky the next'

The Toronto coaching staff echoed Baker's comments. On the flight to Philly, Spencer Smith traded seats with Ron Bailey because he wanted to be on the aisle.

"I got the scoots! I don't wanna be climbing over anybody to get to the john!" he offered.

Ron unconsciously slipped closer to the window at the news of the coach's condition.

The coach noticed that Ron had the paper open to the sports section.

"You don't wanna be readin that at this time of the year, Ronnie," the coach advised.

"I don't know about *that*, coach. At least this paper gives us a chance of winning."

Spencer Smith grinned, as if he hadn't meant to and then went silent for a while. "The biggest decision for me is who to play in goal. I like to go with the hot hand, but right now we don't really have one. Dennis is used to the big games. And he usually does well in them. The kid, Isbister, he doesn't seem to mind the pressure either. Only Rogers seems to be out of the picture."

Ron wondered aloud why the savvy veteran, who never complained about his status as a 'second banana' to John Dennis, and who had always worked hard in practice, was suddenly out of the picture.

"Somebody was telling me the other day that no team had ever won the Stanley Cup using three goalies."

Ron smiled at him and said, "Maybe. But I bet you'd like to be the first."

The Leafs used to dread coming to Philadelphia because it meant playing in that shrine known as the 'Spectrum'. The effect that the crowd there had on the players was the same that a kid pointing a sharp stick had on a hungry tiger. Since the Flyers moved to their new home at the Wachovia Centre, the crowd was no longer a factor. Toronto had lost both the road games against the Flyers.

Before the first game, Spencer Smith stood at the front of the dressing room, near the corridor that led to the ice. He started at the ground until the chatter died down, which didn't happen until Floyd Shoniker told the group to "shut up...the coach's tryin to speak!"

Spencer Smith squinted as if he tried to find the answer to the question he was about to ask *before* he asked it.

"If I said to you guys, 'Could you win sixteen games before you lost twelve?' what would you say?" he asked.

Frank Maleki needed clarification. "Huh?" he grunted.

"I said could you win sixteen games before you lost twelve?"

David Burks was the first to speak up. "Sure!" he responded.

"No problem!" Chuck Andrew agreed.

"That's not much better than five hundred. We're better than a five hundred hockey team!" John Hill observed.

The coach grinned, as if he had asked the answer to a riddle that only he knew the answer to. "There's one catch," Floyd Shoniker added, "If you lose three in a row, you'd then have to win four in a row before you can lose another one." The coach's point was now clear.

"This team is good enough to win sixteen out of twenty-eight. We just have to avoid those three-in-a-row losing streaks that hurt us this year," Shoniker stated.

Before anyone could speak up, Tim Horton yelled out, "Well let's start by winnin the damn game tonight!"

Some of the veterans were surprised that this came from the rookie, but Conacher and Jackson were not.

The line-up had been tinkered with somewhat—the coach decided to go with a few players that he thought were more suited to the style of play Philadelphia thrived on. He inserted 'the beefs' as he called them, Randy Rettig and Lou Zanardo, to play with John Hill. With the exception of spotting Greg Sawchuck for Dennis MacDonald, he kept the other three lines intact.

On defense, he paired Maleki with McKenna, Burks with Horton, and Ragulin with Gusarov. Barilko was the odd man out on this night. In goal he decided to go with John Dennis, but wasn't keen on staying with him if a change was merited.

The Flyers scored first in a wide open first period, which saw them out shoot Toronto 17-7. Mike Knuble beat Dennis with a nifty wrap around that the goalie didn't recover well on.

The coach talked it up good with them between periods, reminding them that, 'they can play with these guys if they want to'.

Greg Sawchuck, playing with Serge Moit and Benoit Marlet for the first time, took Marlet's pass across centre and scorched in on Niittiymaki, firing a low snap shot past the goalie to tie the score.

Up in the visiting team's private box, Walt Fisher remarked, "They finally found someone that could take advantage of Marlet's speed!"

Indeed, Sawchuck looked as if he belonged. Spencer Smith was not one who believed in juggling his lines; in fact he believed in finding the right combination and keeping it intact. For that reason, the regular season had been a trial for him. And it was only because Dennis MacDonald was not use to the rigours of a seven game series that the coach felt it necessary to rest him on this night.

The tempo picked up after the Leaf goal as Philadelphia was playing as if there were only a minute left in the game. The play

359

became more physical, and it seemed just a matter of time before something spilled over.

The hits became harder, and the sticks a little higher. The Flyers enjoyed a wide margin in shots on goal (it was up to 29-11 at one point during the second) yet the scoring chances were about equal, thanks mostly to the steady goal tending of John Dennis.

Philadelphia earned a power play when Donald Brashear nailed Randy Rettig in an attempt to get to the puck. The referee didn't see the play, but he did see the retaliatory shot that Rettig delivered. And who should score on the power play but Donald Brashear.

When Rettig returned to the bench, the coach couldn't help but comment, "He suckered you, Randy, and you went for it, big-time."

The truth really hurt Rettig. And it was unlikely the coach would give him the opportunity for revenge, especially if it meant another stupid penalty.

Chuck Andrew tied it for the Leafs early in the third, as it appeared, as if Philadelphia's defensive shell was a little *too* restricting. It was Andrew's sixth of the playoffs, and most important to date.

Both teams traded chances in the third, but overtime would have to decide it, despite the fact that Philadelphia had out shot Toronto, 52-24.

The Toronto room was surprisingly quiet during the intermission that ensued. The group was thankful that John Dennis had saved them some embarrassment with his play. There was a great deal of determination being felt to pay him back by scoring an early goal. Dale McCaine's line didn't get on the ice until the third shift of overtime, at which point the Flyers had only managed one harmless shot on goal.

Before a face off in the Leafs end, Busher Jackson went over to Mike Richards of the Flyers and said, "I bet I can dump the puck from here and beat you to the other end of the ice for it."

The Philadelphia rookie looked at him like he was crazy.

"I'm serious! I've got a hundred bucks that says I can!"

The kid looked at Eric Desjardins, who told him to go ahead and take it.

Dale McCaine lost the draw, and the puck went back to the point, but Jackson intercepted it, and dumped it down the ice. Richards took after it, looking over his shoulder to see where Jackson was. As he turned to see, a dark blue streak tore past him, and both Philadelphia defenders. Jackson went straight to the corner to negate the icing, and Niittiymaki had to stay put, as no defender was close enough to help him. Jackson turned around to find Dale McCaine trailing. Both Flyers' defenders and Richards went after Busher, who flipped the puck to Dale McCaine, who drilled it into the top of the net, almost taking out the net cam. Just like that, the Leafs were up, 1-0 in the series.

In the dressing room, Charlie Conacher denounced Busher Jackson for his bet with the Philadelphia player. "How are you gonna collect on that one, Busher?"

Jackson just shrugged, and added, "I'd rather have the goal than the 'C-note' anyway!"

After the game, Ron Bailey was invited to join Burks, Kent and Shoniker for a few 'pops'. He met the group at the hotel, where they started out from Shoniker's room. Floyd Shoniker sat on the edge of the bed, the TV remote in his hand as he flicked channels looking for highlights of the game. He cheered when he found it.

"Watch that Bodine kid beat Radivojevic to the puck," he laughed. Shoniker finally got up when the bathroom came free.

"GEEEEEZ—what the hell is this?" Shoniker screamed from the bathroom. Ron and Joel Kent looked at each other, and then at Burks.

"Jesus Christ, Burksie. Flush the god dam toilet when you lay a brick like that monstrosity!"

Burks wasn't embarrassed, and didn't see what all the fuss was about.

"I thought it was a god dam python or something!" When Shoniker returned from the bathroom, Joel Kent wanted to know why the captain had been so frightened by a 'turd'.

"It's gross—it, it reminds me of when I was a kid. We had this aunt, really weird, Bohemian type. She used to come by our house when we weren't home and put shit in the toilet. You'd find it when you got home."

Kent laughed, "What do you mean she '*put*' shit in the toilet? You make it sound as if she walked around with a bottle of it and dropped it in, like a bomb!"

"Hey," Shoniker added seriously, "when you come home after a couple of hours and find one of those brewing, you'd be better off if it *was* a bomb."

In the second game of the series the inevitable happened. Philadelphia displayed precisely why they finished twenty-five points ahead of the Leafs in the regular season. They skated away with a rather easy 6–3 victory that evened the series.

The line of Shoniker, Kent and Andrew contributed one goal each, while the other lines took turns in being unable to handle the Flyers depth. Richards scored twice, while singles went to Forsberg, Knuble, Carter and Savage. The consensus among the players was that they had done as well as expected in the first two games on the road, by breaking even.

"But now we have the pressure on us, to keep the same thing we did to them, from happening to us," Floyd Shoniker told *Hockey Night in Canada* after the game.

Spencer Smith was back to his waffling over goaltenders. John Dennis didn't look particularly sharp, but the defeat could not be solely blamed on him.

"Against the Devils we put McCaine's line on Brylin's. It may have cost us some scoring but it negated theirs. We may have to do the same against Forsberg."

During practice for the home game against Philadelphia, the coaching staff decided to experiment further. They packaged John Hill, Lou Zanardo and Tobin West as a checking line, while keeping the other lines intact. And the decision after the morning skate was that John Dennis was to remain in goal.

"He deserves it. I'll only pull him if he's struggling," the coach told Ken Butler when they met before the opening face off

The pace of the game was furious. The Flyers came out hitting; even their smaller players were taking the body. The result was that the Leafs, in trying to keep up, were ending up on the short end of the man advantage situations. Before the first period was over, Philadelphia had scored on four of the seven power plays they were handed. The checking line idea did little, as Forsberg scored twice with the extra man, as did Richards. Simon Gagne also scored at even strength. Toronto did manage some offense of their own in the wide-open period, getting goals from Benoit Marlet (a pair) and Joel Kent.

Between periods, the Leaf dressing room was like marine boot camp. Spencer Smith looked at each of them individually as he circled the dressing room. He didn't reprimand them individually, but kept his remarks to the team as a whole. He criticized their lack of effort, their getting beaten to the puck regularly, and the lack of physical play. He ranted from the time last player sat down until the trainer had to come in and fetch them to return to the ice for the start of the second period. It was the first and only time that season the coach had behaved in such a manner.

The Leafs were a silent bunch when they returned to the ice, but they seemed determined to let their play do the talking for them. Before the period was a minute old, Benoit Marlet completed his hat trick, and drew the Leafs to within one goal.

Shortly thereafter, Toronto got a rare power play when Donald Brashear roughed up Serge Moit right in front of the referee. John

Hill scored to tie the game when he stole the puck from Forsberg. The elation was short lived. Forsberg completed his hat trick, despite having Lorne Graham draped over him like a toga.

With Philadelphia up 6-5, Spence Smith called a time out. But instead of continuing his barrage from the dressing room, he chose instead to praise them for their hard work in tying the score.

"Don't let up on these guys and don't give up! We've almost got them. Niittiymaki isn't having a very good night. Stay in front of him—he's having trouble with the traffic."

The coach's positive motivation seemed to be just what they needed, as the Leafs tied it before the end of the second on a goal by Tim Horton. The husky defenseman carried the puck on a rush, passing it off to Busher Jackson, who went in on goal, but carried the puck too far to have a chance for to score. Instead, as he raced behind the net, he fed a long pass to Horton, who swooped in, and delivered a quick wrist shot that beat Niittiymaki.

The tone in the room changed dramatically after that period as expected, and the feeling was that the third could be the Leafs period, just as it had been in the first game in Philadelphia.

Midway through the third, the checking line completed its' work when Tobin West intercepted a pass that Knuble had intended for Gagne, and wasted no time if firing it past Niittiymaki to give the Leafs their first lead of the game. The Flyers called a time out at this juncture, but it didn't seem to help, The Leafs controlled the play for the rest of the game. When Niittiymaki was pulled for the extra forward with just under two minutes left, Dennis MacDonald fired one into the empty net from centre ice, to preserve the improbable 8-6 win.

The Leafs being up two games to one in the series was more than some people could handle.

One of those people was Gil 'The Thrill' Baines. "Enjoy the ride, my friends!" the Thrill advised, "because when it's over, all you'll have to remember it by are the 'Kodak moments'."

Ron Bailey listed to the slanted monologue for as long as he could stand it. More and more the callers were starting to disagree with and question the Thrill. Even though calls were screened it was becoming harder to find any Leaf bashers to agree with the Thrill. This was evident by the decreasing number of calls taken on air. And for some unexplained reason, the Thrill began having more guests in the studio. Perhaps the most interesting was Billy Sinfield.

The old goat had been a stranger to Ron ever since their falling out over the team ownership issue. The entire thing had almost blown over for several reasons. The success of the team on ice had diverted attention, while the whole ownership process was still mired in league red tape.

The Thrill began with his introduction of Billy Sinfield. "Ladies and gentlemen, we have with us tonight, perhaps the oldest living (and I think that I could add just about anything here and be correct) reporter, late of the *Toronto Star,* Billy Sinfield! We'll dispense with that ugly 'Old Goat' metaphor."

Radio was not something new to Billy Sinfield, as he had once been the play-by-play announcer of the Toronto Marlboros in their heyday. But on this occasion, his awkwardness provided some comic relief to the overbearing Thrill.

"Well thank you, I think, for that introduction. You know, a lot of people are talking about the Leafs these days, and the consensus of the average Joe is that this hockey team may just surprise some people."

The Thrill had to interrupt; it was written into his contract. "And may cause some coronaries, strokes, manic depression—they are certainly good for that!"

"But the consensus also is this; in general the media have turned the other cheek so to speak, that is to say they've stopped the cutting and started to speak of the team in a more, shall we say, *positive light?* But I note a glaring exception to this rule. And my friend, you're it!"

"And for that, I thank you, Mr. Sinfield."

Billy Sinfield wasn't finished. "And I suppose we have to give you some credit for sticking to your guns, even if the Leafs play is starting to improve."

"Your sympathy is not needed," the thrill humbled.

"But by the same token, only a jackass would fail to realize that this team is as hot as any in these playoffs. And if they can get that one necessary ingredient."

"And that would be?" the thrill interjected.

"Goal tending—no team has ever won a Stanley Cup with three goaltenders."

The thrill was getting excited. It seemed as if the Old Goat was on his side after all.

"So you're point is what? That this team should drop a goalie so they can win the cup?"

"No, my point is that they should decide on one, and stick with him. It doesn't matter to me which one, although it appears that it may be Lars Rogers."

"Good grief!" the thrill shrieked "The man has yet to play as much as a minute in these playoffs, and you think he's the man to go to?"

Billy Sinfield went quiet to collect his thoughts. He had a habit of stuttering when his tongue tried to go faster than his mind.

"I think John Dennis is still suffering some of the aftershock of the capital punishment he received in Washington, and this kid Frank Isbister, well he looks like a stand up goalie in an era when the butterfly is the vogue. And that leaves us with Mr. Rogers."

"Yes it's a beautiful day in the neighbourhood," the Thrill began to sing, completing almost the entire song before the old goat interrupted.

"The point is that Lars Rogers plays better under pressure, when he is the number two man, and now that he's number three. Well there's no telling how good he can be. He could be like Ken Dryden in '71—you remember, when he came in and supplanted the veterans Phil Myre and Rogie Vachon, and led the Canadiens to the Stanley Cup!"

The Thrill was busy adjusting his headset to make sure he had heard the old goat correctly.

"There's only one thing *wrong with* that analogy; *Isbister* is the rookie goalie, not Lars Rogers!"

"Yes, but Rogers went to an 'Ivy League' school—just like Dryden, and they're both tall."

"Yeah," the thrill agreed "And they both put their pants on one leg at a time. Why they're practically twins. We're going to take a break, and we'll be back with more of Billy Sinfield and his look at more tangents and vectors in a moment."

The goal tending question remained in the minds of some of the media, but Spencer Smith was not swayed. And it wasn't just because he didn't read the papers or watch the sportscasts on TV. He decided to stick with John Dennis in game four.

The hype surrounding the game had caused the fans to emote far beyond the actual significance of the game.

It was not a cup final, or even a series clincher, but it was the farthest the team had advanced in the playoffs in years. And so the pre-game ceremonies were as intense as if this game was going to decide something important. And perhaps it was.

The first period was as wide open as any in the series were. The Leafs took an early 1-0 lead, courtesy of Floyd Shoniker, who was responding with the kind of leadership that every team hopes that their captain can aspire to. His goal was followed quickly by a marker from the 'junk line' as it was called, made up of West, Rettig and Graham. Tobin West ended any hopes the Philadelphia players had of taking the crowd out of the game early when he put Toronto up 2-0.

The Flyers were too good a team to be denied, however. While the first period ended with the Leafs up by a pair, the second period was surely the character acid test. Philadelphia was the benefactor of a couple of questionable calls. Bill Barilko took out Jeff Carter behind the net. Quickly the Flyer players' stick came up and nearly took off the Toronto defenseman's helmet. Barilko reacted the way players did in the old days; instead of retaliating with his stick, he popped him one on the nose.

Barilko easily won the ensuing fight, but was unfairly tagged with being the aggressor, and Gagne scored on the ensuing power play. Shortly thereafter, Sami Kapanen scored to tie it, and the Leaf fans were deflated for the moment. And to really ruin the momentum that had been built, Niittiymaki robbed Busher Jackson on a breakaway. The entire Leaf team, it seemed, followed on the rush, and when the rebound came, Eric Desjardins was there to snag it. He raced untouched to the other end to put Philadelphia up 3-2 before the period ended.

The Toronto dressing room was full of cursing, bowed heads and glances upwards to the ceiling for answers to all kinds of questions. Over in his cubicle Benoit Marlet looked calm. He was the only player who didn't seem to be fazed by their predicament. He quietly told his line mate Serge Moit, "I heard them say, 'Just watch McCaine. We take him out and we win'"

Serge Moit replied, "I think they forget all about you little Ben!"

The words were prophetic, as early in the third Moit and Marlet worked a give and go at the Philadelphia blue line, and Marlet wasted no time converting the pass into a snap shot that beat Niittiymaki and tied the game. And it also woke up the crowd.

As the game progressed, and as overtime loomed it appeared impossible that Toronto could get any breaks. The penalties had been one sided in Philadelphia's favour. And suddenly they evened out. Forsberg was called for high-sticking Chuck Andrew, who remarkably restrained himself from returning the favour. The call was questionable, but the Toronto side wasn't complaining.

Valeri Ragulin scored his most important goal as a Leaf when his point shot made it past Niittiymaki, thanks to a well-timed screen by Chuck Andrew.

The fans were now completely behind the Leafs, and the furious chants of 'GO LEAFS GO 'echoed throughout the building. As the clock worked against Toronto the Leafs increased the pace. Spencer Smith shortened every shift, and Toronto kept the puck in the Philadelphia end except for the occasions when the Flyers were forced to dump and chase it.

As the last minute and a half were played out, the Flyers were desperately trying to get Niittiymaki out of the net for the extra attacker. With 1:59 remaining, he managed to get as far as the blue line when Benoit Marlet stole the puck from Patrick Sharp and broke in on Niittiymaki who skated backwards as if he were in the *Ice Capades*. Marlet beat the goalie to the net, and deposited the winning goal.

The Leafs celebrated on ice, but Spencer Smith was anxious to get them to the room. He stood near the entrance slapping backs and shaking hands, but didn't seem as emotional as usual. Once inside the room he ordered them all to 'listen up.'

He quickly congratulated them on the victory but wanted to leave them with a thought going into the next game.

"The toughest thing to do in a series in to clinch it—especially when you're going into the other guys building, and you think, even if we lose we come home for the next one. Wrong. You get them on the ground. You gotta step on 'em. No mercy. That's the way we have to play game five. End it there. That's it!" he concluded.

Ron sat beside Ralph Newton in the GM's box, perched high above the Gardens' ice. The crowd had filed out by now, with visions of making it to the next round, and speculation that the Leafs would be facing the New York Rangers in the conference final.

"I just can't believe what I'm seeing, Newt!" Ron confided.

The coach was gathering up his headset and game sheet, and agreed.

"Your guys from the rock, Bachmann, Bodine, Mouton, Hansky,—they're not the ones scoring the goals and getting the credit, but have you really *watched* them out there?"

Ron confessed that he had, but he wanted another opinion.

"The way they played," the assistant coach continued, "they're opening things up for the other guys, but its subtle stuff—some of it happening just behind the play, or just before a play develops. I see Hansky finishing a check, or Mouton out-muscling a guy who is five inches taller. And that Bodine, beating just about everyone to the puck to avoid the icing, Bachmann—he never gives up along the boards or in the corners. Your kid McCaine has what, six goals? I bet Bachmann has set up all of them, one way or another, but only has a couple of assists to show for it. They have been the difference, I think. And the way they have played has let the guys who are supposed to score, Andrew, Shoniker, do their job."

"And what about Marlet—he's found the touch he had in junior!" Ron added.

"Yeah," Newton continued, "and it's because Moit is setting him up instead of having to do what Bachmann and Bodine are doing. It all comes back to those guys."

Despite the fact that the coaching staff recognized the importance of the ex-Leafs, the media were not.

Neil Powers could only write about the resurgence of Leaf captain Floyd Shoniker, and how Joel Kent was once again winning fights, scoring goals and not missing games.

The flight to Philadelphia was quiet, considering how upbeat the players all felt about their situation, heading into a game that could clinch a berth in the conference final. Barilko, Busher Jackson, John Hill and Frank Maleki conducted business as usual, holding their semi-regular, in-flight penny ante poker game. Joel Kent liked to use the time to respond personally to his huge volume of fan mail. David Burks and Mike McKenna were talking shop, about what to do about the Forsberg-Gagne scoring machine.

Ron was summoned to listen in on a conversation that Spencer Smith and the assistant coaches were having about the game.

"Lookit the stats Bo here, has got," he said referring to Ridley by his nickname, "he says that Desjardins and Hatcher are loggin 38 to 42 minutes a game. I want our guys to dump the puck and make those two chase it every time they're on the ice. We're gonna wear those two down by the third. And we have to get in Niittiymaki's face more. I want Andy to pitch a tent there if he has to. And we'll keep McCaine's line on longer if we have to, so's we can match 'em against Forsberg's line. And every time they're on, when Ragulin is on, get the kid to pinch in. I want our European on theirs. When he does pinch in, we'll have Bodine come back. There's nobody on that Philadelphia team that can stay with him."

Spencer Smith wasn't exaggerating; there was no one faster on either team than Busher Jackson.

The game did go somewhat according to Spencer Smiths' plan. The Leafs scored early in the first—Floyd Shoniker getting the early marker on an even strength goal.

From that minute on, the Flyers tried to out-muscle the Leafs, who had decided on a line-up without Lorne Graham and Randy Rettig.

Donald Brashear, Mike Knuble, Denis Gauthier and Turner Stevenson all took turns in trying to goad the Leafs into something, but it backfired. Although Philadelphia evened the score before the period ended, the second was all Toronto's. Chuck Andrew took advantage of the power plays afforded the Leafs as they kept their cool and chose not to retaliate. Andrew notched the 'natural hat trick', as play-by-play man Jim Gerber referred to it.

Toronto led 4-1 by the time the Flyers realized that the goon act was not going to work.

Jim Gerber observed, "Chuck Andrew has been absorbing a tremendous beating in front of that Philadelphia net all night, and he'll have the welts to prove it tomorrow. But it's been paying off on the score sheet. He has converted point shots from Mike McKenna, Valeri Ragulin and Gilbert Mouton and turned them into goals!"

Bob Swanson added, "When Andrew is given room to work like that, he's unbelievable. He's like Merlin the magician, turning lead into gold. And a good part of it is thanks to Shoniker and Kent who have been drawing the attention of the Desjardins and Hatcher. Those two look pretty tired out there!" he commented.

The third period was almost a moot point, as Benoit Marlet provided the only goal, as he drew even on his quest to claim the goal scoring lead on the team.

As the game drew to its conclusion the Philadelphia players had the look on their faces that Spencer Smith described in the video clips that he had shown his team before the playoffs. The Wachovia centre began to empty proportionately with the amount of time remaining on the clock. The fans expressed their displeasure vocally. After all, this team *had* finished first in the conference during the regular season, and was expected by most to win this series in as few as five games.

The reaction in Toronto was predictably, the opposite. The sports bars, papers, television updates and phone-in shows were heady. The town had not seen this kind of excitement since the Blue Jays emergence in '85.

'That's the closest thing in recent memory I can compare it to' wrote Billy Sinfield in his 'Sin Bin' column the next day. *'However, I expect that the band will stop playing soon when the Leafs have to face the New York Rangers in the next round. The Leafs won only one of four matches from the blue shirts during the regular season, and despite their improved play against Philadelphia, it's highly unlikely they can pull another upset. Still, they have afforded their long suffering fans with some decent playoff hockey that almost makes it worth the hijacking they are getting for the price of a playoff ticket'*

Billy Sinfield's column was lacking in just one bit of accuracy, though he did not know it at the time.

While the Toronto-Philadelphia series was over in a surprisingly short five games, the New York—Montreal set was going to a seventh and deciding game at Madison Square Garden.

Joel Kent invited the entire team over to his Mississauga spread to watch the game. Although the invitation was extended to the coaching staff, they all politely declined. Spencer Smith did not believe in associating with the players when it came to having a few drinks.

The coach rationalized it this way: "It's tough enough to have to coach someone, and be everything from their shrink to their boss, never mind being their friend. I know I can't be somebody's pal one day, and chew them out the next for leaving their man in front of the net, or benching somebody. That's when they'd take it personally!"

Ron Bailey did accept the invitation, however, to view the game from Joel Kent's home.

John Hill explained why it was Kent's place that became the unofficial team headquarters for socializing. "We used to go to Superman's apartment, before he got married, and drink our faces off," he explained. "His wife was the only one that would put up with us when we went 'offside'. But now that we're older, and hopefully wiser, we've mellowed a bit, and his wife's used to us."

The large recreation room in the Kent's basement looked like a genuine sports bar, decorated with memorabilia that would put many hall of fame's to shame. Of course it contained items from Kent's own career; his scoring title with the Swift Current Broncos, his gold medal won with the Canadian Juniors, and Molson Cup award from four years ago. And he had a splendid collection of Leaf items, including a game-worn jersey of Tim Horton and Johnny Bower, rookie cards of Howe, Hull, Orr, Beliveau and his childhood idol Mike Bossy.

But the item that piqued his teammate's curiosity was the display of Leaf cards. Inside a huge display case shaped like a Maple Leaf, and lined with blue velvet were over fifty cards of players from the thirties right up to and including the present season. All of the greats were represented; from the thirties and forties such as Red Horner, Hap Day, Ace Bailey, King Clancy, George Hainsworth, Turk Broda; through the fifties players like Harry Lumley, Teeder Kennedy, Syl Apps; the sixties greats like Keon, Pulford, Armstrong, Mahovlich, Stanley; the seventies including Sittler and Salming and right up to date. Andrew had included cards of many of his teammates, including Shoniker, McKenna, Andrew, Burks and Dennis. Dennis MacDonald, who had only been a Leaf since the trade deadline, was fascinated by the display.

"This is fantastic. Where the hell did you get all of these? They ought to have this thing in the Gardens," he praised.

"I started collecting some of them when I was a kid," Kent said. "When I joined the Leafs I got interested in all of the older Leafs, especially when you see all of the pictures all over the Gardens."

Lars Rogers was quick to pick up on the structure of the display. There was a different card of each year—from the 1933-34 *Canadian Chewing Gum* set (the first set that included the Toronto Maple Leafs) right up to this years' *Upper Deck* set. And only one card was featured of each player, and the year selected of that player was also significant, either because it was a rookie card or because it was a season that the player led the team in some statistical category.

Rogers further noted that the set was conspicuous because it did not include a card of Joel Kent. The big right-winger explained the reason while he changed the hoses on a new keg of Molson Ice draft.

"Naw—let somebody else have me in their set," he said.

As game time neared, the crowd around the big screen television began to increase, while those around the billiard and Ping-Pong tables, and table hockey game began to dwindle. Only the poker game involving the Barilko gang was ignoring the broadcast, for the time being at least.

Dennis MacDonald was still studying the cards with Lars Rogers, and he could not help but notice some startling revelations. "Hey Kent, come over here!" he shouted. He also pointed out his finding to Rogers.

"What the hell is this? The picture of Conacher, that's Bachmann!" MacDonald exclaimed.

The three of them studied the card that said 'C.CONACHER' on its front.

"It doesn't look like Bachmann!" Kent stated.

MacDonald disagreed, "Well, except for the *hair* it does—look at the eyes!"

Joel Kent shook his head in disbelief. It was fortunate that MacDonald didn't examine the cards of Jackson and Horton as closely.

The group began to pay more attention to the game as it started to develop into a very lively contest. The Leaf players were divided on whom to cheer for—the general consensus was that Toronto would have an easier time with the Canadiens than they would with the Rangers.

Those watching the Canadiens lose were somewhat taken by surprise at the jeering the Habs were taking from there fans.

Joel Kent had an opinion on this, "The fans in this town are no better. They like to *think* they know everything about hockey, 'cause most of them have played at one time. But they don't know what it's like to play here. The game's a god dam religion to some people! Everybody wants a piece of you. It's like, when we first moved out here, and I'd be on the road or whatever. Karen would be getting kid's hanging around the door all the time looking for autographs, ringing the doorbell in the afternoon as soon as they got out of school. And it would always be just when she was trying to get the baby down for her nap," he said while sipping on a beer. "She's used to it now, and because most of the people around here know me by now, we don't get bothered as much."

The subject really hit a nerve with Lou Zanardo. "What gets me is how the fans equate you to your game. Is it reasonable to think that because I have a lousy game that I'm a lousy person also? What do they think, because I take a bad penalty and the other team scores on the power play that I go home and hit my wife and kids, and kick the dog?"

"Naw, I've seen your wife, Lou—she can take you!" Floyd Shoniker chipped in.

The seriousness of it wasn't lost on Dennis MacDonald. "I sure didn't miss it in Bern. You play your games there, and go home. Nobody bothers you. Hell, nobody recognizes you, at or away from the rink. But here, it's as if all of these fans own a piece of the team or something-like they live and die on each game."

"The fans in New York, at the Garden, they're the worst. They boo the home team even when they're winning!" John Dennis remarked.

"Not even close." Chuck Andrew countered, "It has to be Boston—they get on the visiting team like nowhere else. I've had things thrown at me; flashlight batteries, condoms, unbelievable!"

Alexi Gusarov had kept quiet during this exchange. Being new to the country, he couldn't comment. But when it came to describing the drawbacks of being a hockey player, well, he just had to set these guys straight. "I maybe should not say nothing," he began.

Dennis MacDonald, who knew him the best, invited him to take part.

"Here, in Canada, they treat the hockey player very well. They put your picture in newspaper, and on box of cereal. They give you money for it. But in my country, if you are good enough you can get single apartment, instead of have to share with wife's father and mother. Is true is hard to have people knock on door and want autograph when baby is sleeping—Is not good to do that. But it is also not good, like my brother, to have door knocked late at night and have two men say 'Your son, he no longer play for Gorki Torpedo. He come with us to Moscow now to play for Dynamo.' That is what is not good about being hockey player."

No one had a comeback for that. Dennis MacDonald nodded to Gusarov, and said, "Goose, we're glad you made it over here!"

Valeri Ragulin gave a respectful nod to his older countryman, and Joel Kent got Gusarov another beer.

The poker game in the corner was still going strong—apparently Barilko was doing quite well and this wasn't going over big with Busher Jackson, who was the big loser. The cheer that went up when the Rangers made it 2-0 didn't even distract them.

Rookie defenseman Ian Moriarty looked on at the game with Ron Bailey "It doesn't look good for Montreal, does it?"

"We'll have to play a completely different game against either one of these teams than we played against New Jersey and Philadelphia. These guys will kill us in a shoot-out!" Ron remarked.

Serge Moit was getting a round of beers, and couldn't help taking a shot at the host over the recent developments in the team Memorial Cup pool.

"I told you, man of steel, look out for Rimouski! They are just three wins away from it!"

Kent rolled his eyes upward. John Hill could not resist getting in a shot for his beloved London Knights. "Hey search me! When it's all over it'll be those Knights. You can bet on that. When's the last time you frenchies took the cup anyway?" he asked.

The poker game broke up as the game drew to a close. Busher Jackson was a little lighter in the pocket, but was more interested now in whom their next round opponent was. As the game drew to a close, the players began to cheer for the Canadiens. And then it was over, a 2-1 the final for New York.

"Hey Hilly, have you got a song about New York?" Chuck Andrew asked.

John Hill broke into a surprisingly good, very bluesy version of the *'New York New York'*

"Tuesday, in the 'big apple' boys," Floyd Shoniker concluded.

'Start spreading the news'

Before practice the next morning the coaching staff reviewed some video clips that the pro scouting staff had put together along with the teams' video coordinator, Mike Wardyz,

"He's given us some great clips of the Rangers first round against the Lightning, and the Montreal series." The coach remarked.

After reviewing the video with the coaches, they had a brief meeting about the proposed line-up for the opening game of the series.

"It has to be close checking. We need Zanardo, Bachmann, Hill, Bodine, Kent, and Sawchuck in there. We may have to mix the lines up a bit."

The two assistants looked at each other in surprise. It wasn't like the coach to make such drastic line changes.

"Do you want to keep McCaine's line intact, or Shoniker's, or Marlet's?" Brian Ridley asked.

The coach scribbled some line combinations on the lined pad of paper in front of him, while letting his glasses slide down on his nose. He looked more like a history teacher grading papers than a hockey coach preparing his team for a Stanley Cup semi-final game.

"Keep Shonny's line, and try Zanardo between Hill and Sawchuck. Hilly can play the wing—he's a right-handed shot. But he can play on the left side, and that puts Sawchuck on right wing, and he's the natural right-winger. That's the line we put on their second line."

Ralph Newton had assumed that this was the line that would go up against the Jagr line.

"Hell, no Newt! I want McCaine's line on them, just like we put them on Forsberg!"

Newton was surprised. "But Spence, Forsberg scored a few goals in that series, but he didn't beat us! I know what you're going to say, 'Why put a forty goal scorer on the other team's best line—it'll count against us'. But McCaine's line can do it. Look at the balance we have with them checking. Marlet has ten goals, Shonny's got eight, and Andy's gotten. I don't think it's gonna take a lot of goals to win this series, but it'll take a lot of defense."

"Which brings us *to* the defense," Ridley remarked.

"Yeah," the coach continued. "I want to use just about everybody. Keep 'em fresh. Keep the Russians together, but give the old guy the every other night off—same with Maleki, and Burks. Get the kid Moriarty in there, and Andersson to spell them. I want to keep Mouton and Hansky together. The more I see of those two the more I like them I've never seen two kids who play so well under pressure. They remind me of—"

"Of Spencer Smith!" Ralph Newton quipped.

"No, Mouton reminds me for all the world of—"

Before the coach could finish his sentence, the door to his office burst open. Nevell Carpenter stood panting in the doorway, and had to catch his breath before he apologized for the intrusion.

"I've called the doctor! I think maybe it's his appendix!"

Spencer Smith jumped to his feet. "*Whose* appendix?" he demanded.

"Dennis'!" the trainer puffed.

"Dennis MacDonald?" Newton asked.

"*John* Dennis!" Carpenter wheezed.

The three coaches hurried to the dressing room where the goalie, half dressed in his equipment was sprawled on all fours as if he were looking for something on the blue-carpeted floor. A small group of players formed a semi-circle around him, though not so close as to steal his air.

The coach knelt beside him, though the player did not raise his head. "What is it?" Smith asked.

"Holy shit—it feels like something inside me is trying to get out—with a can opener!" Dennis grunted.

"I got hold of the doc. He says to get him to emerg at Wellesley. He'll meet us there."

Spencer Smith ordered Nevell Carpenter to get an ambulance, and to accompany the player.

"You let me know as soon as the doc comes. Take my phone from my office!" he ordered. The team was on the ice with the assistant coaches by the time the ambulance arrived. John Dennis lay on his back with his feet pulled up to his knees. The trainer had to remove the goalie pads before the ambulance arrived, because the player could not lie comfortably with his legs out straight.

"Jesus, what timing!" the coach cursed after they wheeled the gurney out of the room.

It was not the way the coach had planned it, but when the Leafs stepped onto the ice at Madison Square Garden the next night, Frank McCool was in net, and Lars Rogers was his backup. John Dennis remained in hospital; the early diagnosis being severe intestinal cramping caused by flu. More tests were being conducted, but the goalie would likely be discharged the next day.

The teams played a scoreless first period, as they experienced the usual game of cat and mouse, testing each other at every opportunity. Spencer Smith was able to match lines as he changed on the fly. It was a necessary evil, one that the players grumbled about, but it seemed to be working, as the Jagr line was given no scoring chances at all.

In the second period, Chuck Andrew tallied on a scramble in front of Henrik Lundqvist to open the scoring. It was short lived, however, as Dominic Moore caught the Leafs on a line change and converted a two-on-one to tie the game before the second was over.

The score stayed that way through regulation, and the dressing room was quiet in the intermission that preceded overtime. The coach gave a brief speech. "The first chance could win it. These guys won two OT games so far, both of them in less than five minutes—that's what our scouts tell us."

Floyd Shoniker piped up, "Who starts, coach?"

"They're late submitting the line-up. If they start Jagr, then McCaine's line—if they start Straka's line, then I want Zanardo's, that'll put you up third."

The Jaromir Jagr-Michael Nylander-Martin Rucinsky line took the opening face-off for New York, and Toronto countered with their best checking line. McCaine stuck on Straka, and kept him from getting the puck to Jagr. When the lines were changed, Straka's trio came over the boards first, and Spencer Smith countered with his group.

From the face off in the Leafs end, Lou Zanardo won the draw, and got the puck back to the point. Tim Horton was there to take the puck and he carried it quickly into the New York end, avoiding not one but two attempts to steal it. All the time he was looking for a forward to pass it to. He found Greg Sawchuck beside the net. Horton fired a high shot at Lundqvist. The drive was so hard that it bounced off the goalie, which had to reach up to try and handle it. Instead the puck dropped to the ice and Sawchuck one-timed it into the net. He was mobbed by his line mates, and a group of blue shirts that rushed from the bench to greet him.

"It wasn't pretty but we'll take it!" Sawchuck told the *Hockey Night in Canada* audience as he was interviewed in the hallway before he made his way to the dressing room. He was slapped on the shin pads by teammates as they passed.

Inside the room there was a celebration that began to equal the one for the series-clinching game against Philadelphia, until the coach came in to cool things off.

"It's only the first game!" he reminded them. "When you win a fourth game, then—" The coach did stop by Frank McCool's stall and offer a handshake in congratulations for shutting out the Rangers for two-plus periods.

"I told you when you stopped the other team big, then I'd get your name right Isbister," he laughed.

"You just keep doing that and I'll call you anything you want!"

"Just don't call me *sweetheart!*" the goalie laughed.

Sweetheart or not, Frank McCool was going to be the goalie, at least for the next few games. John Dennis had been discharged from hospital, and was resting at home. The diagnosis was still incomplete, but he was feeling better, albeit weak from dehydration. The earliest he was projected to return to the line-up would be game four of the series.

Game two of the conference final started much like game one—a scoreless first period. The Rangers had some great chances in the second, but were foiled either by spectacular saves by McCool, or by some great defensive play.

The Leafs rested Gusarov, Maleki and Burks in game one, and inserted Andersson, and Moriarty. Tonight the coach rested those two, and Maleki, and re-united Gusarov with Ragulin, and Burks with McKenna. The rise in the energy of the rested players didn't go unnoticed, especially by play-by-play man Jim Gerber.

"The Leaf defenders really have that extra kick out there tonight, and it's likely because Spencer Smith has been giving his 'longer in the tooth' blue liners the odd night off. Here's a chance for McCaine, in over the line with Bachmann, he fakes the shot—HE SCORES!"

With that goal the Leafs went up 1-0 and from that point on the defensive shell that Toronto went into was un-penetrable. No team had greater coaching depth than the Toronto Maple Leafs had in the art of defensive play. While the Leaf forwards were good in these playoffs at scoring, they all had equal abilities when it came to covering a man.

"It's the kind of thing that never shows itself when you're losing," the coach used to say about the defensive responsibilities of a forward's game. "And when you're winning, it's overlooked as well. Show me a forward that knows how to protect a lead, and I'll show you a complete hockey player," he professed.

Spencer Smith would love nothing better than to have an entire team of Bob Gaineys to coach. In fact, he kept a photograph of Gainey in his Canadiens uniform on his office wall, for inspiration.

Floyd Shoniker scored the only goal of the third period, and McCool stopped all twenty-one shots as the Leafs escaped with a 2-0 win, and more importantly, the same count in the series.

At home, the media were in a state of shock—how could the Leafs be just two wins away from going to the Stanley Cup final? All of this was not lost on their harshest critic, Gil 'the thrill.' On this night the listeners, including Ron Bailey, wanted to hear if he was going to change his slant and jump on the Leafs bandwagon. But it wasn't easy to negotiate such a drastic turn without capsizing the ship. And the 'Thrill' knew it.

"If you look outside your window today," he began, "you'll notice that the sky is still blue. The calendar will tell you it is not April Fools' day, and the sports section will tell you that not only are the Maple Leafs still alive in the playoffs. But they are leading the Conference final two games to zip over a much superior, at least in the regular season, New York Rangers team. We have to pinch ourselves, and ask ourselves, 'How is this possible?' The answer is that this team accomplished exactly what I suggested they had to in order to be competitive, except that they did it a few months late. Did they sign some free agents last summer? No, they waited until the trade deadline to acquire some talent like MacDonald, Gusarov and Ragulin."

The 'Thrill' was just warming up in the humility bullpen.

"I suggested that they needed more goal-scoring, because they weren't getting it done with the group they had. And low and behold they go out and have themselves a find like Dale McCaine. And they must have heard me when I said that this group was too old and too slow to go anywhere, and they come up with some speed and youth like Bodine, Bachmann, Hansky and Mouton. But don't get me wrong. I'm not trying to grab *all* of the credit for where the Leafs are today. But strangely enough, they followed my lead, and just look at where they are."

Ron wanted to reach through the speaker of his Sony portable and strangle Gil Baines, if it was possible.

"Ladies and Gentlemen, I happen to know that at least *one* member of the Leafs management team listens to this show on a regular basis—a coincidence? I don't think so. In a moment, we go to your calls."

Ron desperately tried to get on the air, pressing the re-dial button on his portable phone until it almost stuck in the in position.

While he was dialling a rather nervous sounding caller caught his attention.

"Bud is on the phone from Leaside. Bud, what is your take on all this, *Bud?*" the 'Thrill' asked.

"Yeah, uh, well, what you said about the Leafs, uh, I mean, them listening to what you said—"

"Yes, what can I say? They finally saw the light."

"Yeah, but you said before that this team, and this management group would never win a Stanley Cup with the stupid management group they have—"

"Whoa, wait a minute there Bud! Never did I say the Leafs would never win the Stanley Cup with the stupid management group they have."

"Yeah Gil, you did!"

"Well, *Bud,* I beg to differ."

"You did Gil—early in the year after they played Washington-"

"Well Bud, if my producer can pull the tape-"

"Oh, I have it right here, Gil!"

And with that, *Bud from Leaside* pulled the tape, and played it, too. The voice sounded a bit different, because of the recording quality, but away it went.

"When are *you* people going to get it? This team is *never* going to win a Stanley Cup with the line-up they have, with the management group they have! End of story."

Momentarily, the 'thrill' had been silenced. "Bud—get a life! We'll be back after these messages!"

With that, the 'Thrill' signed off for a few minutes, but regrouped remarkably.

"I hope I wasn't too unkind to our last caller. In case you missed it. I was called to task about something I said on the air back on the first night of the season," he began. "And, as often happens in the media, we are confronted with our own words. However, I stand by what I said at the time I said it. And if the Toronto Maple Leafs go on to win the Stanley Cup this year or any other, I will—what will I do? Yes I will wear a Leaf jersey on the air for a year, and invite each and every member of their organization on this program to have their say."

Ron had wished that he had taped the segment.

Game three of the series was back at Maple Leaf Gardens. It afforded the media coverage of the Leafs playoff run the exponentially driven hype factor that was in need of with each further step the team took. The CKFH talk shows virtually ignored baseball, the NBA playoffs and every other event in favour of more Leaf coverage. *Hockey Night in Canada* was relieved not to have to expend much of their travel budget in covering the games in Toronto.

For so many years the program spent much of the regular season focusing on the Leafs, only to have to drop them once the playoffs arrived. For a change, the spotlight was once again on Toronto. In the western conference final, the Detroit Red Wings and the Chicago Blackhawks were tied at a game apiece, as the series headed to Chicago. If the Leafs made it through this series their reward would be an 'Original Six' Stanley Cup final. But game three proved to be something of a setback. Spencer Smith cautioned his troops not to let up just because the game was at home.

"They're just as capable of winning on the road as us," he surmised. "They'll want the first goal badly; they'll want to take the crowd out of the game early."

That statement sounded strange to many of the players; since when was the crowd a factor at Maple Leaf Gardens?

New York *did* score the first goal, a rather weak shot from outside the face-off circle that Frank McCool seemed unprepared for. Ex-Leaf Dominic Moore made it 2-0 before the end of the period on a goal that McCool gave a big rebound on, that probably should have been cleared by Mike McKenna.

Between periods, the big defenseman blamed himself for the goal, but Floyd Shoniker was quick to deflect the criticism.

"We haven't been helping you out any. We've got to put some traffic in front of Lundqvist!"

Indeed, the Leafs had been bottled up by the New York fore-checking. It had been nearly impossible for the Leafs to break out of their own zone the way they had in the games against Philadelphia.

In the second, Mike McKenna made amends for his first period mistake, finding the net with a slap shot to earn his first goal of the playoffs.

The Leafs headed into the third on an upbeat note. The coach urged them to jump on the puck early, as the Rangers would probably try and sit on their lead. Instead, the Rangers were the ones with the third period jump-start. Petr Sykora intercepted a clearing attempt by Dale McCaine and broke in on a surprised Frank McCool. He made it look easy as he deked the goalie dizzy, and made it 3-1 with just over a minute gone in the third. Spencer Smith was uncomfortable with what was taking place, and he called a time out.

Up in the press box, Neil Porters of the *Globe* was speculating.

"Smith's about to take a page out of the Mike Keenan book—I bet he puts Rogers in now to try and give the team a lift."

Billy Sinfield was in earshot. "Not likely my friend. Coaches are a superstitious lot. No coach has ever won a Stanley cup by using three goalies. I don't think Spencer Smith is brave enough to want to be the first."

On the ice, the Leafs were changing goalies. Lars Rogers was about to get his first game action since March 24th, against Atlanta.

"I'm afraid you're wrong, Billy," Porters shot back. "I guess Smitty's more concerned about winning games than he is about superstition!"

Sinfield was temporarily the butt of the jokes around press row. "You'd be surprised how concerned they are with superstition, my friend," he returned.

Changing goalies did not affect the score, either way—the Leafs still went down in defeat 3-1, and allowed New York to get back into the series.

John Dennis was pronounced fit to practice with the team the next day. His illness had been traced to an allergic reaction to a food additive.

"Eat salad from now on!" the coach suggested.

There was no decision to be made regarding the starting goaltender for the next game—it would be John Dennis. Frank McCool would be the number two man, based on his play in games one and two. And Lars Rogers, despite Billy Sinfield's suggestion that he may be the man to go to, and despite the fact that he had looked remarkable in his only relief appearance, was number three.

"All of a sudden, defense isn't the biggest concern. We have to find a way to get some goals on these bastards," Spencer Smith said the morning before game four, as he met in his office with Newton and Ridley.

"Maybe we've been too concerned lately with our defensive play up front," Ralph Newton suggested.

Spencer Smith frowned at this, but Brian Ridley agreed. "You know, we've managed to keep Jagr's line off the board, and Straka's, but all of a sudden they're not the guys who are doing it for them. I mean, going in, did you think that Dominic Moore and Petr Sykora would be their leading scorers?"

"No, but its only one game—I say we keep it the same for tonight. And see where that gets us," Spencer Smith decided.

What it got the Leafs was exactly the same result—another 3-1 loss, which evened the series at 2-2. Jason Ward, Tom Poti and Martin Straka scored for the Rangers, while only Chuck Andrew was able to beat Lundqvist, who really wasn't tested all that much by the Leafs.

Even though the players were predictably dejected after the loss, the coach chose not to speak to them. After the media conference, he called the assistants in to his office for a late meeting. He changed out of his suit, and got into a dark blue tracksuit, bearing the Leaf's logo and the word 'Coach' scripted over the heart. He grabbed the telephone and called up to the GM's box, and requested that Ken Butler attend. The GM had kept a low profile during the playoffs, ever since his meeting with the coach after game two of the New Jersey series.

Ken Butler opened the door to the head coach's office cautiously, and Spencer Smith rushed to close it behind him, as if secrecy was paramount.

"I wanted you here, Ken, to take part in this," he said as he removed a bottle of *Captain Morgan's* dark rum from a bottom drawer in his desk. Ken Butler raised his eyebrows at this.

"Do you always keep that there?" the GM asked.

"Only since this series was tied!" the coach answered as he poured a shot and retrieved a can of Coke from the bar fridge.

"No ice," he commented. "Know where you can find us some ice, Newt?" he asked.

Ralph Newton confessed that he did not.

"Hell, there's almost forty thousand square feet of it out there! Grab a skate and go chop us some!"

For a moment, Ralph Newton thought the coach was serious. The assistants both accepted a drink when Spencer Smith poured, but Ken Butler declined, instead preferring a soda water.

"So I want your honest opinion, Ken. What are we doing wrong all of a sudden?"

The GM thought about it for a moment then spoke up. "I think you hit on it a minute ago. There are forty thousand square feet of ice out there, but you're not using all of it."

Spencer Smith took off his glasses, held them up to the light, and began rubbing them with the corner of his tracksuit top.

"I see," he said, though it was not clear if he meant he saw what the GM was referring to, or if he could now see out of his glasses.

The GM continued. "I think that you had a terrific game plan. It worked well in game one and two. But the Rangers have adjusted, and sooner or later Jagr and company will break out of their slump, and—"

"You think I oughta let the guys open up more, not play such a close checking game in the other end of the building. Maybe open up a few scoring chances."

Ken Butler smiled. "Well if you had the answer, why did you ask *me* the question?"

"Because these two poor assholes here have been trying to tell me that for the last couple of games, and I didn't agree," Smith answered, as he finished his drink. The two assistants looked at each other uncomfortably, and Spencer Smith poured himself another drink.

"I just wanted another opinion Ken, that's all," he answered.

The GM thought it was time for some positive reinforcement. "This is anybody's series, from what I've seen. I don't think we're playing over our head. This is going to stay a low scoring series, that's the Rangers' style. They like to win 2-1 games. That's how they beat Montreal."

"No shit," the coach decided.

Ken Butler thought that was the rum talking. "But the way we're playing, we're going to be the team that gets the one. If we open it up more, like your assistants here suggest, you have a bit of an advantage. You have guys like Shoniker and McCaine that can put the puck in the net *and* defend. That's a weapon the Rangers don't have. Just let them be a bit more creative."

Spencer Smith was a proud man, but not stubborn enough *not* to admit when he was wrong. That was one of the reasons he had lasted so long as a head coach in the NHL.

Game five of the series, in New York saw the Leafs remain with the same line-up (except for the alternating nights off the older guys were getting) but the strategy had changed, as it had been discussed after game four.

"Don't worry so much about what they're doing," he told the group before they took to the ice for the first period. "Just make it happen for us *first*."

While the scoring chances were plentiful under this more relaxed style, the goals were not. The shots were even after the first two periods, but the game remained scoreless.

"It's gonna come, Spence, I can feel it" Floyd Shoniker boasted in the dressing room before the third period. "They aren't getting to the puck any earlier than we are. I think that we're being like you wanted, what did you call it—*proactive?*

Spencer Smith had used the term, but he really had no idea what it meant—he frequently heard Ken Buttler say it. The third period was much more to the Leafs liking; they out-hit, out-shot and out-chanced the Rangers. But after three periods, there still was no score.

"Got them right where we want 'em, right Shonny," Chuck Andrew laughed before the first overtime period.

"Let's see," the captain recalled. "Sawchuck got the OT goal in the first game, McCaine got the one against the Hawks, and who got it against New Jersey?"

"Little Ben!" Serge Moit shouted, referring to Benoit Marlet.

"Well, it looks like one of the old farts is due!" the captain said, looking at Chuck Andrew and Joel Kent.

At 2:16 of overtime, Tim Horton's pass went right between two New York defenders at the blue line and found Floyd Shoniker, who straddled the line to avoid the offside. He faked to his backhand and delivered a rising shot over the shoulder of Henrik Lundqvist to regain the series lead for the Leafs.

"This is it!" John Hill bristled afterwards in the room, as he led the cheers when the players filed in.

"I can feel it, we're gonna do it back at the Gardens!" he shouted.

The feeling was not lost on the rest of the organization. The realization was starting to sink in, slowly.

For the only the second time in almost forty years, the Toronto Maple Leafs were one game away from going to the Stanley Cup final. And this time, they told themselves; they weren't going to be denied.

The aura that surrounded game six of the series was strained. Too many times in the past the franchise had failed to deliver on promises, but few of them were this close to delivering before they failed. Spencer Smith had managed to instil the fear of losing in his players. This fear would be the motivating factor that would keep them from having to go back to New York for a game seven that would in effect have the Leafs already down one goal on home ice advantage to the Rangers alone.

It would be impossible to achieve this same result with a young team. The veterans had been through so many game sixes that they knew that there was one way and one way alone to help their own cause—win the game.

The Leafs quietly went about their mission. Some of the younger players were surprised by this almost laid back approach to the game. While it may have seemed like cockiness to rookies like Tobin West, Ian Moriarty and Valeri Ragulin, in reality it was not. The old guys were pacing themselves, like a veteran boxer that knew the only way he could go fifteen rounds was to start slowly in the first five.

The first period saw the Rangers gain the upper hand in scoring chances, albeit only by a couple. New York looked like they were going to come up empty for their slight edge in play when, toward the end of the first period, Toronto was given a penalty on an almost un-noticeable holding call against David Burks. The penalty was almost necessary, as Burks had inexplicably let his man get by, and the hold was more instinct than thought process.

For the first time in the series, Jaromir Jagr scored a goal, and his shot made it through so early and so easy on the power play that it looked like a statement. It looked like there were more to come.

Between periods, the coach was silently beginning to worry. Maybe he shouldn't be matching his leading goal scorer against the other teams, even *if* he has only one goal in the series to show for it.

"I'll be damned if they're going to dictate the play to us!" the coach said, not realizing that he had spoken out loud.

"Damn right!" Frank Maleki agreed.

The coach looked surprised to see the defenseman on the same wavelength. "Let's go get 'em! Shonny's line's up first."

The crowd was behind the Leafs like they had not been all season. The noise was deafening, even by the standards of other arenas. From the opening face-off it was clear that the team had turned the energy level up a notch. This was going to be the Leafs period, no question about it.

Chuck Andrew had been held to just two goals in the series so far, after having racked up five in five games against Philadelphia. The big winger took a pass from Barilko as all three of the Leafs forwards broke out together on a rush. Andrew, who as a rule, would not carry the puck for so long on a rush, made a move on Sandis Ozolinsh that he had *never* made on him in his twelve years in the league. Andrew kept the puck and instead of shooting, faked once, but then fired a low shot that just found room under Lundqvist's pads to tie the game.

The crowd went berserk. It was what they had waited for, for almost an eternity—a reason to become as unglued as the fans in other cities had been doing for so long. The crowd was now like a man advantage for the Leafs. Their noise seemed to follow the Rangers wherever they went; into the corners, on the bench, even during stoppages in play, the volume *increased* sometimes.

Several of the Ranger players from southern Ontario looked around the building as if to ask themselves if this really was staid old Maple Leaf Gardens that they were in. And to top it all, the crowd was rewarded for their fanaticism when Floyd Shoniker stole the puck from a Ranger defender who was clipped by Tim Horton. The defenseman had his head down, and didn't see the Leaf coming. Shoniker raced to the net as Lundqvist raced out to try and poke the puck away. Shoniker got there with a burst of speed that many thought had long since lost him, and the Leafs had the lead for the first time in the game.

The celebrations were beginning. The Rangers began to get that look of panic that sets in when a team knows that their season is melting right before their eyes. And as the clock counted down, the noise increased proportionately, and so did the Rangers frustration. It got to the point when referee Gary Blackstock could no longer turn a blind eye, and the New York club spent two of the last five minutes killing a penalty for roughing that Toronto didn't really want.

"Let's decline it and keep playing!" Joel Kent suggested.

The Rangers were unable to get the puck out of their end, even when the penalty was over, and Henrik Lundqvist had to remain in the net. Floyd Shoniker lined up for what would be the final face off of the series and he paused to enjoy the moment. He was treated to the sound of 16,485 screaming fans that were a minute and forty-two seconds away from realizing the dream of just seeing their team get to a Stanley Cup final.

Two hundred and fifty miles away, at Joe Louis Arena, the Red Wings were hammering a stake into the heart of the Chicago Blackhawks, with a series clinching 4-1 win that saw them take it in five games.

Up in the gondola, Jim Gerber grew hoarser by the moment as he tried to count down the last few seconds of the game in unison with the fans. It sounded as if he missed 'one' before he shouted, "THE TORONTO MAPLE LEAFS ARE GOING TO THE STANLEY CUP FINAL—OH MY!"

He then allowed the radio audience to listen to the improbable cheering of the crowd, while he silently looked on as the Leafs mobbed John Dennis, who was declared the *Molson Cup First Star of the Game*, though the goalie could care less.

The bench emptied and the celebration began just outside the Leafs blue line. Brian Ridley tried to throw his arms around Spencer Smith, and they almost made it. The coach grinned so wide it appeared as if his face might shatter like a Toby mug.

Floyd Shoniker quickly organized the troops to partake in the obligatory 'line-up for the handshake,' and it was dispensed with rather quickly so the festivities could begin.

There was supposed to be a presentation of the *Prince of Whales Trophy* at centre ice, symbolic of the championship of the eastern conference. In fact, Hockey Night in Canada announced on air that it would take place. The Leafs were already in the dressing room at this point, and Frank Maleki took off his sweater and placed it over the dressing room camera to black out the home audience.

"I don't want some 'carney' woman with no teeth sitting there in her trailer, wearin her best bingo tracksuit gettin the hots because I'm sittin here balls naked havin a pint!" Maleki told anyone who would listen.

Even though the coach had forbidden champagne to celebrate, the bubbly stuff did manage to materialize, according to a 'screw up by the LCBO', Nevell Carpenter explained to the coach.

There were a few moments for the team to celebrate alone before the HNIC cameras and the media descended. Horton, Barilko, McCool, Conacher and Busher Jackson sat and enjoyed the moment, wondering what the big deal was all about. They had been there, and done that, more than anyone else could count. They took more joy in seeing Dale McCaine realize the moment than anything else.

Tobin West and Ian Moriarty were standing in their street clothes, along with Alexi Gusarov—champagne-soaked, all three of them, and were going to have to take a shower and change into the spares they kept in their cubicles.

Greg Sawchuck, Dale McCaine and Valeri Ragulin toasted Floyd Shoniker, their captain and leader who had shown these young Turks how to do it, and do it with class. It wasn't even considered disrespectful when they poured the remaining contents of their paper cups over his head as he was being interviewed by Ron Maclean.

High above the Gardens, in the GM's box, there were Cuban cigars being removed from a rarely used humidor. Ken Butler struck a silver Zippo lighter, emblazoned with the crest of the WHAs' Winnipeg Jets, and lit cigars for himself, Walt Fisher, Ralph Newton, and Ron Bailey.

"Remind me to give these to Spencer and Ridley!" he said to no one in particular, as he placed two cigars in his jacket pocket.

Ron Bailey celebrated only briefly with the brass, being anxious to get down to the dressing room before the players departed. His timing was good, as there was no Champagne to be soaked in by the time he arrived. Many of the players had departed for showers, and a few of the older guys had left the building. Ron was able to have a moment, almost alone, with Dale McCaine.

"I don't know what is surprising me more: the fact that you are here and playing the way you are, or the fact that this team is playing the way it is!" he confessed.

Dale smiled, and said, "I really have to thank you for the chance. You stuck your neck out for me, and I won't forget it," he said, shaking Ron's hand.

"The ride's not over yet," Ron added, "We would not be here without you. And we still have the most important series to play of all—it's the only one that matters now. Do you think, I mean, is it inevitable?"

The look on Dale's face was sincere. "Is anything, other than maybe death?"

Ron almost wanted to laugh. "But you've beaten that!" Ron whispered.

"I haven't beaten anything, Mr. Bailey. I don't know why or how any more than you do. I don't know what's going to happen during the next series—or after it. I don't know when this season is going to end," he said, as he strode off to the showers.

Ron realized the truth in that statement as it applied to everyone who was mortal. He did not know if it applied to those who appeared not to be.

Never on a Sunday

The Stanley Cup final was a cherished Canadian tradition, even if the trophy was now contested for mainly by American based teams. It had been almost a century since exclusively Canadian players or teams contested the trophy. Yet despite that, the fact was that it had more social significance to Canadians than to any other nationality. It mattered little if all of the players were not Canadian, or even if the teams were all American. The cup belonged to Canadians, and always would, it seemed.

For this reason, many people north of the 49th parallel were angry when it appeared that the NHL was going to give in to the American Fox television network and begin game one of the final in Detroit on a Sunday afternoon.

The league was faced with this decision when Fox wanted to exercise a little-known clause in their broadcast rights agreement. It allowed them to dictate the date for one game of the Cup final, and they chose to exercise that right in game one.

As expected, the executives of *Hockey Night in Canada* argued. They didn't want to give up their biggest ratings night, and have their advertisers stuck with the much less attractive Sunday afternoon.

It was Ken Butler who helped resolve the matter by proposing a compromise—the game should be played on Sunday *night*. In order to settle the dispute, the league decided to settle the thing by a straw vote via conference call, by the leagues' board of governors.

This is when the whole thing became exiting, at least for Ron Bailey. Ken Butler received a call from the executive producer of *Hockey Night in Canada*, Steven Hortop.

"I need a favour on this one, Ken. Do what you can to convince the other governors not to go with the Fox thing!" he pleaded.

Ken Butler was in a pickle. He knew the American governors regarded Fox as the biggest butt they had to kiss. Television rights in the US were nowhere near what they were in Canada, to say nothing of the ratings. *Hockey Night in Canada* did not stand a chance if it went to a vote.

"You'll have to convince the others that it would be more beneficial to Fox if they picked game seven to be their choice for exercising the 'Sunday' clause.

"But there is no guarantee of a game seven!" Ken Butler shot back.

"Ken," Steve Hortop implored, "Don't sell your team so short. Give them some credit."

"Hardly the point—how can I sell them on something that may not come to pass?"

"Appeal to greed—they will be getting the NHL CHAMPIONSHIP GAME, or the SUPER BOWL OF HOCKEY if they get game seven. *That,* their advertisers will buy."

Ken Butler spent the entire day on the phone. It was the longest duration he had spent talking to other GM's and governors without discussing a player move. He called in favours, made threats, reminded certain people that he still, 'had the negatives' and even stretched the truth to a few of the newer members of the board, in order to convince the membership that Fox should be talked into the idea of a game seven.

The ploy worked, for the most part. The CBC did not get their way, but neither did Fox. The Sunday night idea was the solution. The only concession that was made (and this chiefly involved the Leafs) was that game seven of the series, which would be in Detroit, would also be a Sunday afternoon, played the day *after* the sixth game in Toronto. This would clearly be an advantage to the Red Wings.

Around Toronto *all* of the talk centred on the Leafs—the hockey team was on everyone's lips. The marvellous May weather that the city was enjoying was on page two behind the headlines the hockey team was making.

Ron Bailey tuned into Gil 'the thrill' while he was packing for the three days he would spend in 'hockey town' with the Leafs. The thrill had a decidedly different edge about him than he did during the regular season.

"Tomorrow night, this city will be fed what it had been starving for—for almost fort years—a taste of the Stanley Cup. And like the guy who hasn't had a drink in ages, the first thing he does when he gets a taste of it is, that's right, he gets drunk. Crap faced, wasted, hammered,—whatever. That, my friends, is what is happening to our beloved die-hard Maple Leaf fans. So if you know one, or are married to one (God forbid) please be patient, and help them through the next week or so," he continued.

Ron wasn't sure if the thrill was really jumping on the bandwagon, but there was evidence that he was at least pricing the tickets.

"There is no real reason why, in a seven game series, these Leafs could not outlast the Red Wings. The Leafs have beaten some better hockey teams along the way," the thrill conceded, "though they didn't have to face the Stanley Cup Champions."

No, that's right, 'thrill,' Ron thought, as he debated whether or not to pack shorts. We've beaten the team that *beat them*!

"And if you compare the respective line-ups," the thrill went on. "You list the Red Wings: Datsyuk, Zetterberg, Shanahan, Yzerman, Holmstrom, Lidstrom, Legace, and see a veteran core that stacks up with anyone. Outside of that, well...they stack up with anyone on the mediocrity scale. Like the Leafs...they had an easy road to the final, in that they did not have to play the cup finalist from last

400

year. And if you use the regular season as a measuring stick, well, the Leafs finished twenty points ahead of the Red Wings in arguably, a tougher conference. Now subtract from this equation the fact that Detroit defeated Toronto in their regular season meeting, by a convincing 5-2, when of course the Leafs were without Shoniker and Andrew."

The fact that the thrill was being impartial for a change distracted Ron to the point that he forgot to pack his toothbrush.

"So the net result, well, the Leafs have won some bigger games in these playoffs—and have beaten some better teams. But I still have to go with the guy who has more cup rings than the entire Leaf team combined, and pick the Red Wings in, say, seven games."

Ron heaved a sigh of relief. The mere thought of the thrill being in the Leafs' camp was more than he could bear. As it was, the fact that he had chosen not to hitch a ride was a good omen for Toronto.

Before game one, Ron received a long distance call from Calgary. Red Garrett, his mentor (and future father-in-law) called to wish him good luck.

"And that was a nice touch, bringing MacDonald into the fold!" he added.

Joe Louis Arena was the site of game one of the Stanley Cup finals, but Toronto was getting ready to be the centre of more Stanley Cup parties than anywhere in the world was. It was impossible to talk to anyone in the city who would admit that they weren't going to be watching the game.

"Dominos and Little Caesars will be jumping tonight," Spencer Smith said from the visiting coaches office, as he and their assistants talked about how the games would be received back home.

"What gets me Spence is how big a deal they are treating it down here!" Brian Ridley exclaimed.

"It's like, what—only three years since the Red Wings won it? You'd think it was the 1954 drought all over again."

Ralph Newton added, "This city isn't exactly stocked with winners."

"Yeah, but it's still not that often that your team makes it to a championship final," the coach countered.

"You look down our roster, and we have one guy who has played in a final before—John Hill, back when he was a rookie with the Flyers—hell, that's eight years ago."

"And how many do the Red Wings have?" Newton asked.

"Datsyuk, Shanahan, Lidstrom, Holmstrom, Yzerman, Draper, Chelios, Legace, Williams, Maltby, Fischer—" Smith replied.

Ralph Newton's face went white. "What did you do—look that up?" he asked.

Spencer Smith grinned a big toothy that made him look as if he had a piano keyboard stuck in his mouth. "I heard it on the elevator on the way down to the game."

"On the elevator?" Ridley wondered.

The coach scratched his head with the pencil he used to fill out the line-up sheet. "Two guys were talking about making a bet on the series, and the short one wants the Wings. His buddy asks him why, so he says it's because the Detroit has twelve guys on their roster with cup rings, and the Leafs have none."

"So who's the twelfth?" Ridley asked.

"What?" Smith said.

"You only counted eleven. Who is the twelfth player?"

"How the hell should I know? Those are the names the guy said. Why, do you think it matters?"

Ridley admitted that it did not, and they returned to discussing the line-up for that evening's game.

Spencer Smith took a big gulp from his water glass. "We agree on the Ruskies on defense—Burks and McKenna, Mouton and Moriarty."

"No Hansky?" Newton enquired.

"No, I want Ian in there. He played steady against them this year, and the lines, Shoniker-Kent-Andrew # 1, McCaine-Bodine-Bachmann # 2, Moit-Marlet-McDonald # 3, and Sawchuck—Graham and Hill #4."

"And in net?" Ridley wondered.

"Dennis—Isbister as the backup. We'll see where it gets us."

The goal tending decision really should have been a 'no-brainier'—John Dennis had earned his reputation as a big money goaltender in early in his career *because* of how he performed in the playoffs.

This was Dennis' chance to show he could still do it. If there had to be any added incentive it would be this; it was also the option year of his contract. Ken Butler was more concerned with getting through these playoffs that he was about acknowledging any of the media pressure that surrounded the future personnel status or the current ownership transition. The new owner, H.F.Potter, had wisely kept his profile low. If he associated himself too closely with the success of the team at present, he would be seen as endorsing the present administration. That might not be a good move if the team failed to bring home a cup. And if he denounced it, or distanced himself too much from the team, then he would be accused of 'absentee-ownership', which was as much a pariah as the dreaded 'meddling owner.'

Potter's group felt the owner was a 'no-win' situation, so they approached his image from another angle. They made sure that he was seen to be attending all of the games, but was not made accessible to the media.

Potter did issue statements about how exciting it was going to be to have the Leafs and Raptors together under one roof the next year, but would not take questions regarding how the Leaf season-ticket holders would be accommodated.

Ken Butler was fine with all of this. It simply meant one less thing for him to deal with. At present he was concentrating all of his efforts into seeing that his coach had every comfort and situation looked after so that the team could focus on just playing.

To this end even the minuscule details were addressed; everything from ensuring that the correct brand of contact lens solution for Chuck Andrew was packed by the trainer to checking with the hotel to be certain that no conventions were booked into it, thus preventing any sleepless nights.

When Spencer Smith addressed the guys in the room just before they took to the ice, he did it with a smile.

"Do you all know how good it feels just to get here?" he asked as he cast the smiling glance around the room.

Although he was met with everything from nodding heads, to blank stares, to nervous tapping of sticks on the floor, the consensus was general agreement.

"Then let's make the most of this—GO OUT AND WIN IT!" he screamed. His words had to have been heard all the way to the stands.

He began anxiously drawing out plays on the white hockey rink shaped memo board on the wall. He drew the Leafs in blue, and wanted to show a contrasting colour for the Red Wings, but didn't have one. He quickly adjourned to the visiting coaches' office and returned with a red marker. He drew the Yzerman line in red, and demonstrated how he wanted the checking line to take only the other two forwards on the line, and to have the third forward, the centre, play closer to the blue line in anticipation of a breakout pass.

Floyd Shoniker was the first to express his alarm at the thought of leaving one of the leagues' all-time leading scorers unprotected while he had the puck.

"You want us to lay off Stevie Y, while he has the puck? Spence its suicide!"

The huge coach laughed his bellicose chuckle. "If he has no one to pass it to, he'll try and make the play himself. Stevie had exactly fourteen goals this year, and only four of them at even strength. And how many of those do you think he engineered on his own? Exactly four, that's what our scouts have told us, I guess time can catch up with even Stevie. Do what you have to do, but if it's a question of who to double up on—leave him alone."

The group was in shock. All of their collective careers they had been told to look out for number nineteen. No matter what, do not to let the Y guy handle the puck; he will beat you. But it is said that time is the great equalizer, and perhaps for number nineteen the time had come.

The first period ended 2-0 Detroit. Nick Lidstrom and Chris Chelios set up both Wings goals, and both were scored by a young looking forty-year old; number nineteen.

Spencer Smith made no comment about the apparent gaffe when discussing the strategy for the second period. He did however make the passing remark about what was written on the wall.

"Look at this!" he remarked pointing when he pointed to the memo board that displayed his formerly brilliant idea "It's the same everywhere you go in this city—stuff written on the walls that makes no sense. Who are the idiots that write this shit?"

There were a few chuckles from those who had temporarily forgotten the score of the game.

After the players filed out of the room, the coach took the eraser and began to rub the board clean. Everything he had written in red remained; the marker he had retrieved was not the type for erasable boards!

"Well lookit that; my stupidity is imoralized," he said to no one in particular.

Ron Bailey watched the start of the second period in anticipation of some sign that Doug McCaine's curse on the team might be any small step closer to being lifted. The score in the game was no indication. Beside him sat assistant coach Brian Ridley, who was wired to Newton on the bench via a radio headset.

"What's the feeling in the room?" Ron asked.

Ridley turned to Ron and answered. "They seem to be upbeat; it just seems to be a big hill to climb against a team that doesn't give up any easy goals."

The consensus was correct. The Leafs managed a goal in the second, a power play marker by Charlie Conacher, who rifled a feed from Tim Horton past a partially screened Manny Lagace.

"I don't think he ever saw it!" Conacher remarked, as Jackson, McCaine, Burks and Horton mobbed him.

"It wouldn't have mattered, Bomber!" Horton said. David Burks didn't notice the nickname that Horton called Conacher, until much later.

Though the Leafs were back in the game as far as the score was concerned, they were being slightly out shot, and worse, out-chanced. The Red Wings definitely had more jump, and even linesman Curly Howarth noticed this.

"You guys had more hustle against the Rangers Thursday night!" he told Joel Kent.

It was hard to argue with, but the Leaf winger had to agree. "Is it just me Curly, or is this ice like Wasaga Beach?"

"Yeah!" laughed the linesman, "it *is* slow."

While the slushy ice conditions were supposed to be the same disadvantage to both teams it was clearly helping Detroit. They were no longer the speedy team that won the cup in '02, while the conditions took away one of the few distinct advantages the Leafs had—their ability to out skate the opposition.

The topic came up in the room between periods, and the coach tried to deflect the attention from the ice and to the Red Wings inability to clear the front of the net.

"You have to get in Lagace's face!" he roared.

Instead, in the third, it was Detroit creating gridlock in front of the Toronto goal. And as a result, Burks, Gusarov and even McKenna were making regular trips to the penalty box for holding, hooking and high-sticking, as frustration mounted and tempers flared.

The Red Wings took full advantage, going up 3-1 on Lidstrom's power-play shot from the point, and Jason Williams' marker from the face-off circle.

Jim Gerber summed up the disappointing result on his post-game show. "The Toronto Maple Leafs were the victims of *twos* tonight— two goals by Stevie Y and too many short-handed situations, as Detroit drew first blood on a muggy night in Motown. The ice conditions were appalling, and seemed to worsen as the game went on. But by then the Red Wings had built a comfortable lead and the Leafs seemed to accept this defeat rather easily. On a brighter side, the weather forecast calls for cooler temperatures this week, and game two should have ice conditions more befitting a Stanley Cup final than a Pina Colada. Reporting from Joe Louis Arena, this is Jim Gerber for 1430 CKFH."

Spencer Smith was so revolted by his team's lack of drive in the third period that he cancelled his plans to visit Greek town, and instead stopped by the bar at the hotel for a nightcap after the post-game media circus.

"I don't know how much longer I can answer those stupid questions without losing it!" he told Brain Ridley as they sat beside across from each other at one corner of the huge rectangular bar that formed the centre of the lounge.

The coach quietly sipped his *Captain Morgan's* dark rum and Coke. "You have to tell me what it is, Newt!" he called to Ralph Newton, who was further down the brass railed bar, trying to locate a dish of cashews to munch on.

"Tell you what, Spence?" Newton replied, obviously happy to notice that the dish contained *only* cashews.

Spencer Smith stabbed the lime with his plastic cocktail sword, and deposited it in the ashtray.

"What is it about this team that causes it to lose when you think they'll win, and—"

"And take one when you think they're going down?" Newton added.

"Yeah, I mean, these Red Wings, they're not the team they used to be. Hell, I still don't know who the favourite is in the series, should there be one. Who cares? But the thing that was doing it for us all year when we got in trouble, that thing that I told you guys before that I just couldn't put my finger on. It just wasn't there tonight, you know?"

They knew, but they couldn't define it either.

Halfway across town there were other conversations going on at the same time. At *Ty Cobb's*, the *'Dead Leafs Society'* was holding a wake for the game.

Conacher ordered the meeting, and he sat at the head of a large round table, flanked by Busher Jackson and Tim Horton. Frank McCool was also seated. Bill Barilko was up requesting a country and western song, though his chances of getting the band to play 'Hey Good Lookin' weren't great.

"I sent the kid to get McCaine. Where's he goin?" Conacher asked.

"The kid's lookin at all of the stuff on the walls!" Jackson replied.

The restaurant was decorated in a sports motif that was popular long before the term 'sports bar' was ever used—autographed black and white framed photographs of some of the most famous 'prize fighters' in history decorated the place like a hall of fame.

Some of the centuries' greatest Detroit based athletes had frequented the place, and their autographed pictures were all there—Hank Greenberg, Denny McLain, Joe Louis, Mickey Lolich, Jack Morris, Lou Whittaker, Isiah Thomas, Barry Sanders, and Gordie Howe. And it was there that Conacher decided to hold the meeting that ultimately would determine the fate of the Stanley Cup that year.

Barilko was back, his song request having been turned down. He dragged McCaine along with him.

"We have to decide, right here and now!" the former captain dictated, "The only fair way is a vote," he decreed.

Before they went any further, Horton had to get something straight. "I know we agreed, that if we were coming back, it would be for one reason, and one reason alone: to help young Dale here win the cup. To get the chance he was supposed to have. But I don't think I'm the only one here that feels that there is more to it."

Horton looked into the eyes of his teammates one by one, and took their nodding reactions as acceptance of his statement.

"I know we're all reluctant to step up and steal the kid's thunder, but dammit, we're down a game now, and this thing could get away from us unless we do something about it."

Conacher was the leader, and it was time for him to quietly assume it.

"Superman makes good sense. Dale, this is for you. What are YOU gonna do about it? The spotlight should be on you. Are you going to step up, and grab it?"

Dale McCaine seemed almost embarrassed by the suggestion. All of his life he had wanted to play for a Stanley cup winner. He had finally been given the chance, and they were asking him if that was what he really wanted.

"Of course I do. It's just that, well, it doesn't seem right. It's like its *fixed* or something."

Busher Jackson didn't know whether to smack some sense into the kid, or to hug him.

"Kid, do you know how hard it is to win a cup? Hell, this is all about you! You aren't being handed something. You're working for it and you don't even realize it. Nobody ever said they were gonna *give* you the Stanley Cup. The deal was that you were gonna get a *chance*. Don't blow it!"

Dale McCaine glanced at the others, and could see the pain in their expressions that another campaign had given them. It was eighty-two games, instead of fifty or seventy. And there was more travel, and the hits were from bigger and faster players than they had ever played against. And ghosts or not, they felt every check, slash and spear. And the only reason they were doing it was because they wanted the kid to have what was rightfully his—the *chance* to earn a championship.

"It seemed like it was all a, well, like a play or something. Like all I had to do was touch the puck and it would go in!"

Frank McCool was unravelled. "YOU MEAN TO TELL ME YOU JUST *EXPECT* TO WIN?"

The kid ducked because, for a moment, it looked as if McCool was going to knight him with a beer bottle. Dale didn't want to admit it, but he *hadn't* been going all out—he thought that as they inched along the playoff road, it was pre-determined that they would win.

"My God, you sound just like Bailey! He thinks we know what minute of what game the winning goal is gonna be scored, like we should tell him so's that he doesn't miss it while he's out getting popcorn."

Tim Horton added, "Kid, next game, I want you to go out there and show everybody, that coach, those guys wherever they are, that *didn't* put you on the team, how wrong they were!" Dale promised that he would.

Closer to the Leafs hotel, Ron Bailey sat in a sparsely populated brass rail type bar, and was quietly enjoying a glass of *Stroh's*. He silently wondered how the cup final was going to play out. Had the Leafs really come this improbably far only to *lose,* was a win guaranteed just because some ghosts had appeared?

What if, after all these years these guys weren't good enough anymore? After all, modern players were bigger and stronger and faster. And it wasn't as if these ex-Leafs were exactly setting the score sheets on fire. As he recalled, the five of them (not counting McCaine) had exactly two goals in nineteen playoff games, hardly the stuff those legends were made of. Instead of another Stroh's, Ron tried a Rolling Rock this time, as he pondered the question that was eating at him.

And the more he drank, the more it ate at him. And then he began to get hungry.

"Well, well, Ron Bailey!" he heard a familiar voice call, as he felt a slap on his back, though he felt it only awhile after it happened.

"Billy Sinfield! How are ya, ya old goat?" Ron slurred.

This reaction alone should have told Sinfield that his fellow Canadian had reached his limit. Instead, Sinfield eased his lanky frame onto the bar stool beside Ron, and ordered a round of Gin and tonic and "whatever colour bottle beer my friend here is drinking."

Ron was jerking his head in all directions as he looked for a dish of peanuts, pretzels—anything to stem the hunger.

"Wanna order a pizza, Billy?" he asked.

Sinfield tossed some cash on the bar in the direction of the bartender, and replied "If you want a nosh with your drink then you should have gone to the bar at your hotel. They throw out better stuff than they serve here."

"Too crowded," Ron answered.

"Maybe so; at least no prying reporters that would ask you about a curse that had been placed on the Maple Leafs."

Ron was in no condition to quickly pick up on what the old goat was driving at.

"You remember that conversation we had over lunch back at *Tim Riley's* bar? You told me that a fan had placed a curse on the Maple Leafs. That was why they hadn't won the Stanley Cup since '67. Well I just wanted to ask you: has the curse been lifted, or should I be going to Las Vegas and putting my Toronto Star pension holdings on the Red Wings?"

Ron was sobering up rather quickly. Perhaps it was because he got his hands on a large bowl of some very decent pretzels that the bartender had sympathetically placed in front of him

"Nothing's been lifted as far as I know. I haven't even seen any signs that we're going to win this thing," Ron answered truthfully. He was being very careful not to let any more secrets be known; he remembered how much grief he had taken over the Potter ownership announcement back in Ottawa.

Billy Sinfield was near the end of his drink, and was about to order another round when Ron stopped him.

"No thanks Billy. I can't afford to tell you anymore."

"Anymore?" the reporter asked. "You haven't told me anything yet!" Just as well. There'll be a story, someday, and I bet that you'll be the one to write it. I just don't know who'll believe it," Ron said, as he staggered off to find a cab.

Game two of the series did not take place until three nights later, thanks to the Fox TV deal. The Leafs decided to practice at the arena in Windsor, and bus it back and forth to the Pontchartrain hotel. Most coaches would have had the team stay closer to the practice site, but Spencer Smith insisted on staying in motor city. As much as he was a workaholic (he had the team's video coordinator Mike Wardyz play highlights of the loss to the Red Wings until the players screamed for it to be turned off) the coach did enjoy a good meal—and the *Tunnel Barbeque* in Windsor was his kind of place.

The morning of game three, the coach met with his assistants at the hotel coffee shop for breakfast. "Some line-up changes I'm thinking about," he mumbled, as he took a bite of a grapefruit-sized blueberry muffin.

"I think we need a little more zip in there; whattya think about Zanardo in there instead of Graham?"

Neither coach answered right away, as they were tempted by the thought of eggs Benedict, or Belgian waffles to start.

The coach answered his own question by mocking, "Great idea coach, a *mannequin* would be a better choice than Graham."

Just then the assistants realized they were needed. "Sorry Spence!" Ridley answered for both of them.

The coach continued, "And I want Hansky back in there, and the Swede, and Frank Maleki. He has a real hate for the Detroit."

"Why is that?" Ralph Newton asked, having gotten the real question, French toast or western omelette, out of the way.

"Something about Yzerman—can you imagine? Anyway, that leaves us sitting Moriarty, Gusarov, and Burks I guess."

"So what are we gonna do about Yzerman?" Ridley wondered, stating the obvious.

"We know what *not* to do," the coach laughed, as he took a gulp of his second cup of coffee. "I've been thinking about McCaine's line on him. It's funny you know, but Dale and him are alike in a lot of ways."

"Yeah," Newton interrupted, "they're only about five hundred goals apart."

"You phony bugger!" the coach laughed.

The strategy to put the McCaine line on Yzerman's was a good one, except when he was being double-shifted. That's when the coach would have to decide if he wanted to double-shift McCaine.

The first period started with the Detroit faithful in a fanatical mood; they sounded more like the crowd at a Saddam Hussein rally than a hockey game.

The Leafs were not fazed by this, and very quickly settled in to a rhythm, one that was missing in the first game. And there was no mistake where it came from. It was Dale McCaine who was setting the tempo for this game.

Early on his second shift, McCaine stole the puck from a Red Wing forward who was trying to dump it for an easy line change. He skated up to the centre ice red line and was being pursued hotly by Daniel Cleary.

413

McCaine made a move as if he was going to try to go between the boards and Cleary, and the Detroit forward went for it. At the last second, McCaine changed gears and pivoted away from the boards. It all happened so fast; it appeared as if Cleary just fell into the boards. McCaine skated in over the blue line and found Charlie Conacher trailing. He used the Red Wing defenseman as a decoy and then threaded the pass over to Conacher who more or less steered the puck past the sliding Manny Lagace.

"Now that was goal worthy of a Stanley Cup final," Billy Sinfield declared from his roost in the press box.

"That Bachmann looked for all the world like the 'Bomber' on that play," he remarked to Neil Porters of the Globe, who was sitting in earshot.

"Who?" The scribe asked.

"The Bomber, Charlie Conacher. Geez, you young guys haven't heard of anybody who wasn't playing when they started broadcasting NHL games on Fox for crying out loud!"

With the Leafs up 1-0 the Red Wings started to press. They didn't want to see the Toronto club develop any momentum. It was at this point that Detroit tried to use their supposed physical advantage to give them an edge. Kirk Maltby took exception to being nailed by Bill Barilko at the blue line, and responded with a slash that earned the Leafs their first power play. The Leafs passed the puck around for almost a minute without taking a shot—frustrating the fans but also unnerving the Red Wings. When Tim Horton finally let a rising blast go from the point, Dennis MacDonald was there by the crease to direct it home for a 2-0 lead. It was only MacDonald's third of the playoffs, but like the others it was a huge goal.

Between periods, Spencer Smith said nothing. Instead, he went over the line matchups from the previous period, reviewed the statistics on face-offs, and looked at the time logged by each player. He did not want to miss a trick.

In the second, Detroit got a gift goal when referee Bob Edwards looked the other way when Chuck Andrew was hauled down as he tried to break out of his own zone. Robert Lang ended up with the puck and was home free on John Dennis, who wasn't ready for the resulting deke, and moved late on the play. The Red Wings had moved to within one, as Floyd Shoniker followed the referee all the way to the scorers' bench to voice his complaint at the missed call. Andrew kept up the verbal assault on as the teams lined up for the ensuing faceoff, and the pay back for the missed call proved only to be the referee's restraint at not awarding an un-sportsmanlike conduct penalty to Andrew.

The period ended 2-1, but the advantage was still Toronto, as they out-chanced and out-hit Detroit in the period.

"It's in our hands!" Spencer Smith said, as he stood in the room in front of his team, his hands cupped. He looked unintentionally funny as he did so. At this point, Floyd Shoniker wanted to make a point, but he too was unfortunate with his timing.

"What you wrote on the board there last game, coach," he said, referring to the message written in indelible ink, "We should try it tonight!"

The suggestion got a few laughs, but Shoniker was trying to diffuse it; he was serious.

"You've got McCaine on him, but Dale set up the goal while he was doing it—if Dale was to leave him *alone?*"

"I think we should let it go for now, and see where it takes us," the coach decreed.

Where it took the Leafs was overtime. Yzerman tied the score midway through the third, but it was the Red Wings who had to withstand a last minute barrage around the goal that almost saw the Benoit Marlet line tie it.

"It should be time and a half for overtime," John Hill argued, "be careful with those passes out there fellas. Have an eye."

The coach addressed the group briefly before he went off to consult with Newton and Ridley. "If we go after them quickly, they might not be up to it," the coach inferred.

"They'll probably—" Before he could finish his sentence, Spencer Smith let out a tremendous fart, and commented, "Oh, *Geeeeez!*" He could not continue, as everyone in the room had succumbed to laughter.

Outside the dressing room, in the hallway, Scott Oake of *Hockey Night in Canada* was trying to conduct an interview with David Burks of the Leafs, who was not dressed for that game. The uproar of laughter could be heard even outside the room (though surprisingly, the fart could not). Oake was visibly bewildered by the occurrence, but Burks just took it in stride.

"It often happens when Spence tells one of his stories from his days as a Red Wing. You know, like back when he was a rookie you had to let the veterans get on the bus first, or whatever. It really breaks the guys up," he deadpanned.

Oake did not know how to comment on that, luckily for him, they had to go to a commercial.

When the overtime period started, the fans rose to the occasion, delivering an ovation right from the faceoff. Detroit had the first good chance, as if they were trying exactly the strategy that the Leafs had planned to employ. Yzerman actually had a good chance, as Mike McKenna collided with Zetterberg, letting the Stevie Y in alone on John Dennis. The big goalie made the save look easy though, and the period continued.

When the lines were changed up, Benoit Marlet decided to try and end it, and although both he and Serge Moit had excellent chances, Manny Lagace was equal to the task. Despite the importance of the period, the play was fairly wide open, much to the delight of the fans. And to add to the excitement, the period enjoyed a stretch of almost four minutes without a play stoppage.

When the Leafs went back to McCaine's line on the Yzerman line once again, it was clear that the Leafs were getting the better of the matchup. Time after time they picked up the rush, after yet another stymied Red Wing effort, and Jackson, Conacher and McCaine took turns setting each other up. On what was likely to be their last shift of the period, McCaine spotted Busher Jackson on open ice just near one of the centre ice faceoff dots, and quickly fed him the puck. In what seemed like a split second, he had his man beaten, and curled in around the Detroit defender. He went straight at Lagace, who tried the poke check as his last resort, and Jackson fell over him after he had put the puck upstairs in the net for the win.

The Leaf bench emptied, while the Red Wings tried in vain to protest the goal. The Leafs confidently celebrated, while Detroit lobbied for the dreaded 'video replay.' To no one in the Leaf camps surprise, the Red Wing captain's appeal was granted; the play was going upstairs for review.

In the Leaf 'executives' box, Ken Butler was silent, moving his glasses up and down on his nose to relieve the tension.

Walt Fisher remarked, "If that's anybody but number nineteen down there, the period is over. It may sound like sour grapes, but I'm sorry, it's a fact!"

The Leaf brass saw exactly the same replay the officials were viewing, and to their relief, there was no question; it was a goal. Their opinion however was not the one that mattered.

Because it was taking an excruciatingly long time for a verdict, Spencer Smith had not only pulled his team from the ice, he ordered them to the dressing room, while the Red Wings milled around their captain and the referee's semi-circle. When Bob Edwards got the verdict, he ignored the question, and waved his arms, the way a baseball umpire would indicate 'safe'.

At first, some of the Red Wings thought that this meant that the goal was waived off, and celebrated for half a second, until Edwards finally followed his gesture up with the words "Game Over!"

Brian Ridley had stayed in the runway to the dressing room, and thrust his fist into the air with the announcement.

He pounded the door to the room, and entered shouting, "Tie series, boys!"

"Hello, Canada"

The series resumed in Toronto, but not until Saturday night. The delay permitted three days of media hype to get the Leaf fans whipped up into a proper frenzy. The intensity that the series was bringing grabbed the city like CNN biting into a breaking news story. Suddenly all media focus, not just the sports sector, was focused on the Leaf's drive to the cup—it made the hype surrounding the Blue Jays World Series experience seemed like a rumour in comparison.

"Enjoy the ride," Spencer Smith advised his players, as he spoke about the entire cup experience.

"I played with and against some great players who never were on a cup winner. They all said, at least the ones who'd been to a final, to savour every moment of it. It may be the best moment you ever have in hockey."

If you drove down Yonge Street from highway 401 to Carlton Street, it would have been interesting to count the number of Molson Canadian 'Go For The Cup' signs with the Maple Leaf logo that were displayed in the windows of taverns, pubs, sports bars, restaurants, and even hardware stores along the route. The city was experiencing 'cup fever' as it never had before.

Game three of the series was a watershed as far as Spencer Smith was concerned. To him, a win in game three was more important than a win in game one. Partly it was superstition, but the statistics also backed him up. And even if they didn't the coach was stubborn enough to believe so anyway. He went with essentially the same line-up that had produced the win in game two, except that he made one change on his defense, inserting David Burks and Alexi Gusarov back into the line-up in place of Christian Andersson and Bill Barilko.

Overall, *Hockey Night in Canada* was reaping a huge benefit of having a Toronto-Detroit final. And even the American networks (Fox, ESPN) could not complain, as even though Toronto was not an American city it had perhaps the highest profile of all Canadian cities, due to its hockey heritage and it's 'place in the American psyche due to the Blue Jays.

The CBC broadcast that evening was a classic. To add to the mystique of the 'Original Six' theme, the Leafs had requested through their director of marketing Mike Lengell that they receive permission to use a sweater style from the past for the game. The league and the Red Wings had no objection, so when the Leafs skated out for the warm-up, they wore their usual home white. But when they came out for the opening faceoff, they were clad in what was then the road white shirt from the 1967 season, which featured a centennial-looking maple leaf, and a blue shoulder yoke. The fans cheered even the choice of sweaters. The players were inspired by the selection (last worn when they won their last Stanley cup) and by the fan reaction.

Harry Neale of the HNIC crew would later say that game three 'was one of the greatest games he had ever seen, let alone broadcast.'

From the opening faceoff, the tempo was quick. Observers felt because three days off at this stage of what was now more than ninety games since the season opener, was exactly what the weary players needed. Both teams made substitution to help the fatigue factor as well. The Red Wings were intent on getting the first goal, but John Dennis was equal to the task early, stopping Henrik Zetterberg and Pavel Datsyuk on good chances in the first period.

The Leafs had some good opportunities as well, but the period ended scoreless and the shots on goal were even.

The second saw things open up a bit, as the home crowd lifted the Leafs spirits with the chanting of 'GO LEAFS GO', and go they did.

Bob Cole of the CBC described the first goal this way. "The Leafs on the power play, less than a minute left in the penalty to Chris Chelios. Toronto has yet to get a shot on goal with the man advantage...McKenna plays it over to David Burks...Burks looks like he wants to shoot it...there's a crowd in front of the net...he lets it go...wide of the net...it's out in front...THEY SCORE! ...I didn't see how that happened..."

Burks had pulled his 'Three Musketeers' play that he had demonstrated to Ron Bailey.

Harry Neale, with the aid of a replay, explained it as best he could to the viewers.

"David Burks fired that shot. It almost looked like he *meant* to miss the net it took a crazy bounce out in front, and Chuck Andrew was in the right place at the right time, and steered it home to give the Leafs a 1-0 lead—a very big power play goal for Toronto, who haven't been equal to Detroit with the extra man."

Up in the Leaf V.I.P. box, Ron Bailey was recounting his experience of the Burks goal with Ralph Newton.

"Never doubt Burksie," Newton said, "I've never met anybody with more patience. He would have waited all series, until the time was right, to use that."

Emotionally it was a huge lift for Toronto, as the fans became louder. People were still pinching themselves to believe that this kind of noise could come from a *Toronto* hockey crowd.

Floyd Shoniker was as electrified as any of the veterans by the reaction of the crowd. He had been there many nights when the reaction was no reaction at all, or even worse, silence, broken only by a single obscene comment by leather-lunged idiot in the greys. But this reaction raised the spirits, and Shoniker turned his game up a notch. He flew up and down each shift as if it was his last in the game. He hit anything in his way, and the reaction he got from the opposition was that they were not up to the level of his game, at least that night.

Maybe Shoniker could have beaten Detroit all by himself that night, but the Red Wings had something that a few other championship teams had on their side. And even though Steve Yzerman could no longer do it all by himself, he was still a great leader, and the Red Wings could be inspired. It was Yzerman who made the play that indirectly led to the tying goal. Brendan Shanahan took a pass that Serge Moit tried hard to intercept, but instead was left on the fringe. He moved over centre, and was looking to pass to Yzerman. Young Valerie Ragulin was there to defend the three-on-two, and had to make a choice. He knew he was supposed to play the pass, and let the goalie take the shot. He was closer to the shooter and therefore was going to let his partner, Gusarov, take the other wingers. But the uncovered guy was Yzerman, and Ragulin knew that somehow he would be involved in the play.

Ragulin moved over to cover Yzerman, leaving Shanahan and Samuelsson to work a two-on-one with Gusarov. They drew the Old Russian out too far, and Samuelsson was able to work the puck by the sprawling John Dennis.

Harry Neale immediately saw the significance of Yzerman's involvement in the play, and told the viewers. "Assists aren't awarded for savvy or respect, but Yzerman just earned one for that, and you won't see it on the score sheet."

The score remained tied, and the teams went into the third period with the game and series even.

"Think of it as overtime," the coach said, "except that, if we get the goal in the first minute, we have to keep playing for a while longer."

Many of the players could not grasp this, but the coach knew that the momentum generated by the first goal could lead to another, or put the team that scored it into a defensive shell that would be difficult to crack.

"And if we get it, then we play puck control. You dump it only inside their blue line."

Unfortunately, the period did not unfold as the Leaf coach had hoped. Almost from the puck was drop until the final whistle, the play was inside the Leaf blue line. Toronto spent eleven of the twenty minutes killing penalties, as they were charged with everything from too many men, and boarding to a five minute hick sticking major to Lou Zanardo (the first of his eight year NHL career).

"Clipping?" The coach screamed at referee Scott Aberdeen "Where did you dig that one up? When the hell have you seen that called before? Did you look it up in the archives?" He fumed.

The referee cut the coach some slack, but quietly told himself that if the coach kept it up he would have no choice but to assess a bench penalty. Before the faceoff, Floyd Shoniker tried to calm the rift, talking to the referee first, and then the coach.

"Spence is getting frustrated. That's all Scotty," he told the official. "He wants to take it out on us, but at the same time he wants to keep us up. So instead, he vents on you."

The referee, for now, would buy this. "Tell him to keep it on the bench!" he advised.

After his next shift, Shoniker got the coaches' attention on the bench. "I talked to Aberdeen out there," he began. "He admitted that he overreacted on the clipping call. But he wants you to stop riding him. Let it go—you know how these things have a way of working themselves out."

The coach accepted the explanation. The captain, through his white lie, was able to diplomatically diffuse a potentially damaging situation.

Spencer Smith was able to focus on the game and not the officiating, and he began to tinker with his line matching. With the last change, he had been putting Shoniker's line out against Yzerman's and this was drawing to a stalemate. He wanted to see McCaine's line show the offensive thrust it was capable of, but against the Red Wings' checking line, it didn't seem to have enough room to operate. So Spencer Smith decided to put the Zanardo-Hill-Sawchuck line on Yzerman, thus freeing up one of his best two scoring lines, one of the two would be able to operate without Detroit's checking line on it.

Red Wing coach Ted Pye put the Kris Draper line on Shoniker's line, and that left McCaine's line up against a Detroit line made up of three young guys. It was the coaching mistake of the series.

When Dale McCaine jumped over the boards, with Busher Jackson and Charlie Conacher, the Bomber told the kid that he would take the faceoff.

"What's Bachmann doing out there?" Spencer Smith shouted on the bench. He was trying to get the wingers' attention. He let it be known on no uncertain terms that he wanted *McCaine* to take the draw. Conacher pretended that he didn't hear, and he was urged on by Tim Horton who shouted, "Better make it good Bomber, or you'll be doing the wild thing with the bench for the rest of the series!"

"Just make sure you don't trip on it when I get it back to you!" Conacher shot back.

The Bomber won the draw, and it did go back to Horton, who carried the puck in over the Detroit line. He spotted Busher Jackson, who was drawing attention from the Red Wing defenseman. Conacher trailed a bit on the play and was well covered by a Detroit forward doing a good job of back checking. Horton waited until the last possible second, being careful not to permit an offside and he at last fed the puck ahead to McCaine. He took the pass on his backhand, but quickly drew the puck to his forehand as he raced in from the left wing. He faked like he was going to the front of the net and then pulled back to his left. But instead of shooting the puck right away, he hesitated as he switched to his backhand. The goalie had committed by now to the move, and as he went down the puck sailed into the top corner, courtesy of the angle created by the backhand.

The entire building seemed to elevate when the fans rose to their feet for the ovation. The coach forgot whatever it was he was upset about, and the Red Wings were the ones who were feeling cursed. They had done everything to control the period, but one play had put them in a hole that it did not look like they could quickly climb out of. There were three minutes and twenty-one seconds showing on the clock when Paul Morris announced the goal, Dale McCaine from Charlie Bachmann and Gilbert Mouton. It would have sounded so much nicer if he had been able to say, 'from Conacher and Horton.'

Three minutes was either a lot of time or next to nothing, depending on whether or not you were a Red Wing or a Maple Leaf.

Detroit sent out Yzerman's line, intent on getting the tying goal on this shift. Spencer Smith countered with Hill, Zanardo and Sawchuck. But just after the three were in the play, the coach motioned for Sawchuck to come back, and Smith replaced him with Dale McCaine.

Jim Gerber in the Leafs radio booth was the first to pick up on this.

"Dale McCaine has just finished a very big shift and he's out there again, on the checking line. Could Spencer Smith be telling his team, and the Red Wings, that not only can these Leafs score, but they can play defense as well?"

That seemed to be the only explanation, as now it was the Red Wings who were bottled up in their own end. The lines were finally changed, when rush after rush of the Detroit team was stopped at the Leaf blue line. And the last Toronto forward to come off the ice was: Dale McCaine.

The Red Wings tried desperately to pull the goalie, but Chuck Andrew kept dumping the puck back into their end, just close enough to avoid the icing. The fans triumphantly counted down the time until the final horn went, as the Leaf players poured over the bench to congratulate John Dennis.

The *Molson Cup Three Star* selectors had a difficult time choosing between Dennis, McCaine and Shoniker for number one, but finally chose Dennis; he had stopped thirty-seven of thirty-eight shots for the win.

Spencer Smith greeted his players as they came off of the ice, patting each one on the back, or high-fiving them. Inside the room, the cursing was as plentiful as if it was a loss, but the emphasis was positive. The coach addressed them briefly before he headed off to the obligatory media scrum, and just said, "Two in the bag, we're halfway there boys!"

Spencer Smith was careful not to let his exuberance get the better of him at the press conference. He sat patiently listening to questions, as stupid as some of them were, and answered slowly and carefully while sipping the coke that had been placed in front of him. Little did he know that it had been spiked with *Captain Morgan's*, courtesy of Tim Horton.

The coach gave the players the next day off (after all it was Mothers' Day) but expected a brisk early practice on the following Monday. It was on this unique occasion that Chuck Andrew decided to unveil his pride and joy, the new special edition Ford Expedition *Eddie Bauer* model, with all of the toys on it. He drove it to practice this day with the unashamed purpose of showing it off to his teammates. Andrew had been bragging about the vehicle since he placed the order, just after Christmas, and he had finally taken delivery of it.

Andrew took special care to arrange for a parking spot that was not in danger of having any other vehicle in close proximity. He bribed the building manager to re-arrange the spots so that smaller cars would flank it on either side. And he had been boring his fellow Leafs to insanity with his descriptions of the vehicle, and his promise to 'drive it to work' when he picked it up at the dealership.

Unbeknownst to Andrew, however, there would be a strange twist to the unveiling of the vehicle after practice. For perhaps one too many times that season, John Hill had been on the wrong end of a Chuck Andrew practical joke. The two had been mild adversaries when Andrew was with Hartford and Hill was with Philadelphia, but the feud really stemmed from their days in junior.

Andrew was a Windsor Spitfire, and Hill a rival London Knight, and they had seen just about enough of each other over the years.

For Hill, the time for a *piece de resistance* had come. When he heard about Andrews' purchase, he placed calls to more than twenty auto wreckers, towing services and body shops looking for a Ford Expedition in any sad state of body damage. And when he got lucky, he waited for the right opportunity.

On this beautiful spring day, Chuck Andrew, still beaming from the Saturday night victory, was ready to bring his baby with him.

He carefully parked it at the pre-arranged spot, and hurried into the Gardens to spring the news. Much to his dismay, his teammates showed little interest in seeing the vehicle whose description most of them had memorized from the incessant drilling they were given over it. They feigned indifference, but promised to see it, 'after practice.'

Andrew felt it was sheer jealousy, but his moment could not be ruined. He bent over lacing up his skates, telling himself that, when they saw the beauty out there sparkling in the sunshine they would appreciate what a marvellous piece of machinery it was.

When practice ended, Andrew was the first one off the ice.

"What's he got, a date with one of them Slice Girls?" Spencer Smith asked, as he saw the big winger leave the ice as quickly as if he was on a breakaway.

"No, no, 'Spice' Girls," Brian Ridley corrected. "He wants to show off his new wheels!"

"Oh yeah," the coach remarked, always appreciative of a fine automobile, as long as it was a truck, "let's go and see it!"

Andrew was ready to rush out the door, his hair not even dry yet.

"Wait up Andy! What's your hurry?" Floyd Shoniker asked, as he tried to keep up with the big winger while struggling to zip up his fly.

"He's afraid somebody will kidnap his baby!" John Hill shot back, as he pulled on his Kodiaks.

Chuck Andrew led a procession from the dressing room, down the corridor that led to Wood Street, past a few reporters who skulked around looking for a story.

"What's the parade for? Are you guys practicing for when you take the Cup down Bay Street?" one reporter asked.

"We're going to see Andy's new machine!" David Burks answered.

"Yeah, what was that you said about the paint?" John Hill asked Andrew from the back of the pack.

Andrew didn't acknowledge who had asked the question, and responded, "Yeah, in the right light you can see a different colour. It's a new high tech paint from Du Pont."

As they headed through the glass door onto Wood Street and walked up to the spot, they all came to a stop at once.

The parking attendant had been considerate. To display the Expedition in all its glory he had arranged for the vehicles that would normally be parked on either side of it, to be relocated to a lot across the street. It allowed the players to view the spectacle in front of them from all angles.

Sitting in Andrew's spot was what could be more accurately described as a mangled piece of automotive sculpture. The driver's side door was bent inwards like a 'V'—the hood, on the other hand was folded up into a letter 'A', perhaps for 'Andrew.'

None of the tires were flat; they just touched the ground at forty-five degree angles. Other than that, the Expedition was pretty much as Andrew had described it.

"Just look at that paint glisten in the sunlight!" Floyd Shoniker commented.

"Andy, you sure drive the shit out of your vehicles," John Dennis added dryly.

Andrew, of course, didn't get the joke—especially not when Mike McKenna commented on the personalized license plates.

"Nice touch, Andy—not too pretentious!"

Up until then, Chuck Andrew was filled with only anger and disbelief. But for a brief second, when he saw the piece of scrap bearing his own plates, personalized with 'ANDY 14' on them, he thought that this really was his truck that had come to such an untimely end.

It was a nice touch; he would have to admit later. Now that he had overcome the shock, there was only one thing to do—seek out John Hill, and kill him.

Hill was one step ahead of Andrew, and was down the street and into his own Corvette in seconds. He drove around the block once, and then came back to where the players were still laughing, and said.

"This almost makes us even for the OHL final!" he shouted, as he drove away.

"It was the semi-final, you moron!" Andrew returned.

Game four of the final was going to be monumental. If the Leafs could win at home, it would give them the leg up that every team took as the signal to go in for the kill. And if they lost, well, at least the series would still be even.

"In this series we have seen a bit of everything," Jim Gerber remarked in his pre-game introduction.

"We have seen some great goaltending, by both goalies, and some scoring from some fellas who really know how to put the puck in the net. Mr. Yzerman, Lang, Shanahan, and on the Leaf side of the ledger, well, therein lies the problem. The guys who were doing in the regular season, and in the series leading up to the final have been silent for the most part," he concluded.

Gerber was right; other than Dale McCaine and Chuck Andrew with one goal each, the Leafs had seen no numbers from the likes of Joel Kent, Floyd Shoniker, Benoit Marlet, and Greg Sawchuck—to the rescue were Charlie Conacher and Busher Jackson, with two goals and one respectively.

"If the Leafs were going to get a stranglehold on the series, then the guys who did it during the season are going to have to do it in this Stanley Cup final," Gerber reasoned.

The Leafs were pumped for game four like they had not been for any game of the series so far. Their confidence and consequently their cockiness had been increasing exponentially with each step closer to the pinnacle.

The pre-game hype only served to fuel their self-assuredness. The Leafs had even brought in a 'crowd warmer' to enliven the audience—a college student from Ottawa who worked the Senators' games. He paraded up and down the aisles in synch with the Leafs audio director, dancing in the aisles to blaring, fan-baiting music designed to morph the throng into a screaming mania that would be like a man advantage to the team on the ice.

The Leafs had adopted the practice, of playing the kind of music over the PA that lifted the crowd. Not just the usual 'Rock n Roll Part II', but also TV themes and video clips that related to player nick names. The favourites were the 'Dennis the Menace' theme for John Dennis, and the 'Rifleman' for Dale McCaine. It was quickly becoming McCaine's official nickname, when the old black and white video clip showed an actor saying, "Why do they call that McCaine the Rifleman?" which was quickly followed by a clip of McCaine scoring some of his forty-seven goals, followed by the TV theme. It did raise the clubs' spirits, but it also had an effect on the Detroit. They were more accustomed to playing in front of such a noisy audience; indeed the crowd at Maple Leaf Gardens at times could be better compared to a golf gallery than a collection of the world's most rabid hockey fans.

Whether or not it was the crowd that distracted the Leafs, or the pressure of trying to forge ahead in the series while they were at home, was not clear.

From the opening face-off it appeared that the Red Wings wanted this one more than the Leafs.

Detroit was taking no prisoners. Their coach had unceremoniously lambasted his players for not capitalizing on their opportunities in game three, noting that Detroit failed to profit from their advantage in scoring chances.

But on this night they cashed in early. The Leafs seemed content to let the Red Wings make the first move on almost every shift. Toronto's defensive style worked much better when they were protecting a lead, and in this game Detroit scored first.

Henrik Zetterberg jumped on a rare giveaway by Joel Kent, who seemed to have lost his focus so far in this series. The Red Wing forward used Mike McKenna as a perfect screen and fired a rising snap shot over the surprised goalie's shoulder to open the scoring.

McKenna smashed his stick over the net, and apologized on the spot to John Dennis.

"God dammit! I thought I had more room. I couldn't hear you yelling at me!" The angry defenseman explained.

John Dennis was notorious for instructing his defensemen where to be and when they were screening, always at the top of his lungs.

The unnatural crowd volume made the inside of Maple Leaf Gardens sound like an airport runway, and the goalies' warning went unheard.

The period ended 1-0 for Detroit. Spencer Smith left things alone in the room between periods. He let the players sort this one out. Joel Kent accepted full blame for the goal, and pleaded with his teammates to be patient.

"Every time we get behind, we feel like we have to get it back right away. Let's be patient. If we press, we'll end up giving *them* chances."

Smith could not have said it better himself.

The Leafs were patient in the second, and the scoring chances were about even, but the period remained scoreless. The tension of the period was starting to wear on the fans. Suspense is a feeling that most can tolerate in gradual doses, but when it builds to a climax and the relief is not fast enough in coming, *then* the nerves begin to snap.

The idea of entering the third period still down one goal was too much for the faint of heart. And early in the third those fans got some relief.

Just after Tim Horton was given a questionable holding penalty, he was getting ready to return to the bench, but Mike McKenna was hit from behind by Thomas Holmstrom, and had to make it to the bench, or collapse. There was no penalty on the play, but Horton stayed on the ice, and Bill Barilko saw him leaving the box with no one covering him. Barilko fed the pass nicely up ice, and Horton streaked off towards the net, with few in pursuit and only one defenseman between him and Manny Lagace in the Detroit goal.

Horton ignored the defender, who was bowled over in his attempt to separate Horton from the puck. The Leaf defenseman made a good move on Lagace and fired a low blast at the five hole, with the puck squirted through as the goalie squeezed the pads together like elevator doors closing, as he fell to the ice. Horton skated past the net, thinking that the puck was in. Even the red goal light flashed. But as Lagace toppled over onto the ice, the puck lay just outside the goal line, and he reached back with his huge glove to smother it.

The Leafs were inspired by the fact that they had come so close. Spencer Smith on the other hand was becoming more concerned. He knew that chances like that one were few and far between; it was the kind of play that was talked about after the game as an 'if only.'

The Red Wings had a couple of good chances as well, but John Dennis was equal to the task. And shortly after one of his outstanding saves, Detroit was ready to go farther ahead.

Alexi Gusarov attempted a clearing pass that was intercepted by Detroit rookie Valerian Filppula who looked like Pavel Bure as he rocketed in alone on John Dennis. Burks did what he had to do; he caught the kid from behind and hooked him to the ice.

Up in the Leafs executive box, Walt Fisher was shaking his head, but Ken Butler disagreed.

"He saved the goal, the kid made a helluva play to pick up that puck. I'd take our chances with our special teams any day."

The GM's sentiment was well placed, but the situation on the ice proved otherwise. The Red Wings quickly had the Leafs bottled up, and set up patiently, passing the puck around in a precision manner while waiting for the perfect shot. The Leafs were working the box well, but the Red Wings were going to find the open man; it was just a matter of time. Nick Lidstrom let go a shot from the point that looked as if it would make it through, but instead it hit a leg, and when it did so it deflected off the shin pad of Thomas Holmstrom, and into the bottom corner of the net.

While the Red Wings were celebrating, Floyd Shoniker was protesting vociferously that the goal be reviewed; it did appear as if Holmstrom was at least partially in the crease. The Detroit players were still mobbing Holmstrom when referee Bob Edwards signalled that he was going for the review, and he skated over to the timekeepers' bench to make the dreaded call upstairs. Now it was the Red Wings turn to complain. Yzerman went over to plead his case, and up in the Leaf V.I.P. box the brass anxiously reviewed the same television replay that the officials would be looking at, just a few boxes away.

It seemed like an hour to the Leaf faithful while the play was being reviewed, and the obligatory, 'Final Jeopardy' theme was played over the P.A.

And all of a sudden Bob Edwards gingerly waived his arms and pointed to centre ice; the goal was waived off!

It was the second time in the series that Edwards was the presiding judge that handed Detroit a decision that they could not accept. And he was gracious; normally the profanity that followed the Red Wings' protest would have resulted in an unsportsmanlike conduct penalty.

It was evident that the verdict gave as much gas to the Leafs as it sapped from Detroit, and the momentum shift led to some good chances for Toronto. Time was working against them.

"It seems like yesterday since we scored on them!" Chuck Andrew observed on the bench.

At the other end of the bench, Benoit Marlet was having other ideas He was being short-shifted by the coach, as it was clear that he was struggling against the Red Wings who employed a good checker, Daniel Cleary on him.

In this series, there was no rival from Marlet's Quebec league days to do battle with. His feud would be with Cleary alone. Up until this shift, Cleary had won all of the battles. But finally Marlet was about to break free. With only three minutes left in regulation, and Detroit hanging on to their one goal lead, Marlet lost the draw just outside the Red Wings' blue line. The Detroit player that won it was in a bad position, as Serge Moit separated him from the puck, and almost from his teeth, with a vicious hit that included what should have been called an elbow to the head. Edwards didn't see the elbow, and the play continued. Dennis MacDonald, who spotted the flying Marlet across the rink, picked up the loose puck, put on the brakes, and slid it across to Marlet, who let go a shot that just kept rising until it just made it under the cross bar.

Life was breathed into the Leafs again. The Red Wings could only protest the missed call; they complained up and down that they didn't want to see refereeing decide the series. And as it turned out, it would not.

Overtime seemed inevitable. During the intermission, the Leafs remained confident. As Harry Neale of *Hockey Night in Canada* pointed out, "The Leafs are perfect in overtime so far in these playoffs."

Ken Butler did not have the same confidence as the commentator. "The goal that was disallowed," he commented, "will have a bearing on this game. I have a bad feeling about it. Call it Karma, retributive justice or whatever; we have to score on our first chance."

Walt Fisher was amazed. He had never heard his boss speak in such a negative tone about the hockey club.

When overtime, started the fans had their second wind, as did the players. They, like the players, were filled with confidence. There was something about the way they had come back in the game that gave them a good feeling.

And that feeling climaxed when Joel Kent took a pass from Mike McKenna, and broke away cleanly from the Detroit defense. Kent's breakaway lasted only from the blue line in and he let go one of his patented wrist shots. A lightning strike of flashbulbs went off, but Manny Lagace robbed him with an almost impossible glove save.

Ken Butler didn't say it out loud, but he thought 'That was it!'

Shortly thereafter the Red Wings brought the puck over the Leaf line on a rush, and when Steve Yzerman crossed the Leaf blue line he circled several times while looking for the perfect pass. The Leafs seemed mesmerized, as no one moved forward to pick him up. Finally Dale McCaine crossed over to take the Detroit captain. Conacher and Busher Jackson had their men tied up, so Stevie Y had one had no one to pass to, except Nick Lidstrom.

Yzerman fed a pass under McCaine's stick across to the former Norris trophy winner, who let go a slap shot directly at the five hole of John Dennis. The goalie appeared to have time to set up, but as he went down the puck changed direction like a knuckle ball, and when the goalies' pads met the ice, the net behind him rippled with the movement of the puck. At 9:09 of overtime, the Red Wings evened the series.

Disappointment covered the faces of the Leaf players as vividly as the blue and white makeup that coloured the faces of some Leaf fanatics. It was an expression that they had not worn for a long time. They had suffered other significant losses since the season began, and even though the series was only tied, there was a feeling among the veterans that this thing was slipping away.

There was an uneasy silence in the room that was broken only by equipment hitting the carpeted floor, some of it being slammed but most of it falling, as if it wouldn't be picked up too many more times.

Floyd Shoniker looked gloomier than he had been at any time during the playoffs, even when they lost game six against the Devils, when they were blown out 6-3 in Philadelphia, or when they dropped two in a row to New York. There was almost a hint of the 'well, we gave it a good ride but I guess this is it' sentiment.

While the veterans were almost resigning themselves to a fate, others were not. He had not said much up until now, even though he was once the captain of this team. But Charlie Conacher wasn't about to see this team pull itself into the dumps.

"I haven't been here as long as most of you," he began, with the authoritative sound of someone that was used to addressing the team as a captain would. "But I can sense that there is a bad feeling here that maybe we just lost more than one game. I don't think we have. Those bastards got some good breaks, and we're gonna get ours, you can bet your life on that!"

The more Conacher spoke, the more attention he received.

"We're going back to their rink, sure. They'll think they have the upper hand, why not? But that only works if you let it. And it didn't stop us from winning game seven on the road in New Jersey—or game five in Philadelphia—so why not Detroit? Hell, I even *like* the place!"

It was not as noteworthy as a 'Knute Rockne' address, but Conacher said something that needed to be said. He knew that if a team thinks like a team, they could play like one too.

Due to the awkward scheduling to suit television, there was only one day off between games four and five. The Leafs left for Detroit the next morning, and held a late afternoon skate at the Windsor arena.

The media in the 'Motor City' were getting ready to award the cup, based on the Red Wings' gritty performance in game 4. But Spencer Smith had other plans. When he met with the coaches for coffee the morning of game five, he floated another one of his 'wild ideas' for their consideration.

"We've done everything to the Red Wings but get tough with them," he said, adding a third cream to his coffee.

"What are you suggesting, Spence?" Brian Ridley asked cautiously.

"Not a goon act. I mean more 'in your face' or whatever the kids call it now. When I played, we made them pay each time they beat us to the puck. I don't see a whole lot of it out there. Oh I see finishing checks, but where are the hits that put people out of games."

That statement made the hair stand up on Ralph Newton's neck. That was exactly how *his* career as a Maple Leaf had ended.

"Those hits are mostly in black and white highlight videos," Newton answered.

"We know our guys—we know who can deliver what I'm talking about. I know Hilly and Kent will, I know McKenna will, I know Rettig will—if we put him out there.

And I bet that those kids Hansky and Mouton will cause I've seen 'em in practice. All I'm saying is, let's unleash 'em a bit."

Though the line-up change involving Rettig was made (in for Greg Sawchuck), and the players who were mentioned by Spencer Smith were talked to before game five, the source of the much needed physical presence came from another, improbable source.

During the warm-up for game five, the Leafs worked out the starting goalie first, as usual, and then the backup (in this case Frank McCool, as Lars Rogers was with his wife in Toronto, where they were expecting their first child.)

Before the session ended, John Dennis asked McCool to come out; he wanted another short round of shots, to give him an edge. The warm-up was almost over, as game time neared. Left on the ice for Toronto were Dennis, defenseman David Burks (usually the last off the ice) and forward Randy Rettig, who was working the pine-splinters out of his behind.

At the other end of the rink were Detroit backup goalie Chris Osgood, forward Kirk Maltby and defensemen Kyle Quincey and Cory Cross.

As the two Detroit defensemen headed to the net, Maltby tried to hit Quincey with a pass, but sent it too far as he didn't notice Quincey departing the ice. The puck went all the way to the Leaf end, and entered the recently vacated net.

John Dennis didn't see the attempted pass; all he saw was a Red Wing firing the puck into his empty net. And he took exception. Dennis took the puck and fired it right at Maltby, hitting the forward in the back.

Maltby turned, and seeing the goalie with his body poised in the shooting position, began to skate the length of the ice to have words, or worse, with the angry goalie.

Rettig was no longer on the ice, but made a mad dash to return when he saw Maltby going after his goaltender.

He began to chase after the Detroit forward, and intercepted him before he reached the goalie. It was at this appropriate moment that the three game officials appeared, standing near the boards at the centre red line, preparing to step on the ice. Referee Don Money saw all he had to see, when John Dennis skated up to the two combatants and piled onto Maltby.

There it was, Money said,—third man in. The three officials headed onto the ice, as the linesmen moved to break it up, while Money signalled for Osgood, Cross and Burks to stay out of it, though the three of them had already formed a dance team.

By this time, word had reached both dressing rooms, and the crowd noise had also tipped them off.

Spencer Smith was the first to arrive, and he confronted Money who gave him the bad news.

"They each get majors," he said, referring to Rettig and Maltby, "but the goalie's third man in—he gets the game."

Smith was going to blow a gasket. He popped the top button on his shirt as he reached new decibel levels as he lambasted the referee.

"YOU CAN'T TOSS THE STARTING GOALIE BEFORE THE GAME STARTS!" he boiled.

Money tried to remain calm, but by now league security was getting ready to intervene. The supervisor of officials was on the scene, and the leagues' vice-president, also in the building, had been summoned.

Up in the visiting V.I.P. box, Ken Butler had witnessed the entire scenario, and was on his way to plead the case for his team.

When the crowd around the timekeepers' bench had reached numbers that resembled a battalion, the league V.P. declared a solution. The area was to be cleared, the start of the game was to be delayed, and a meeting was held in the Pistons' dressing room to settle the mess.

Despite the Leafs protests, the referees' decision was upheld. Ken Butler was as concerned about another matter; third man in would automatically generate a one-game suspension. The Leaf GM wisely suggested that this should constitute a hearing with the league, and not be decided right there and now.

Spencer Smiths' concern right now was for the game at hand. He was going to have to go into game five, the pivotal game, without his number one goalie.

The Leaf coach met briefly with the GM, as Ken Butler tried to get his coach to ignore the decision, and get the team to keep their head in the game.

"It's a god dam travesty!" the coach fumed. "I've never seen such a fucked up call in my life!"

Ken Butler wisely let his coach vent then added. "We still have a game to play. You need to be with the team and get them ready, Spence. I know you *know* that. And there isn't much time."

Smith stormed off to the dressing room, almost flattening a HNIC cameraman in the process. John Dennis was probably angrier with himself than anything. He knew that he had ultimately let the team down by his actions, but none of his teammates were thinking that.

"We have to play like the goalie's made of glass," he ordered, referring to the fact that they now had no backup goalie. "Unless one of you guys wants to don the pads."

John Hill shrunk a bit in his seat; he was the only player who had played goal above the pewee level, and he didn't want to make an encore performance at the NHL level.

Frank McCool took it all in stride. "Score me a goal, and we'll all go home happy," was all he said.

Busher Jackson nudged Charlie Conacher in the ribs. "They don't know Bomber, do they?" he grinned.

Conacher shrugged sheepishly. It was true. The Bomber had been forced to replace a penalized goalie more than once.

"Let me see," Busher Jackson recollected, "there was the time you went in for Old Bulwarks, twice I remember, and once for Hainsworth?" he smiled, shoving Conacher in the shoulder.

"Quiet Busher—they'll have me wearin' that Halloween mask and working the door on the bench if you don't pipe down!" he scowled.

"But you never even gave up a goal, in three games!" Busher laughed.

The pair began to draw attention. Bill Barilko and Tim Horton were about to vouch for Conacher. And Dale McCaine had no reason to doubt him. The situation was quickly diffused by one of Spencer Smith's more wolfenly growls.

Back in Toronto, the soap opera that had been unfolding almost before the very eyes of millions of CBC viewers was causing a greater unrest than the implementation of the GST.

Fans who tuned into the game late were given the incredible explanation. And as the lined up for the opening faceoff, it was apparent that the Leafs were now playing for a cause. Had the Red Wings truly realized this, they may have chosen to decline the penalty.

As it was, the Leafs rallied around their rookie, seldom-used goaltender, who had last played in the 3-1 loss he shared with Lars Rogers in game three of the New York series.

He was also, however, the goaltender that held the NHL record for most shutouts in a Stanley Cup final, with three (consecutive).

After the puck was dropped, some of the Detroit players began to drop as well.

Joel Kent started it when he drove Robert Lang into the Red Wings' bench with a vintage open ice hit.

Floyd Shoniker caught Jason Williams looking the other way after a shoot-in, and levelled him. And on his first shift of the game Busher Jackson did the unthinkable; he put the body on Steve Yzerman. Chris Chelios was quick to retaliate, and incredibly the Leafs were awarded the extra two minutes.

The Red Wings were licking their collective chops at the prospect of a man advantage with a rookie in the Leaf goal. They fired an amazing nine shots at McCool while Busher Jackson was in the box, and he stopped all of them. His throwback stand-up style was throwing Detroit for a loop, as he made turning aside the shots that came along the ice look easy.

"Seventy-One percent of all goals are scored along the ice," Brian Ridley remarked to Ron Bailey, who was seated next to him in the V.I.P. box.

"And if McCool keeps on his feet, he'll stop 'em," Ron answered.

Even though Ridley wore a headset, he had heard what Ron said.

"Who?" He asked.

Ron quickly recovered. "I mean, if he keeps his cool, on his feet!"

The first ended in a scoreless draw, but the Red Wings had a 17-8 advantage in shots, due primarily to their one power play chance.

In the second, the Leafs kept up their physical play, and it seemed to finally be rattling Detroit, even if it did give them a 4-2 power play advantage in the period. It mattered little, as Frank McCool kept kicking out the shots while standing tall in the net.

Harry Neale of *Hockey Night in Canada* made an interesting observation during the second period of the broadcast. "The Leafs are now in an interesting position because of all the injuries and call-ups they've had this year." he observed.

"Chuck Andrew, Floyd Shoniker, Mike McKenna and John Dennis; four key Leaf veterans missed a combined one hundred and twenty-eight man games this year, but what that also means is, they were rested, even though due to injury, for a large chunk of the season. They have to have more stamina and zip, and less fatigue at this late stage of the playoffs than do the Red Wings, who have for the most part been in there all year. And add to this guys like Dennis MacDonald and Alexi Gusarov, who played a short season in Europe, and the call-ups like the kids Mouton, Hansky, Bodine and Bachmann, and these Leafs are practically in mid-season form. At some point this is going to be a factor."

Bob Cole added, "And that includes the goaltender in there, Frank Isbister, who has been magnificent so far tonight."

In the Leaf radio booth, Jim Gerber was making a similar observation. "Spencer Smiths' line-up juggling is really starting to play dividends. The way that Frank Maleki, for example, and David Burks are playing after having game four off—they look like they've taken five years off of their lives!"

The Red Wings, on the other hand, were tiring by comparison. Midway through the third period the shots on goal were even, as the Leafs had tightened up defensively to the point where Detroit practically had to dump the puck in from centre ice in order to get a shot on McCool.

The Leafs did make one critical mistake in the third, but even that worked out in their favour. As the Red Wings offensive frustration mounted, they began to object to the beating they were still taking. Brendan Shanahan even took exception to a Bill Barilko smash into the boards, and answered with a two-hander that the referee missed. He was all eyes when Barilko nailed him with an elbow, and Toronto was once again on the short end of the penalty tally.

The Leafs were forced to begin playing a man down with their second penalty killing unit, but Spencer Smith wisely decided to double shift Dale McCaine. Benoit Marlet, Tim Horton and Busher Jackson joined him.

The Red Wings won the draw at the faceoff circle to the right of Frank McCool, and Zetterberg controlled the puck while Yzerman set himself up beside the net. Too many times in Yzerman's career this had resulted in misery for the opposition, but this was different. While Marlet covered Zetterberg, Jackson took Samuelsson and Horton took one point man. McCaine was left to cover his opposite, the centre man.

But instead of staying put, and waiting for Yzerman to either do the magical wrap around, or deliver the pin-point pass that would result in a goal, he headed straight for Yzerman, who didn't have time to move. The pass came, but it was McCaine who received it. He pivoted while building up steam, a seemingly impossible task. As he raced up ice, he noticed that Tim Horton was trailing. All that stood between them and Manny Lagace was one of the Detroit defenseman, who quickly anticipated the breakout pass, and recovered enough to be there to try and break up the two-on-one.

443

Horton pulled even with McCaine, as they broke in over the blue line, and the Red Wing defender was positioned beautifully to intercept the pass. Dale McCaine looked over at Horton, who had a wicked shot, and he prepared to feed the puck while the Detroit back liner could almost feel it hitting his stick.

McCaine barely took his eyes off of Horton, and he pulled his stick towards the defenseman, as he readied to make the pass. And all in one motion, he transformed his motion into a backhand, which lifted the puck high over the startled goalie's shoulder, and knocked the water bottle from on top of the net.

Horton lifted McCaine with a bear hug, and the Leaf bench emptied to celebrate with the two rookies.

Up in the HNIC booth, the commentators were reliving the moment, as the replay flashed.

"Watch Dale McCaine as he uses Gilbert Mouton beautifully as a decoy." Harry Neale observed.

"He looks as if he's going to make the pass, but the rookie with the savvy of a veteran wisely decides to keep it himself, and why not? McCaine is a forty-seven-goal scorer. Why pass it to a defenseman who scored only twice?"

There were now less than seven minutes between the Leafs and an all-important three game to two series lead.

But the Red Wings were not going to be counted out easily. They shortened their shifts, and began to find a little more open ice as they did so. They somehow managed to avoid the Leafs physical contact, and set up inside the Leaf blue line while controlling the play. They tried to get Lagace out of the net with just under two minutes left, but each time they tried, the Leafs would dump it in while sending one speedy forward to beat them to the icing call.

As the clock counted down to the final minute, Lagace made it to the bench at last. The Red Wings put all of their big guns on the ice at one, for one last assault. Yzerman, Zetterberg, Datsyuk, Shanahan, Lidstrom and Chelios were working against Andrew,

Shoniker, Kent, McKenna and Burks. And though Detroit had the extra man, the Leafs had Frank McCool. Detroit managed six shots in the last forty-five seconds—McCool stopped them all.

The final buzzer went, and Frank McCool had one last shining moment in the Stanley Cup final against the Red Wings. He was named the *Molson Cup* first star, and in a post-game interview on HNIC, commented that he 'knew he had to come up with a good game, because if he had so much as a bad period, Spencer Smith was going to come in and play himself—and that scared the team more than anything else.'

As the Leafs filed into the room, the energy was like static electricity.

"Let's go out and play game six, right here, right now!" Floyd Shoniker screamed to a rousing cheer.

Spencer Smith wasn't so cocky, but the grin he wore could not be erased even with plastic surgery.

Up in the V.I.P. box, there was quiet celebration, though the GM, his assistant and the director of player personnel knew that there was nothing to celebrate, at least not yet.

"But we're close," Ken Butler told the group, "and it feels good, doesn't it."

The quirky playoff schedule now gave two days off until game six of the series, and thanks to the ridiculous Fox TV deal, it meant that game seven would be played the following night, but two hundred and fifty miles away.

Since Thursday was a travel day, the Leafs did not arrive home until almost noon. Spencer Smith gave the team the day off, and took one himself. He headed far north of the city, and spent the remainder of the day fishing. A few of the players took advantage of the great spring weather and played golf. And the ones with families chose to spend it with them, including Lars Rogers, who now had a new family to spend time with. But the assistant coaches were at the Gardens, holding an optional skate attended by players who hadn't seen much ice time in the final, notably Greg Sawchuck, Tobin West, Ian Moriarty, Randy Rettig, Christian Andersson and Lorne Graham.

The day off proved to be a tonic. The pressure associated with a potential series clinching game was monumental. Around the city, players and fans alike were almost afraid to even to *think* that they could possibly be this close to winning a Stanley Cup.

On his radio program, Gil 'the thrill' Baines refrained from even mentioning the 'S' word, and also forbade callers from doing the same.

"There will be no jinxing, of anything on this program," he told the listeners, which included Ron Bailey, on the day before game six.

"I have said all along this year that this team was not going to get here…but here they are. And I am not going to be blamed by rabid Maple Leaf nuts for raining on the parade. So on this program, and until this series is over, no mention of the word that begins with 'S.'"

Ron Bailey spent most of the day before game six with his future in-laws, as wedding plans were being discussed. Kelly would be arriving from Vancouver on Monday. Ron was allowing himself to think that wouldn't it be ironic if he were returning from Detroit on the same day, with the Stanley Cup on board the plane.

The Maple Leaf Forever

ame six was played at the Gardens on a Saturday, a result of the deal between *Hockey Night in Canada* and Fox.

Floyd Shoniker had some trouble sleeping the night before. And he arrived at Maple Leaf Gardens more than two hours before game time. He had tried to kill some time that day by getting his hair cut, and by getting an oil change on his '57 Thunderbird. But at the barbershop and at the garage they only wanted to talk about the series, and the game, until they realized that the Leaf captain did not.

When he arrived at the Gardens, he climbed the stairs to the red seats, and sat staring out onto the ice. He remembered the first time he had come to the Gardens as a kid, and had sat somewhere in these same red seats. His dad had taken him to see the Philadelphia Flyers.

Shoniker's favourite player was Bobby Clarke, and he disliked the way that then Leaf captain Darryl Sittler was compared to the Flyer great.

Years later, after having met Sittler as a member of the organization, Shoniker's opinion changed considerably.

Shoniker was not alone for long. Spencer Smith had also arrived early for work, and when he spotted the captain, he had to go and see why he was there early.

"Same reason as you, I guess," Shoniker answered.

They two of them sat silently a few seats and one row away from each other, until the captain broke the silence.

"This may sound stupid Spence, but I can't help feeling that even if we lose this thing, it feels so great just to be here, to be in it, ya know?"

The coach could have nipped that one in the bud; to not allow any kind of negative thinking on this day, but instead he responded. "I know what you mean. I played against some great hockey players, Ratelle, Gilbert Perreault, and with some like Dionne, and Park, who never won a cup. They had great careers as individuals, but never played on a Stanley Cup winner. But you're right, just to have the chance. I guess that's why it is so special. I just want to soak it all in. I don't know if we'll ever get this close again."

The pre-game skate was quiet. And compared to a regular season game, with all of the blaring tape decks and clowning around in the room, this game was a comparative funeral viewing.

It was as if there was a job to be done, and they all knew it— better to get it done and move on, to whatever conclusion. There was no talk in the room about what would happen if they won. No one wanted to jinx it. Even the coach had made some special arrangements. Even though the cup could potentially be awarded that night he did not want it in the building. He had arranged, through Ken Butler and NHL security, for the cup to be kept in its' armoured car, parked *outside* Maple Leaf Gardens, unless needed.

The hype leading up to the game seemed to build exponentially; could the game live up to such expectation? Cottages were being opened for the season; what better way to celebrate the coming of spring (and the end of another Ontario winter) than to have a party? And to cap all of this off with a Stanley Cup—well it could not get better than this for hockey fans, could it?

The Gardens had been papered with faxes, e-mails and letters of support from all over Canada. Outside of Montreal, since the NHL had set up shop in Vancouver, Calgary, Edmonton, and Ottawa, the Leafs were still largely 'Canada's team.'

While most players were silently preparing in the room before the game, Joel Kent read one well-wishing fax out loud.

"It's from a guy in Seaforth, named Brad. He says he has a bet with his wife on the series. If we win, she'll give him the divorce. But if we lose, she gets to stay—keeps the bedroom and he has to move into the room over the garage. Shit, I don't know if we'll be doing the right thing by winning or not!"

The coach gave no pre-game speech, instead saying, "I have no wise words for you guys. You know what to do. You know what has to be done. Let's do it."

Even during the player introductions, with the obligatory laser and smoke show, there seemed to be more concentration on the player's faces. They wanted to get on with the game. The line up would be different than in game five. John Dennis was cleared to play, as Ken Butler has wisely appealed to the league that any such suspension resulting from the game five ejections could be served *next* season; there was a league precedent for it. Frank Maleki was out and Alexi Gusarov was back in on defense, and up front Greg Sawchuck replaced Rettig.

A collective 'here we go' was heard around the province, and in fact the country.

Up in the Leaf executive box, Ron took up his usual spot beside Brian Ridley and his headset.

Walt Fisher and Ken Butler were absent, having accepted an invitation to watch the game from the new owner's private box.

From the opening faceoff, the play was brisk. Each team wanted to get the early advantage—it was of course more urgent that the Red Wings did because they were the ones that faced elimination.

The Leafs went into their defensive mode early, the same one that they had employed for most of the low-scoring series. It had served them well; indeed they only seemed to get into trouble with it when they fell behind. The coach knew that they were not, as a rule, a comeback team.

On this night, they would have to be. Detroit took the lead only five minutes into the period when John Dennis was beaten by a seemingly harmless shot from outside the faceoff circle. Johan Franzen let go a wrist shot that got by on the goalie's stick side, just below his blocker.

Dennis did not react emotionally; instead he turned around and took a nonchalant swig from his water bottle. Inside he was upset, but he knew that one bad goal does not always ruin a game. The fact that they were trailing did not start panic to set in, at least not yet. The Leafs maintained their close checking style, although not as physical as they had in the previous game. Joel Kent tried to enliven his fellow Leafs with some spirited hitting, but most of the other forwards were content to play the puck and cover their man.

The period ended 1-0 Detroit, and the shots were almost even, though the Red Wings did have a wide margin in power plays at 3-1. The Leafs excellent penalty killing was saving them again.

"We need to open up a bit in the second—get in front of Lagace more. Andy, you'll have to take a stick in the ass now and then," the coach said to some mild laughter, as he chewed on a few ice chips.

The scoring did open up in the second, as Chuck Andrew did get in Lagace's face, and when Valeri Ragulin spotted him parked in front of the crease; he let go a point shot that Andrew skilfully directed down and to the right of Lagace's out-stretched pad, to tie the score.

The Leafs were back in it, but only for a moment. Detroit took advantage of their slight edge in speed, when the Hudler-Franzen-Filppula line found them matched against the Leafs on a line change that accidentally included their three slowest players, Serge Moit, Lou Zanardo and John Hill.

The three young Europeans worked a good three-on-two as they circled like a circus act, and got the puck to Filppula who put it past Dennis by directing a quick pass between the goalie's legs.

By now many who were watching the game were beginning to wonder why the coach had not decided to stick with Frank McCool, who had shut Detroit out in game five.

Dennis could not really be blamed on the second goal, however.

Spencer Smith knew that the next goal was critical; it would have to be scored by Toronto or this game was likely over. He called a time out following the second Red Wing goal, and cautioned his troops to exercise some patience. They did *not* have to get the equalizer right away. But when the period ended, the score remained 2-1, and it meant only that the Leafs now had only twenty minutes to tie it.

The coach did not have to say anything during the second intermission. The players took turns blasting themselves as a team, and directing their anger at Detroit.

The Red Wings quickly went up 3-1. Horton and Barilko were bringing the puck out of their end, when Brendan Shanahan intercepted Barilko's pass. He rocketed in alone on Dennis, and pulled a great deke that saw the goalie do the splits. The puck was wobbling as it went under the goalies' pants. Dennis thought that he had stopped it—he thought that he felt the puck under him. He looked over his shoulder to see where it was, and the puck rolled slowly over the line as he watched helplessly, as if it were a dream.

"If Tiger Williams were here, he would say 'stick a fork in 'em, they're done like dinner'!" Bob Swanson observed from the Leaf broadcast booth. Jim Gerber looked at him, as if to say, 'you idiot!', but did not. Everyone listening at home likely did it for him.

Spencer Smith looked up at the clock, and the HNIC cameras caught him doing so.

"That may be the goal that clinches it for the Red Wings...at least this game," Bob Cole remarked.

There were only nine minutes remaining. And whatever sparks the Leafs had seemed to be dimming. On the bench, two of the Leafs were not thinking that way. At one end, it was the captain, Floyd

Shoniker. And at the other end, it was the former captain, Charlie Conacher.

Both of them were leaders, and both of them were not going to see this end, this way.

The teams staged a seesaw battle for the next seven minutes, but no great chances came out of it for either team. Detroit was obviously trying to protect the lead and force a game seven; the Leafs were pressing hard, but it looked like they really didn't know how.

Steve Yzerman was taking charge out there, and the rest were following orders. As they prepared to take a faceoff deep in the circle to the right of the Red Wing net, Yzerman was carefully directing the positions he wanted everyone in. Floyd Shoniker did the same for the Leafs, though he never said a word. When the puck dropped, he won the draw and sped right to the corner of the crease on the goalie's glove side. The puck came back to David Burks who shot it right at Shoniker's stick, which was positioned about two feet wide of the Detroit goal.

The puck hit the blade and Shoniker actually drew the blade back, and as he did so, the puck went left, and down, and past the Red Wing goalie. The players celebrated, but it looked to be too little, too late.

The fans got some of their momentum back, until they looked at the clock. There was only two minutes and forty-three seconds left. How had the clock gone down so fast? Detroit called a time out, and Spencer Smith was telling John Dennis not to come to the bench for the extra attacker until one minute thirty seconds remained. And he was carefully planning to work the lines so that Shoniker's could be the one out there at the end.

Marlet, who lost the draw but stayed with his man even after the shoot in, took the faceoff at centre. The problem was the Leafs could not get the puck out of their end for the next two minutes. The fans were screaming, and the Red Wings got away with mayhem. There was some doubt if the referee even *had* a whistle on him at that point.

There would be another faceoff just outside the Leaf blue line, and therefore no chance yet to lift John Dennis. As the players lined up for the faceoff, there was some problem on the ice and the referee skated over to the timekeepers' bench. During the delay, the picture of the new Air Canada Centre was flashed on the video screen above the scoreboard, and the notation was made that this would be the last playoff game ever played at Maple Leaf Gardens.

Ron Bailey reacted as if a curtain had been removed from in front of his face. He thought about Doug McCaine. What was it he had said, 'Dale McCaine would have to realize his dream, and his dream was to play for the Leafs; to win a Stanley Cup in Maple Leafs Gardens?' Well unless he could make *that* happen, that team was *never* going to win another Stanley Cup, he swore it. That meant that the Leafs would have to win it in Maple Leaf Gardens, *not* the Air Canada Centre, and not Joe Louis Arena, but *Maple Leaf Gardens!* They would have to win it, NOW!

Right away, Ron looked at who was on the ice—it was Shoniker's line. He turned to Brian Ridley and said, "Get McCaine out there!"

Ridley looked at him as if he was speaking another language.

"Bo, I'm not kidding, you have to get Dale out there, NOW!"

"Ronnie...I'm talking to...yeah...Newt...I..."

There was no time, he grabbed the headset away from Ridley and shouted at Ralph Newton.

"Newt, there's no time to explain, MCCAINE HAS TO BE ON THE ICE NOW, OR WE DON'T WIN THE GAME... GOT IT?"

Ralph Newton did not get it, but he listened.

"I can't Ron, Spence would..."

"You HAVE to! Just go over and tap him on the shoulder. Spence will thank you for it later—believe me."

Ralph Newton went over to Spencer Smith, and said something in his ear. The coach shook his head and Newton looked up at the box. He looked at Ron and shook his head.

Ron wanted to run down to the bench, but he knew he would never make it in time.

"Bo, help me convince him!" he implored to Ridley.

Ralph Newton had never seen Ron Bailey this way. He was behaving unusually, but it made sense to him just the same.

"Go ahead, Newt, send him out there instead of, I don't know, as the extra man!"

Shoniker, Kent and Andrew were the forwards on the ice, with Horton and Barilko on defense.

The faceoff did go into the Detroit end, and John Dennis raced to the bench. Spencer Smith went to tap Benoit Marlet on the shoulder, but before he could, Ralph Newton told Dale McCaine to "GO!"

The coach was astonished, and not half as much as Newton looked.

The Red Wings didn't seem worried; in fact Daniel Cleary saw a brief clearing and tried to fire the puck the length of the ice. But McCaine trailed on the play, and he picked the puck out of the air like a centre fielder. He carried it up ice carefully, striving not to go offside. Barilko trailed on the play, and when he tried to feed a pass a head to Shoniker, Mathieu Schneider tripped him. As Barilko fell he let go a shot, and Legace was screened briefly, and never saw the shot whiz by his shoulder. The Leafs had tied it with seventeen seconds remaining.

The team poured off of the bench, but the referee signalled that they must regroup, because there was time left on the clock. If they didn't return right away, he said, there would be a bench penalty.

Floyd Shoniker didn't argue, and instead had order restored in no time. The ice was cleared, and the all-important faceoff at centre took place, and overtime was looming.

"And the buzzer goes, can you believe it?" Jim Gerber asked the radio audience.

Ron Bailey took a deep breath, and looked at Brian Ridley

"What was that all about?" Ridley asked.

"It had to happen, I just knew it. I can't—"

Just then, Ridley motioned that someone on the other end of the headset wanted to talk to Ron. It was the coach. "You just earned your god dam days' pay!" the coach growled.

In the dressing room, the coach was going over the lines, and realized that with the rest, it would be possible to go with Shoniker's line right away. In the corner of the room, Barilko was still beaming. Horton looked at him and said, "How the hell can anybody score the same goal, *twice?*"

Barilko smiled a gap tooth smile, and began to sing, "This is for the Detroit goalie...*today I passed you on the street, and a puck fell at my feet. I can't help it if I scored a goal on you...*"

Horton threw a paper cup full of ice at Barilko.

Spencer Smith wasn't about to make any heart wrenching speeches at this point. His address to the team before they went back on the ice was this: "You guys know I love Detroit, and there's a bus outside waiting to take us to the airport when this one is over. BUT I DON'T WANNA GET ON IT, SO WIN THE GODDAM GAME...AND I WON'T HAVE TO!" There was a collective cheer at this news.

Charlie Conacher felt that it was going to be up to him to make sure that the goal was scored, even if he didn't score it.

The intermission was over too quickly, it seemed. Red Garrett watched the game from his cottage in Huntsville, cheering for Ron's Leafs. Kelly was watching on TV in her apartment, though she couldn't bear to look as overtime passed the second minute mark. In Mississauga, Terry Oddy and a few of his neighbours sat around the big screen TV in his living room, his friends feeling sympathetic that Terry was not out there. Leslie Winston, in the den of his Oakville condominium, sat in his lazy boy chair, clutching a Rye and Ginger in his hand. Dan Cameron and Al Swartz watched from the legion in St. Johns', ecstatic about the fact that one of their own, 'David Hansky' had scored the tying goal.

Doug Forster viewed the game over his satellite system from his Boston home, cursing the fact that the Ragulin trade had worked so well for the Leafs.

Shithead Moore didn't watch the game; he was too busy drinking while driving his boat on Georgian Bay. At Reds' Hotel in Cobourg, they watched as the puck was dropped for the start of the first overtime period. Thorny sat at his usual barstool, an empty one reserved for Doug McCaine beside him. From where he was watching it Doug McCaine had a better view of the game than *anyone did*

And Ron Bailey held his breath as Henrik Zetterberg got a breakaway on John Dennis when Dennis MacDonald coughed up the puck at centre. Both teams seemed to be frozen, as they watched the goalie back up into his net, as the speedy winger planned his move. It seemed to take forever, though it lasted less than three seconds. Zettterberg drew to one side and tried to deke the goalie as he went down, and as quick as if it had been Johnny Bower, out came the stick and the poke check knocked the puck all the way to centre. Dale McCaine scooped it up, and fed it ahead to Charlie Conacher, who waited until the last possible second before returning the favour. McCaine looked like he was going to his formidable backhand, but instead pulled the puck back to his forehand, and popped the winner on a low shot to the stick side corner.

Maple Leaf Gardens had not experienced a feeling like that before or since. It was more than a sound; it was a rumble that rattled the structure to its very foundation. Dale McCaine held his stick high, and he was bowled over by the players on the ice and those that flowed from the bench. And then the crowd joined in, as if invited. The security staff could not have prevented it if they had wanted too. And many of them did not want to. Soon there was not one square inch of white ice visible to the TV viewers, as the crowd mobbed their heroes.

On the bench, Spencer Smith lifted Ralph Newton in the air, and slapped the backs of Nevell Carpenter and his assistants.

Jim Gerber did not really need the radio to reach his listeners, though he was being overcome by hoarseness, as he bellowed "THE TORONTO MAPLE LEAFS HAVE WON THE STANLEY CUP...AND THE THIRTY-SEVEN YEAR DROUGHT IS OVER!"

The Cup was coming in from the armoured car in the garage, and the commissioner was moving with his entourage towards the ice for the presentation, just as soon as it was cleared. David Burks had enough presence of mind to retrieve the historic puck, though only Ron Bailey knew *how* historic it was.

Up in press row Billy Sinfield began writing his column for the next day, 'How the Curse of the Maple Leafs had been lifted.'

Long after the Cup was paraded around the rink, with each player (including Dale McCaine) getting their turn, and the speeches made, and the Conn Smythe trophy awarded to Chuck Andrew, and the ceremonial team handshakes with the Red Wings made, the real party inside the Gardens was confined to the dressing room. The fans celebrated on the streets, and the Leaf brass in the Private Boxes, but in the room, the last men left standing sat down and enjoyed a drink from the Cup.

And this time, the coach let them drink *real* champagne. They were still pinching themselves, and trying to believe that it was really happening. The scene outside Maple Leaf Gardens was unparalleled. The streets were so jammed; it looked like the city was being evacuated. The party was bigger than any World Series, world cup or world war victory that had ever been celebrated in Toronto.

As dawn was beginning to break outside, only Spencer Smith, Ron Bailey, Dale McCaine, Tim Horton, Bill Barilko, Charlie Conacher, Busher Jackson, Frank McCool and Floyd Shoniker remained.

"You guys are lucky," the coach slurred, after so many sips of champagne, beer, Captain Morgan's, and Gatorade. "You, except for Shonny, get to taste this in your first year. Do you know how lucky you are, right Shonny?"

Shoniker didn't answer—he was half-asleep with his arms hugged around the cup.

Conacher smiled. "I think we do. Coach, it's been a pleasure. We really have to go. We're gonna miss you."

"Yeah, yeah, have a good summer, 'cause we're gonna work your tails off next year, to try and keep Mr. Stanley."

"I'm afraid you'll have to do it without us," Busher Jackson added.

"Aw, c'mon, you can't quit now! Because you think it'll be too hard to repeat?"

"It's not that coach. We were only here to give the kid a chance. And he got it, thanks to you," Barilko said.

"Now you guys stop shittin me. I may have had a few, but I know you'll be back. Hansky, Bodine, Bachmann, Mouton, Isbister. See I got the name right!"

"It's McCool," Frank McCool corrected, "and he's Charlie Conacher, and he's Tim Horton, and that fella there who scored the tying goal is Bill Barilko, and that ugly guy is Busher Jackson!"

Smith laughed an intoxicated belly laugh. "Yeah, Yeah, and I'm Fido Purpor, WOOF!"

Ron sat smiling in the corner, and finally passed out. And as Spencer Smith got ready to give one more coaching bit of advice, the five players vanished right before his eyes.

"Wholly shit!" the coach exclaimed, "I'd love to see them do that on the ice!"

Dale McCaine stood close to the coach. "I'd like to come back!" he said.

"Well, son, we'll see you in September. That would make me very happy!"

THE GHOSTS IN MAPLE LEAF GARDENS

Long live the Maple Leafs.

Rick Ferguson

September, 1998

The Toronto Maple Leafs have not won a Stanley Cup since 1967—that is a burden that all long-suffering fans of the Blue and White have had to bear. This is the story of what was supposed to happen in the 2004-05 season—the year that a lockout prevented the Stanley Cup from being awarded.

The Ghosts in Maple Leaf Gardens uncovers the reason for the team's long drought, and how Ron Bailey, the Leafs' young director of player personnel, accidentally uncovers a 'curse' that has been placed on the team. Can the curse be lifted? Before he can find the answer to that question, Ron Bailey must investigate how the curse involves a former player—Dale McCaine.

The Dale McCaine saga is tragic—a player who due to circumstances was never allowed his chance to play for a Stanley Cup winner before his untimely death. It is also the story of how five former Leaf greats' band together to try and help Dale McCaine get his chance.

Author's note: The book takes place during the 2003-2004 NHL season which history confirms, was cancelled by an owner's lockout of the players. The league did produce a schedule that season, and as purists will note, this book does not follow that schedule. That's because this book is a work of fiction, and not a transcript.

CPSIA information can be obtained at www.ICGtesting.com
Printed in the USA
LVOW13s1423021213

363533LV00002B/19/P

9 781491 707104